The Approaching Tide

Doug Thompson

Matador
9 Priory Business Park,
Wistow Road, Kibworth Beauchamp,
Leicestershire. LE8 0RX
Tel: 0116 279 2299
Email: books@troubador.co.uk
Web: www.troubador.co.uk/matador
Twitter: @matadorbooks

ISBN 9781800462120

British Library Cataloguing in Publication Data.
A catalogue record for this book is available from the British Library.

Printed and bound in Great Britain by 4edge Limited
Typeset in 10.5pt Adobe Garamond Pro by Troubador Publishing Ltd, Leicester, UK

Matador is an imprint of Troubador Publishing Ltd

BY THE SAME AUTHOR

To the Great Sea: A story for Christmas (Troubador, 2016)
Sensing he has fallen from favour and that his life may be forfeit, a
high-ranking minister flees his homeland, entering into the wilderness.
Chance knowledge and a chance meeting change the course of his
journey and of his life, leading him onto the stage of what many have
argued was the most significant event in the history of mankind.

Checkmate: Three Portraits of Power (Troubador, 2013)
What can you do when all of your conditioning, fuelled by desire, or
desperation, tells you that the Interviewer, like God, holds the keys
to whatever paradise it is you happen to be seeking?

What can you do when, believing implicitly in your own
importance and in the absolute nature of your power, you suddenly
find yourself a prisoner of the will, the absolute enigmatic power of
another or others?

What can you do when you are young, idealistic, inexperienced in
the devious ways of the world, and out of the blue comes the chance
of fulfilling your wildest dreams, not only with such an eminent
teacher but in the arms of the naked, most exquisite creature you
have ever set eyes on?

These three black comedies explore the nature of the relationships
between those who wield power and those who are powerless, its
effects and its implications, and not only for its immediate victims…

A Time for Role Call (Troubador, 2017)
The year is 1946, and a former debutante, Sally Jardine-Fell, is in
prison awaiting trial for a murder she didn't commit…

Set mainly in wartime Italy, *A Time for Role Call* follows Sally's life
in London, and in Yorkshire, where she falls in love with the enigmatic
Adam. Returning to blitzed London, she is eventually recruited by
Special Operations Executive (SOE), to undertake a bizarre mission
in Rome, seeking to win the confidence of Count Galeazzo Ciano,
Mussolini's Foreign Minister. However, history shuns this game-
plan, and she is forced to quit Rome, to try and 'disappear' during the
savage German occupation of Italy. Fate, however, has other things
in store…

In loving memory
of my dear brother,
Dave
(1948–2018)

and of
William (1875–19??), Alice (1894–1958) and Lilian Crosby (1918–98),
in the hope that with them, at last, all is now well.

Their understanding
Begins to swell, and the approaching tide
Will shortly fill the reasonable shores
That now lie foul and muddy.

(W. Shakespeare, *The Tempest*, V, i)

Acknowledgements

Novels frequently come out of a hinterland of events and people, and *The Approaching Tide* is no exception. Its *sine qua non* was a memorable stay on Stradbroke Island, in 1998, for which my ever grateful thanks to Mike and Cynthia Levy, and subsequently to Cynthia for uncovering further vital information about the *Emigrant* and its ill-fated voyage in 1850, once I had decided to write the novel.

The story has seen many changes during the intervening years, and I am most grateful for the many suggestions from friends and family, especially John Gatt-Rutter, June Thompson, Gareth Whittaker, and Andrew Thompson, all of which have played some part in shaping the novel.

My thanks too, to Jeremy Thompson and Sophie Morgan at Troubador Publishing for their much-tested patience and professionalism throughout the publication process, and to Jane Rowland for her imaginative cover design for the novel.

A special thank you to Elisabeth Gondwe at the North Stradbroke Island Museum on Minjerribah, and the Ask Us team at the State Library of Queensland, for their very generous responses to my requests for nineteenth-century photographs of particularly the Dunwich area of Stradbroke Island.

As always, with my writing, I owe an immense debt of gratitude to Gillian, my partner, for the hundreds of hours she has spent reading and re-reading the novel at different stages in its development, always with an astute critical eye and a wealth of suggestions. Any residual blemishes, I am afraid, are the sole responsibility of the author.

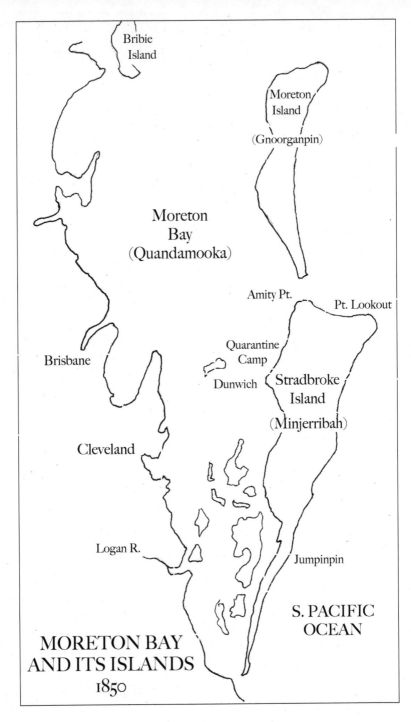

Bribie
Island

Moreton
Island

(Gnoorganpin)

Moreton
Bay
(Quandamooka)

Amity Pt.

Pt. Lookout

Quarantine
Camp

Brisbane

Dunwich

Stradbroke
Island

(Minjerribah)

Cleveland

Logan R.

Jumpinpin

S. PACIFIC
OCEAN

MORETON BAY
AND ITS ISLANDS
1850

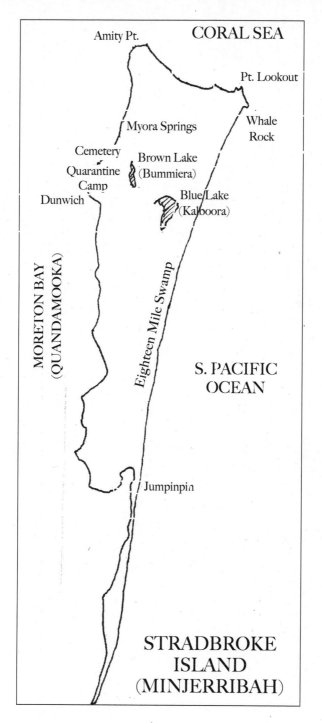

Prologue

Captain Kemp catches the sound of the latch being raised, then of someone struggling to open the wheelhouse door against the force of the gale, but he cannot leave the wheel to assist, not for one moment. His eyes stare straight ahead, straining to pierce the blackness through the driving sleet and the water sluicing down the glass pane, the whole of creation seemingly bent on sinking back down into the darkness and the deep.

A backward half-glance tells him that the man has finally managed to get inside and is now fighting to fasten the door behind him. The wind's howl is deafening and within it the crazed piping through the rigging, the frantic slap of ropes against wood and metal, the groan of a thousand boards, as the *Emigrant* heaves and tosses and ploughs its defiant furrow.

But the wind's whine is now playing more softly, in a minor key. The door is closed fast, then.

By his side is the young boatswain, fiddling with the tags of his sou'wester.

'Would you believe it, skipper, on such a night as this, they have not the gumption to keep below, coming and pestering the men who are doing their damnedest to make sure we all come through... I've just given a couple of 'em short shrift... Asking me if the lifeboats are ready... if there are sufficient for all...' He snorts his contempt.

Kemp laughs quietly. 'I doubt it'll come to that...'

'You should have seen their faces when I suggested they'd be better employed praying, below...' The young man giggles. 'Anyways, sir, the boats are at the ready, with their crewmen standing to... just in case. The topsails are down, the hatches battened... And I've got a couple of men below, checking for leaks...'

'Quite right! Complacency mustn't prove our undoing... So back to it, eh, Mr Williams?'

The wan light of the moon, racing ragged clouds, briefly illuminates a portion of the foredeck, now seemingly alive with flitting shadows, through the prism of watery glass in front of him. He cranes forward, squinting, even as the clouds drown the light in a newly flooding darkness, seeking to discern, to clutch at momentary knowledge that might reassure, or confirm, in this well-nigh, universal blindness.

The light comes again, scudding, shafting, and again the shadows, and the captain stares into their floodlit arena, aware that whatever his eyes suggest is not wholly to be trusted. And yet, for all that, he fixes on a figure, or more than one, darting or slipping ... a grey shape at the prow fraying into spray.... But when he looks again, the figure is gone... if ever there at all.

In this other dimension, where he alone exists, Kemp fancies the nearness of those souls who had earlier perished from the epidemic now clambering back aboard, seeking shelter from the surging chaos into which he had tumbled each in their turn, once the epidemic had begun to take its toll. He smiles at the superstition, but crosses himself as best he can, none the less. His left arm is stiff as a ramrod, steadying the hand which holds the destiny of all aboard in its grip on the wheel. Yet, slackening every minute or so to allow a slight tacking to port, or a compensatory correction to starboard, to relieve the strain on the tiller.

Suddenly, the ship dips into a trough with a sideways lurch and shudder that have him staggering to his left. A momentary pause, then it ploughs on, through and up, and out the other side. Kemp's right hand clamps down hard on the topmost spokes of the wheel, and he prays, silently, that the rudder will hold. If he falters the ship will be engulfed and every soul aboard – whether of the living or of the dead – will be shed upon the waters to sink down, down, down many a fathom into the pitch-black ooze at the bottom of the world.

These fleeting half-thoughts Kemp brushes aside, like intrusive cobwebs, and sets himself, once more, four-square behind the wheel, his mind fixed on their still far-off landfall.

I

The timbers creak softly every now and then as *The Emigrant* rides at anchor in the shallow bay, waves lapping gently against her sides.

Occasional cry of a seabird or shriek of some unimaginable creature, hidden away among the mangroves or in the forest further off...

Intermittent murmur of voices drifting over the water. But chiefly, now, the silence, in those few moments before the curtain of darkness finally falls.

Leaning upon the rail, the smoke from his pipe curling away behind him, William Crosby contemplates the scene along the island shoreline. Lamps being lit, here and there a fire flares; shadowy figures passing through its glare to be lost, at once, in the thick, dark backdrop of the forest beyond.

Will had earlier been a part of that scene, raising tents, carrying blankets and buckets of water, wheeling the truckle beds inside so that the women could begin making them up to receive the sick being ferried across in the longboats.

These practical things, though so ordinary, had proved exhilarating, if finally exhausting, after months of helpless inactivity at sea. Then, only Dr Mitchell, the ship's surgeon, and his few brave helpers, had toiled long hours, in their attempts to stem the vile epidemic that had come so calamitously upon them – yet with inadequate equipment and medicaments, in impossibly cramped conditions...

For so many it is already too late. Yet there is now, at least, some chance of fighting back, of not having to wait until death taps you on the shoulder to lead you into oblivion.

Most reassuring of all, perhaps, as Will's eye lights on the *Aurora*, the fact that other help is at hand.

And with this brighter thought he pushes himself up off the rail, a tall, spare figure of thirty years or thereabouts, and crosses to the other side of the ship to peer through the gloom at the few, barely discernible lights flickering over on the distant mainland. Yes, sure enough, there is some real comfort in seeing the ketch, her keel end-on to *The Emigrant*'s starboard, not a hundred yards away.

Immediately, however, he checks his wandering thoughts. There is no place for complacency or fanciful illusions. The pretty scene has momentarily beguiled him, and he shakes his head in disbelief at his naivety... After all they have come through!

The sound of footsteps mounting the ladder up from the galley, and he turns, and almost at once the head of the purser appears, bending through the low doorway.

'A job well done, Sergeant Crosby, wouldn't you say?' And the purser stretches, then stifles a yawn. 'The captain's providing some refreshment below, afore supper, and invites us all to join him. Please do come down; you've earned it!' And with this he strides off along the deck in search of others who have returned to the ship for the night.

'Sergeant' Crosby was somewhat premature, for his appointment to the Royal New South Wales Constabulary would not finally be confirmed until after his medical examination and other formalities had been got through, but it pleases Will none the less. It gives him a certain status among both the crew and his fellow passengers. It gives him back a little of the self-respect he has sorely forfeited in the attrition of these three years past.

Tapping his pipe against the outer edge of the rail, he watches the embers fall away into the water. Re-crossing the deck he kneels beside the nearest of the still-trussed, inverted lifeboats, to reach beneath it and replace the pipe and pouch among his bundle of things.

This small, uncluttered space has been his shelter and refuge for the past four months, even before the outbreak had been confirmed. Rightly or wrongly, he attributes his continuing survival to his decision to quit the dingy, airless, fetid lower deck into which over two hundred souls had been crowded. Right enough, he has passed some cold, some exceedingly wet and comfortless nights beneath this lifeboat, yet it has served his purpose, that it has. And Will is thankful to have come through this far.

The gathering below is not quite what the purser's words have led him to expect. A ship's council of war is clearly in progress and instinctively, almost, he recoils, neither wishing to be a part of it nor, as a passenger, after all, feeling he has any right to be there. He turns to leave, muttering an apology, but the purser – just now returning below – signals that he should sit, and makes a point of pouring him a measure of rum even as he takes his own from the flagon passing along the table.

'As I said above – *you've* earned it!'

Will takes stock. The Captain, seemingly presenting a summary of their current situation, looks grave, drawn. Kemp has the riveted attention of all present.

'...But we are full of gratitude for the swiftness of the response to our plight by Dr Ballow here, and the good people out of Brisbane.' And Kemp turns his head in the direction of the man sitting to his immediate left and pauses.

Several of the officers, taking their cue, clap or make assenting noises, tapping glasses on the tabletop, all of which the man acknowledges with a curt nod. His stern looks perhaps conceal his true age, for Will's closer scrutiny of his face suggest a man not much older than himself.

'A state of quarantine has now been declared,' Kemp continues, 'and will be maintained until it is deemed safe for the afflicted passengers and crew to complete their journey up-river to the township...'

Much more than frustration runs through the sudden murmur

as the men round the table receive this news. All of them weary, and anxious – for their own safety and that of their passengers too, for whom, willy-nilly, they are still responsible. All the same, Will muses, it was hardly news, rather what the more experienced travellers among them would surely have known must now ensue.

'Would not the epidemic abate more speedily if the passengers were widely dispersed, instead of being herded together in such close proximity?' the First Officer inquires.

Captain Kemp frowns and makes as if to reply, but Dr Ballow indicates his wish to speak, and the captain waves him to his feet.

'The answer to that question must necessarily remain a question mark.' Ballow pauses, places his hands squarely on the table, and leans forward. 'Two overwhelming factors must at this stage determine our conduct. Firstly, we already have more than thirty likely or confirmed cases among the passengers and these require urgent treatment. And... you should be in no doubt about this... our resources here are already stretched to crisis point! For we do not yet have the hospitals or the doctors to treat them, other than in a group, in the one location...'

Again, a sudden buzz, like angry bees, greets this information as the shock of it drives home. Dr Ballow patiently bides his time until the noise has again subsided.

'Secondly, as Coroner of the Brisbane District and Resident Surgeon for the Moreton Bay Hospital, it is my statutory duty to protect the populace from contagion and epidemics coming in from the outside world. This I could not do if there were any dispersal, beneficial though that might prove in individual cases.'

All is silent again, the company fully attentive, as this new, stark reality displaces – Will senses – earlier vague hopes founded, very likely, on even vaguer, if natural, assumptions.

'Just how many more among the passengers – and crew, I might add – may already be harbouring the disease, is impossible to tell, but what is certain is that such latent cases undoubtedly exist.'

Plain truths, Will recognises, that at a stroke must inevitably rekindle all the fears the euphoria of landfall had understandably all but displaced.

'With only sixteen deaths thus far – a figure attributable in no small measure to the skill and unstinting dedication of your Dr Mitchell – you have been exceedingly fortunate, however terrible that number may seem...'

Ballow clears his throat, an operation that seems to take an age.

'But, as I say, there are going to be more, and we must and will do everything within our means to restrict their number, to reduce the suffering of those afflicted and the anguish of their families.'

The doctor sits down slowly, warily, perhaps anticipating further questions, but for the moment none are forthcoming. However, a general murmur, rising steadily, once again courses round the table, then falls away as suddenly as it had begun.

Ballow rises to his feet again: 'Gentlemen, I almost forgot. I have to remind you that you are all bound by Her Majesty's Law applicable in the District of Brisbane and Moreton Bay, as in the rest of the State of New South Wales, so...'

Yes, well, it had to come sooner or later, Will thinks. Always the hint, if not the outright threat of coercion. For God's sake! Wasn't everyone tired, downcast, each the victim of his own false hopes? And now this surely unnecessary 'reminder'?

Will had had enough prating, preaching. and bullying in these latter years to last a lifetime... A man mounting a rostrum was, for him, like a red rag to a bull... and a sharp exhalation signals his irritation. He turns his head away, his eyes fixing on the golden liquid he swirls gently, absently, round and round in his cup.

'... we can undertake the process of fumigation. This will begin as soon as possible tomorrow morning. The ship's personnel...'

As the doctor's voice drones on in its marked, lowland-Scots' accent, Will toys once more with the thought of leaving.

'...Furthermore, it is imperative that the medical staff be informed...'

'Imperative,' Will repeats, under his breath – as in all such catechisms: the commands of the few, the obedience of the many, filtering down and downward through the layered ranks of the cowed, the subdued, the humiliated...

And all his old hatreds are up again, bristling again, prickling back into life...

'...I shall endeavour to find some help for Dr Mitchell among my colleagues in Brisbane, but, well... I'm not over-hopeful that any will volunteer...'

Not over-hopeful? Will's silent anger brims and simmers. Nor would I be, doctor! Who in his right mind would choose to step into a cesspit? Not you, doctor, I'll be bound! Nor your comfortable colleagues either...

Ballow looks across in his direction, and then away. 'Gentlemen, do you have any further questions...?'

'... Can you not give us a little more hope than...?'

'... Will any sort of segregation be...?'

Several speak at once, and some desultory talk follows, chiefly regarding details of the steps to be taken over the next few days, after which, to Will's relief, supper is called, and the meeting gradually disperses into smaller groups.

Setting himself apart, being in no mood for company, Will eats quickly then leaves, intent on penning a letter to his sister, since one useful bit of information the doctor had imparted was that a postbag would be travelling speedily on to Brisbane and thence back home by another route. Knowing Mary, doubtless she would already have presumed the worst – after almost four months of silence.

II

Writing letters is always something of a toil for Will, and last night's had proved no exception. He must be sure, however, that in it he has said all he must say, for how his eyes had drooped over its last few paragraphs! The long time it must travel, negating its very self with each league that passes, demands as full a picture as possible of how things stand with him up to the moment of its despatch.

For his sister, indeed, for all who eventually read it, it will be a history, though his family will doubtless treasure it as though he has handed it to them himself, this very morning.

He reads. But it seems so inadequate, a mere glimpse. Not even a whole book, however, would suffice to embrace all that has befallen him since he left them, back home. But, for all that, has he managed to convey the essentials, of the voyage, and arrival…? Surely, it is so.

But one final scrutiny… before he goes to drop it into the bag by the purser's door.

Stradbroke Island
New South Wales

13th August 1850

Dearest sister Mary,
*   I think you must long have despaired….* (he reads) *For this I am truly sorry, since I am mindful of the anguish… However,*

as you will soon realise, my silence has not been a matter of choice. Much less of thoughtlessness...

His eyes traverse the page rapidly.

We have arrived at last off the eastern coast of the Australian continent, at Stradbroke Island, which lies near the mouth of the Brisbane River. It is here that I and my fellow passengers must now spend an unknown period of time...

Yes... and yes... Then on to the next page, his finger running over the lines.

... One could not but be moved to pity at the sight of so much suffering, on The Emigrant. Naturally, you wished to do whatever was possible to help those who were afflicted, as well as their relatives, yet there was always the fear you would catch it from them, so that you usually avoided... as mothers attended the deaths of their children, or wives of their husbands. Worst of all was the lot of those who were travelling alone, for their deaths were so lonely, to be much pitied, but still the fear we all felt... the succour which was their due and our Christian duty to provide. This new layer of guilt, and I'm sure you will understand this, when added to that I already bear, did nothing to raise my spirits...

Yes, it seems to be all here... the camp... my lifeboat...

... it is believed that these ship-diseases are spread through bad air and, as you can imagine, with little ventilation, particularly in the tropics, the quarters soon stank abominably. In any case, fleas and lice abounded, making for comfortless, often sleepless nights. To be rid of these loathsome creatures I spent a whole day washing everything, including my blankets...

Then a bit about the place itself... Yes.

It is said that the island is quite large but apart from an unknown number of the aboriginal people, who are thought to be living in the more distant areas, there is only a tiny cluster of buildings around a small natural harbour, which goes by the name of Dunwich. God willing, I hope to be able to keep free of the sickness and to explore the whole island which, if I understand aright, was the first place in the northern part of this continent come upon by James Cook, some eighty years ago. I remember hearing about his exploits when I was in the first standard at Queen Street school, in a life which now seems so terribly remote...

This mention of school reminds me of Alice... Do you...?

And here, Will pauses, turning his face toward the mainland. After a moment or two, the back of his right hand is swept brusquely across his eyes.

The last time I set eyes on her and little Lilian, she pulled the child away indoors and would not even speak to me. Yet, in truth, I cannot blame her... Though at the time, it seemed such a cruel thing to do. It had taken me almost a whole day to reach them at Redhills. I beg of you not to lose sight of them and to let me know how their lives are faring. If you think it opportune...

And so to the conclusion...

I do not know whether I shall survive these coming weeks, but I shall try. God willing...

And not ten paces away from where Will stands reading, another more pressing drama is rapidly drawing to a close.

The flame. The flickering shadows. Over the timbers. Each time the wind shifts, the shadows shift too. After the candle has sputtered, guttering almost, the shadows shift. But always dancing, mimicking the flame.

9

The cabin on the poop deck has a sole occupant now. And with her, leaning over her, always attentive, this man several years older than she, even though her pallor seems to add to her years, using them up all too quickly, all too soon.

Here, with the stout planking between, the man had believed – had hoped – she would be out of harm's way, above the fever that rampaged through steerage. But it had stalked her, even here, and brought her down.

Before leaving for the island, some three hours ago, now, the surgeon had made his final visit, shaking his head, laying his hand briefly on the man's shoulder....

But at least she has the comfort now – or is it the man himself who has it? – of the last Absolution. That, at least, he has managed to perform for her... but there's not much time left... Touch and go whether the candle, or whether she, will go first. But whatever, now, their dancing shadows are lost forever – those larger than life shadows her light had cast against the blank wall of their future here, together.

'How shall I go on without you, Love, Life, Purpose?' the man murmurs.

Again, he leans forward and clasps her hands in his own.

Your hands, my love. So cold. Your breathing so flimsy. Imperceptible... Incredible that so late, so late, you should have taught me what love is, really is, and now that self-same breast and heart... that warmth barely flickering. How can it all...? How can all this that was so alive, so very alive, just suddenly not be any more? Your laughter alone, it made the whole world sing for me...

Gently, he relinquishes his hold and lays her hands upon the counterpane.

Could it be a punishment? God-sent? A punishment it is, sure enough, but banal whether sent or no. Not your God of Love, then. God of wrath, is it? Mindful of broken vows? And we reaping the whirlwind?

But what, dear God, could I have done differently? If Joanna appeared to me here, now, as she did then, the dying child at her milk-less breast, slumped against my garden gate, imploring my pity, I would do no different. What she craved, what I craved, but never really knew it till she taught me... All these wonderful things we are... have been... together; all those joys the world had denied us, apart – had hidden, forbidden...

If a punishment, I spit on it! I spit on any wrath or condemnation that has intention behind it, human or divine... Yet, in truth, it is worse if there be none... just nothing at all...

In his sudden anger, the man makes as if to rise, but then sinks back down onto the stool, aware that these are truly her last moments, too precious to be sacrificed to a useless anger... or to anything – there would be time enough for such railing, hereafter. Too much time. All time running to waste...

But any notion of God's wrath, it is childish, isn't it? Silly superstition. Ireland's ghostly legacy. Just chance. Like everything else. Why he goes on and she, who is so much younger, does not – just chance, in all its banality. God in his absence. Our *Deus absconditus!*

Again he reaches for her hands and strokes them, as if, even now, seeking to transmit some of his own living warmth into her.

So cold. Your hands. Breathing so shallow it barely draws on the air about us... Oh if I had known. If I had only thought, Love. Taken heed. Listened. For all the evil we lived through back in that other life, we would never have taken ship to this extreme edge of oblivion...

But these 'ifs'... are they not the very essence of our groping, human futility...?

And he smiles, bitterly.

Goodbye then, Love. God – in his absence here – be with you, now, since I cannot be... being the death of you. The madness of it. My Joanna, fading away... back into the misty day you came out of. I will remember. Always remember. Always hold you in my heart... My Life, my Love.

And here he remains, lost to time, his eyes never leaving her face... until, resigned to the futility of it all, when he gently places her hands beneath the sheet, unfolds it, and draws it up to cover her dead, white face.

After bowing his head momentarily, he rises and shuffles his way slowly along the narrow passage between the beds, the tables, and the bulkhead, to step out of the cabin into the new day that is just now breaking.

The candle stub goes on flickering in the empty silence.

And here's the lifeboat man... like old Diogenes, in his barrel. A quare fellow... But alive still. Breathing still in the still breathing air...

'Not a bad sort of day,' the lifeboat man says, cheerily.'

'Aye, you could be right... weather-wise,' he answers back, over his shoulder. Then groping through tears, his fingers find the rail of the ship's after-deck, and once gripping hold of it, his gaze fixes on the side-slipping dawn wind's rippling passage, over the waters of the bay.

Will's eyes follow the man to the rail, but since he makes no further attempt at communication, he rapidly scans the final sheet for one last time... Yes... All appears to be in order. And thrusting the letter back into its envelope, he seals it, then heads off towards the Purser's post box.

III

Even before the longboat reaches the shore, a white smoke is pouring from several of the portholes, as if the ship has suddenly caught fire. The fumigators' tackle had been ready the day before, but their purpose had been thwarted by the plight of a female passenger who was too ill to be moved, but who had apparently passed away at first light. Now they are losing no time at all.

Waiting to receive the longboat's occupants as they come ashore are a constable from the mainland and two of the ticket-of-leave, convict volunteers they had been told – and warned – about before they left *The Emigrant*. These men are acting as porters, in the first instance, assisting with the movement of cabin trunks and other heavy effects over to the tents.

The constable has a list of names and allocates each person to a tent by number as they disembark. Although he has not thought of it till now, Will realises that his own boatload must be the very last, and that may augur badly for the quality and location of his quartering.

And yet, none of the cohort that has come ashore with him has been assigned to the same tent as he, and for a fleeting moment Will entertains the hope that he must share his living space with no one. In the event, it proves a forlorn hope. When he pulls back the tent flap to drag his two trunks inside, he finds that some other person's things are already lodged there, and one of the three low beds has been claimed.

Damn it! Well, what's it to be? The bed nearer the entrance, he supposes. And he arranges his belongings in such a way that his occupation of it would be obvious to any third comer... God forbid! He then stands on the threshold for several minutes, getting his bearings, and observing random moments in the lives of his fellow castaways. Observing, but feeling no desire to hasten contact with any of them.

At times his reticence surprises him, even now, even after these three years of steadily increasing suspicion and caution. Yet – he acknowledges – it is a long-standing habit, not simply born out of more recent adversity. The devil-may-care behaviour of his younger days had gradually given ground to something like sobriety, even well before his marriage to Alice. Yet, the collapse of their world and its consequent hammer blows have greatly intensified that process, and for some time, now, his first reaction to any new situation is to back away and observe it at a distance.

And thus it is that in this moment, a walk – with all the regained freedoms that implies – suddenly becomes his highest priority. And he strides off, over to his right, leaving the tents and the hubbub behind him.

He has been walking for only a minute or two when, nearing the point where the great clearing ends and the forest's coolness beckons, a cluster of figures catches his eye, away over to his left, close by the water's edge. Standing in a small circle... he counts four figures in all, facing each other, two and two... but quite still. What can they be up to...? After a short while, one of them finally moves, raising his right hand, and at this sign, the other three bow their heads.

Yes, of course! A burial. It has to be – immediately confirmed when the figures move, and one of them begins shovelling earth from a mound, which had lain hidden behind them, into the grave around which they are gathered.

After standing – heads bowed – for a little while longer, three of them cross themselves then begin walking together, very slowly, in a line parallel with the sea, back towards the encampment, leaving a lone figure to his labours, refilling the grave.

That one, the tallest, is almost certainly Dr Ballow... and the second, the priest… taking off his stole, or whatever they call it. Too far off to make him out properly… Yet, there had been no priest on board… surely? One must have come over from the mainland…

Shaking his head, Will resumes his walk, but at a brisker pace.

As the trees close in, the path narrows, and yet it looks as though horses have passed this way recently enough. Entering a patch of deeper shade, Will remembers he is unarmed, but then, he has heard tell, there are no large land animals to fear, only snakes, scorpions, and spiders… and he grimaces at that far from reassuring thought and continues on his way.

After another hundred yards or so, the towering trees have fallen back again, and beyond them, to his left, through the undergrowth, his eye catches the glint of sunlight off water… And suddenly, his mind lurches into confusion, as it veers sharply along another path, glimpsing another sea through other trees, with Alice at his side, Lilian on his shoulders…

Sweet sorrowing memory. And he stops, trying desperately to rein in his now stampeding emotions.

And he sees that further on still, the track broadens out, surprisingly, into what appears to be a regular roadway; light has returned, and with it a sense of reassurance, of security, almost. Here, he feels, the tensions and cares of life aboard the plague ship could easily slip away, though they remain less than a quarter of a mile behind him.

Those more distant cares, however – as he has just been reminded – could doubtless ambush him anytime, anywhere…

Alice: so far away, so long ago… Would she always remain lost to him, now?

Coming suddenly upon a roughly-hewn, painted sign announcing 'Amity Point 10 miles', he almost gasps, brightening immediately at the enhanced sense of security this casual reminder implies: the island, though remote, still lies within the compass of the civilised world.

The path is opening out, hugging the coast, and following it awhile yet, he tries to think his way ahead for the weeks, maybe months, to come.

IV

The sun is well up. The bustle and noise of breakfast time has abated. Will judges he has been away for maybe an hour and a half, yet there is still no sign of his as yet unknown messmate. Taking off his jacket he sits down on his closed trunk. Must make a start getting myself organised. But howsoever organised, comfort would be well-nigh impossible here.

A sudden commotion draws him outside, though it seems to come from some little way down the line of tents and on the seaward side of the narrow roadway. A rapidly growing cluster of people is converging on the tent from which the sound is coming – plainly that of a woman wailing. His near neighbour, just then emerging from his own tent, is shaking his head and says something Will cannot quite catch. But then the man comes towards him, hand outstretched.

'I know we shouldn't in these harrowing times,' he says, looking ruefully at his hand as though – Will imagines, in a flight of fancy – it were some capricious creature that at any moment might strike and wound, 'but it's not easy to get out of the habit… Besides, it seems so un-mannerly. I'm James O'Rourke… Jimmy… and that's my brother, Johnny, inside. We're blacksmiths by trade… from Stowmarket, in Suffolk.'

Will meets his hand firmly, responding to vague feelings of solidarity, stirring within him. 'And I'm Will Crosby,' he says, 'from Whitehaven, in Cumberland.'

'Here's a sad business though,' the man continues, jerking his head in the direction of the noise. 'The poor woman has both her husband and her child down with this damned pestilence, and it seems likely the worst has befallen one of them, judging by her keening. I just hope the onlookers are not there out of mere morbid curiosity… That's something I never could abide… people swarming to others' misfortunes like flies to carrion.'

'Aye, 'tis indeed one of our less-appealing habits,' says Will with feeling, glimpsing again, in his mind, the jeering onlookers as he was being bundled into the Maria, to be driven away to the gaol to begin serving his sentence.

But at that, the conversation dies.

James, who a moment ago has seemed like a man full of confidence, and words, is suddenly struck dumb and starts to fidget with his hands, eyes fixed upon them.

'Ah, well,' he eventually manages, ''tis indeed all a bad business, there's no denying…'

And again, the embarrassed silence, broken by and by, equally lamely, by Will: 'Aye, and 'tis likely there will be many more afore the disease departs…' And then, not wanting to prolong the awkwardness: 'A bad business, right enough… Well… best be getting back to unpacking my things.'

The two nod curtly, smile, and thus released, turn away into their tents, Will closing the flap, consciously sealing in his privacy – the habit of the prison cell.

Yet he is restless, with no enthusiasm for 'unpacking his things' or the other trivialities even this limited domesticity requires. Opening the trunk, throwing back the lid, he abandons it at once, turning his attention, rather, towards the large chest he had so casually acquired on board The Emigrant, after the mysterious disappearance of its owner. Up to now, there has been no opportunity even to glance at what his nominal shilling had brought him, for all heavy baggage had been stowed in the hold and, in accordance with custom, access was allowed on but one day a month.

Curiosity rekindled, sitting on the corner of the bed he has claimed as his own, he reaches over to drag the bulky chest towards him. Ah yes. The stencilled name and address, reminding who and what its late owner had been: 'Mr Justice P. Rosper-Sandys, Duke's Mansions, The Chantries Mews, London', and he delays a moment before turning the key that will admit him to the last tangible remnants of a life that had ended in such uncertain and tragic circumstances in one of the remotest quarters of the globe. It would never be known whether his loss overboard was by accident or design. But this man, by all accounts, had been travelling to the northern sector of the Colony to become its Chief Magistrate.

Will shakes his head, musing on that void, on the vast, leaden, empty skies, the grey, storm-tossed seas boiling up in his mind's eye.

A stiff lock, visibly rusted; must take care not to break the key in it. But now, with patient coaxing, yielding at last; so what have we here? Hmm! Just books – Plato's *Republic*, Machiavelli, foreign stuff mainly, by the look of it… *The Complete Works of Shakespeare*… Ah well! Luck of the draw… But what's this? Fine binding, no title? Metal clasp, its own lock and… brass key. Looks more promising, some private inner sanctum, likely enough. A diary or some such, for why else the key?

And he holds off for a moment or two, conscience pricking, before turning it.

How strange. A moment's whim, nothing more than that, and I've become the custodian of the latest memories… of thought and feeling… of a life that came to its sudden end within such close proximity to my own and yet never touched me. And yes, a diary is what it is, its opening date and its brief first entry – "*17th April 1850: So goodbye to England and the torment it has brought me these three years past*" – announces the Judge's record of his journey to oblivion. But Will holds off still, wondering. Though the Judge is dead, is not even this step one too many, a trespass… on the man's soul?

But now, the sudden sound of someone approaching. Muffled words. And Will turns towards the tent's entrance, just as the flap is pulled back and a figure backs half in; some garment or other draped over his visible arm; still speaking to someone outside.

Laying the diary aside, Will rises to his feet, in anticipation.

Standing there he hears the half-figure's words, catching the brogue with its musical lilt. So, his companion-to-be... clearly Irish; stocky build, from what he can see, and probably, by his voice, several years his senior. But now, with the parting shot, 'it seems there is to be no let up yet awhile,' the whole man is revealed.

'Oh, I'm sorry,' the man falters – seeing Will standing there. 'I had not realised... I mean...' And his voice trails off into a helpless shrug.

Will smiles, thrusting out his hand. 'It seems we are to be messmates for the duration. I'm sorry if you were not warned... My name is William... Will... Crosby.'

And even as he speaks, he wonders if this isn't the man he had greeted on deck, as dawn was breaking... how many hours ago? But then this half-suspicion is immediately supplanted by another, that this is also the man he had witnessed, by chance, conducting the burial...

Will glances at the black garment still hanging over the man's arm and falls into consternation; for a churchman would never be his choice of companion. He turns away, his confusion accompanied by an acute sense of disappointment, the threat of restrictions, when he most needs to be free.

Yet these conflicting, stirring emotions have no time to develop, as a torrent of words starts to pour from the man, throwing him into further confusion.

'This fucking fever, Will, this fucking awful pestilence that scythes us down, young or old, rich or poor, innocent or greedy – in its very democracy it derides all promises mankind was ever made, or believes were made, by our Deus abscond... ye know, our ever-absent god... Lord Cop-out... the great empty chasm the Churches would have us believe in as presence... as guarantor of all future happiness! Well, I spit on it all, Will, I shit on it all! Just babies' babble, all of it! Oh, but... Holy Moth...I hope you're not ... I mean... I do not wish to give offence...'

The man's sudden embarrassment brings a slow grin to Will's face, despite his shock of words...

'Oh, what the hell does it matter? That's the truth of it, as I see

it. No point beating about the bush. Anyways, for better or worse –
and you must decide, Will Crosby, you must decide – I'm Thomas
Sheehan... for far too long the parish priest in a fleapit you've never
heard of and I never wish to set foot in again, in the County of
Tipperary.'

V

Dumbfounded, Will sinks back down onto his bed. The silence is prolonged as the priest seems fully occupied opening his own trunk, rummaging about in it, then pulling out a bundle of clothes, which he throws onto his bed with evident disgust, before closing the trunk again and dragging it into the furthest corner of the tent.

'Mildewed!' he declares, glancing at Will, 'rotten, like every other bloody thing that came off that stinking hulk!' And he proceeds to unfold the clothes whose acrid smell, even at a distance of several paces, has Will turning his head away.

'They'll probably be all right after a good soak,' Will ventures, 'though that's no help right now. Borrow something of mine if you wish, though it'll hardly be... bespoke wear!'

Sheehan nods and smiles his thanks, an almost absent smile, Will thinks, as the man starts to separate each item from the bundle, examining it minutely before consigning it to one of two newly forming piles. 'Some things look as though they'll see service again, others are too far gone,' he announces, then stands and goes outside for a moment, carrying the smaller bundle with him.

Perplexed by the immediate contradictions so apparent in this man, Will greets his return by voicing his own curiosity: 'Did I not see you... at a burial... ceremony, an hour or so ago? That was you, wasn't it?'

'Aye, you did that,' Sheehan acknowledges, suddenly agitated, his face transforming into a mask of anguish, tears swimming in his eyes. 'I was burying... the woman... the woman... who was to have been my future life, who had been the whole of my past – at least, that small part of it that ever counted for anything...' He cannot carry on, for his words choke, yet his anguish seems loaded with anger too.

'I'm sorry, truly sorry...' Will falters, yet in the same moment realising he is unable to square the man's words with what little he knew about Catholic priests. 'I didn't mean to pry... I had no idea...' and his speech falls away into yet another uneasy, questioning silence.

Sheehan looks at him direct. The tears welling, overflowing, then spilling down his cheeks as he speaks.

'We were looking to start again here. New world... New life... Like everyone, I fancy, who undertakes that infernal journey half round the world. We were running away from the tyranny of our past and the continuing tyranny of our present. Simple as that! I'd seen enough in Ireland's Great Hunger over the past three or four years to know, once and forever, there is no loving God. No nothing. Just misery, chance, then the endless dark. I knew these things even before she fell into my life, but her very coming – the manner of it – simply confirmed it all. Cast out, sickly child at her breast, half dead with hunger and fatigue... She had been on the road for several weeks, begging mostly, having walked the hundred or so miles up from Cork. I nursed her back... back to something like health on what meagre rations I could scrape together. And somewhere along that road I realised she had joined my life for good and all, and that the only parting would be that which came a few moments before you and I greeted each other on deck, early this morning.'

Will nodded. 'I see... but I had no idea that you...'

'Only,' Sheehan went on, disregarding Will's further attempt at apology, 'neither of us ever dreamt that that parting would come so soon. You see, we travelled separately. I bought her space in a first-class cabin, on deck, so she didn't have to experience the foulness below. When the epidemic was confirmed I was sure she would be safe. We were bound for Brisbane, where I was to offer my services as a schoolmaster; the priest – we were sure – could safely be laid to rest. But it was not to be. For some reason... or more probably, for no reason at all, it was not to be. And that's the bloody fact of it.'

Will's mind whirls about this story, told so matter-of-factly, yet nothing less than the flaying of a man's hopes, his belief and motive.

'So what will you do now...? I don't suppose you have any idea, have you...?'

'In the longer term, no, I don't know. I can't yet even grasp the notion of her... not being here... What strength that woman had! She could have propelled me to the moon if she had had a mind to; I could do anything at all, anything, with her at my side – that I could! But for now, well, it looks like there'll be more than enough to occupy me here...'

'You mean... what? I'm not sure I follow...'

'I mean that even if the priest is dead for me, he isn't for most of these simple country-folk who, through no fault of their own, find themselves in this hell-on-earth. I don't imagine the priests of Brisbane will be queuing up to serve on Stradbroke Island, do you? Same as the doctors. Like it or not, unless I'm very much mistaken, Mitchell and the young matron are going to have to see us through this on their own. And in such circumstances the dying and their folk are going to need something to keep utter despair at bay. In me, to be sure, they'll see the collar and the robes and the book, not the man – God forbid! So here, I guess, I shall be of much more use to my fellow men than I was even in my time with the Hunger... And if we come out at the other side, then there'll be time enough to think about the future. And if not, then it hardly matters.'

As he struggles to take this in, Will senses the complexity of the man – what manner of man? – but also, despite his pre-disposal to the contrary, his admiration for someone who could translate such immense personal loss into help for others. And the thought shadows through his mind that Sheehan's 'absent God' may still be just one jump ahead of him in all of this...

Then the priest's mood appears to shift suddenly, as his eye lights on the chest that Will still has open in front of him. 'Books?' he inquires in amazement, his sorrowing eyes lighting up once more. 'Real books! But how did you come by them? Forgive me for saying so, but you don't strike me as being a likely reading man, Will Crosby.'

'Oh, a spur of the moment decision… It seemed like… I can't really explain… but, saving something of that man who died such a lonely, awful death. I didn't know what was in the chest, of course, but, well, I saved it, them, its contents, from following their owner to a watery grave…'

'Ah! *That* one, was it?' the priest exclaims; 'Did he fall, did he jump… or was he pushed? I ask myself – and maybe others asked themselves the same question, at the time…'

Will regards him quizzically, for it is the first he has heard of this third possibility. While suicide was mentioned, at the time, the consensus was that the judge, foolishly on deck, had been washed overboard in one of the many gales they had passed through in the Southern Ocean, that he had missed his footing and rolled overboard unbeknownst to anyone else aboard. 'Do you think that likely? Why would anyone want to …?' But before he can finish his question Sheehan interrupts him.

'What you probably don't know is that our Mr Justice Rosper-Sandys had demonstrated a very keen interest in the Australian colonies for quite some time previous to his posting here. Many's the poor wretch he sentenced to deportation during the early and middle forties, more often than not for no worse a crime than stealing a crust to keep his wife and children alive as the potato crops fell to the blight. You see, he was Resident Magistrate for a time – too long a time – in West Cork and had a reputation for the utmost severity in upholding the law… a reputation that reached us even up in Tipperary – our very own Judge Jefferies, you might well have thought.'

Frowning, perplexed in the moment by the reference, which is beyond him, Will decides to let it lie.

'It's not beyond the realms of possibility that someone aboard harboured a grudge against him and took advantage of adverse conditions to tumble him. To be sure, opportunities were not lacking, while the chances of detection, well, remote to say the least.'

But now, suddenly, voices outside… two certainly, maybe three, conversing in whispers. And the priest leaps to the doorway of the tent and whips back the flap, almost knocking over a dwarfish man standing there, cap in hand. 'And what would you be doing here?' Thomas inquires, none too friendly. 'Cannot a man have a little peace, just once in a while?'

'Sir,' the man begins, 'oh Father, it is our poor neighbour, James Real... a Limerick man... He is fast nearing his last breath, God help him! And is calling for a priest to confess him. Dr Mitchell has sent me to ask if you could come with all speed, for the man is in some distress, something he needs to tell badly, before ... the good Lord takes him.'

The priest darts back inside and picks up the stole he had carelessly discarded. 'Yes, yes man, where is he...? I'll come at once.' He turns back to Will and opens his mouth to say something. But then, away he darts, followed by the messenger and the two other men who had accompanied him on his errand of mercy.

VI

A good deal later that same day, with its many twists and turns, Will is at last able to give his attention to the judge's trunk and its contents, still pondering the priest's surmise about the manner of the man's fate.

He picks up the journal once again, opening it at random then flicking quickly forward. He sees that the last entry had been made on 13th July, a month ago, in fact, and for a moment he fancies that must have been the day the judge had gone overboard. But then, leafing back more slowly through the pages, he sees that the entries had been intermittent, with no clear pattern to them, so that the judge's demise might well have occurred even several days after the 13th. That last entry was odd, though, not easily intelligible, but whatever else, it was evidence enough of a tangled, anguished mind:

Lost at sea. 'Land Ho!' reveals no land a Christian soul would ever wish to set foot on. The vicious storms of late and the absence of a noonday sun have made it well-nigh impossible to set a course, the captain says. If the captain has gone astray what hope for the rest of us? It was always going to be approximate. Charting a course is always approximate – more hope than certitude. You start out from a point you think you know and have a vision of a point you would reach by and by, but with no notion of how, what route, what storms, what shores, will bring you there, if at all.

Oh Emma! Emma! On what tide did you come to drift

away after such perfect beginnings? What storms blacked out the sun for you? Through the murky air I fancied I saw you there, waiting – they said it was called Kerguélen Island; stark, snow-capped mountains sheer out of the water and you high on a promontory beckoning. Should I have come to you there, then? Was the course that was charted for me from the very beginning to end there? Is this vast emptiness the spot, among the grey rocks and pure snows? Unsullied by human footprint, presence, perversity, dross? This aimless wandering, forever trying to set a new course in a leaking boat, with inadequate equipment, to see the sun again; is this all there is to be? If only you had...

And there it breaks off. Clear enough what the words say, but what did they mean? The entry immediately prior to this, penned three days earlier, offers no assistance that Will can fathom, referring to things apparently unrelated, and equally obscure:

I have always suffered with those I condemned to suffer for their own good and for the good of those whose lives they tainted by their continuing presence. Evil has to be contained always, close confined, since it cannot ever be vanquished outright. Not on this earth. There's no harm done, then. None.

As to the rest, I have done nothing but in care of thee, to shield thee always from the consequences of this fallen world. Yet, perhaps, this simple fact escaped thee in all our time together. Would that I could know for sure, for it might yet provide some little shred of comfort.

Baffled by the thought, or, at least, by the strangeness of its expression, Will turns more pages, and more...

A loud thunderclap startles him. 'God in Heaven's name!' And heavy drops of rain begin immediately flailing the tautening skin of the tent. Laying the diary aside, he goes to the entrance to close the flap, which had remained open after Thomas's hasty departure, hours before. And he sees the priest just now hurrying towards him, accompanied by the haggard-looking, desperately overworked, Dr Mitchell, who is trying to keep a cape over his head with one hand while gesticulating vigorously with his other. Will holds back the tent flap to admit them, both drenched and dripping pools of water.

'Ah Will, thank you kindly! A harrowing day it has been. The man I was called to this morning – you remember? – was barely coherent, but what little I understood of his confession, well, it was obvious why he felt the need to get it off his chest, poor wretch! I only hope, for his sake, I did not fail him, because by now he may well be quaking before his Maker, and that's a burden – however carefully wrapped – I wouldn't have fancied hauling into that company!' And he laughs wickedly. 'But now,' he goes on without pause, 'of more immediate concern is our promised rendezvous with a bottle of pochen I've been keeping by for a rainy day – and what more rainy day than this one? 'Tis somewhere among my things – let's hope it too hasn't succumbed to the mildew like the rest of 'em...'

Will smiles knowingly, while the doctor looks mildly perplexed. 'The good doctor, here, is in need of a little something, to lift his drooping spirits... So, come now, off with your cape, sit yourself down, and make yourself as comfortable as these cramped quarters will allow. By the way, the bed's yours – if you lack one, George...'

First sitting, then unable to resist the temptation, Mitchell stretches himself out on the bed, muttering his apologies. And by the time the priest has managed to lay hands on the elusive flask and tipped a generous measure into an ornate, antler-horn cup, the doctor has plummeted away into sleep.

'Well, poor man, that's really what he's short of... The drink can wait till later,' he murmurs, clumsily laying a blanket over their exhausted companion. He makes as if to return the contents of the cup to the flask but then, on second thoughts, tilting it, regarding it reflectively, he changes his mind – 'Oh... but... t'would be a pity to let the Holy Spirit lose its fire, so it would...' And he drains it in an instant, refilling it at once and handing it to Will, who takes it gladly.

'A little early in the evening for me, though, Your Reverence.

Nevertheless… I'll make the sacrifice…' Will raises the cup to his lips. 'Your health..', and glancing to his left, 'and the poor doctor's, too,' he toasts, with exaggerated ceremony, before filling his mouth and tipping his head back sharply. At once he falls into a fit of gasping and coughing… 'Good God! What is it?' he manages, at length. 'I've never known potatoes like it! So that's what happened to all the spuds in Ireland,' he says, still gasping, dabbing at his eyes, 'the blight was just a story put about by the whisky-swilling priests…'

But Sheehan's face clouds visibly. He laughs a little, a strained laugh, evidently more out of politeness than conviction. 'If you say so, Will. If you say so…'

The mood of the moment has clearly shifted. And Will senses his companion's discomfort, a suppressed anger even. Inadvertently, he has again touched a raw nerve. 'Well, not really, I mean… Not really,' he flounders, though suspecting no words he can find will redeem the situation… whatever that is.

Later, in the night, lying awake with his own perpetual torment, and yet newer, ill-defined confusions, Will hears the muffled, half-choking, gasping sound of the priest's lonely grieving.

VII

The day came dreary and heavy with a rain-filled mist sagging over the encampment, so thick one could neither see, nor hear, the sea.

Will realised he must have dozed off sometime towards dawn, for Thomas and the doctor had already left, doubtless to confront yet more hopeless emergencies somewhere among the tents or in the large, round tent, the makeshift hospital down by the water's edge.

His whole inclination, from the first days of the outbreak, had been to distance himself from it, and from his fellows, not least because it offered a plausible enough justification for his habitual reticence. Now though, brought by chance into the orbit of those who were most in the thick of it, he was beginning to feel uneasy. His unexpectedly kindled liking and growing respect for the priest was going to make it more and more difficult to maintain this aloofness. If the priest and the doctor collapsed – as well they might, from what he had seen last night – the prospects for all would be that much bleaker... The risks the two of them ran, selflessly, with their own lives, surely demanded some more responsible attitude from him, despite the fact that, in their last night's conversation, not a word or a look of reproach had come his way.

Cursing this realisation, he threw back the covers and reached for his boots.

As it happens, these creakings of conscience have their immediate origins in a false premise. Thomas, after an almost sleepless night, had indeed risen at first light – a habit long rooted since his days at the seminary. Covering his nightgown with a cape, he had picked his way through the murk and mist up into the little burial ground to stand before the raw grave of his lost companion.

His tears now blinded and choked him. The words he tries to utter emerge distorted or are lost entirely in a low, gurgling rush, his futile attempt to stem the flow of emotion that he had yesterday kept more or less in check, deadening himself through the plight of others. Yet, even if the words had come, he had no idea what they might have been, for the harsh truth of their sudden separation, and the manner of it, had left him quite incredulous, and floundering.

Strange for her not to go on wishing our wishes, thinking our thoughts... What had it all been for – our daily routines, the anticipations, the roses, and the briars, thrust brusquely aside, forever, like a broken pot?

His mind is back in those final moments, yesterday morning; as it ever would be, he fancies; she already departed into the mist and he straining to catch a last glimpse of her... The sputtering candle... The flickering shadows...

He has known death before, many deaths – given his calling how could it not be so? Yet never of someone on whom the myriad strands of his very being depended. This abyss he can only curse and contemplate, the blackness by which all, with our exhausted, unique, unrepeatable natures, are swallowed at the last. And we who are left, he thinks, must free ourselves as best we may and endure a while longer. But how? How? How? For we have no earlier experience to call upon for strength...

'Ever-present help in time of trouble,' he begins, but then, spitting forth the bitter words: '*Deus absconditus*, fraud, locus of all hatreds, of all deprivation, lend us thine aid...' And he stands, arms outstretched, drowning in mist and futility, shaking his head violently from side to side, with tears streaming down his unshaven cheeks. And those dancing shadows lost forever...

What, my dearest, my only love, can I do with this silence that now eternally divides us? What vibrations will ever again shake this emptiness into life for us?'

Dr Mitchell had risen only a little later, his feather-light sleep disturbed by the priest's movements. Assailed immediately by guilt at having slept when so many in his care had need of him, he had dressed hastily and stumbled away towards the hospital tent in which the worst cases were treated. Yet, even as he went, he realised that if any had had need of him then most surely someone would have been sent to fetch him; and that it had not happened was perhaps cause for small rejoicing. Maybe yesterday's seemingly hopeless cases had come through the night, outstripping their crisis; faint rays merging into the feeble light of the new day...

A flickering optimism that was to be short-lived.

Arriving at the tent, Mitchell learns that one of the two patients he had left there had died suddenly, within a few minutes of his departure with the priest. The matron had thought it preferable to let the doctor be, since there was nothing more he could do.

Beginning to protest, he is at once silenced by the patient young woman.

'The poor man had no family. He was of the dissenting faith, and so sudden was his departing that neither you nor the priest could have been recalled in time. Truly, Dr Mitchell, it was a merciful release, as you must realise. You have nothing to reproach yourself for. Nothing at all... George...' And shyly, hesitantly, she lays her hand lightly upon his arm.

At this mild recall to common sense and a right perspective – by one so young and inexperienced, at that – he calms a little and begins his examination of the young man in the only other bed now occupied, who seems brighter, more alert than yesterday; he even manages a smile, a ray of light that sends the doctor's spirits soaring. 'I think we might even shift you back with your family, today or tomorrow, or maybe the day after... What do you think?' he asks, and the youth nods vigorously, taking this concession as a sign that he has already come through.

Pulling on his boots, Will catches sight of the diary he had thrust aside the evening before, when the priest and the doctor had entered so suddenly from the squall. Opening it at the first page, he begins to read the dead man's words over again:

17th April 1850: So goodbye to England and the torment it has afforded me these three years past. That a brother could be so perfidious! To steal my life, my comfort, my happiness! That she could have betrayed me who was my every concern. And both, seeming pure, proved hideous in their joint perversity. But the Lord provides, as is fitting, and their incestuous passion did not go long unpunished. Yet that she should have died, not he, is no comfort at all, seems no justice at all, for his sense of desolation will undoubtedly be little different from mine own, though mine is lawful and just, and his nothing but the long, howling echo of the Fall.

If aught is clear from this, it is that belief in the perfectibility of mankind is folly; nature, not nurture, as the bard so rightly concluded. Behind the smile lies the leer; beneath the skin slides the serpent. Guilt must know no mercy. Sentence with the compassion owed to all human folly but sentence you must – to the very limits the law allows. The Brisbane district will not tolerate even the seeming least of crimes since crime is its own absolute, it shows no degrees – in truth, it has no lesser nor greater; it is or it is not, and that is an end of it. Sin must be confined at all costs and guilt can be safely presumed in all who come before the Law's Majesty, it little matters whether in the particular or the general. Our mission is clear. That much, at least, thine evil deeds have taught me, brother!

Will is alarmed at the harshness of the tone, the hardness of the will that shaped it. And flicking forward, again at random, he finds page after page of this same obsessive vengeance for a personal wrong suffered to be wrought on all mankind in the guise of a spurious, biblically inspired crusade against the sin of the world.

In spite of the neatness of the hand it is difficult to read in parts, and on one page there are several sporadic crossings-out, which make it almost impossible to connect the bits that remain intact.

If this was the man who, had he lived, would have donned the robes of the judge, the prisons in Queen's Land thereabouts would have been filled to bursting, the public executioner would have known no rest. It was a mercy the judge had never reached these shores, though oddly, none but he, Will, would ever realise this. Or… unless, of course, the priest's hints had some foundation in certain knowledge, were maybe the veiled testimony of the confessional, and it had indeed been the man's record and reputation that had done for him. If it were so, then here was a crime that had surely prevented the perpetration of many others. And again, if so, then someone may well have wrought his own personal vendetta, yet taken particular satisfaction from it, since it redounded also to the general good. But this was all surmise, for he could never know for sure.

Will shakes his head in recognition of the tenuous connections binding one cause to another effect, the very mistiness of truth itself. Such thoughts, he reflects, will scarce be tolerated when he takes up the office *he* has come to fill, as another upholder of the 'Law's Majesty' – as the ill-fated magistrate had so pompously expressed it.

And there was, he owns, a certain sense of discomfort in this knowledge, something stemming from the changes his voyage and its many anxieties had imposed upon him, a growing tendency no longer to see the world as the huge parade-ground of his soldiering days. But no – and, of course, yes – aboard *The Emigrant*, certainly, yet even before that sea-journey had even been contemplated, in the seemingly endless months he had languished in Carlisle gaol. There he had had much time for reflection, but also for reading other men's reflections about the life he had hitherto only ever encountered head on. And the no-nonsense, do-it-now-without-question sergeant the army had forged had looked about him with new eyes, and glimpsed a different world.

That slow process had then compounded all his immediate pain and sense of shame. It had tunnelled into his future, forcing him to recognise the many trivialities the military life embodied, those things in which he had formerly taken such pride – its pomposities and blind disregard for human weakness. Yet, it was all he had known, and though cashiered from that life because of his own failings and frailties, nevertheless he had somehow counted on that knowledge and those attitudes, which bound it together, to furnish him with a livelihood, if not in his own country then elsewhere, in the colonies. Only now, he realises, had that process, progressing unabated, leaching former certainties, been accepted even before he embarked on this new venture. Nothing now could ever tempt him back into the stiff high collars and gold-braid he has come to despise.

Will flicks through several more pages of the diary, but his mind can no longer fully engage with their tainted words.

There was no doubt, he had lost much, his self-esteem above all, when they had hauled him before the judge and pinned the 'bigamist' label upon him; and when the judge, and even earlier, the court martial, had made much of the fact that this crime was worse than most, for it was also a heinous sin, expressly forbidden in the scriptures. Intentionally or no, the 'Law's Majesty' and its Advocates had endeavoured to destroy the whole man completely.

But it was one thing to recognise his guilt and pay the penalty, quite another to bow his head and his knee and accept the tag of 'moral degenerate' they sought to impose upon him in perpetuity, these men of rectitude. Their cruel persistence and his dogged refusal had been the white-hot furnace from which the new man had emerged.

In retrospect, he thanked them with all his heart...

No, if excessive, none the less, Mr Justice P. Rosper-Sandys had been true to type, so arrogantly self-assured, so perfect a representative of his class and his country.

And in coming so far away from all of that, Will hopes he has cast off its shackles for good and all!

And yet, he muses, was not Rosper-Sandys also a man to be pitied? His life had been awash with hatreds, it seemed, even though he had had wealth, position, and privilege – all the advantages that the vast majority could not even dream of – and it had availed him nothing, nothing at all.

Will closes the diary sadly, reflectively, aware that somehow or other, just as the plight of the priest and the doctor and their joint charges all touched him, so too did the life and death of this other, not very good man, despite all his presumptions to the contrary.

Then suddenly, struck by a forming thought, he reopens the book – at the last entry – and slowly leafs through the many blank pages which follow, those that had been saved from the bile and bitterness that would surely have filled them, the noxious distillations of days that would never now be lived. And in these very moments, an idea is slipping into his mind, not over-insistent, but there, hovering at the edge of consciousness.

What is it? What does it want with him? These pages, these days they might well still represent, but differently, positively, constructing not destroying… Yes, Alice (he finds himself thinking), the book of *my* journey – back to you, if God and good fortune will it. If not, at worst, a chronicle of how I fared, what I sought to atone, to rebuild respect upon self-respect, until death – however it came – claimed me also. And peering into the judge's chest, he begins taking out the books one by one, placing them beside him on the bed, until his hand lights on what he has surmised must surely be there somewhere, a writing box – beautifully bound in calf's leather and tooled gold. Lifting it out onto his knee he turns the silver key and opens it to find the quills, the inkhorn and the sand sprinkler, which will transform the idea, now it is fully revealed, into the new reality, turning the judge's Hell into, at very least, his own promised road to a hoped-for future.

He sits back, elated.

Then, carefully unscrewing the cap of the ink horn, he selects a quill, and, after a few scratching, preliminary strokes, solemnly, purposefully, writes on the first blank page:

Journal of the New Life of William Crosby, dedicated in love and absolute fidelity to his former and future wife, Alice Fallowfield, of Redhills in the County of Cumberland, England.

Alice, so perfect, and so peerless.

Stradbroke Island, NSW, this fifteenth day of August in the Year of Our Lord, 1850.

And he regards his words in wonder, marvelling at this new, small, yet, he feels, most significant turn in his foundered life and fortunes.

Thomas Sheehan comes to himself after standing for an age like a statue of Grief, and looking about him, he sees that the mist has all but cleared, the drizzle has ceased, and an intensifying brightness promises the start of a new sunlit day. He smiles down at the grave: 'Perhaps I do you wrong to wish you here again. Perhaps lying here where the light sea spray daily flecks and salts your grave is enough… but I shall come again, my love, rest assured,' he murmurs before turning away, over towards the sea.

The tide is out and a considerable stretch of sand, with islands of water, lies before him. He lets the cape slip from his shoulders, then stooping, he raises the hem of his nightshirt and lifts it the whole length of his body and clear of his head, letting it too fall where he stands, and in a fit of physical euphoria, he hurls himself, naked, down onto the sands. He heads for the nearest rock pool, and having reached it, scrutinises it minutely for signs of unknown, alien life, before plunging in up to his thighs. An immense shiver courses through his body and his bravado freezes. He stumbles, cursing, towards the edge to make his escape; but then, thinking better of it, gently lowers himself onto a convenient rock and begins timidly to splash the icy water over his body, gritting his teeth as he does so.

VIII

Mindful of his niggling resolve, Will leaves the tent at last, and stands before the morning. The freshness of the breeze almost stings his face and hands after the enclosed, still clammy feel under the canvas. This latter awareness prompts him to fold back the flaps as far as they will go and secure them with the tapes attached for that purpose, to flood the damp space within with cool air.

Then, looking about him, he searches for the priest and the doctor, but sees neither among the few people as yet astir. At the hospital tent, likely as not… and he pivots momentarily on this thought. And yet, he finds himself reasoning, the newness of his resolution did not require quite the urgency of action that it had seemed to suggest at its birth. Deciding it could wait a little while longer, he starts off towards the brighter sky now advancing over the sea.

Approaching the gently rising embankment which marks the land's edge, he catches sight of what appears to be… a heap of clothes, could it be? Or – and the terrifying thought strikes him – maybe even a person, lying over yonder, to his right. Increasing his pace, his breathing noticeably quickened, he comes up with it and is at once relieved to find that it is not some poor child or unfortunate wretch in a state of collapse or worse. Yet this sense of relief is instantly dispelled as he recognises the priest's discarded cape and nightgown.

Several explanations flash through his mind, one after another, none of them good, as he remembers the priest's nocturnal anguish. Fearing the worst, he takes the last few steps towards what he imagines must be the water's edge. And once again he is shocked.

Firstly, to find the sea far off, then, almost simultaneously, to see the naked priest and, intermittently, hear his rollicking, almost tuneless voice vying with the wind and the far-off sound of the waves, the rustle of leaves in the forest behind, bellowing some song which, whatever else it might be, is surely no morning hymn of praise.

Will's face, for just a moment, lined and taut in anticipation of some yet lurking terror, relaxes at once into a snicker of laughter, as he recognises yet again the stalwart, seemingly unshakeable sanity of the man. And he censures his own ridiculous fears, slackens his pace, and ambles out towards him, shouting 'Madman! What are you up to?'

Sheehan, barely glancing in his direction or interrupting his chorus, yells back at him, 'Up to? I'm up to me arse in water, that's what!' before resuming his bellowing with a renewed vigour, fit to drown out the sea, almost.

On an impulse, Will tears off his own clothes and plunges into the pool – 'to drown the bloody lice!' he exclaims in mid-flight, whereupon the two fall to splashing each other furiously for several minutes, like giddy children, before finally subsiding exhausted, though laughing still, up to their necks in the by now quite turgid waters.

For several minutes, neither speaks, as if each were collecting himself up, and his thoughts, once more, from wherever their splashing had conveyed them. Then the priest suddenly heaves himself up out of the pool to sit on one of the rocks that ring it on three sides, his feet dangling in the water.

The silence is finally broken by Will, anxious to pledge his support and strength to the more serious business that awaited the priest just over their present horizon. And he stood – to make his offer – but this suddenly seems overly formal, a little ridiculous – being naked – so he too sits himself down on a rock facing his companion.

'Ah!' Sheehan acknowledges the sincerity of his words with a nod, but to Will's astonishment makes no further comment. After a pause, however, leaning forward, the priest says: 'But tell me how *you* come to be here, Will… at the wrong end of the world? For I cannot imagine anything other than… well… adversity, could tempt a man to such a desperate leap. Was it lack of work…? A woman? Or… what?'

A new gravity steals over the two as they sit facing each other in what both tacitly, if separately, perhaps recognise as being – in the wider circumstances which engulf them – a wholly incongruous, not to say ridiculous, attitude.

And yet neither shows any inclination to move.

The sun has at last risen above the distant trees and its warm light floods over their bodies. And Will has a sense of basking rather than bathing.

But Thomas Sheehan is still waiting for an answer.

Will shakes his head. 'You may well ask,' he sighs. 'It's true enough, I am here under sufferance. It's like this, you see…' And the priest hears how, at the age of seventeen, when Will had but lately joined the army and was still wet enough behind the ears to think he was somebody, strutting up and down his home street in his bright red uniform with its glinting buttons and badges and braid, for all their poor neighbours to marvel at, he had had the misfortune to encounter a woman several years older than himself. 'It was in a tavern; where else? In Carlisle, the home of my regiment,' he says, unhappily. 'She was there with friends,' as had he been, he recalls, 'but it was obvious from her manner and from her speech that she didn't belong there, Thomas, that… Well, Nancy later led me to believe she was used to much more gracious surroundings and a more… modern… way of life. And…'

Thomas regards him, as Will falters, but he makes no comment. He shifts his position on the rock, a bit awkwardly, and splashes his toes about in the water.

'And so?' he says eventually.

Will makes a gesture of disgust. 'Nancy was an actress, on tour in 'the provinces' – as she put it – and was then playing at the theatre in town.' She'd told him her home was in London where – as her friends had also assured him and his companions – she frequently played in all the famous theatres and rubbed shoulders with the best playwrights, artists and actors in the metropolis.

'Carlisle was but an interlude for her, her friends told me, something of a holiday from the demands of work and parties and other social functions that the life of the capital imposed upon one of her profession – and standing, within it.'

Despite his discomfiture, Will does not underplay an irony that is directed principally at himself.

'She herself said little, merely simpered modestly at the huge claims being made in her name – all the actors she'd worked with, supposedly of national and international acclaim – their names lost on me, however!

'Although she was more striking in appearance than beautiful, I was none the less bewitched by her from the first few moments of that first encounter. What totally undermined any, well… sensible judgement I might lay claim to was the fact that she seemed to single me out for her little attentions…' He swallows hard. 'Yes, her whispered asides, the raising of her eyebrows at some of the more outlandish things her friends were saying… Well, by the end of the evening we had become close friends and by the end of the week we were discussing marriage.' He shakes his head, wistfully maybe, certainly with regret.

'Can you credit it, Thomas? I was quite bowled over by the swiftness of it all – not least, of course, by the suddenly impending realisation of all my adolescent fantasies… In these matters Nancy was greatly skilled, though I never thought to ask how so, believing, I suppose – if I thought of it at all – that they were things an older woman would know instinctively, by virtue of being… older…

'Then, one day – not three weeks after we had first met – and completely against the mood of intense rapture that shaped our every assignation, Nancy came to me in tears, and for a while I could not persuade her to tell me what ailed her. But then, all of a sudden, she blurted out her – our – plight.'

Suddenly changing the pitch of his voice to mimic that of poor Judy pleading with Punch, his hands clasped over his heart, Will continues: 'I very much fear, dearest Will, that I am to become… a mother, and you… Oh, I am so very, very sorry to have brought this upon you... and you, my dear love, a father...'

Thomas chuckles appreciatively. Will clicks his tongue derisively. 'Oh yes, it was a fine performance…! But you will understand, I'm sure,' Will continues, resuming his normal tone, 'that such consequences of our joint bliss had never once crossed my mind, or if they had, had been speedily dismissed, since I felt securely cradled in Nancy's much greater wisdom in these matters of the heart… and the bedroom.'

Will had not had the slightest notion of what to do in these earth-shattering circumstances and it had been Nancy, when she was calmer, who had suggested a possible way forward.

'Nancy said I must speak to my commandant, inform him of the situation in which we now found ourselves and, effectively, I was to throw myself upon his compassion, begging his leave to marry as soon as was possible.'

This he had done in great embarrassment and trepidation, having to bear the man's ranting and raging, for what seemed an age. 'Of course, I was given extra duties to perform by way of punishment, for a whole month, but I came away with his permission and, well, we were married as soon as the formalities of the banns were got through. In less than a month after that I was posted to Malta, where Nancy was eventually to join me after the birth of our child. And…'

'And did she?' Thomas enquires, slipping back down into the water.

Will shakes his head. 'Thomas, this is a bit… You see…'

But Thomas, waving his companion's misgivings aside with his hand then hoists himself back up onto his seat.

And Will notices the water running down through the dark hair of his friend's thighs, in little, sandy rivulets.

'Holy Mother of God!' Thomas yelps, 'You sit there, prating away, while I am beginning to sizzle! Can you not hear it?'

Will chuckles, but then realising the performance – like all good comedy – holds its own bitter truth, and a hot one at that, he starts to suggest they wait till a more opportune moment to complete his story, thinking now they should take refuge from the burning sun. But the priest – and Will is aware how, increasingly, he has consciously to remind himself of this incongruous fact – will have none of it.

'Oh, now don't get me wrong, Sergeant Crosby, I'll not be after spoiling a grand yarn, to be sure I won't! But I'll just remind you, since it obviously would not dawn on you otherwise, we neither of us have to die shrivelled up in bloody forfeit!' Thereupon, he slides once more down into the pool. 'I swear I heard the water hissing, did it not, as I sank down into it…?'

Will follows suit, then leans back on his rock, his hands behind his head.

When their laughter has at last subsided, he seeks to make a quick end of it. 'The baby was still-born – or so I was told. Then, before Nancy could join me, I was whisked away to India, to the North-West frontier… And, well… by the time I returned to England, after three years away, I was a different man, more worldly-wise, I suppose, more confident in my own judgements… as well as being full of ambition… of determination.'

Even as he is speaking Will realises there are other things he would rather not confess to, and he censors his words, skirting around his shameful acts and omissions, compressing all into the moment of his return to England.

'My first meeting with Nancy… after India… was something of a shock… She had grown stouter, and her dress, which I had thought of as immaculate and elegant, had become careless, even slovenly. She was visibly older – and it was only then, Thomas, that I really appreciated she was… twelve years my senior. Twelve years!' He shakes his head in mock disbelief. 'The house she had rented for us on the allowance I made over to her was… well… squalid and dingy.'

'And how did she receive you?'

'Oh… it was odd, I can tell you. It soon became apparent we were complete strangers to one another, and violent rows would flare up continuously out of nothing, so that…'

Thomas has his hand in the air, and begins waving it in front of

Will's face, excusing himself for the interruption. Raising his head, Will sees two small boys, just below the slope down onto the sands, looking in their direction, but hesitating, clearly perturbed at the curious sight of two men up to their necks in the water.

'So what is it that you want, boys?' Thomas shouts, 'Is it me that you're seeking or are you just intent on spoiling our bath? Cannot a man have a bath in something like peace?' And the boys hesitate, backing away a few paces even. So, manoeuvring himself towards the rocks, he eventually stands upright on the sands and shouts, again: 'Come here, then. Tell me what it is that you'd be wanting.'

The children, still plainly unsure of themselves in these daunting circumstances, shuffle slowly forward, their heads down, seemingly, not daring to look upon a naked priest. And even when they are standing before him, shifting uneasily from one foot to the other, they continue to look at the ground directly in front of them.

'Please Father, the doctor has asked us to find you to ask you to come at once to the hospital tent. It is a matter that is very... very...' and the speaker turns to his companion for assistance, but he too is unable to supply the word. And so they stand, fidgeting, utterly uncomfortable until the priest instructs them to return at once to the doctor to say that he is on his way.

Once the scurrying boys have disappeared over the brow of the banking beneath the cemetery, Thomas begins to look about him. 'Now, where the Hell did I put me bloody things, for God's sake...?'

IX

It was Will who remembered, chuckling at the priest's raillery. 'In fact,' he confided, 'it was your "bloody things" that led me to you, imagining God knows what, seeing them lying there all of a heap.'

'Ah, well, I was in need of a new birth in that moment and those things – and now I think of it, all they represent – seemed an absolute encumbrance. Still, I'd best put the bloody things back on if for no better reason than to maintain the illusion that priests, like angels, have nothing between their legs!'

And away he went over the sands, up the bluff, to stand silhouetted against the skyline. Then he turned to look back towards the pool and shouted, gesticulating wildly, 'Ah, for God's sake, I'd forgotten! It's me bloody nightshirt not me cassock at all! I'd best get back to the tent and put on the uniform. Are you coming or will you stay and take another dip to finish off your de-lousing?'

'That's up to you, really. Remember what I said. If there's anything I can do, to...'

But Thomas, walking part way back over the sands, towards him, cuts him short. 'To tell you the truth Will, there's nothing you can do that's regular, to help me – unless, of course, you'd like to apply for the job of sexton? Though I warn you, it's a job without any prospects...'

Will laughed, catching his drift. 'No, that's not what I had in mind, frankly. Besides, that grim-faced Stevens and the other ticket-of-leave man seem well fitted. And, with the practice Dr Ballow is predicting, they are certainly going to have much opportunity to hone their skills!'

Thomas came up with him in this instant, his face alight, and stood watching Will hopping around, swinging his arms wide then back against his chest, hoping to dry off in the sea-breeze sufficiently to put his own clothes back on. 'I think I can see an opening for you as an entertainer, Will Crosby, music hall maybe – the poor people here have too little to laugh at,' he suggested in mock seriousness. 'But no, Dr Mitchell is another matter. It's likely he will be able to give you work a-plenty, though obviously it will be work that puts you in constant danger of contracting the sickness yourself. He needs people he can rely on to nurse and observe his patients and administer whatever comforts are to hand. We'll talk to him if you like. I know he'll be only too grateful to you if you think of taking on that kind of responsibility.'

Will nodded, reflectively. 'Truly, Thomas, I feel I have no choice in this matter.'

Yet, if 'no choice' were indeed the fact of the matter, an added 'no stomach for' would have brought him even nearer the truth of it.

And shortly, when Will was ready, away they went, hurrying towards their tent, so the priest could dress.

They are not at all prepared for the sight that awaits them at the hospital tent.

The young doctor, who had appeared fit enough when they had seen him last night, despite being utterly worn out by his constant calls to duty, is stretched out on one of the beds. He is sweating profusely, and in some obvious distress.

'Ah, Thomas, I fear I too may well have succumbed to the fever,' he croaks. 'Certainly, I feel distinctly unwell and the symptoms are… suspiciously like those at the onset of the disease. I have had an incapacitating headache these two hours past, am running a high temperature and am aching in all my joints.' His tone is matter-of-fact. 'It could be the influenza, but I doubt that, frankly. So please… No… don't!' he says, refusing Thomas's hand as he eases himself gingerly into a semi-upright position.

'And Dr Ballow…?' Thomas begins.

'Dr Ballow returned to Brisbane at the turn of the tide late last evening, hoping to persuade one or two of his colleagues to come and assist us here. I only pray he is successful, for I fear I shall soon be of no use to anyone, if… if, as seems likely, I am sinking into the inertia the pestilence imposes.'

Thomas is silent for a moment then speaks quickly and quietly, chiefly to the doctor but also so that the anxious matron, and Will, coming closer now from where he'd been standing, know what is in his mind. 'George, I hope for all sorts of reasons that you are mistaken about your condition, but you and I both know that in these already straitened circumstances we must now make plans to face even greater difficulties, as contingency, at very least. I am no doctor but have obviously some authority by virtue of my calling, and some little experience of the disease from my days in Ireland. You must instruct us now what is to be done, not only in caring for yourself but also for the many others who are, or are to become sick, if we are to believe the warning given by Dr Ballow.'

He then signals to the matron that she must endeavour to make a note of the points as the doctor speaks them.

There was already a list of patients who were regarded as critical and the doctor detailed what little could be done to best help each of them. Additionally, however, he explained how to detect the onset of the disease and what to do with patients suspected of having contracted it. He talked about the few medicines available to them, hoping that more would soon be on their way from Brisbane, on the returning *Aurora*. Chiefly, though, he was concerned to minimise the number of new cases rather than deal with the disease where it had already struck.

'Little or nothing is known about its causes,' the doctor explains. 'As you are aware, it is thought to be carried on the air and thus, it would seem, there is little can be done to prevent it. I am not so sure about that I have to say. I have observed that it always strikes in crowded and filthy conditions. Constants are uncleanliness of person – infrequent washing, especially of the hair – unwashed clothing, and the presence of lice both on the person and in the bedding. My intention is... was... to seek to eliminate not one but all of these factors.'

It seems an impossible task.

'Such action would undoubtedly require a regime of enforcement... and here I would appeal to both you and Sergeant Crosby, in your respective authorities... but also you must enlist the aid of Mr Weatherall, the immigration agent – when he gets here – and whatever police he brings with him. I am afraid that people will have to be forced to... I suppose... change their ingrained habits. And given the dire consequences of their failure to do so, I should be inclined to ignore their protestations, and to use sanctions against those who refuse to conform, withholding food and drink and other necessaries...'

He spoke urgently, in short gasps, and the matron barely looked up from her pad.

'Only by eliminating the conditions in which the pestilence thrives shall we be able to defeat it, since once it catches hold treatment is largely ineffectual. Not surprising when we have only the vaguest of notions what it is that we are fighting.'

And after maybe a quarter of an hour's hurried, unbroken, almost whispered speech, Dr Mitchell falls back on his pillow, exhausted, and sinks at once into a deep, though from the outset, uneasy sleep.

Thomas beckons to the other two that they should follow him outside and, once there, permits himself a long sigh. 'This is indeed a bad business. We had need of better. From what I have seen of this fever, here and during the Great Hunger in Ireland, it is almost certain that Dr Mitchell has indeed succumbed to it. Inevitable, I suppose, for one who, day and night, is exposed to those who have already fallen victim to its ravages.'

Turning then towards Will, he continues: 'We need time and better fortune – and more expert assistance than is immediately to hand. But we three must do something.' He pauses. 'I think, in these circumstances, we have no option but to try and put into action what poor George has just explained to us. Unless, of course, either of you has a better plan....?' He looks from one to the other but, after a moment or two's silent reflection, it is clear that nothing further is forthcoming.

All three are in agreement about their immediate course of action. The matron is to remain in charge of the makeshift hospitals in both hut and tent. They then divide the camp into four notional sectors, one of which Will and the priest will immediately begin visiting, homing in on particular families, and in the name of 'The "Authorities" demand their espousal of a strict regime of cleanliness.

Still addressing the matron, Thomas asks her to make the doctor as comfortable as possible and to keep them informed of his condition, suggesting, at the same time, she refrain from spreading the news of his lamentable state, 'so as not to cause panic among people who are already sorely afraid.'

She nods, though visibly distraught, and goes back inside, followed closely by the two men. And after briefly checking on the doctor, Will suggests they add credibility to their subterfuge by posting notices in prominent places, summarily outlining the new discipline required by the "Authorities" and the consequences of failure to comply with it.

By the time the notices are written the morning is all but over, and, to add to their new sense of crisis, no fewer than four new calls have been made on Dr Mitchell's assistance. These are dealt with, in the short term, by suggesting that the doctor is already busy elsewhere and that he would come as soon as he was able. But it is clear to the three of them that they would not be able to conceal the doctor's illness for long.

Time was forever running out. The notices were posted in three different locations, and together Will and the priest finally began their visitations.

The light is fading fast on another scene, in another far distant place. The little girl's eyes close at last and after keeping her habitual, nightly vigil for some few moments more, Alice rises silently from her chair and lifts the candle away from the bedside locker to the dressing table, at a safe distance from the sleeping child. At once the small room is reconfigured, an abyss of deep shadow separating the bed from the door, but with the tiny, flickering beacon suggesting safety and comfort for an hour or two more.

Not quite conscious of the motivation that underlies it, the mother senses the importance of this and other little daily routines in her daughter's fractured life and so takes the necessary trouble to maintain them. Yet, for herself, they are hateful, stark reminders of the slowly eddying, well-nigh static nature of her days during the last three years, waiting, always waiting, afraid to move away in any direction, clinging still to the lengthening interlude, yet hating it – and him – him especially, for imposing on her still young life this inexorable longing.

X

Even by the time he had left for Malta, Will had begun to realise how blind he had been in accepting, without demur, the urgent dictates of a first love affair in full spate. The matter of the coming child and the responsibilities of fatherhood had started to weigh heavily on him, as it had gradually become clear that he knew nothing of life, had experienced nothing, and was thus far from ready to settle into the kinds of routine all of that would demand of him...

Thoughts passing through his mind as he hammers home the nails that Thomas passes him and fixes the notice at eye level.

And he remembers too how grievous that parting from Nancy had been, and sincerely so; yet, once away, he had quickly begun to feel that a burden had slipped from him. Yes, he had taken readily to the life of a young soldier in his first overseas posting, especially in such a delightful spot. Valletta harbour... and the pleasures that life offered in its vicinity. Even before news of Nancy's stillbirth had reached him, he had formed the habit of visiting the brothels there from time to time, encouraged and schooled by older, more experienced comrades.

Of course, he admits to himself now, his letters home had long maintained the fiction of his love and longing, and a regret at the loss of the child, his child – or so he had believed it then – a regret that, in all truth, had not touched him very deeply. With every week that went by, the ties had grown less, and he remembers having dreaded the time when his wife would join him there, when, he had fancied, he must devote himself to a wholly restrictive home life with Nancy, centring upon her and, presumably, the children she would have desired, and demanded of him.

Will's face, even now that all was known and long past, registers a cold, suppressed anger.

At the very last minute, it had been the increasing troubles in the Indian States that had saved him and changed his life forever: his regiment being redeployed from Malta to the garrisons of the Northwest Frontier... where families were not able to follow.

And thus an anticipated separation of but a few months had turned into one of three years – a 'sacrifice' he had willingly embraced.

'Good day to you, neighbour!' calls the priest to a man of middling years, who was sitting on a low, three-legged stool before an open tent, smoking a clay pipe. The man fixes them with a steely glare but says not a word. Nothing deterred, the two approach him, smiling all the while, but the man's look never falters, his eyes remaining fixed upon them.

Feeling that something must be said to deflate the fellow's obvious hostility, Will tries another tack. 'So what brings you so far from home – wherever home is?'

The man snorts audibly, uncompromising still. 'And what is that to you?' he challenges. 'For surely, 'tis none of your business.' He turns his back, swivelling round, awkwardly.

Will looks at Thomas, who grimaces and shrugs, but goes forward all the same. 'To be sure, it is not,' he says, 'and I'm sorry we asked, for it was kindly meant. Honest to God, we have no wish to intrude more than we have to...'

The man rises to his feet and faces them squarely. Squat, rather ill-clad, and as they can now see, bearing a deep red birth mark on the side of his face, which had been in shadow as they came towards him; but he shows not the slightest glimmer of friendliness.

'And in what manner do you have to intrude at all?' he demands.

Abandoning all attempts at civility, and looking the man directly, coldly, in the eye, Thomas asks whether or not he has read the notices lately posted, and understood the instructions they bear – 'About the washing, and all?'

'The washing? That I have not,' the man snaps back. 'Nor do I have any intention of doing so.'

Thomas nods slowly, reflectively, and, muttering to himself, scans the list of names he carries with him, mentally checking the number on the tent pole. 'Wilfred John Farmer, is it not? From East Langton, in the County of Leicester?'

'Aye, that's me. So, what of it?' the man growls, making as if to enter the tent.

'Not so quickly, Mr Farmer,' Will intervenes, summoning up the memory and tone of a sergeant's authority, 'for unless you accompany us now to read the notice and to confirm not only that you have understood its instructions but that you will swear to carry them out to the letter, then I'm afraid... well... your daily ration of flour will be halved from tomorrow, and if you have still not complied within three days, it will cease altogether. We trouble you on a serious matter, sir,' he adds, 'and wish that it did not have to be so, but what we are about is for the good of all.'

The man hesitates at the threshold, fiddles with the tent flaps, then turns back to face them. 'You asked what it was that has brought me so far from home; well, I'll tell ye.' His tone and stance speak defiance. 'It is to put as much distance as I can between the likes of you and the likes of me. I have no cause to love either priests or policemen, believe me – and he nods pointedly in Thomas's direction, and then at Will, summarily – for those I have known have ever been lickspittles to the gentry, turncoats to their own people, ever a... a burden upon the poor.'

He spits, noisily.

'And here y'are, telling me about notices and instructions and swearing and conforming and withholding what is mine and my wife's by right...' The man's tone has sharpened noticeably. 'Well, whilst ever we are imprisoned here, you clearly have us by the throat, hounding us... but we shall yet get beyond your reach, if we pull through this latest trial of our patience and our lives. You mark my words, we shall...'

Thomas raises his hand to arrest this angry flow. 'Had we more time – and were you a modicum more civil – my companion and I might well disabuse you of the presumptions you make about us. That we would. But 'tis no great matter, as there are graver problems at hand. You have heard what we have said. So… Are you coming with us or will you choose rather to impose needless hunger on your poor wife, as well as upon your discourteous self? Decide quickly, Wilfred Farmer, for we have many such calls to make this day.'

'You give me no choice.' Farmer shakes his head. 'My wife is sick and needs nourishment. But you wield your authority sharply… sir. Lead on, and let's get this tedious business over with.'

The three of them turn, and Will, playing out his part, leads the way to the nearest of the notices he had pinned to a huge tree, a hundred or so yards along the roadway in the direction of their own tent. Once there, Thomas begins to read the notice aloud – to save the man the possible further embarrassment of having to confess his illiteracy, Will surmises.

When the priest has finished his litany, he looks at Farmer. 'So, what is your response? Will ye conform or no?'

The man looks incredulous. 'This is an affront to human dignity!' he blusters. 'Compelling people, who are supposedly free agents of their own destinies, to… to take baths every day and wash their clothes, first in this water then in that… and twice a week at that! To what avail? What… what is the purpose of this deliberate annoyance?'

Thomas will not be drawn. By this time entirely out of patience with the man, he states bluntly: 'At five of the clock this afternoon, Sergeant Crosby and I shall set up a table in the middle of the encampment and you… you will be there to swear the oath on the Bible, so you will – on your own behalf and that of your wife, if the good lady is not well enough to do so herself. Is that understood?'

Wilfred Farmer nods curtly and stomps away, clearly cursing under his breath.

Will removes his wide-brimmed hat and wipes his perspiring brow, shaking his head, yet grinning broadly. 'Thomas, my friend, I admire your forbearance, but… if they are all as stubborn as that one, we shall soon have a rebellion on our hands.'

'True enough. True enough.' The priest shakes his head, ruefully. Then he manages something of a smile. 'Let us hope Dr Ballow and Mr Weatherall, and whoever else, will not delay their coming overmuch. We have tense days ahead, to be sure.'

They fall silent.

'Awkward customer though he is,' Will says, by and by, his thoughts moving on, though also back, 'I understand well enough what he means, for I have felt similar hatreds myself, especially during these most recent years.' He glances at Thomas. 'There is a harsh oppression of the poor at every turn, Thomas, whether it is the law, the police, the army – as I discovered to my cost – the city fathers or, indeed, the Church... whatever the Church.' Will steps back to lean against the tree's cool, smooth mottled trunk, though taking care not to disturb the notice.

'Well, what is your explanation for it, Sergeant Crosby?' The priest affects a mock solemnity, peering out from beneath his bushy eyebrows.

'As I see it,' Will answers, trying not to be distracted, 'well... it seems that 'sin' and 'poverty' have the same sense in the minds of all of these... Authorities. Aye... and in spite of what is actually written in our country's laws, there is an assumption of guilt – of sin, that is – or, at best, of likely or inevitable guilt. It's plainly there in the Judge's diary I've been reading. It amounts to nothing short of... of an undeclared civil war. Just look at what happened to the leaders of the Chartists, and before them those poor devils from Tolpuddle – and Peterloo afore that. Do you know about the excessive cruelty, the spitefulness, with which their just demands were treated? The working man... who is, well... without question, the cornerstone of our country's fame and prosperity, is ground down... is frequently trampled upon by his so-called betters.'

Thomas's face looks grave: 'Aye, that he is! Believe me, Will, I need no lessons on that subject! I'm Irish, remember...'

But Will must make his point. 'You know, inconvenient though his attitude is, I admire – and in some measure applaud – the defiance of a man like Farmer. Do you, as well? Can you...?' With all his dormant rancour aroused again, it is suddenly important for Will to know his friend's views.

'Aye, well...' he goes on, almost without pause since Thomas does not answer, ''tis ironical, if you think about it. That we two, with our own particular reasons for leaving the old life behind – fugitives, not unlike Farmer, apart from the particularities of his case, whatever they may be – should find ourselves, well, thrust into this role of "lickspittles" to the "Authorities". For that is undoubtedly the way such as he will see us...'

He turns away. 'But it isn't as simple as that, is it?' he murmurs. 'No, most certainly it isn't. As I see it, Thomas, in this action of ours, well... whether it succeed or no, we have responded to necessity by... by assuming authority ourselves – even if we are doing it in the name of some unstated, truly non-existent "Authorities" – because we know, instinctively, maybe, that the greater part of these downtrodden people about us here will likely conform in their habitual, cowed manner to whatsoever thing such "Authorities" demand. Is that not so?'

Thomas smiles, his head tilted to one side, acknowledging the truth of Will's self-criticism. 'Quite the philosopher, when put to it,' he declares, his smile becoming a grin.

'Is it dishonest of us?' Will persists, stooping to fasten one of his boots. 'In truth, it never even occurred to me to ask, till now – and that says a lot about corruption as creeping habit, whatever our minds may wish for ideally.'

A sudden shiver courses down his spine, and unsure whether the priest is really listening to this stabbing conscience of his, he steps out of the shade of the tree into the glare of the midday sun as if to move on to their next appointment.

Given as he is to long solitary musings, it was probably the longest statement of his opinions he had uttered in a long time.

'So is it... dishonest?' he asks again, turning as Thomas comes up with him.

'Of course it is Will. To be sure it *is*. Yet desperate situations demand desperate measures, do they not? And knowing what may well ensue if we do not enforce these measures, by whatever means available to us – and he nods sagely – I feel certain our deception is justified. Indeed, the real "Authority" here is common sense, is it not? Or the pestilence itself… whatever fancy garb we dress it up in!' And with a flourish of undoubted self-irony, he begins adjusting his cassock.

'Yes… and of course, you are right,' Will concedes, smiling. 'Yet it's still galling to be ranged, in the eyes of one's fellows, among the ranks of the enemy. Lickspittles… indeed!'

'Well, then' Thomas concludes solemnly, 'Whatever the enemy, we had best seek out more souls to save with our Inquisition and its ordeal by water – their baptism into a new, lice-free world. For the sooner it becomes common practice, this bathing, the more quickly will its results begin to be felt. At very worst, our fellows will smell less foul than at present, even if poor Dr Mitchell were to be proved entirely mistaken in his other prophylactic surmises…'

He consults his list, his finger running through its names – 'Right. Let us pay dear Mrs O'Leary, from Ennis, a call, for she might seem a likely candidate for the ducking.'

XI

The rest of the day, as they had surmised, was fraught with difficulties. Yet in the majority of cases it had not been so much the demand and all that it implied about the long shadow of a rigid authoritarianism, cast apparently even to the ends of the Earth, which had upset them all, but rather the substance of what was demanded – its 'unreasonableness', its 'unnaturalness', even its 'immorality'. Surely, the body gained its resistance, its strength, precisely from the natural film of grime that stood like a bulwark between it and the world beyond with its pernicious rheums, its currents of chill air, its many evils borne upon the wind? Why else would colliers never scrub their backs? – And they should know. Surely?

And with those many who reasoned thus, when they came to the table in their twos or threes, or alone, Thomas's eloquence came into its own, gaining in authority with each supplicant that passed.

'The science of medicine,' he declares confidently from a fund of near total ignorance, 'is ever moving, Mrs O'Leary, ever evolving, making new discoveries, and we now know for certain that far from protecting us and giving us strength, dirt enters our bodies through our skin and is cause of all kinds of ills that until now we had attributed quite wrongly to other causes.'

And as if fired into belief by his own invention, his 'science' grew and expanded prodigiously, with his audience all agog.

'It is proven beyond all reasonable doubt, Mr Coleman,' he proclaims, 'that the lice and fleas, which are our common lot, are not just a constant irritant, but that they feed upon our body's dirt, and when they bite, they inject all manner of germs into our blood, including this pestilence!'

'Mr and Mrs Frith, if the body's dirt – a bountiful food supply to these tiny pests – is eliminated,' he asserts, sagely, 'as it is by frequent exposure to water and soap, then the vermin will cease to trouble us, and the risk of infection will be gone! It's all quite simple, quite logical, really,' he adds, for good measure, 'salt water, and then fresh water, lots of both, that's the answer!'

'So – he concludes, reasonably – just put your name, or your mark, here. Yes, that's right, just there. And now place your hand on the Holy Book and repeat after me...'

Will sat beside him, marvelling at his effrontery (and benign hypocrisy), from time to time nodding wisely himself, or making a sound or gesture of agreement. Most, it has to be acknowledged, went away persuaded, if shaking their heads regretfully at the 'advances' of science and the thought of what the morrow held in store for them. Some few, however, departed as visibly sceptical as they had come; they signed, they swore – because Authority demanded it – and they left, but both Will and Thomas recognised that their reluctant signature or mark was but a tiny gain. The real test would come when they, like Moses, sought to lead their charges into the water.

Wilfred Farmer did not come. So, when everyone else they had visited that day was finally registered, and after small deliberation, they determined to seek him out once more, taking the Bible and the register with them.

As they went, they passed by a group of five or six children playing leapfrog, rowdily, enthusiastically, like children anywhere. Watching them, hearing them, Will found it hard to believe, for these children were not 'anywhere', they were here, with sickness and death all around them, perhaps even now a participant in their game whose end, for one or more, might not be far off.

Thank God that Lilian was not among them.

It was clear, immediately they arrived at his tent, why Farmer had not come. Two or three women were back and forth, trying as best they might to alleviate the sufferings of his wife, Hester, who – Thomas whispered, retreating from the tent doorway, where he had briefly peeped in – was certainly near to death.

And after standing there a moment, as if collecting his thoughts, Thomas leads Will inside.

Farmer is sitting beside his wife, his head in his hands. Becoming suddenly aware of the presence of the two earlier intruders he rises angrily and comes towards them, shaking his fist.

'How dare ye! How dare ye come pestering us now with your petty whims! Can you not see how things stand with us? We have sent for the doctor several times, but he does not come. His delay has almost certainly cost my wife her life, and me...'

Thomas takes a step towards him. 'Mr Farmer, we are truly sorry, and would not have come bothering you had we known. To be sure we would not. As to the doctor, well... unfortunately... I must tell you that he will not come, for he cannot. He too has been struck down... as a result of his selfless devotion to the rest of us.'

Farmer gapes incredulously.

'We can only hope that succour will soon arrive from Brisbane. I am sorry to bring you these grievous tidings, honest to God I am, but, in any case, from what I have just seen, I think there is little he could have done, by this time.' He pauses, clears his throat, then very quietly, very gently, says: 'As you observed before, I am a priest, and if you think I can bring any comfort to your dear wife, well, I will gladly try and do so.'

Farmer stands where he is, his face sunk in his hands, yet again, his body convulsed in an uncontrollable sobbing.

Thomas speaks some words of comfort, crooning, almost, and at last the man's shoulders are still.

And thus they stand, the three of them, for what seems an endless time. When Farmer again feels able to frame his words, he stammers a grudging thanks, but then explains, apologetically almost, that his wife, though a believer, is not of the Roman faith.

Thomas steps close to him and puts his hand on his shoulder, so as to relieve the man of the necessity of further words: 'I care not what faith she is of, Wilfred Farmer, she is one of God's children and sorely in need. Let me, please, minister to her now, for her comfort, and for your own. Please!'

The man's bewilderment is evident in his face, being unable, in the moment, to comprehend this break with long established forms.

'Please,' Thomas begs again, 'before it is too late?'

Farmer cannot bear up any longer. He nods his consent then turns away, once more reduced to a violent sobbing.

Thomas signs to Will to do what he can for the man, himself asking one of the women to bring water quickly. He then approaches the bed and sits down on the stool Farmer has vacated. He begins talking softly to the dying woman whose laboured breathing seems to steady somewhat, as she listens to the words he speaks. Without formality or show, but with definite purpose, he constructs an absolution that seems to soothe her, and when he has finished, he holds her hand and calls for her husband. Farmer now comes over and kneels beside his wife, taking her other hand and bowing his head over her face. She smiles, whispers something to him, closes her eyes, and slips silently over the border into death.

Will, witnessing these rapidly enacted events, feels impelled to turn away. It is not just pity for the man and his wife but also the profound humanity he sees at work in his companion who, not many hours before, had suffered an identical loss. It humbles him, and overwhelmed, he walks away, in the direction of their tent and the sanctuary it presents.

'Whoever would have believed it?' he finds himself thinking, 'Me, of all people, admiring... let alone sharing a dwelling with... a Catholic priest!'

But he does not go far. For once he has brought his own emotions to heel, he turns back towards the Farmers' tent, pauses, then enters once again.

The corpse has already been shrouded in a sheet and the priest sits beside the grief-stricken Farmer, talking to him in subdued tones, an arm about his shoulders, ignoring the comings and goings of the women helpers. Seeing there is truly nothing he can do there, Will signals to Thomas, who, however, is too absorbed by his immediate task to notice. So away he goes, for the second time, though now towards the hospital tent.

And once again his mind returns to the account of his own misfortunes he had begun to give, and not give, to this wholly commendable stranger, the priest.

Life at home with Nancy, on his return from India, had been even more unbearable than Will had anticipated, even in his worst moments. Not surprising, then, that only three months later he had volunteered for another tour of duty overseas – to Gibraltar, this time. Glad to be gone. Like a millstone fallen from his neck, it had seemed… and with no farewells at all on either side. Oh, he did not blame her overmuch for taking up with a tradesman whilst he was in India, even having him live with her, in *his* house. His own habits, in those intervening years, would hardly permit such condemnation…

Nevertheless, there had still been times, in Gibraltar, when his heart was heavy. That all had gone so badly awry after such beginnings. That he had not tried hard enough, had not exercised sufficient moral responsibility to accept the road he had taken – however unprepared he had been.

So, he had written to her, at least once a week for the first three or four months – in all maybe twenty letters, all of them full of descriptions of the way things were on the Rock; but increasingly, of endearments too, born, no doubt, of nostalgia for what had now come to seem like a fairy-tale past.

But from her, not a word. Not one.

Will had written, then, to different friends and to his brother Joseph in London, asking for news of her, eventually discovering she had almost certainly returned to London to try and take up her stage career once more. He had wanted to feel himself distraught, destroyed even, but had to admit to himself how quickly he had adjusted to the fact that Nancy had gone from his life, perhaps forever. And within a very short time he'd found she barely entered his thoughts.

When he arrives at the hospital tent, the doctor is still sleeping, fitfully, he notes, showing signs of delirium, and he is soaked in sweat. The matron, whom he fancies he has wakened from dozing, shakes her head sadly, then, after a moment or two, breaks the silence.

'He is in such torment,' she says. 'Poor, poor Dr Mitchell!'

'Is there nothing that can be...?' Will knows the answer to his question even before he has framed it. He realises too, looking at the woman, that she has been there in attendance for too many hours and that she must be near to dropping with fatigue. Tired though he himself is, he cannot, in all conscience, bring himself to abandon her. After some minutes have elapsed, the doctor appears less restless. 'Perhaps you should go and get some sleep now,' says Will. 'I will sit with him a while.'

The woman begins to protest, and yet her gratitude is obvious; but still she does not move.

'Away now!' he insists, 'I will call you in a couple of hours or so.' And when she has left, he settles to his desperate vigil, and surging thoughts.

XII

It was to Wilfred Farmer and the roots of his repressed anger that Will returned now, in his mind. The man's story, though its details were entirely unknown to him, must contain that kind of hurt that Will himself had become all too familiar with – the hurt of constant humiliation by 'Authority' in its diverse forms. In his own case, it had chiefly been that of the law, but the law's fiercest tormenters were not the judges or the barristers. Their involvement was soon over. Rather were they those of one's very own background and class: the policemen and gaolers, and the bystanders outside the courts and the prisons, hurling violence and abuse, venting their hatreds – direct consequence, in all probability, of their own humiliations – upon their own kind, as Farmer had suggested.

In prison, Will had had much time to think, to perceive and understand the functions and the functioning of the seemingly innocent, entirely normal, everyday transactions and interactions which bound them to the masters and made each of them mindless agents of their own slavery to the power, ambition, cruelty and contempt of the few. Even kindness, even generosity were harnessed, and a host of dancing emotions which caused the lowly to value the tiny concession of the high-born far above the spontaneous gift of their fellows. It was insidious but far too huge an edifice for one man, the likes of Will, to penetrate and demolish. He knew that for a fact. Yet once perceived, there was no living with it any longer; self-respect would not allow it. In his own case, the double stigma – of imprisonment and dismissal from Her Majesty's service – would doubtless have reduced him to beggary, to an ignominious existence at the very margins of what passed for a civilized, Christian society...

Gently, gently, Thomas Sheehan tries to move Wilfred Farmer's mind away from his present grief, and to draw his smouldering anger by getting him to talk about his and Hester's reasons for leaving England. It proves, or rather, promises to be a story of extending sadness, and Thomas begins, too late, to question the wisdom of his ploy. Mercifully, Farmer's stumbling grief is halted in its tracks only a few minutes after it has begun.

A cry close by, followed immediately by confused shouting and the sound of people rushing about outside; then all at once, the priest is aware of a flash of light against the tent wall, behind him, the sudden whoosh and crackle of fire. Both he and Farmer dash outside to find that the cookhouse tent, not a hundred yards away, is all aflame. A crowd has converged upon it, but they are clearly helpless, being driven back by the conflagration which, in a matter of seconds, has convulsed the tent and its awning.

Incongruously, bizarrely, however, everyone's attention and concern seems to switch seamlessly to two men rolling about on the ground, close to the scene of the fire. It takes Thomas a moment or two to realise that a fist fight is in progress, and that people's momentary awe and alarm at the fire and its consequences have quickly fallen away into eager fascination and a banal partisanship. Cheering and jeering and ignoring the crackling fire the rapidly swelling crowd thrusts itself into a circle around the combatants, who are going at it hammer and tongs.

A surge of revulsion takes hold of Thomas. 'For God's sake!' he exclaims, between clenched teeth, and he dashes forward, closely followed by Wilfred Farmer. As they push through the blood-lusting cordon, Thomas becomes aware that a burly, red-headed man has now decisively gained the upper hand, sitting athwart his helpless opponent's chest, raining down blows on his unprotected face, which is oozing blood.

'Let's put a stop to this,' says Farmer. Thomas signals his agreement, and they plunge into the arena. The priest, coming up behind the red-headed assailant, locks the man's head firmly against his own thighs, with his right arm tightening like a vice around his throat, so that he is soon choking, gasping for breath. Farmer, at the same time, shoves his hand up beneath the man's nose and presses his fingers hard into his eye sockets. Between them they manage to haul him off, amid cat calls and jeering from the baying crowd. They dump the man like a sack several feet away from his bloodied opponent, to whom they now turn their attention.

A woman steps forward from somewhere among the spectators. 'Here,' she says, 'let me help you with him... I'll bathe his face and try to staunch the bleeding... if we can get him to our tent... just over there.'

Thomas nods his thanks, but even as Farmer is helping the sorely pummelled man to his feet, he is aware of the red-headed man approaching him from behind. 'Look out, Father!' someone yells, and he whirls round to face the bully, who is clearly bursting with anger and indignation. But if the man's first thought had been to attack the priest, he has evidently thought better of it as they stand almost chin to chin. Swearing and boiling with rage, he steps back a pace and thrusts his tightly clenched fist just beneath the priest's nose.

'Ye fecken papist bastard!' he spits. And continuing to shake his fist in front of the unflinching priest, he adds: 'I'll be lookin fer youse. So youse'd better watch your step...' He spits on the ground and glares his defiance.

'Give him one, Sean!' a voice pipes up from among the crowd.

But the man backs away, inexplicably deterred, despite his show of bravado, yet still shaking his fist, then he turns on his heel and stalks off.

Will is distracted by the sound of the doctor's voice, but the moaning subsides as suddenly as it has erupted, and the poor man sinks yet again into heavy slumber. Will then takes up a damp towel and gently wipes the man's brow, then he sits awhile beside him, his eyes fixed on the pallid face, his own thoughts stilled for the moment.

The trouble was, although a period of honest toil, and accumulation of some fortune here in the colony might well rehabilitate him in the eyes of the society that had to all intents and purposes shrugged him off, Will now felt it was unlikely he could be reconciled with it ever again. And in this realisation lay his deepest dilemma. If that society had cast him out because of his transgression, he himself had quite consciously, indeed willingly, finally come to accept the role of outcast. His own admitted and expiated fault had unearthed layer upon layer of deceit at England's roots, which, rightly or wrongly, he judged to be... yes, far more pernicious than his own...

It is hard enough for him to turn his back on what means most to him, and all he has ever known. But, consequentially, to turn away too, from the love he bears Alice and the child, bears no thinking about. Then again, given his abhorrence of a world that has dealt with him so harshly, in what *acceptable* circumstances might his purposed return to Alice and his child be accomplished? Clearly, love and integrity were full set to collide within him, since his release from physical imprisonment has had the effect of thrusting upon him the freedom to choose or reject. And... to flounder endlessly between them...

His head is in a whirl. He leaps to his feet and paces back and forth, and it is thus that Thomas finds him as he steps into the tent.

He looks from one to the other of its two occupants for a moment or two, then inquires what change, if any, there is in the doctor's condition.

Will, dragged away from his own preoccupations, shakes his head, looking grave. 'None for the better, that's for sure,' he says. 'Indeed, at times, he is quite delirious, moaning and shouting. Just now, as you can see, he is quiet, but that won't last long, I shouldn't think.'

'I went looking for you up at our shelter,' says Thomas, 'thinking you might have returned there. Poor Farmer... he has taken his wife's death very badly. He had it fixed in his head that her illness was nothing to do with the fever but was something else, something that would pass in a day or two, when things would return to normal.

I'm not sure he is convinced, even now...' Will raises a quizzical eye. 'No, really, I'm not... As we discovered earlier, he's a headstrong character, sure of his ground, even when he stands in quicksand. At one point he broke away from our conversation and actually tried to rouse her, shaking her, even as the women were dressing the corpse for burial in the morning. Ah – poor man! They, simple souls, were quite outraged by his behaviour, and I had the divil's own job to calm him and persuade him to let them get on with their necessary tasks. But...' He stops, changing tack. 'Did you not hear the commotion a little while back, over at the cookhouse?'

'Commotion...? Ah, well, now you mention it, maybe I did... but I didn't attach any importance to it... Should I have? At the cookhouse, did you say...?'

'Well, insofar as the cookhouse went up in its own smoke and flames... maybes you should have...'

'Up in its... whatever do you mean?'

'Burned to the ground in a matter of minutes... '

'What...! But... how so?'

'It seems – from what the cook says – he had just got the fat hot for frying tonight's potatoes when he heard someone in the tent behind him. He jerked round and saw two fellows helping themselves to some of the bread the *Aurora* brought across. Well, he's not too sure how it happened, but in that moment, he somehow upset the big pan of fat straight onto the fire and a great sheet of flame shot up and set every bloody thing alight. He says they were lucky to get out alive, so swift was it.

'Anyhow, once outside, the cook went for one of the two thieves – a tall, redheaded Ulsterman – you may have seen him about. The other one, the "rat-faced ticket-of-leave man", as the cook described him – so Stevens, I presume – must have slipped away into the crowd that had flocked to the fire in moments. Well, when Farmer and I got there, this hulking brute was pummelling the livin' daylights out o' the cook, who's only a slight man, you'll recall, and not in the first flush of youth... pummelling him to death as far as I could see...'

'But didn't anyone try to stop him? You say there was a crowd... what the Hell were they playing at?'

'Oh, people, Will... and not just the men... they were blood-lusting, that's what. They were none too pleased when Farmer and I rushed in and pulled the big fellow off the cook – whose face already looked like a battlefield. The Ulsterman then threatened me. I thought he was going to have a go at me but, in the event, he backed down. But maybes I'd better start watching my back, especially on dark nights...'

'Aye, maybe you had... Do you think he was serious? What did he say?'

'Oh, something like... 'I'll be looking out for you'. Hard to tell really, maybe it was just anger talking – he'd lost face, after all... – Well, I suppose we shall see in due course... But, what of yourself? I found you... well... elsewhere, if I'm not mistaken.'

'True enough, you did – with what was, but chiefly with what still is... Although, in a manner of speaking, I too had been occupied with Wilfred Farmer... What manner of man he is, I have no idea; he is certainly surly, opinionated, not a companion I would choose...' And he shifts his weight from one foot to the other. 'Still, having suffered much myself from "Authority" for a good three years, and having understood something of the complexity of its workings I cannot help seeing in a man such as Farmer a... a comrade – if not in arms, at least up in arms; someone who – as he said – is seeking to get himself somewhere beyond the reach of such oppression.'

Thomas nods in agreement. 'Farmer... yes, complex all right, but you know, he made no bones about the fire or the fracas. He came with me spontaneous like... all the way, and had a go at the big fellow himself, so... I don't know. One thing for sure, though: he and his wife had suffered some great tragedy that made them leave England. He'd just started to tell me about it when the fire broke out...'

Thomas looks about him then plumps himself down on a chair in the corner of the tent. 'But what were you meaning, Will... about your own experience...?'

Will pulls over a chair and sits down by his friend. After a moment or two, seemingly collecting his thoughts, he begins to explain. 'You know, Thomas, while I was in prison, I made up my mind I would not remain long in that state of almost complete ignorance which, conveniently for our masters, enclosed me – and I've no doubt, millions like me – in a crabbed little vision of the world. And I'm not talking, now, in terms of geography, for I have travelled more than most – Her Majesty's Service afforded me that opportunity, at least. No, it's rather about the things I don't know that I ought to know… to be able to make my way with confidence in a world always controlled by others… Am I making any sense to you?'

'Perfect sense! So what about schooling? Did you have any schooling, in your little corner of… Cumberland, was it?'

'I did… although my schooling, like that of all of my kind, was rudimentary, and pitifully short. So I set about trying to change that when I was still in… in… I was in Carlisle gaol, for a time, you see… And – he continues quickly – in that respect, our unfortunate Judge's twenty-odd books look like a godsend to a man like me… at least, from what little our continuing tribulations have hitherto allowed me to see of them. But once all of this is over… if I come through it… I shall put them, and any others that come my way, to good use. Because I reckon that if one is to stand any chance of competing against the privileged of this Earth, one should at least know how to know about, let alone make use of, their sharpest weapons!'

'That's right enough, Will! Indeed it is!' Thomas has clearly warmed to this swelling theme. 'And, you know, there are undoubtedly parallels with my own quite different experience. If it was the army, in your case, that nurtured your ignorance and exploited it, it was Holy Mother Church in mine! Pinned down by a host of "Thou shalt-nots" I became the living instrument of that self-same negativity for my parishioners, the guardian of the gate through which, if they ever got near enough, they glimpsed the wonders of life as it could be, as it should be. And, well, it took that good woman who was taken from me the other morning, my lovely, incomparable Joanna, to make me see the utter iniquity of it all. And I assure you, Will, once the need for... this... play-acting of mine is over here, I shall never go back to it.' His face darkens. 'Remember, Will, I have lived through the iniquities and injustices the English masters and their native arse-lickers have wrought in Ireland, especially in these past few years.' He shakes his head, in sorrow, though his eyes show a burning anger and contempt.

They sit on in a brooding, but not dividing silence. Eventually, Thomas speaks, the tone of his voice quite changed: 'But you mentioned gaol, Carlisle gaol, you said. Tell me... was it for some misdemeanour in the army that they put you away there?'

'Ah no, not as a soldier, for in those quarters I was generally considered exemplary – which, like a fool, I thought was important! No, Thomas, as a man. Or rather, as a citizen, which – I have come to realise – is not quite the same thing.' And his eyes twinkle mischievously.

Thomas smiles. 'A nice... distinction, Will Crosby, but I think I know what you mean, nevertheless...'

'Aye, well, you'll recall I was telling you about Nancy... Yes? Well, it was partly because of her. While I was abroad on my third tour of colonial service, in Gibraltar, I lost track of her, and yet, despite my – on the whole – sense of relief, I couldn't settle to life on the Rock, as I had in my other overseas postings – pleasant place though it was. So, as soon as my time was up, I went back to the garrison in Carlisle. There, once again, out of a sense of duty, bad conscience rather than desire – and with something like trepidation lest my quest proved fruitful – I made enquiries about her, even seeking out the man she had lived with whilst I'd been in India...'

Thomas – or the vestiges of the priest in him – raised his eyebrows.

'...but no one had any idea what had become of her. Not a glimmer. Among other things, I wrote to my brother Joseph who, by that time, had been living in London for several years, working as a clerk in the Admiralty. He had known Nancy slightly, even before I had met her, since she had at one time been an acquaintance of his wife's, but they had no knowledge of her whereabouts. She had vanished, I hoped, for good and all.'

'And had she…?'

'So it seemed. Yet none of this would have mattered overmuch had I not, within a week of my return to Carlisle, met someone… Someone I fell in love with, even at our first introduction.'

XIII

Will had needed to say this, Thomas realises, so he does not ask the questions that are rapidly filling his mind.

'I had gone with a friend to a birthday party – his sister's, in fact, and it was there I first set eyes on Alice. She was a trainee teacher in a village Infants' school, not too far away, though her home was near Penrith – a way off, near the south-eastern border of my county, Thomas. Well, Alice, Alice Fallowfield, as she was... is, perhaps...' Will falters but steadies himself at once... 'Alice had some connection with my friend's family and was then lodging with an aunt of his, whom she had accompanied to the celebration. As we stepped in, my friend confessed to having designs upon her himself, but as the evening progressed it was clear her eyes were on me... almost continuously.' Despite himself, Will blushes.

'So – what did you do? Did you risk approaching her?'

'Aye, I did. Emboldened, I suppose, by the drink I had taken, towards the end of the evening I spoke to her, and I told her I should like to see her again. To my great relief, she readily assented.' He smiles wistfully at the memory of that beginning. 'We met frequently, whenever we could, and soon we became lovers. In some ways, it was like living through the dreamy days of my early courtship with Nancy, except that by this time it was I who was the worldly-wise one. Not that Alice was either ignorant or weak-willed, anything but – he hastens to add – it was just that I had a certain authority, a brash sort of confidence with her, I suppose, which was owed to my having experienced a good deal more of the world – and its women.'

Thomas, a playful glint in his eye, affects a sudden cough, which Will acknowledges with a peremptory nod, a knowing grin. And he relaxes into his account, grateful to be speaking his memories aloud.

'Well, not so very long into the courtship, Paradise took a tumble when Alice told me she feared she was pregnant. Yes... You may well shake your head. The way we had been... oh, rash but cautious... as we thought – if you can accept the contradiction – meant that sooner or later it was bound to happen, I suppose. And I did not doubt her. But, of course, that was no answer to the problem we now faced. And for a moment, aye, it indeed seemed as if my history was repeating itself, and yes, I admit it, I was afraid.' Will grimaces. 'I would only too readily have suggested marriage, but of course I could not. So that, in something like desperation, the request had finally to come from her – to my regret, and shame. In truth, there had been nothing in this life I had wanted more.'

'I see. So...?' Thomas prompts.

'I remember all the details of that particular summer's evening,' says Will, staring into the space ahead of him. 'I see it as if it were happening now. We had gone for a walk, at her suggestion, into the country on the edge of the city. I had shown great concern, had spoken about what we could do, even about where we might live, but I hadn't actually mentioned wedding her. Alice had listened, had commented occasionally on what I had to say, but, I sensed, with no very great enthusiasm.' He looks up at Thomas, whose questioning eyes, he sees, are fixed on his face. 'I was standing on the edge of a precipice, of course,' he says, attempting levity.

'We arrive at a glade and I say we should sit down and try and come to a rational decision, even work out some sort of timetable. And indeed, I do sit, motioning to her to come and take her place beside me – and Will makes the gesture – but she will not. She stands leaning with both hands pressed against the bole of an oak tree, her face clouded, her brow puckered in an unspoken question. A vision of judgement, if ever there was one, as clear to me now as it was then...' And for a moment or two, he closes his eyes. Then, without warning, he gets up and walks over to Mitchell's bed to glance briefly at its restless occupant. After a moment or two he turns back to stand behind his chair, leaning upon it.

"'Will,' she says to me at length, her eyes holding mine, "what is it? Do you not wish to marry me for some reason? I must know because most certainly I shall have to give up the idea of a teaching career, nor can I know how my family will react if I am not to be married, being in this condition."

Will glances at Thomas, shaking his head. "'They are very strict, as I told you,' she says, "and are likely to take a strong stand on what I must do. I fear I shall become a prisoner of their beliefs, in their house, perhaps for the rest of my days, in these circumstances...'"

Thomas is clearly perplexed. 'But... had you never made any mention of... Nancy, to her... at all?'

'No, I had not,' Will confesses. 'It had crossed my mind to do so, and more than once, but no... I hadn't. I know...' he acknowledges, catching his friend's astonished look, 'irresponsibly; and I have long had cause to rue it. The moment never... never seemed quite right. Yet, it had nagged at my conscience, believe me, for I knew that sooner or later, even without the compulsion of her being with child, I would want to marry her.... And in that moment, standing... leaning against that tree, so earnest, so vulnerable, I could have denied her nothing. "What are you saying?" I protested. "Have I not this last half hour been examining our situation in order to find the best way of proceeding?"

"'You have, indeed, William Crosby,' she retorts, "and it is that which disturbs me, for to my mind the solution is simple enough. We should announce our engagement and at the same time have the banns published. We could have our difficulties resolved in... six weeks, if both of the same mind... Do you not love me, Will?", she says. "I am your wife, if you will marry me..." Will winces at the memory, the directness of her plea.

'Of course, she was right, Thomas, insofar as what she knew, and believed of me, was concerned. It was, of course, that little, very substantial truth withheld which stood between us and the... mutual bliss we craved. My back was to the wall, right enough, and I either capitulated there and then or tried to fight my way out, using whatever prevarications I could arm myself with in that desperate moment. If I chose the latter, I ran the risk of losing her trust and her respect, in which case the whole nature of our relationship would take a change for the worse. No, I could not risk it. I cursed my folly at not being completely open with her from the start, yet no amount of cursing could now alter what was done... and not done.'

'So... what... how did you answer her?'

'I said that I loved, prized, and honoured her beyond all limits... or words to that effect. "You are quite right," I say. "All this planning... these details... are of secondary importance and can wait. Aye, they can. We have a little time yet before your condition begins to show. We'll do as you say, love, and then look to the practical matters of where and how we shall arrange our life together." And so... I asked her to be my wife.'

Thomas shakes his head in disbelief, perhaps already surmising what is to follow.

Will looks away, his eyes smarting.

Alice had sunk down beside him on the warm grass, visibly relieved, but his mind had been in turmoil.

A risky course, clearly, but the consequences of not following it would have been more immediately and irretrievably dire, in his mind, than those more remote ones which would emerge if his deception ever came to light... which had not quite seemed possible in that sun-dappled, enchanted glade. And when her hand reached out and took his own... Oh, God, what a fool...

Dr Mitchell cried out in that moment, waking himself from his delirium and Will from his reverie. He sat bolt upright, the perspiration glistening on his forehead and on his chest. His nightgown was wringing wet and the two moved with one accord to remove it. Thomas sponged his body with cold water, and assuaged his desperate thirst, but in a steady manner, in sips rather than the great gulps the doctor plainly craved. He had regained a measure of control in his awakening and was able to co-operate with them, and indeed, by the signs and gasps he made, approve what they were attempting for his greater comfort. But this respite was all too short, and their ministrations completed he fell away again into incoherence.

The matron came scurrying in, then, fastening her robe as she came, still only half awake. 'Is he in pain?' she asked, hurrying to him. 'His cries... they woke me...'

Thomas tried to persuade her to return to her bed, for they could manage a while longer, but she would hear none of it, and took her place beside the doctor, gently dabbing at his brow with a cold, damp cloth.

When he was once again settled and more or less quiet, the priest entreated her, yet again, to return to her bed: 'You will be needing all your strength, for the doctor... and for others, Miss Labone, to be sure you will, at least until help comes from the mainland...'

She glanced at the priest, tears in her eyes, then made a show of smoothing out the doctor's covers before retiring to her quarters, with no further protest.

And on the other side of the world a child woke and cried out and was comforted and held in the dark by her mother's reassuring arms.

XIV

Late that same evening, Will's story – and the memories it stirred – quite overwhelmed him.

'Thomas, if you'll excuse me a while, I have a mind to take some air. Do you mind?'

Thomas nodded. 'I understand...' he said, 'it must be hard...' but Will had already stepped outside into the star-spangled night.

He hesitated for a moment, then set off in the direction of the sea, going cautiously, for he had a horror of snakes, and was not yet aware of their hibernation. 'Every single one of them,' he had been told, was deadly poison. 'In the colony, there are a thousand things waiting to kill you,' the First Officer had said. 'You must ever be on your guard, always armed, and never reach out to touch anything you do not know, however innocent it may appear.'

'So much for the new Eden,' he remembered thinking at the time, 'The snake obviously got there before us!'

He therefore made a good deal more commotion, in his going, than he would normally have done.

Soon, his eyes had adjusted to the dark, and although there was no moon the myriad stars gave out light enough. He followed the meandering path hugging the shoreline, in the direction of the cemetery; then passed through its little gate, until he came to what proved to be a way down onto the beach, not far from the rock pool where he and Thomas had frolicked and basked, early that morning. The tide was still some way out though he could hear it was already well turned and coming in fast. He headed for a large, rounded rock near the banking, and there he sat, glad of the cool breeze on his face. He was tired, right enough, but he knew the memories his tale had revived would not let him sleep, not until he had had it out with them.

The heavens were alight and unusually free of cloud – which would account for the decided nip in the air. Yet it was welcome. There were no sounds that he could hear other than the rush of waves, galloping in towards him, devouring all in their path, yet far enough away still to leave him time and space for contemplation.

But still he remained troubled, even in, even by, this haven of tranquillity.

And what was it? The helplessness: Alice, Lilian, a life away, on the other side of the world; the deaths, and the sickness all around; and especially, the plight of the doctor whom he hardly knew but greatly respected. So much had happened in such a short time. And Thomas, well, it was he, certainly, more than any other, who disturbed his already tenuous mental equilibrium… though not just because he had urged him to relive his story through the telling of it. It was the man's solidity, his humanity, in reaching out…

Will drew his feet up onto the rock and wrapped his arms around his knees.

Thomas. The many contradictions he embodied, and so boldly: his anger and his patience; his blaspheming and his eloquence; his bluffness, and his… yes, tenderness. The man left Will wholly bemused. Most surprisingly of all, however, his active ministry here, despite his professed atheism… if such it truly was. What did the man believe? And all this responsibility he had taken upon himself, when he could have remained on the side lines. Yet the loss of his Joanna, it seemed, had thrust him back into his former role… In the absence of anyone else, clearly, but in the name of what cause?

Will knew that, had chance not contrived to bring him into the fizzing orbit of this enigmatic priest, he himself would not have become involved with the sad events now unfolding around them. And he was not involved willingly, not like Thomas. He had chafed against it; and would still, no doubt, though for now, his battle with conscience had got the better of him.

Yet the war was by no means over...

He turned his head, then slowly, his whole body and looked out towards the dark sea. Its lulling waves. Its purposes – if such they might be accounted – so far removed from anything remotely human, and that awareness of his, in itself, in the moment of its realisation, amounting to a vague sense of infinite loss...

He had come to these shores in search of a kind of freedom he had never known. In search, too, of a new... what was it? A new sense of... cleanliness? Yes, maybe that was it. Like starting out again in a new body, with a new mind, unburdened by any concern he might encounter or by any living person within hundreds of miles of where he stood, if that was what he chose – and it was this potential, of course, that inclined him still towards aloofness from the unfolding tragedies about him. After everything that had befallen him it was that cleansing distance above all else that he craved. And strangely, the epidemic would allow him that, if it were not for his conscience and something in him, he could not quite understand, much less name. His destiny had not been his own, even though it had been he who had failed in that one decision which had brought him so low. But Justice, the justice of the realm, had heaped injustice upon injustice upon him, and had very nearly destroyed him.

But what's that? Will cocks an ear. In the momentary lull between the rushing waves, he is almost sure he has caught the sound of voices. It seems unlikely, given the hour – and what might that be? Eleven? Midnight even? Indeed, he concludes, extremely unlikely. But no; there it is again, clearer, and nearer than before.

Then he sees them: two shadowy figures coming towards him, quite unhurriedly, deep in conversation. Almost certainly, they have not realised he is there. Not wishing to startle them, should they become aware of his presence, he coughs, then slowly slides down the rock onto his feet. The two figures stop instantly.

'I had not thought to find anyone else abroad at this ungodly hour,' Will calls out. 'Indeed, if truth be told, I'm quite surprised to find myself here at this hour. But so it goes...'

The two men – for so they prove to be – come on towards him, apparently sufficiently reassured. 'Aye, indeed, but sleep is hard come by in this place, now,' says one, 'with the groans and moans and screams of suffering all about us... People, I hear, are saying already that it is little better than it was on the journey out, eh?'

Will feels stung to the quick, hearing this, although, in the moment, he would have been hard pressed to explain why. 'If it is so,' he counters, rapidly assembling his thoughts, 'then they are quite definitely wrong. They all have more space, for one thing, even if to suffer in, yet space enough which may yet prove the salvation of many. Once we have more practical help and provisions from Brisbane, then surely...'

'In truth, neighbour,' the second man cuts in, 'I'm in full agreement with you... though that said, I fear the help from the mainland will not amount to much; not from any want of charity, mind you, but rather the result of a general ignorance about what should be done. And the dire lack of anything of use other than basic foodstuffs... This emergency has caught us on the hop most cruelly. Six months ago, well... hardly anyone here had ever given a thought to the need for a quarantine station...'

'Ah, so you are not from the ship, then...' Now it is Will's turn to interrupt, ruffled still. 'So, what is to be done?' Receiving no answer, he adds: 'Did you know that Dr Mitchell, our only doctor, has himself succumbed to the fever? In truth, we are floundering... maybe sinking fast.'

'Is that so? Then it's a worry, right enough!' the second voice comments, a heartfelt note of commiseration in its tone. 'But I tell you, in Brisbane we all thought we would have more time. We two came here only a couple of weeks ago to site and, eventually, begin constructing the quarantine hospital. Ironically, with all available assistance and resources going into meeting this present crisis, we can now make no headway whatsoever. Our labourers are gravediggers and odd-job-men now...'

'Aye, that's the truth of it... gravediggers,' echoes the first man, his head shaking in bemused disbelief.

'My name is Ridley, by the way,' the second man volunteers,

somewhat against the run of the conversation, 'Joseph Ridley. You know, in Brisbane things are still in quite a raw state! Because I appear to have been the only man in the township with any real experience of construction work back home, they gave me a grandiose title and a grand assignment, but little in the way of cash or labour. Besides, surveying is really outside my boundaries. We sorely need more immigrants if this colony is to survive, let alone thrive. Maybe, when the urgency of our present plight has sunk in, the council will take a more professional attitude in these matters – sadly though, it seems likely to prove a lesson high in human cost!'

His thin laughter knives the soft night air.

Will nods thoughtfully, strangely appeased. 'Pleased to make your acquaintance, Joseph...'

'Joe,' the man corrects him. 'Everyone calls me Joe.'

'And I'm Barney... the rest of the construction team!' puts in the other man.

Will laughs. 'Two men to build... to build a hospital!' he exclaims, feigning incredulity. 'I see what you mean, then, about "professional attitudes..." Anyway, I'm Will Crosby.'

'Well, let's hope necessity does indeed turn out to be the mother of invention, Will Crosby, or something like it,' says Joe. 'Anyhow, we had best bid you good night – or good morning – and be on our way. Strictly speaking, we are not supposed to have any contact with the passengers. Yet, who's to say whether or not any of the crew down at our end are harbouring the fever too?'

And with this, the two men move off again, resuming their leisurely pace, making their way along the beach.

Will saunters back to his quarters, where he undresses slowly, but in an instant, once abed, is asleep.

And when Thomas enters, somewhat later, Will does not stir as the priest stretches himself out, fully clothed, upon his own bed.

It would not be until late afternoon, the following day, that Will saw Thomas again, when the priest came to retrieve his stole, and then only briefly, before he was away again to yet another burial.

Until then, however, Will found it difficult to launch himself into any purposeful action, starting one thing then dropping it in favour of another which, before many minutes had passed, was also abandoned, incomplete. And, not very far back in his mind, the previous night's conversations pushing forward, half claiming him, so that his day was spent, for the most part, in a kind of no-man's land mid-way between now and then, here and somewhere always other.

As evening fell, he finally dragged himself over to the hospital tent to see how Dr Mitchell was faring. And there he found Thomas, sitting at his bed head, a book open on his knee. The priest's head slumped forward, and Will smiled. Dr Mitchell was asleep too, so, at a loss, he went in search of the matron. Not finding her, however, he retreated once more inside the tent.

Thomas was now sitting upright, awake and trying to read in the fading light.

'Good evening, Will,' he said. 'I had forgotten what a sharp mind Thomas More has... if quite at variance with his passion for roasting heretics!' He chuckled, nodding down at the book. 'I hope you don't mind, I borrowed it from the Judge's ghost...'

Will barely glanced at the book Thomas thrust towards him, saying nothing about his earlier entrance into the tent. 'How is the good doctor, do you think? He seems calm enough, just now.'

Thomas looked down at the sleeping figure, as if only now recalling his presence. 'Well yes,' he replied, after a moment's scrutiny. 'For the time being the doctor seems comfortable enough.' He put the volume down on the bed and rose to his feet. 'Come Will, we should just be in time to catch the sunset... Have you not noticed how splendidly golden and scarlet they are here... over the mainland? I doubt that even our Constable or our Turner could come anywhere near them with their palettes, in their... exploding majesty.'

XV

Twenty-four hours later, Will and Thomas come together once again, to stroll out to see the sun's pyrotechnics from a different viewpoint, a little further north, so enchanted by its display had they been the evening before.

Dr Mitchell had slept most of the day away, waking occasionally, wildly; but once, the matron had managed to coax a spoonful or two of broth into him, and then later, some water. But from past experience, Thomas knew that the crisis was yet to come.

The two men stand now, marvelling at the dying sun, at how each moment is different in its chromatic effects from the previous one, the blood-red sea metamorphosing into an ever-deepening green sward, then an oily blue, before succumbing to the final, all-enveloping darkness. And the birds, whose cacophony, not twenty minutes before had all but deafened them, gradually fall silent, the odd one or two flapping up higher or even over to the next tree to settle for the night. And when the show is plainly over, the two men remain rooted to the spot, as if waiting expectantly for some kind of encore. But finally resigned, they begin their walk back to the camp and supper.

'And is all that... that miracle we've just witnessed, quite... meaningless, Thomas? Did it all just come about by sheer chance, do you think?'

Thomas stays silent for a while, then: 'I don't know how to begin to answer you, Will, and that's the truth of it. Certainly, science can now – indeed, for quite some time now – give you answers about how it all happens... It's the why that's the tricky bit...'

He returns to his silence for a while longer, and Will too ambles along, focused as so often of late on those dear, tormenting memories of a time when his happiness approached fulfilment, though was never free of shadows.

Because Alice had easily accepted his suggestion their wedding take place in her own parish of Dacre, it had been so much easier for him to push his grievous fault to the back of his mind, and that such an agreement accorded with her own dearest wishes had given him a degree of contentment – for her sake – contentment to which, in all truth, he himself was hardly entitled. Just before they reach the hospital tent, Thomas stops.

'Will… your tale… *your* history… begs an ending, does it not?'

'Thomas, you're trespassing on my mind!' Will replies, laughing, and shuffling forward a couple of steps towards the tent. To be truthful, its end is still being lived, and maybe always will be… I can't know, can I…?'

Once inside, Thomas checks on Dr Mitchell, who is sleeping, if restlessly. Unusually, the matron is absent.

'Ah, she won't have gone far, I don't think,' Thomas remarks, 'for I have the impression it is more than just duty keeps her near the young doctor's sick bed! But … what were you saying…?'

'What I've been thinking about, was when we went to see Alice's parents – so I could formally ask for her hand in marriage. We'd already agreed that only if there were any objections raised to our union would we acquaint them with the real reason for our haste. In the event, while both her father and her mother cautioned us against hasty action, neither wished to stand in our way.'

'They weren't surprised, or suspicious then… about this haste?'

'Not really, for right from the start Alice had told them of our relationship in her letters home, so they were aware of the developing courtship, and to them, I suppose, our request would seem to come in the natural run of things. So, her father solemnly gave me his consent, appreciating, he said, the difficulties for us that the life of a soldier might otherwise bring.' A kindly man, Will recalls, with his clear blue eyes, a large moustache – so fashionable at the time, and hair greying at the temples. 'Even then though, I had the feeling that if it had been left to Alice's mother, the outcome might have been different – a difficult, sullen, somewhat hard-seeming woman of few words.'

'A shrew, you mean?'

'Aye, maybe that is the word… Well, anyway, you can imagine how relieved I was, yet at the same time uneasy, deeply so, for I could see that many more, good, trusting people were, all unwitting, going to be caught up in my careless deception….'

'Ah, Will…! And Alice's father?'

'Yes, as I say, a decent man – Jonah he's called. And, as a Church Warden – which was extremely convenient – he agreed to publish the banns for us, though reminding us that for the weeks immediately prior to the wedding Alice would have to be resident in the parish. Now, this was a detail we had overlooked, and my heart sank, for I realised it would certainly lead to further delay – Alice could not quit her post without giving the required minimum notice of her intention. Nevertheless, without having any possibility of discussing the matter, we had no choice but to agree to that condition there and then.'

'It must have been a tense time for you, Will, knowing what you knew, living with that. How, in God's name, did you get through it?' Thomas gently lifts the doctor's head and turns the pillow over beneath him.

'Aye, it was that. For me, the thing festered and gravely infected what should have been nothing but joy. I could confide in no one, and least of all in the one person who might, just might, have helped me… us… through it all. Well, anyway, we fixed the date as soon as Alice had secured her release from her apprenticeship and were married in little more than a month after that.'

In all the time of waiting for that date to arrive, Will had suffered repeated bouts of bad conscience and doubt. Several times he had been on the point of confessing his true situation to Alice, yet aware that if he did so, matters having proceeded as far as they had, he would lose her completely. And he couldn't even begin to contemplate that, for she had rapidly become all in all to him. Daily, he had lived in trepidation lest someone from the other end of the county, venturing by chance upon the announcement of their betrothal, might denounce him to the parson or to the guardians of the parish.

Of course, none of his family back in conveniently distant Whitehaven had been told of what he was about, for too many of them had known Nancy, and sympathetic though they all had been towards him in that distasteful affair, he had felt quite unable to risk confiding in any of them.

'All things considered, you must have been a bundle of nerves, Will...' says Thomas, standing up from the table where they sat facing each other, and stretching noisily. 'But how did you explain the total absence of anyone from your own family... or from your regiment, for that matter? Who was your Best Man?'

'The Best Man was no problem, Alice's second brother, Anthony, filled that role well enough. As for my family, I said my parents were too infirm to travel all that way, and besides that, I wasn't particularly close to any of my brothers and sister for it to matter – another lie, of course... and I made more or less the same excuse about my fellows from the regiment...'

'I'm presuming, then, you did manage to carry it off and suppress all your anxieties. Did anyone even notice?'

'My nervousness, though natural enough for any who observed it on the day, had, of course, far more worrying causes than any of them could possibly know... But it was in those moments of silence following the parson's invitation to anyone who "knew of any just cause or impediment" why we two should not be "joined together in Holy Matrimony," to make their declaration, that I died a thousand deaths, for I knew! But to make matters worse during that silence, someone dropped a prayer book, exploding the silence, and I spun round, my body trembling in every fibre. Alice looked at me, perplexed, but squeezed my hand, and the moment passed. We were duly proclaimed husband and wife, and it was the minister's final words I clung on to with all the desperation that racked my being:

"Those whom God hath joined together, let no one put asunder."
And as the weeks passed over into months, and my new state came
to seem more and more like normality, I think I half believed that
God, perhaps recognising the grave injustices I had suffered in my
association with Nancy, had indeed conferred his blessing upon our
union.'

Thomas raises his eyebrows and permits himself a fleeting smile,
before turning to Dr Mitchell, once again. 'Ah, Will, we look for
comfort, in our desperation, in the unlikeliest of quarters. That we
do!' And, as he is speaking, he is sponging the doctor's face and
hands, before wringing out the cloth in the waxed-linen field-sink
standing at the foot of the bed.

Will watches and waits, patiently, gathering in his reeling
thoughts. When Thomas has finished and Will judges him to be fully
receptive once more, he resumes his account. 'Well, as Alice waited
her time, with great patience and fortitude, in the care of her family,
at Redhills, I embarked upon the task of seeking a posting away from
Carlisle, as far away as was possible.'

'That, I can well imagine, Will.'

'And fortune appeared to be smiling on us, yet again – or so I
thought at the time – for the Regiment was just then beginning a new
recruitment drive and sought volunteers to conduct it in all parts of
Cumberland and Westmorland. And thus it was I came to take on
the temporary role of Recruiting Sergeant for the latter area, based
at the castle in Appleby. Not only did this remove me from the ever-
threatening dangers of disclosure surrounding me in Carlisle, but it
also meant I was near enough to be able to spend time with Alice and
her family.'

That time had been short, yet idyllic in its way. The doubts and
fears that plagued him had receded once again, and they had both
looked forward eagerly to the sealing of their union with the birth of
their first child.

But entering upon this sad phase of his story, Will once again falls
into a brooding silence.

Thomas waits patiently, all the while scrutinising his friend's face.

'When Alice was at last delivered of our child, all seemed normal, and over the next few weeks he appeared to grow and to strengthen. But, Thomas, there came a day when Denis would not take his milk, and the doctor could find no reason for it. A number of different remedies were prescribed and tried, but to no avail. The little boy, it seemed, had lost interest in this world and had decided to quit it, which he did within three weeks to the day of that first indication that something was amiss...'

The priest rises and places a consoling hand on his companion's shoulder. 'Steady now, Will... Stop there, if it is all too painful for you...'

Will nods. But after a moment or two's struggle, he shakes his head, briefly pushing his knuckles into his eyes: 'No... I want to tell you...'

'That was a grievous blow, Will, to be sure it was.'

'Yes, it was. Alice was utterly distraught, coming near to collapse; while in me all the old fears resurfaced, if in different form. Not normally a superstitious man, I got it into my head that this must be a punishment wrought upon me for having wilfully turned my back on God's law, and I suffered then as I had never suffered before, for I could confide in no one, and most especially not in that lovely, wronged creature who was – and was not – my wife.'

He shakes his head in apparent disbelief. 'How could I have done that to her, Thomas? How? I've asked myself time and time again, but there is no satisfactory answer... And there is no putting the clock back; those wrongs I did her will stand forever...'

'Ah, Will, we get so caught up in things. In the pressures of the moment, in our emotions, and we often do things that, if given more time, more... space, we would not even have contemplated... and as for "standing forever", well, who can say with any certainty about that? But... I can see the pain it is causing you now...'

'Yes... And I have never before said these things aloud, though I have thought them often enough. And then... still floundering in uncertainties, once Alice had regained some of her strength, I took to returning to her Redhills home less frequently. In her presence, you see, I was constantly reminded of… well, all the wrong I had compounded. I was also fearful of adding to it further, with the ever-present possibility of her conceiving yet again, of course…

But the changes in my regime were noticed. And not just by Alice, but by her family, so that on one of my rare and fleeting visits to Redhills, her eldest brother, Richard, a pharmacist, took me aside. And with great tact and delicacy he made me aware of the deleterious effects such abstinence could have on a young woman's health – effects which were already noticeable, he affirmed, in his sister's increasing depression and uncharacteristic, erratic behaviour, and tearfulness.'

Poor, dear Alice…

And thus prompted, Will's mind had gradually swung back once again towards a different sense of responsibility and towards a more optimistic view of their relationship. The loss of their child, he had reasoned, was but a stroke of ill fortune; so very many children died at a tender age, through all manner of causes.

'And then the idea that the sudden and early departure of Denis from this life was something devised by a just and awesome God, came to seem ludicrous in the extreme…'

Will rises from his seat, to go and stand at the tent opening. His eyes search the horizon, through the tangled branches of the wispy trees along the shoreline, as if looking, almost consciously, for a likely place of refuge from this endless torment.

'Will, I know just what you went through, to be sure I do,' Thomas says eventually, his voice gentle, inviting. 'All your doubts and recantations, and new doubts at every turn in your fortunes… I have been there too, I assure ye, with my poor Joanna, and all. And I tell you, for all the tyrannies that we encounter in our dealings with our fellow men – those tyrannies Wilfred Farmer rails against and runs from – there is none so mighty as that of our own conscience, whatever its composition. I own I have not yet made up my mind about it, whether 'tis a principal force for moral good or for human unhappiness. Certainly, it can make our personal world an exceedingly uncomfortable place to be in! That it can!'

'Aye, how right you are!' Will turns, and scrutinises his friend's face, expectantly. 'But… Thomas, I swear, not a crust has passed my lips since dawn, and… is it not the same with you? Now I think of it I realise I am mightily hungry...'

Thomas moves purposefully, brightly, towards Will, standing at the tent's doorway, and gives a mock salute. 'Right you are, *sergeant!*' And pushing past his companion he steps out into the darkness, heading for the newly sited kitchen tent.

XVI

As Father Thomas is returning along the already well-trodden path to the hospital tent, immersed in his own thoughts, and provisioned with half a loaf, a small billycan of broth and some cheese, he is accosted by two men.

It is obvious, even as they approach him, that they are in some consternation.

'Oh, 'tis Father Sheehan… Thanks be to God we've found you, sir. It's young Elizabeth Wade, see sir. She run straight out o' the tent and into the dark and we can none of us find her, though we have been a-shouting her name this long half-hour past. She was nursing her mother and her little sister… and the little one, she died this morning… Then this evening, 'twas the turn o' the mother, and the girl herself were so distraught like – as who would not be, for that was all of her family gone, and she just run off a-screaming like, into the dark…'

'Right… Come with me. Sergeant Crosby is at the hospital tent, and we'll come up with a plan right away, I'm sure.'

Will rises to his feet as they enter.

'How many of you are there searching for the girl?' he asks, when Thomas has apprised him of the emergency. 'And do you have lamps?' Without waiting for their replies he turns to the matron to ask: 'Do we have any storm-lanterns, anywhere?'

'I'm almost certain there are some – in the store hut. And oil too if I'm not mistaken. We can go and check if you like… I'll fetch the key.'

And she hurries away past the little group clustered in the doorway. And the men follow in her wake.

'There be but four of us, Sergeant Crosby,' one of the two men mutters in belated response, while trying to keep pace with Will's loping stride. 'And 'tis indeed uncommonly dark down the bottom end...'

'How old is this girl we're looking for?'

The two men exchange glances, then the first one says, hesitantly: 'I can't rightly say, sir, for 'twas a family as kept to themselves – and besides, since we all come to this island here, they've had nothing but this trouble... But, looking at her, I'd say... sixteen, or... maybe as much as eighteen...'

The matron bobs into her own small tent, and a moment later comes out with her own lantern, and the key. 'I've not had cause to enter the store hut lately... not since the first week...'

But once at the hut, which backs onto the forest, the lock yields easily enough. Finding the lamps almost at once, the matron passes them to Will, and he and Thomas quickly fill and light them. They then hurry away to the southern end of the encampment, gaining three or four additional helpers as they go, keen to offer what help they can.

They find the two men who had been left searching standing beside the Wade's tent.

'Ah, thank goodness you are back, and with lights too...' says one of them.'

Will explains immediately what he purposes. They will stretch out in a long line, several yards apart from each other, and move slowly through the tents towards the sea, calling the girl's name continually as they go.

Soon, the line stretches out along the edge of the embankment, above the sands and the unseen sea which, by its hushed murmur, is still some way off, though coming in through the darkness. After a moment's hesitation, they all clamber down onto the sands and walk slowly forward, as far as the water's edge. Then, standing closer together, they move up and down the shifting tide line, still calling the girl's name. But the only sound they hear in response is the restless murmuring of the sea.

After several minutes of fruitless searching, by common accord, they turn away and walk slowly back to the embankment.

'That poor girl...' someone says. 'Whatever can have become of her?'

'Aye, poor child... What a tragedy!' their mingled voices echo.

'She may, of course, have run off in the other direction, into the forest behind the camp,' Thomas suggests. 'But it would be impossible for us... in the dark... even with the lanterns...'

'I agree,' Will says. 'Floundering about and getting lost there, ourselves, would serve no useful purpose.' Not in a forest with its many lurking dangers, whether real or imagined... 'Sadly, I think we must call off the search till morning. What do the rest of you say...? Good. Then we'll meet back here at first light. Is that agreed?'

Once back at the hospital tent, Thomas sets a bowl of now stone-cold broth before each of them, and plates of bread and cheese.

Will eats, though with no great relish. 'Of course, the girl may simply have lain down somewhere, and fallen asleep... in her exhaustion, her distraction. Sleep can be a welcome escape from the world's harshness,' he suggests, perhaps clutching at straws, adding – as if scrabbling for conviction – 'as I know well enough myself.'

'But yes... "Sleep that knits up the ravelled sleeve of care", as the bard puts it... Yes, it's possible, and I hope that turns out to be the case. The other alternatives don't bear thinking about.'

And although the fate of the missing girl is still very much on the mind of each, the conversation gradually turns back to Will's own misfortunes.

Determined that their marriage should not founder, now that, for better or worse, it was done, Will explains how he had taken a small house close by Appleby, where Alice had then joined him. They were once again, he confesses, eager, indeed voracious lovers, both desirous of a child which, they had reasoned, would do much to fill the chasm of their sad bereavement.

'Within a few weeks we knew for certain that Alice had conceived, and how we rejoiced in that knowledge…'

'And then… what?'

'And then, without prior warning, I was hurriedly transferred to the Isle of Man, to the garrison at Peel castle; at the same time being promoted to Warrant Officer. I could have refused the posting, of course, and the promotion it carried, and I did consider it. We were happy, wildly happy, in our cottage. But alas Thomas, we sorely needed the increase in pay it would bring… Let no one tell you that a young child is but a meagre expense, for 'tis far from the truth…!'

'And how did Alice react to this sudden interruption in your lives?'

'Oh, she was pleased enough. Even though it meant a separation of about one month's duration – which felt like a punishment – but after that she joined me there and we soon resumed the habitual routines we had established back in Appleby. And as soon as my predecessor departed, we moved into the married quarters that my newly exalted position entitled me. And all of this in good time for Alice's laying in, and the subsequent birth of our daughter. We called her Lilian,' Will rounds off, proudly, his face relaxing, his eyes glistening in the candlelight.

The bread and the cheese are soon gone, but the two of them sit on in companionable silence.

'And your Lilian, she grew healthily, did she?' Thomas asks, by and by.

'Yes, she thrived well enough. But those early weeks of her life were an anxious time, mindful as we were of the sudden death of our first, apparently healthy child… But in her first year, the year we were in Peel, Lilian ailed nothing, and Alice and I were content, at last. So much so that I turned down the next opportunity that came my way – of a further posting to Malta.' Will chokes back a groan. 'And how I have regretted this, Thomas, long regretted it. And I will to my dying day…!'

'So where did you go?'

'Would you believe it? When my new posting came through, as inevitably it must, it was to within ten miles of my home town, and only two from Harrington, where my sister and her husband lived… and still live, for he – Charlie – is a deckhand on the colliers serving the mines a bit further up the Solway coast… And so… as you can imagine… my past fault returned to torment me all over again.'

'Had you not kept in touch with members of your family, during your time in the Isle of Man, or seen any of them, for that matter?'

'I'd written to my sister Mary, occasionally, and more often to my mother, as well as to my brothers in Whitehaven. But no, I hadn't seen any of them, not for almost three years.'

'So they didn't know about your… your new marriage?'

'No. Nothing at all, or about Lilian, or… And so, as you can imagine, I was in one hell of a quandary. My first thought was to tell them that Nancy had died, but then I realised that then her name, and the whole sorry business of my marriage to her, were bound to come out. And despite Alice's undoubted love for me, I was not at all sure that she would forgive me for that omission which, understandably, she would see as a gross betrayal of trust… Less though it would have been, than the full truth – of how things really stood…'

Will's voice falters, and he struggles manfully to control his endlessly bruised emotions.

'Then I decided… after thinking about it on nights when sleep would not come, or came only in snatches… I decided the only solution was to tell the truth – that is, to confide in my sister Mary. And if she were amenable, I would entrust her with the delicate task of informing the rest of my family. I hoped they'd all support me in the maintenance of my deception, since the alternative….'

'So you weren't going to tell Alice,' Thomas says, quietly. But then, quickly, clearly seeing the look on Will's face: 'Will, I'm not judging you. It's more… well, I'm thinking that this would have been Mary's reaction… surely?'

Will is silent for a moment. But, despite his almost recovered calm, the priest has starkly pin-pointed what he himself keeps shying away from, and has done, ever since he set out on this deceitful course. 'I couldn't tell her.' He hangs his head, miserably. 'For all the reasons...'

'Will, as I say, I'm not judging you...', Thomas repeats. 'Honest to God I'm not. I was just thinking...'

'I know. And you're right, of course...'

'So... well, tell me about your sister, then. I imagine it was rather a tall order for her, was it not?

'Yes, my meeting with her was far from easy. I'd had no difficulty in arranging it, as I'd gone on ahead of Alice... to seek out suitable lodgings for us. But yes, after her delight at seeing me again after so long a time, Mary was horrified, and wholly against continuing, much less spreading the deception. I pleaded with her; but she said I was only putting off the moment of truth. But I was adamant, and in the end, she gave in and agreed to help me. I remember that at our parting she said I would live to regret this course of action. And, of course, she was right...'

'And what of the others?'

'Well, by the time Alice joined me at Tithe Barn, where I'd found lodgings – it's near Harrington – Mary had spoken with our mother. And although, like Mary, she was very uneasy about the whole business... she was persuaded, as were the rest of my family; all of them agreeing to keep silent about my former marriage. I was relieved, of course, but the apprehension never went away.'

'And Alice eventually met them all, did she?'

'Yes, gradually; though never all of them together. And as time passed and visits among us became more frequent, my fears began to subside, in particular as Mary and Alice became firm friends. Yes,' Will sighs, 'our life became easier once more. Lilian grew, though not without the usual childhood ailments, some of them quite serious at the time. But all in all we were content.'

'Then, you were a lucky man, if I may say so, Will Crosby!'

'Aye, well, so it seemed... But one thing I must tell you. Lilian was especially mine from the moment she began to toddle. I acquired one of the new-fangled velocipedes and she used to like nothing better than to sit between my arms, perched up on the handlebars, ringing the bell. They were good times, Thomas.'

'Did you stay at the Barn place for long?' Thomas asks. 'Will…?'

'Sorry… I was just hearing her excited little cries… But… no, not for long, no, as I was soon transferred yet again, this time back to Regimental Headquarters in Carlisle. But we decided to retain our Tithe Barn cottage, where Alice and Lilian were closer to Mary and Charlie, and I didn't want to see them uprooted again; young children, I felt, needed that kind of stability; and I could see them often enough.' Will pauses. 'It wasn't the joyous time we had known at Appleby, or Peel – because of my many comings and goings – but our situation was not uncomfortable. And now… Well, the time we spent together there… just a normal domesticity, with long walks in the country or by the sea, Alice's churchgoing, and visits to, or by friends… well, it has in retrospect taken on an air of a land of lost content. Ah, Thomas…' Will's eyes mist over. 'There have been countless times, since, that I would have given anything, anything at all, to have been back there, with Alice at my side, Lilian on my knee. But that time is now past, probably gone forever, for likely as not there will never be any way back to them.'

'You can't know that, not for sure…'

'No, I can't. But I swear, Thomas, everything I do, wherever I happen to be, however bound up in the moment, underlying all is the endless regret, and a certain hopelessness that accompanies it. Always, always….'

Will falls into a lost, self-absorbed silence.

Thomas busies himself gathering together the remnants of their meal, and then leans across and lays his hand upon Will's shoulder.

'I understand, to be sure I do. It is hard to bear such loss, divilish hard; but you must not give up hope, no, you must not. But tell me… what was it that scuttled your bliss and brought you, if I have understood a-right, to prison, quitting the army, and to this unfortunate place?' He takes up the pitcher to replenish their mugs. 'Someone, I surmise, must have denounced you – out of a sense of malicious moral rectitude; was that it?'

Will grimaces. 'Aye, something of the sort. Someone did denounce me, though I cannot believe there was any malice intended.' And he smiles, bitterly. 'Ironically, it was the weekend in which we were to celebrate my mother's seventieth birthday. And though I should have been on duty then, I managed, right at the last minute, to arrange with a friend to take my place. The party was arranged for the Saturday evening, so I was already resigned to missing that... My leave was just for the Sunday,' he explains, seeing Thomas's quizzical look. 'And so late was my "reprieve" that none at home expected to see me there, believing, as I had, that my duties prevented it. But by the time I got to the house, Thomas, it was mid-afternoon, on the Sunday, as I say. And as soon as I crossed the threshold, I could tell something was amiss.'

XVII

Will looks downcast.

'There was no surprised, joyous greeting, such as I'd imagined. My mother – my younger brother John told me as I entered the house – was not well and was lying down upstairs. But when I stepped into the parlour, there was a sudden, hushed silence. Mary was sitting next to her husband, while James, my older brother, was perched on a dining chair beside Charlie. But there also... and much to my surprise... were Joseph and his wife, up from London. As far as I'd understood the arrangements, previously, they had not been expected, either. All of them had clearly been deep in conversation, moments before, and were obviously embarrassed at my sudden appearance...'

'Ah, so you're still here, gentlemen.'

Miss Labone, having heard their voices, perhaps, walks towards them. 'Sergeant Crosby, Father Sheehan... I should be preparing Dr Mitchell for the night. It's about time, now, I think...'

Will blinks and gets to his feet.

'We were just about ready to leave...' Thomas says, apologetically almost.

'...But afore we go,' Will adds, 'is there anything we can do to help...?'

The matron looks at the doctor. 'He seems to have slipped a good way down the bed, and over to one side, and his covers... If the two of you could pull him... gently, mind... back up onto his pillows, and hold him while I smooth out his sheets, it would be a very great help to me…' And she looks expectantly from one to the other.

The manoeuvre proves none too easy. The doctor's inert figure, in spite of his small, slight frame, is a dead weight and it is only when the matron herself has lifted his feet that the two men are able to shift him. But his sheets are once more wet through and the young woman insists on changing them, so that by the time the whole operation is complete, almost half an hour has slipped by and it is close on ten o'clock.

'Thank you, gentlemen… I really could not have managed that without you. I am sure the doctor will pass a more comfortable night, now. Thank you so much, and… a good night to you both.'

Each in his turn bids her 'good night' as they leave the tent.

Thomas stifles a yawn. 'Goodness! It's quite a bit later than I thought! Where did the time go?'

Ever since that meeting in Whitehaven, Will had often been bemused by the role that chance had played in his undoing. For it had come out later that his brother Joseph had only managed to get there at the very last minute. There was an important audit under way at the Ministry, and his brother was too much involved to have any hope of getting away in time for the long journey north. But then the Under-secretary had been called away on other, more urgent business, and so the operation had been shelved for a week.

Will looks at his companion, shaking his head.

'All this has long tormented me. I rake things over and over in my mind. But it was complete chance that caused my undoing. Joseph was relieved of an audit he had been engaged on, and so Arabella, his wife, had insisted they take advantage of their good fortune, and had arrived entirely unannounced. And I remember… I stood there, looking from one to the other, utterly bewildered. And then I asked where Alice and Lilian were. Were they off out for a stroll, perhaps?'

'Mary, looking grave, pointed me to a chair.

'"You had best sit yourself down, Will, for we have something to tell you," she says, "something we would wish never to have had to tell you. But it is best you hear it at once."

'And Thomas, I knew immediately, of course. I knew that what I'd always dreaded... but also half believed could never happen... had indeed come to pass. And I slumped down upon the settee, facing my kin as though they were a jury.

'My brother Joseph then speaks up.

'"Will," he says, "I fear 'tis I who, all unwittingly, have brought misfortune upon you..." It had been close on six years since I'd seen him, Thomas, so he had no idea what direction my life had taken, in all that time. And Joseph tells me that the previous evening he and Arabella had been introduced to Alice as "Will's wife". And of course, so taken aback was he – for no one had thought to warn him – he'd blurted out something like "This cannot be, for Will's wife is Nancy, whom we know well enough."'

Thomas takes a sharp intake of breath.

'Yes, indeed... But then Joseph reprimanded me fiercely. "Alice, your wife... if that is how you describe the poor girl, though you are plainly wrong to do so... turned as white as a sheet; and was quite overcome with embarrassment, and began to cry..." There had been others standing with them, too, Thomas... And, of course, there was nothing anyone could do to console her.' Will sighs, heavily. 'And with genuine sadness, poor Joseph recognised that through no fault of his own, his "few, thoughtless words had destroyed Alice's life utterly", and, of course, there were no other words that could compensate for that.'

'Ah... you poor, unfortunate man...'

Will grimaces, throwing back his head in a gesture of helpless resignation. 'So that was Joseph's part, Thomas,' Will adds, 'but I never doubted his good faith.'

'So, what did Alice have to say... eventually, I mean?'

Will shakes his head. 'At this point, my sister Mary took up the story. "Will," she says, "I am afraid that I am as much to blame for this state of affairs as is Joseph here. For when we agreed never to mention Nancy and your former life before Alice, I was convinced that our mother would secure the agreement of *all* our close family, including Joe and Arabella." Yet our mother, Thomas,' Will explains, 'was under the impression that *Mary* would already have told him... doubtless since she knew Joseph and Mary wrote to one another quite regularly. Thus, neither Mary nor our mother ever told Joseph, each believing the other had done so. And that's why my mother had taken to her bed: out of a sense of guilt and remorse at what she saw as a failure on her part... when of course the failure... was entirely mine.

And poor Alice, yes... When I asked again about her, Mary said "Alice took it extremely hard, as who would not? She retired to her room immediately, locked her door and would speak to no one. She and Lilian had left at dawn that morning – the day I arrived – refusing breakfast or any offer of help and making it clear she held the whole family responsible for the deception. She also said that I was to be told she would be seeking legal advice at once, and that she would not be returning to Tithe Barn." Her final words – though Mary said she could not believe Alice would abide by them – were that she would not see me again, and that I was not to go seeking her, under any circumstances. Poor Mary... my sister's distress was obvious, as she told me all this. She seemed to choke on every word.'

They enter their tent, and Will gropes his way over to his bed and flops down heavily upon it.

Thomas sits down on the edge of his own bed, but then – curiosity seemingly getting the better of him: 'But there is surely more to come, is there not?' he says. 'Matters obviously did not end there...'

'No. They did not.' Will sits up and leans forward to unlace his boots. 'Bad enough though all of this was already, Mary told me that, unfortunately, a few minutes before Joseph had let the cat out of the bag, our vicar, Reverend Davidson, had called in with his wife to wish our mother well. And so he was witness to all that transpired and would most likely inform the Authorities of my... bigamous state – poor Mary had the greatest difficulty saying the word. It seems he had left the moment he understood the situation, without uttering a word of thanks, or goodbye to anyone.' Will shrugs. 'So I was to expect the worst, though Mary told me the family were resolved to stand by me. I was grateful to them, of course. But I feared there was little anyone could do in the face of any action Davidson's denouncement would set in motion.'

Thomas winces. 'God in Heaven's name! What an unfortunate sequence of coincidences…!'

'My head was spinning, as you can imagine. Feeling faint, fighting nausea, I could not think clearly at all. I had no idea what I was to do. My only real concern was for Alice and my child. I wanted to be with them, to comfort my wife, for that is what she was to me… and always will be.'

The priest nods again, on hearing this. 'How would any man, plunged as suddenly into chaos as you were, have felt? 'Twas but natural.'

'Yes, I wanted to try and explain to her that it was my love, my fear of losing her, which had brought this whole shameful edifice crashing down upon us. I did not care what was to become of me though I knew well enough that it would be nothing pleasant.

'My life was quite destroyed during that reunion with my brothers and sister, and any future seemed futureless. I knew Alice: a woman of conviction; honest, true, incapable of any deception herself and thus incapable of understanding it in another. I knew absolutely that all was at an end… So there you have it. I could not have imagined a worse unmasking.'

Will shrugs hopelessly, spreading his hands and arms wide, and exhales deeply.

'And I was not mistaken. The law took its course. Our marriage was declared null and void, and I was put on trial. And had it not been for the very positive testimonial coming from my commanding officer, as well as the mitigating circumstances surrounding my doomed relationship with Nancy, underlined in the testimonies of my family and, I have to say, even the most unlikely witnesses, my sentence would probably have been even more severe. Yet, it was harsh enough. Thirty months hard labour, and, inevitably, a dishonourable discharge from Her Majesty's Service. At the age of thirty-three years, on my eventual release, I was to begin my life all over again, perhaps with a new name, in a new place, having no past and no family. It was a stark, terrifying prospect.'

Thomas shakes his head. 'What a confounded mess. I feel for you, Will, truly I do... For there, my friend, but for the grace of... God knows what, go I; because in the eyes of the Church I was married to the Church, and in my relationship with Joanna was clearly an adulterer... except that such condemnation would only follow if... if I were publicly denounced... which we took very great care never to be; more successfully, of course, than you in your like endeavour; for, you must understand, Holy Mother Church is always inclined to look the other way when the question of the priest and his necessary "housekeeper" arises. And believe me, Will, there are many "house-kept" women serving the Church in that particular way. It is all a matter of words, really... like everything else. A housekeeper is a housekeeper, until she is incontrovertibly revealed to be... a concubine; but that seldom happens since no one is keen to broadcast the Church's hypocrisy in this matter. Like you, I should have been cashiered, except that I was effectively on the side of the angels while you, alas, were always, in the eyes of the Church – any Church, I'm sure of it – a victim, and thus a re-enactor of the Fall. Power, Will, is the key to success in this life, and I fervently hope, to damnation in the next – if there were to be a next...!'

The doctor stirred, groaning in his half sleep, half delirium, as the matron was on the point of leaving the hospital tent. So she turned back and tried to give him what little comfort she could. Water, he had said, was essential in his condition, as much water as they could get into him, and as often as possible. Remembering this again, Miss Labone now held him upright, wedging her own small body behind the dead weight of the doctor's, while she patiently coaxed water from a tin mug into his mouth. Much was spilt, running in rivulets down his chin and dripping onto the newly changed sheets. With her free hand she attempted to stem the flow, though to little avail.

After several minutes' perseverance, the doctor came to something like consciousness and indicated a need to pass water. In this too he required all the assistance she could give him, being as helpless as a little child. She manoeuvred him to the edge of the bed, with the greatest of difficulty, and wedging his pillows behind him she held the chamber pot for him for what seemed an age.

'Such indignities – they come to us all, sooner or later, though much too soon for me... so galling to be felled by our mere physicality...' the doctor mumbled, much to her surprise. Even more surprisingly, he then added: 'It is the love of God... the love of God showing!'

When the stricken man was back on his pillows, once more into his fitful sleep, the matron finally quit the tent. But before retiring for the night, she took up her lantern and walked briskly over to the hospital hut to check on the situation of the sick housed there.

Tired though Will was, sleep would not now come. The priest was not mistaken. Power was indeed the key, not only to success but to its opposite too, for the huge majority who stood outside it. Judges had it; commanding officers had it; priests too, it would appear, in some degree. There were very few of his fellows aboard *The Emigrant*, if any at all, who would not have been victims of someone's power over them. Most were here fleeing from tyranny, as he was, towards the fulfilment of some personal dream of freedom and prosperity.

Ironical, then, that they were still being compelled to follow the same pattern as before, being diverted by other people's legitimate needs, to this island, ensuring that it remained the penal colony it had formerly been, in all but name; still a place for remorse, for regret. Yet (and he clung to this piece of driftwood) if this last place of torment could be got through, the island might yet prove the antechamber to the realisation of many a man's dreams – not least his own.

XVIII

A week later, the *Aurora* returns, coming in on the morning tide. Many of *The Emigrant*'s former passengers hurry down to the water's edge, behind their side of the perimeter fence, which runs at right angles to the shore, and to the forest behind. They watch the ship manoeuvre slowly round to dock at the short, timber landing stage, further along the shore at Dunwich, not far from the unlucky *Emigrant*. Hope and relief and curiosity, as well as anxiety, are all registered in their faces.

Eventually, several men disembark – among them Dr Ballow – and greet Captain Kemp and his First Officer, who move slowly, perhaps hesitantly, towards them. They stand conversing in a huddle, while the ship's crew begin the business of unloading its varied cargo.

The growing crowd of onlookers watch intently from behind the fence, straining to catch the slightest indication of hope or hopelessness that may show on the faces of these men whom they perceive, rightly or wrongly, to be holding the destiny of all on the island in their hands.

Will Crosby was not among the watchers.

For several days he had tried as best he could to assist Thomas in the various tasks that the worsening situation had thrust upon them but had become increasingly impatient at the obtuseness and surly resistance they continually encountered, among people they were earnestly seeking to help. He had seen even Thomas lose his temper on a number of occasions and bully recalcitrant individuals into conforming with his commands, in the name of a nebulous Authority whose existence all, fortunately, presumed and none, thankfully, questioned.

Two days earlier, he and Thomas had sought an audience with Captain Kemp, in which Thomas had explained how they were trying to put into effect some of the points Dr Mitchell had outlined, at the moment of his own descent into the fever, as well as the obstacles they were meeting. Kemp had been sympathetic, partly since his wife had often assisted Dr Mitchell and the young matron during the journey out and had witnessed at close quarters the appalling filth in which many of the steerage passengers lived, seemingly lacking the will to help themselves. He had thus readily agreed to assist them, wielding his own 'authority', whenever necessary... though not even he had been sure of its legality: did the captain of a quarantined vessel retain the same absolute powers off his ship that he had enjoyed when all were aboard it? Given the present circumstances, however, he had declared himself prepared to bluff his way through, 'until some proper Authority arrives from Brisbane.'

For the most part, it had been the women who had objected to the collective, frequent bathing proposed by the new 'regulations', and certainly would not countenance it, they had said, if any of the men-folk were likely to be nearby. There was a question of propriety to be observed, and it had to be acknowledged that their resistance on those grounds was legitimate enough.

It was ostensibly in order to find a workable solution to this problem that Will had set out at dawn that morning, thus missing the arrival of the *Aurora*. Riding one of the horses Ridley had in his governance, he was glad to be off on his own, to be exploring the land to the north of the settlement – in the hope of coming across a convenient bathing-place for the womenfolk, if such were to be found close at hand.

The great clearing was soon left behind, and, at first, he recognised features of his previous short journey on foot, the day he had disembarked. He had not ridden far, however, before he was into new territory, and therefore became more watchful and attentive.

The tall trees and thick woodland quickly gave way to a lower scrub and before long Will caught the sound of gurgling water. He halted and listened more intently, then following the sound, rode slowly into the *mallee*. A hundred yards or so brought him to a spring gushing out of a knoll, to meander away along a sandy-bottomed bed and eventually back towards, and across, the track, after which it suddenly broadened out into a proper stream.

Dismounting, he tethered the horse to a bush, then knelt down by the spring. Cupping his hands he caught some of the water, noticing at once how cold it was. He bent down to taste it. It was fresh water right enough, even though with a faint suggestion of salt. Yes, small groups of women could certainly come here to bathe unobserved, and to wash clothes, since the place would not be much above a mile from the encampment, if that. The spring might also augment the supplies of barrelled water shipped in from Brisbane – always in short supply – provided some means could be devised for transporting it.

Well satisfied with his discovery he stood up and looked about him.

What he had not noticed as he had arrived – being so intent on locating the source of the spring – was that just to the left of the hillock was a circular area that was entirely free of the surrounding scrub, and that towards the back of it, planted at irregular intervals in the ground, were a number of single, round poles, all seeming to have been smoothed and carved, some indeed being also stained with different coloured dyes. This clearing was no accident of nature, and already had some sort of function and meaning different from that he had just assigned to it in his thoughts.

Here was a dilemma, indeed.

Since arriving at the island he had given no thought to the Aboriginal people rumoured to be living in its remoter parts, other than to mention them in passing in the letter he had written to his sister. Yet here was evidence of their recent, if not actual, presence. Might his purposed use of it trample upon their sensibilities, perhaps even lead to conflict? Was the need of a watering place so urgent?

As he stood pondering the possibilities, he had the sudden sensation he was not alone.

Whether it had been some slight movement in the trees, beyond the clearing, or simply the operation of a sixth sense, he could not be sure. It could just have been an animal or a bird, of course. But, what if...?

Momentarily unnerved, he backed towards his tethered horse, never for an instant taking his eyes off the backdrop of trees, and feeling for the rifle in the saddle holster, he drew it out. Checking that the weapon was indeed loaded and ready for use, his confidence returned, and he walked back slowly, cautiously, across the scrub, scrutinising every inch of the tree wall. At the near edge of the clearing he paused, listening intently, then raised the gun into the crook of his left arm, his right index finger firmly on the trigger, before again moving forward. A few paces from where the coloured poles began, he stopped again, though it was certainly not what he had intended.

Later, when he thought back to that moment, he couldn't explain why he had stopped or why he had felt unable to take another step forward.

It was as though something were preventing him from doing so, something physical almost, and so strong was the force of it that his immediate purpose was entirely driven from his mind.

XIX

Will stood rooted there for an indeterminate time, trying to regain control over his own powers but failing to do so. Coming eventually to himself, he backed away, then turned and walked, unhurriedly, towards his horse. Replacing the rifle in its holster he swung himself up into the saddle and, without a backward glance, quickly regained the track and continued his journey northwards.

As he rode, he tried to tell himself he had imagined too much and that now, if he had a mind to, he could go back there and walk quite unhindered into the trees; except that now it would all have lost its point, since had anyone been there, they would certainly have departed by this time. One thing was clear to him, however, that he should not mention the spring or the clearing when he returned to the encampment. His search for a 'suitable' bathing place for the women musts begin all over again.

For a while, the track turned inland, and Will lost sight of the sea, and this worried him for he suddenly realised that the further he had to go in order to find a place, the less practicable it became as a solution. The already rebellious women would not take kindly to anything resembling a route march to enable them to carry out the ablutions they so much resented. And he laughed out loud imagining such a scene.

By the time the path swung back towards the sea, Will had already dismissed his search in that area as hopeless. He was nevertheless still set on reaching the Amity Point indicated by the sign close to the camp, which he had come across, even on that first day. And, if it proved at all possible, he would then work his way back down the coast in the hope of locating a spot much nearer to Dunwich, perhaps even where the stream flowing down from the untouchable spring emptied into the sea.

The silence was intense, the only occasional sounds emanating from the horse's passage: the jingling harness, the creak of leather – or raucous parakeets, startled away in the tree canopy, high overhead.

The sun was already nearing its zenith by the time he entered an area of swampland. At times, the track became indistinct, being lost in black pools of water, and he had to rely on his horse's instinct to see them through. He eventually came to the headland which, Mr Ridley had informed him, was named after a ship that had foundered thereabouts more than a quarter of a century before, and he was surprised to find two or three rudimentary, though derelict huts, likely testimony of a failed attempt at settlement Ridley had also mentioned.

The site was attractive – having a long sandy beach running southwards and along what he took to be the northern shore of the island – yet too remote to be really viable, except for hermits. From the Point itself, he could see what he believed must be Moreton Island to the north and the still unattained mainland of the continent to the west.

Half a mile or so to the south the mangroves began, while inland there was what appeared at first to be a lake but which, on closer inspection, turned out to be a long inlet from the sea, itself quite thickly wooded with mangroves on its northern and eastern sides. This last discovery was, in effect, a disappointment, for it meant he would effectively have to retrace his steps to come down to the shoreline, on the farther side of the inlet, before moving south again, compelled once more to negotiate the insect-ridden swamplands. Yet, even as he thought it, he dismissed the idea yet again, for no one would be willing to come this far out from the camp. How would a mass of people get here, anyway? He would return to the stream by the route he had come and follow it from there, if it were possible, down to the sea.

He hesitated for several minutes, unable to make up his mind what to do for the best. Then he dismounted and let his horse follow him along the sands. Apart from the lapping of the water, the silence was absolute. Yet he was far from alone. Just yards away a pair of yellow-breasted kingfishers sat among the branches of a driftwood tree; on the sands, tiny blue crabs skittered away from him in all directions; and suddenly, a flight of pelicans (he counted eight) glided past him, less than fifty yards from the shoreline. He was immediately struck by the stark contrast between the dark scenes of human desolation he had left behind an hour or two before, and the unsullied nature of this place.

Will's mind drifted back to that strange experience in the clearing by the spring, and the strong sense of trespass – yes, that was it – he had felt there, just before he had stopped (or been stopped – which he now entertained as a distinct possibility) dead in his tracks. Although by no means so strong or compelling, he once again had the sensation that he should not be there, that his very presence was an offence, yet to whom or what he could not say. He retraced his footsteps in the soft sand, regretting them, yet also aware that within a few short hours they would be washed clean away, and then it would be as if he had never been there.

By the time he had regained the main track southwards the sky had darkened considerably behind him, and it was obvious that a storm was imminent, coming down from the north. It would strike within minutes. With this realisation he abandoned all thoughts of cutting through the scrubland towards the coast, and he set off over the uneven terrain back towards the camp.

With the growling storm fast approaching he rode his horse hard. The air seemed to have thickened and though no rain as yet had fallen a thin mist had descended. He could see the lather-like foam about the horse's mouth and nostrils, occasionally flying off past him in the slipstream and he realised she could not maintain such tremendous exertion for much longer. Gently, he reined her in. He had covered four, maybe five miles.

And then the storm broke and in a matter of minutes the ferocious squall had overtaken him and soaked him to the skin.

The going became increasingly difficult as the path quickly turned into a quagmire, and he slowed the horse down to walking pace. Thunder crashed and echoed all around them, causing the animal to start with each new peal, whinnying in fear. He tried to pacify her, patting her, speaking quietly into her ear, and she calmed a little. But suddenly, with the renewed rattling of thunder and first lashes of lightning, she reared almost vertically. And, taken by surprise, Will was hurled from the saddle.

Even as consciousness slipped away from him, he realised he might well drown in the shallow stream the track had now become, but he was too far gone to do anything for his own protection.

A long narrow tunnel whose walls tower away above him, so high their top cannot be seen. Far down the way a blinding light draws him on, and he seems to glide, having no sense of physical being. As he comes nearer, he becomes aware of shadowy figures, deep within the light, beckoning him forward, and his own whirling velocity increases to a superhuman swirl. Then come the sounds, a swishing and a deep droning, enveloping him completely even as he absorbs them to the exclusion of all other sensation; then the two merge into a quietening hiss behind which there seem to be voices, calling, chattering, laughing excitedly, then the blinding light begins to fade, and he is rushing backwards, backwards, backwards at ever-increasing speed.

His eyes opened, though unfocused, seeing nothing. Gradually, his dispersed senses came together near the borderlands of coherence – like Humpty-Dumpty, was his first conscious thought, put together again... But that couldn't be right... He wasn't, was he...? They couldn't... And he gave up on this rambling, realising how nonsensical it was, and slowly he began to take stock of his situation, as eyes and mind refocused at last.

The rain is now falling steadily, although nowhere nearly as fierce as before, nor is there any thunder or lightning. He remembers the horse and turns his head slowly round, first in one direction then the other, acutely aware of a stiffness in his neck and shoulders, a throbbing at the back of his head.

And there she is, only a few yards away, tethered to a tree.

He frowns. And as the memory of what had happened gradually comes back to him, he realises how impossible this is – his horse… tethered? He peers at her again, his eyes still blurring; but in the end he is forced to the realisation that it is indeed so. Almost in the same moment, he becomes aware that he himself is sitting, propped up against a rock at the side of the track, and this is impossible too.

Cautiously, Will moves his legs round until he is in a kneeling position from which, after a moment or two's hesitation, a gathering of determination, he tries to lever himself onto his feet. The pain hammers at his head, his neck, and his shoulders, but, in the end, he manages it, and he stands swaying in the roadway, but faint again, nauseous, with the exertion of it. And all the while, his mind is working on the gaps, prodding at a sluggish memory.

Then comes the realisation. There were voices. In my unconsciousness there were voices.

Will leans against the horse's flank, trying to steady himself, but the weakness in his legs and the haze before his eyes persist. For the moment, at least, it would be pointless trying to lift himself up into the saddle. Even if he succeeded, he would run the risk of another fall, with maybe even graver consequences than the first. He is shivering too, for his clothes are soaked, sticking to his skin, and ice cold.

Groping for the reins he unfastens the horse and turns her in the direction of the encampment. 'Come on now, old girl, gently does it. Must get going… That squall is sure to have spread havoc back at the station…'

It is then that he notices the rifle is missing from its holster.

Re-tying the animal to another low branch, his fingers fumbling with the loose knot, he starts searching about, albeit desultorily, in the undergrowth where he had been. But it couldn't have slipped out, could it? The holster was far too deep, and tightly gripped...

Whoever attended to him – possibly even saved him from drowning – must also have taken the rifle. There was no other possible explanation. Yet the two actions strike Will as being somehow incompatible...

But now, rubbing his eyes, he sees he is back at the clearing, with its painted poles, and this too, he realises, is quite impossible.

He could never have come as far as this from Amity before the storm overtook and felled him. Impossible.

Yet, here he is, for there is the spring, though all but lost, drowned by the sheet of water that still covers the land all about him.

XX

Proceeding as best he could, slowly leading the horse, slopping through mud and water, ankle deep in places, Will eventually came through the belt of trees that led into the camp.

He stopped at once, utterly dismayed at the scene before him. The ground was awash and many of the tents had been flattened, evidently some had been borne away by the flood. He approached slowly, observing that there was a great deal of to-ing and fro-ing, mainly down at the far end of the compound, very likely to bring the sick to more secure shelter in the semi-derelict huts, which had housed the convicts in years gone by. He saw too, through the rain mist, that the *Aurora* had returned and was riding at anchor alongside the jetty that separated her from the deserted *Emigrant*.

His feet now squelching in the soft ground, he went by his own tent, which thankfully still stood, though like the rest, in several inches of water.

Passing slowly beyond the perimeter fence he came at length to Ridley's quarters and tethered the horse to the rail erected for that purpose. Not surprisingly no one was there. He had wanted to explain about the events that had led to the loss of the rifle, but it would have to wait.

Re-entering the compound, Will saw that the hospital tent was still in place, and he made towards it, hoping to find the priest. In the event, there was only the matron, still maintaining her watch – her loving watch, it suddenly struck him – over the gradually failing Dr Mitchell, who was now in an almost continuous comatose state.

Miss Labone rose at once to her feet.

'Thanks be to God, you're safe, Sergeant Crosby! The Catholic Reverend Gentleman – did he detect a note of disapproval in her voice? – was all for sending out a search party...! Come on, let's get you out of that.' And in evident consternation, she began helping his still fumbling, unfocused fingers to remove his sodden shirt.

'And with the return of the *Aurora*, we now have dry sheets, dry blankets, towels and clothing. And we have Dr Ballow back with us, and a young doctor, Dr Mallon, and medical supplies... and a few more tents.' Her relief was all too clear.

The priest and the newcomers were over at the huts, she told him, doing whatever they could for those who had suffered worst in the storm...

Despite the fact that these huts had been condemned for demolition, and there would be fearful overcrowding, it had been decided to use them all, until the ground had dried out. And now, amid all the confusion brought by the storm, another two of the immigrants had expired, bringing the total for that week to nine deaths, with more still expected...

'But you are not to be one of them,' she said, gently but firmly, as though she expected him to rebel against her good sense. 'Wrap yourself in this blanket, now, and take off your wet trousers and underwear while I go and fetch you some dry clothes – if you tell me where I can find them.' And away she went. Will, having followed her instructions at once, sank gratefully down upon the pillow of one of the two empty beds, his back and shoulder full of pain, his head pounding.

When he woke, it was already dark. Thomas was sitting beside him, and a young man, whom he took to be the new doctor the matron had mentioned, was close by. As he roused, the young man came over to him.

'That was a nasty blow you took to the head, Mr Crosby. How did it happen?'

Will told him – of his headlong flight and his fall – and Dr Mallon nodded. As Thomas looked on, the doctor had his patient sit up then carried out a couple of quick tests to make sure that he was not suffering from concussion. He also felt at his shoulders and the upper part of his back to check that no bones were broken or out of place.

Will winced, repeatedly.

Then, even as he was expressing his satisfaction that all seemed well, the doctor deftly jerked and manipulated the left shoulder, and Will screamed at the sudden, greatly intensified pain of it.

'I'm sorry, Mr Crosby, but it was dislocated, and I thought it best to do it without any warning, while you were relaxed. I think you will find the pain now fades quite swiftly. I'm still a little concerned at the double vision you mentioned earlier to the matron, so we'll have to keep a check on that. But are you comfortable for the moment?'

As Will settled back on the pillow, the doctor and the priest acquainted him with what had been done to aid the sick, and their unfortunate families, in the emergency. And this, as Thomas remarked, was precisely to put them back into cramped, overcrowded quarters which, if Dr Mitchell's theories were correct, was more likely to 'aid the spread of the damned pestilence' than lessen it. But given the suddenness of the downpour and the havoc it wrought he owned that nothing better could have been devised for them. There had apparently been talk of reoccupying *The Emigrant*, but Dr Ballow had forbidden this solution, for the ship still required further fumigation before it could be pronounced free of the disease. Their best hope, as all acknowledged, was for better weather; but for now, since the rain persisted, they must do the best they could.

After a few minutes' more discussion, Dr Mallon moved towards the exit: 'I will see if Dr Ballow needs any assistance, over in the huts. More deaths are expected, Mr Crosby, within the next few hours, and I should be on hand.'

'Aye, and so should I,' said Thomas. 'I'll... be along directly, Patrick.'

Will smiled, grateful to have his company a while longer.

'Well then, what happened to you?' Thomas asked, when the doctor had left. 'You were off exploring, I gather.'

'Not really. If you remember, I was actually looking for a bathing place… for the women… At first, anyway…' And then, having explained about the area he'd covered, and his failure to find anywhere near enough, he told Thomas how he'd been caught in the storm, about his fall, and finally, his strange discoveries on regaining consciousness.

'Hm. Quite an adventure!' Thomas acknowledged. Then he remembered: 'Oh, yes, when I happened to mention to Mr Ridley why you had borrowed his horse, he said it was a pity he had not known sooner, for it turns out there is a fresh-water lake about a mile distant, straight out of the camp here, which in his opinion would provide the ideal conditions for our purpose – for both men and women.'

'Is there, indeed?' Will clicked his tongue in disgust.

'So it seems. Maybe, when you feel up to it, you might go and take a look at it, or if not you, then someone else the captain might suggest from his… entourage.'

'No, no, I will go….' Will flinched at the shooting pain in his shoulder. 'I'll speak to Mr Ridley before I do… So, Thomas, what do you make of the strange feeling of… prohibition that I experienced? Was it my imagination, do you think? It was as though something were pressing me back, physically, making me step back. I've never before known anything like it.'

'It's… hard to say.' Thomas seemed to be choosing his words carefully. 'My rational mind tells me the feeling came – for whatever reason – from inside rather than outside you, but our reason is such a paltry thing, is it not? I would not care to press it overmuch. One hears, from time to time, of all sorts of inexplicable, quite amazing things happening in exotic parts of the world, and I suppose this place qualifies as well as any for that epithet; by Jesus, it does!' He smirked at Will. 'Maybe it did have something to do with the Blackfellows who are said to be in the remoter parts of even this island. But, well, I myself have no knowledge of their habits or their culture, so can make no real response.' He looked at Will. 'You really should speak to Ridley about it. He's been here a good while longer than we have. And maybe he'd… have a better idea of what happened to you.'

'Aye, you have a point. I'll mention it to him when I see him.' But Will's attempt at brightness rang hollow even to himself. There was still the matter of the gun to be resolved.

'Right you are, then. So I'll be off, to do what I can to assist the young doctor.' But then, the priest turned back. 'Will – I'm not sure it is good for you to remain in here… with Dr Mitchell so poorly and all. Do you not think…?'

'It had crossed my mind.' Will shifted his position, gingerly. 'I still feel shaken, with a terribly-nagging headache. And I noticed our tent was standing in water… But yes – again he attempted levity – I'll… paddle over there and try to sleep it off…' He hesitated. 'Thomas, I was…'

'Good.' His friend was already half out of the door. 'Tell the matron when you are leaving, so she knows to keep an eye on the poor doctor. Oh, and by the way, there was a letter came for you with the *Aurora*. I put it on your bed.' And away he went.

A letter. Will brightened a little, then realised, at once, that it would be an expression of all the anxiety felt by his sister, and other members of his family, occasioned by his overlong silence. It would, of course, be many weeks before the letter he had written… when? over a week ago, was it…? reached its destination; the curse of all that time and distance that stretched, seemingly endless, between them. He pulled himself up a little, with a sharp intake of breath. Yet, it might contain bits of news that for a little while, at least, would bring them all closer together. It was too much to hope that there would be any news of Alice and his daughter.

And then, despite his resolution of a moment ago, Will's eyes closed, and his hands automatically reached for the covers and pulled them over him.

XXI

Later, maybe an hour or more later, Will dressed slowly, finding the clean clothes matron had brought him, at the foot of the bed. Walking proved less uncomfortable. He alerted the matron, in her quarters, before leaving and picking his way over to his own tent.

The water level had reduced noticeably, but every footfall churned the ground into a treacly mud. On entering he saw at once that someone – probably Thomas – had thoughtfully placed his baggage on top of the judge's chest, so that nothing had been touched by the water. He lit a candle, making space for it on the chest, and sat down carefully on the bed. Then, using his good arm, he opened the bulky envelope, which was, as he had expected, in his sister's hand. It was dated 8 May 1850.

He wondered at the rush of emotion the very presence of the letter caused to well up inside him, since what was news on that date – for she who had penned it – had now, most surely, receded into the great black pit of the past. Its emotions, its urgencies and its immediacy were now dulled, replaced by… who could say what at this impossible distance that was also unfathomable time? But for him, though clearly history, it was new knowledge, although, he realised yet again, he could not quite bring himself to think of it as 'news'. And he realised too that, to all practical intents and purposes, he was as far away from home as if he had been on the moon. In these circumstances – the thought passed through his mind – one must always fear the final full stop, for what had gone on to happen, either in consequence of the intelligence the letter brought, or indeed, in no related sense at all, would surely be cause of more and more desires and anxieties.

He took up the letter and began to read.

Dear William,

I do not know whether you will ever read this letter, though I pray that by some miracle it will indeed be so. Here we are all in despair, not only because we had expected to hear from you before now, but also because our dear mother lies close to death. The stomach pains she had felt for the best part of a year, and which she insisted were nothing to cause concern, have now been confirmed to be a malignant growth. Poor mother has become pitifully thin, wasting away before our eyes, because she is not able to take solid food any longer. She is in constant pain and Dr Loughlin is now compelled to administer ever-increasing doses of laudanum; it will be a mercy when it pleases the Good Lord to take her, William.

We all feel so helpless, foolishly encouraged if she manages to get out of bed or even to smile, but for the most part tending to her needs, to try somehow to make amends for the cruel end towards which her life is surely hastening.

The Reverend Davidson pops in to see her every day and he, more than any of us, seems to bring her some little comfort. It would have brought her great joy in her adversity had she been able to receive word from you – that you were faring well and that your fortunes were at last beginning to prosper (sadly, in the circumstances, I fear that is not to be). We of course tell her that it is as yet too soon for us to expect news from you, but before long such an optimistic interpretation of your prolonged silence will lose its credibility.

Joseph writes from London that he may well be able to make the journey to Whitehaven towards the end of June, and this gives our mother something pleasurable to look forward to, though we know full well – and I suspect she does too – that she will not last until then.

If Will's thoughts had been with Alice as he opened the letter, they were now propelled into a new despair, for when he had last seen his mother, several weeks before his departure, she had been in reasonably good health, in spite of the nagging pain in her side she sometimes complained of. With great difficulty he tried now to concentrate on the rest of his sister's news, reading over the sentence at which he had broken off in his distress, two or three times, before he could bring their sense into focus.

He mentions in passing that though he has made extensive inquiries among mutual acquaintances no one appears to have any news of Nancy. She seems to have disappeared entirely. Joe's other news is mainly about his work duties, though he does tell us that the Prince's dream of a huge crystal palace to house next year's great exhibition is fast taking shape and will certainly be finished in time. He and Arabella made an excursion there to see it only a few weeks ago. How fortunate he is to be living in the city which is the centre of the world. There is so much always happening there – though I must say that it would in no way suit me.

You will be pleased to know I have at long last received news from Alice…

Alice! And Will's heart skipped a beat.

…to whom I wrote, as you requested, no fewer than three times, and had just about given up all hope of having any reply, believing that she must yet continue in her bitterness. It turns out she and Lilian have moved to Kirkby Stephen, where she has a position as housekeeper to a farmer, a widower with three young daughters, and her parents had neglected to post my letters on to her. She found them only when she returned home on one of her apparently rare days away from her duties. As you will see from her letter, this neglect was cause of yet another bitter row and perhaps final breakdown of relations with her mother…

She had written, had she? Will leafed quickly through the remaining pages until he found the all-important communication. And seeing her letter, with its small, neat handwriting… just the fact of having it here, brought tears to his eyes; while, at the same time, knowing all the recriminations it would contain, the unwillingness to contemplate any forgiveness – her constant, stubborn message these three years past…

He placed his fingers gently, reverently, upon the ink, shaking with excitement and dread, as if it were her very hand he was touching.

And then he looked away. Following hard on the heels of the turmoil stirred up in him by the news of his mother's imminent – and by now, almost certain – death, here he was, suddenly being bundled into the presence of the one person in the world who could save or destroy *him*.

Will laid the letters gently down upon the bed, and went outside, choking back the tears, beating back the surging memories and useless feelings of remorse. Time… he needed time to prepare himself mentally and emotionally before taking up Alice's letter. He needed to fortify himself as best he could against the stings and barbs its words, whatever they described, would bear for him. He needed… he was not sure at all what he needed…

In those moments, he bitterly regretted his decision to flee his country to seek a new life, and so very far away. Yet regret was futile. Time and distance nullified it. He could only accept the terms they imposed, he knew that, and live out the consequences of his own freely made, yet none the less imposed, choice.

No calmer, but steeling himself, he went back inside to brave the letter.

Dear Mrs McGuiness…

… it began… ominously; for at one time Mary and Alice had been such close friends…

You may have wondered at my failure to respond to your letters, but it was not, I assure you, on account of any intended discourtesy on my part. It was simply that I did not receive them until I returned to Redhills, only a week ago, the first time in over two months. My mother, with whom relations have become unbearable, had not even the decency to post them on to me at my new address.

Having finally failed to find a way of returning to my former intended profession of schoolteacher, I have been compelled to seek some other form of employment, and for the time being, at least, have a position as housekeeper and governess at a farm near Kirkby Stephen.

After agreeing, at first, to mind the child if I managed to find a post locally as a trainee teaching assistant (as I did, in fact, at Dacre), my mother went back on her word and adamantly refused to help me. The cause was trivial – she made some disparaging remark about Will that did not suit me – and when I retorted, she flared up and poured out a lot of poison – about him, about me, even about the poor, innocent child – that she had been bottling up, evidently, these three years past, and more. Behind it lay the fact that I had declined the doubtless kind offer of our local parson and his wife (who are childless) to adopt Lilian. I admit I was sorely tempted, and gave the matter much thought, but in the end, for better or worse, I could not bring myself to do it.

Will was thrown into yet more turmoil, quite overcome, realising – by Alice's own admission – that his little daughter could so easily have been thrust even further away from him, when he had imagined the situation could not have been worse. He would have had no say...

He might never have known.

And in this sudden, renewed awareness of his own helplessness Will could feel the perspiration rising all over his body. He read on, panic-stricken, yet thankful, at least, that Alice had not succumbed to external pressures nor, indeed, to the temptation to be free.

Certainly, they would have given her a better life than I can ever hope to do, and it would have allowed me to begin all over again, hopefully with some other, worthier man than your brother, but I could not be sure they would give her the love of a mother. She is now six years old and the shock of being given away to strangers would – I am sure of it – scar her for life. I know I shall probably rue my decision many times over in the difficult years ahead, but I believe in my heart of hearts it was the right one. Had she still been a babe in arms it might have been different. I cannot say.

My mother declared me a fool; she said I was selfish to keep her, that they were good people, and she would soon forget me, and a whole lot more hurtful things. She worked herself up into such a fury, provoking me to equal anger, and in the end, she ordered me to 'get out before the end of the week – and take my little bastard with me!' For those words alone, I shall never forgive her.

My poor father, when he came home, tried to pour oil on these troubled waters, but I had already packed my bags and was on the point of leaving. He persuaded me not to go, not then, since there was nowhere that I could go. Next day, however, I took the train into Penrith and placed an advert in the local paper. The idea of governess, then housekeeper, had come to me during an anxious, sleepless night.

A week after placing the advertisement I had three replies and chose this one because it was located on the railway line to Redhills junction, where my father works as a signalman. However, I did not hasten to make use of this convenience and waited more than two months before returning – I suppose in the hope that things would have calmed down, in the meantime. Maybe they had, I can't rightly say; for the moment I discovered that my letters (and not only the ones from you) had been withheld, I could not contain my anger, and in a matter of moments we were right back at the impossibly low point that had occasioned my departure in the first place. I stayed only long enough to gather up some more of my things – and to go up into the signal box to see my father – before taking the next train back. He was upset, as was Lilian, for she is greatly attached to her grandpa, but I have vowed not to go back there again. And that being the case, my father has twice visited us here in Kirkby Stephen, on his free day, but I have no wish to see, much less be reconciled with, that hard, viper-tongued woman; she (like your cowardly brother) has ceased to exist as far as I am concerned.

My only other news is of the routines here. Mr Hewitt, a widower, the master of the house, is a bluff man of few words and has handed his three daughters over to me entirely. Aged between five and eleven they are a handful, and they (and Lilian) and all the other household duties keep me busy seven days a week from dawn to dusk, and often beyond. Yet I am thankful I have a roof over my head, a degree of independence, and a modest income, some of which I am able to save against a rainy day. Being so occupied and, as a consequence, so very tired at the end of the day, I thankfully have little time or energy for brooding over what has been. I hope, in time, to have so distanced myself from it, and from him, that I no longer suffer the hurt that still catches me unawares in odd, always unexpected moments. If only. If only. But the world is a harsh place and takes no account of the ways our hearts work, and there is no sense in dwelling on it.

I have no idea where he is, and have no particular desire to know, for what is past is past. But if you know, you might like to pass on to him some little news of his daughter, who has never ceased to pine for him, and of the burdens he has thrust upon me. Lilian is at present ill with the rheumatic fever and is missing her schooling. She is like to be at home for several weeks yet, maybe even months. But please do not think I am asking for anything from him. I would not accept it even if it came, which, given his proven selfishness, is highly unlikely anyway.

If you wish to contact me from time to time for news of your niece – if that is how you deign to think of her – then all well and good but considering your own part in the deception that *has well-nigh destroyed my life and deprived my daughter of a father, I could never contemplate any renewal of the friendship we once enjoyed. I shall not change my mind.*

I remain,

Yours truly,

Alice Fallowfield

The letter, read quickly, confirmed Will's worst fears. He was deemed a deceiver, a moral coward, and all Alice's heat was turned upon him. Hard. Unforgiving. Her mother's daughter, sure enough!

But when he read it again later, more slowly, sometimes regressing to read a phrase or a sentence over, he felt… yes, strangely heartened.

It was just little, incidental things: what was it her mother had said about him *that did not suit her*? And it was not that Alice didn't want to know absolutely where he was, only *not particularly* – which seemed to him to leave the door open, if just a fraction, whatever she had meant by that odd-sounding qualification. But most of all, the confession (even if couched in terms of its opposite) that she still might be inclined to *brood over the past* and *still felt the hurt* which, he reasoned, would not be the case if her driving passion were hatred – or even a pallid indifference. She suffered, he concluded, because she had lost him, just as he suffered in losing her, and whilst ever those wounds remained open, there had to be some way back. There had to be! Alice was as proud as she was honourable and upright in her conduct and Will knew that only by proving himself to be a man of integrity, and being publicly acknowledged as such, might he ever hope to win her again, if at all.

He laid her letter aside, on the judge's chest, and, after a moment's more contemplation, turned back to his sister's, skimming through it to the points at which she relayed other bits of news:

I almost forgot, Will. Our brother John's wife, Sarah, was delivered of a baby boy, six weeks ago, and almost died of the milk fever. It was touch and go for a while – but she has managed to pull through, though she still continues frail. They have decided to call him John, like his father. He, at least, seems healthy enough. Charlie is much saddened by all of these changes. As I'm sure you are aware, he was ever fond of you, and greatly misses the pleasant times we all used to enjoy together when you and Alice were living at the Tithe Barn. Our mother's affliction seems to have hit him hard too, and he has recently lost much of that alertness and joviality which always made him welcome wherever he went. God only knows what is to become of us all in these troubled times.

I shall write no more for the present – I have not the heart, not knowing whether you are living or dead. Nothing from you again today. But we must not give up hope, not yet.

One thing more before I close. Alice's letter, for all its harshness in your regard, seems to me to convey another message too, one which is in direct contradiction of all of that. The fact that she wrote at all, but at such length, does nothing to make her unforgiving words ring quite true. Do not give up hope Will, if indeed you are still of the same mind you were when you left us all those months ago.

God be with you.

Your ever-loving sister,

Mary

So, he had not been mistaken; Mary had sensed it too. Between the lines of Alice's letter there was a hankering, despite herself, which brought him some little hope and determination to yet prove himself well worthy of her. Yet, there was something else, more immediate in his thoughts. The condition of his child, her health and her pining. She, he knew well enough – more than Alice, more than himself – had been and would doubtless long continue the prime victim of his deception.

What futures lie hidden in our present follies, in our immediate vision that never penetrates the shadows that hover about us!

Sometime later, Will read Alice's letter over again, then again, and newly elated by its few crumbs of hope, placed it carefully back in the envelope, alongside his sister's. He lay back on his pillow, his shoulder stiff, his head still throbbing. Then, suddenly feeling the damp cold, he stripped off his outer clothing and slid down between the covers, and into a restless, churning, sleep.

XXII

Suddenly, Will was wide awake, aware that Thomas had returned and was muttering to himself, trying to light a candle. That finally accomplished, the priest glanced in Will's direction and, seeing his eyes were open, apologised for having wakened him. 'Truth is,' he whispered, 'it's so long since I was here, I can't remember where anything is – so, after spending a fruitless age groping about in the dark, the candle was my only hope! I'm sorry, truly.'

Will pulled himself up, leaning on his elbow. 'Ah, 'tis no matter… I'm sure I'll have no difficulty sleeping again. But… when was it you last slept? What time is it anyway? Is it late?'

Busying himself in his search, Thomas did not answer immediately. 'Agh! Bugger it! I can't see a bloody thing in this pathetic light'.

'So, what is it you're looking for that can't wait until the morning?'

Thomas straightened himself up and turned to face him, 'Well,' he said, his pitch rising, 'I'm looking for some soap, for my razor and for a towel. Because not only have I not slept for two days, Will Crosby, but I haven't washed either, so far as I remember, and the bloody lice must be thinking they've ended up in some sort of paradise garden! I'd like to give meself a treat and them a shock, late in the day though it is… Ah, but there you are, hiding away from me! Sometimes, Will, the perversity of things… They hide away from us, I swear they do!' And he picked up his chronometer from among the objects strewn about his bed. 'In answer to your last question but one, it is almost eleven o'clock – the eleventh hour for my horde of vermin… if I ever find a piece of bloody soap!'

'If you can't find your soap, take mine – it's in my kit, here, on the judge's chest. And watch out for the snakes… if you're going over to the water troughs.

'Ah, you're a saint, Will Crosby, that you are!' and so saying Thomas unwrapped Will's kit, took out a bar of soap, lit a lantern from the candle, and went off outside.

After twenty minutes or so he was back, naked apart from his heavy boots and the towel around his waist. He found Will sitting up in his bed, swathed in his topcoat, reading by the light of his own candle.

'By God but it's cold! Is that your letter, then?' Thomas nodded at the papers Will was holding.

Will glanced up. 'Oh my! And he began to laugh. 'Very fetching attire, if I may say so, Your Reverence.'

'Aye, well, I dumped the cassock, and the rest, in one of the troughs; I'll see to them in the morning. I only hope there are no further calls to duty, tonight, otherwise I shall be scrounging from you again.' He sat down, trying to maintain some little dignity, as might a woman arranging her skirts. 'So, Will… what is your news from home?'

Will shook his head. 'Oh… not what I would have wished for, and that's for sure. My mother is dead, and my sister has forwarded a letter she received from Alice that is, well, as unforgiving as ever. It's as though my prison sentence had never ended. And yet, I think – and in this my sister agrees with me – Alice leaves me not without some shred of hope for the future…' He looked up at his friend and shrugged helplessly.

There followed a moment or two's silence. For Will it was an expectant silence – of some comment, and understanding, perhaps. Yet Thomas's face registered anxiety.

'Will, forgive me if I speak bluntly but I feel I must. I would have been insensitive in the extreme if I had not gleaned from our previous conversations on this matter that it is your intention to return at some future date and reclaim Alice to resume what you remember as an idyllic life. Am I not right?'

Will nodded, though wondering at this shift in his companion's mood.

'Indeed, it seems to have been the avowed intention underlying your decision to come here in the first place,' and again he paused awaiting Will's acknowledgement of this surmise also. When he had it, he too nodded his head, more perhaps at his own satisfaction than at his friend's truthfulness: 'Have ye not had sufficient sadness in these past few years to last you a lifetime?'

Will looked searchingly at his friend, surprised by the seriousness of his tone. 'Well... yes, that is so...' His headache, he realised, was still with him, though perhaps not quite so severe as it had been before he slept.

'I thought as much,' said Thomas, nodding yet again, his eyes fixed on Will's own. 'If you will allow me to indulge in a parable – that would seem a fittingly priestly thing to do now, would it not? Now, there was a certain priest who suddenly stopped feeling he was a priest; indeed, he realised he no longer wished to be a priest. The reason for this revelation was not hard to find. He had suddenly discovered "woman" – a woman – and realised that the emotionless abstraction which was known to him as "Love", the Love of God, and which had hitherto been the cold guiding principle of his every thought and action, could, in fact, become a powerful energy within him, not as Love – with the usual capital, indeed, Holy Roman L – but as "love", in the humbler, much more effulgent, lower case. Now... do you follow me?'

There was a definite twinkle in his now smiling eyes.

Will smiled appreciatively at his friend's self-mocking tone, then sat upright in his bed.

Thomas paused briefly to accommodate Will's move. 'That wholly new sensation – he continued – was fired and fuelled by the sure knowledge that the feeling was wholly reciprocated. And from that moment on he became two people, living two quite incompatible lives: the loving husband, when his door was shut and locked behind him, and the ministering priest, the moment he crossed the threshold out into the world. He soon learnt, however, that a revolution of fact is not necessarily accompanied by a comparable adjustment in moral principle. "Once a Catholic, always a Catholic," is a common enough saw, but imagine how much more truth there is in it if the Catholic also happens to be a priest! You see, Will, the hypocrisy of my situation – and here he dropped all pretence at parable – plagued me, as it did Joanna, and it was not helped by the knowing or suspicious looks that sometimes passed between our parishioners, even in our presence, and the whispering campaign that came eventually to our ears. Joanna was young, and uncommonly good-looking.'

'Ah, I hadn't realised… But that surely wasn't why…?'

'I can't be sure, Will. But sooner or later, I had to choose between those two modes and being true to myself for maybe the first time in my life – as well as to the woman whom, you may remember, I had saved from grinding poverty and almost certain death. And so I chose; I chose the private rather than the public life. And from that moment on – and herein lies something that is pertinent in your own case, Will – my life was detached from present reality and hitched to that cerebral hotch-podge of surmise, hope, fairy story and gross improbability that we call "the future". But Will, "the future" is a lie, a utopia; and the harder you cleave to it the harder you fall when the only reality time affords – the here and now – reasserts itself, as it always does. There is no bloody future, Will, only a long succession of "nows", and these we can only direct more or less minimally towards our dreams and aspirations; for the rest of reality is totally ignorant, and, what's more, utterly careless of them. And thus our dreams begin to be shredded and tattered from the moment they are conceived.' He paused, then, to secure the towel that barely covered him, and which seemed to be slipping away from him on account of the vigour of his gestures.

'In my own case, Will, the process began in elaborate comedy, bordering on farce. And it ended in undignified, chaotic tragedy! And you see – Thomas's voice assumed a bitter edge – we knew it would be impossible to fight the Church, for my release; and even if we'd been successful, we should have been hounded out of Ireland. So, we worked out a careful plan to escape… into our rose-tinted future.'

Will flinched, unable to miss the irony.

'Joanna would leave for Cork, where I was to join her, two or three days later,' Thomas explained. We would then take ship for Bristol or Plymouth and thence, at the first available opportunity, one for New South Wales. And since it was not uncommon for a priest to be away from his parish on occasion, on Church business, all of this part was easily accomplished. Of course, we packed only a few essentials between us, so as not to arouse suspicions, and, in any case, we wanted to shed as many reminders of our old life as we possibly could.'

'So you... you told no one, no one at all that you were... leaving?'

Thomas raised a bemused eyebrow. 'Oh, to be sure I did, Will, I most certainly did! Just before our ship left Cork for Plymouth, I posted a brief letter to my bishop explaining my loss of vocation and my determination to make a new life in "the Americas", where so many of my fellow-countrymen had already fled in the past few years. I made no apologies and asked for neither forgiveness nor blessings. Of course, I had some qualms about leaving my parishioners in the lurch; the potato situation had gone from bad to worse and neither the government in London nor the local gentry had so much as raised a finger to alter it. Cruel indifference was the best they could manage between them. In those circumstances, the priest's role had been shrunk to muttered words of solace and... well... conducting funerals. I knew also, though, that the Church would soon plug the gap. And God help the poor, unfortunate boy-priest who would come to replace me!' He looked long and earnestly at Will, dipping his head reflectively, mechanically almost.

'The rest you know, more or less. But you see, don't you, the very tenuous hold we have on events, even at the best of times. You and Alice. Joanna and me. What Joanna and I had purposed we had achieved to our satisfaction, but the road to any future is always full of unseen potholes and other lurking dangers. And once we had set sail on our long voyage from Plymouth these began to emerge and waylay us like so many hideous demons.'

'You refer to the pestilence, I imagine.'

'Aye, that. But also, Will, I had not realised how much I would come to despise the manner of my leaving, and neither of us really understood what miseries such a journey entailed. When the pestilence broke out and turned plain adversity into a living hell, it sapped our remaining confidence and our resolve. The unknown towards which we were moving so slowly shed its magical, liberating allure to take on, more and more, an air of menace, to seem like the land of the lost. I myself sank into deep depression brought on by my profound sense of guilt – both at turning my back on my calling and at exposing Joanna to these horrors against which we had no defence. The ship was our prison, our hell, and we were at the mercy of blind chance, of sheer bloody chance, Will. You see... Joanna and I... we had made of each other the sole condition of our future happiness, and it had never crossed our minds, not until our fellow passengers began to die around us, that one of us might have to face that future alone and unconditionally. And so it has proved.'

'Are you saying,' Will asked, leaning forward, resting his chin on his hand, his crooked elbow on his knee, 'that you should never invest exclusively, or too narrowly, when looking to... the future?' Suddenly shivering, he sank back down further into the warmth of his bed and pulled the covers up to his chin.

'Well', he persisted, 'is that it?'

'More than that, Will. I am trying to say something I do not yet fully understand myself, but it is to do with the uncontrollable nature of even our own lives because our lives are so dependent on so many hidden or chance factors. Most of the time, these can cause us disappointment, for they destroy what we had purposed, but we adjust and move on. In my case, however, building a whole future on such narrow, shaky foundations, whose solidity I had not even thought to question, was sheer folly. And I'm telling you this, most especially since... well, I should hate you to be brought low, yet again, as I have been, through making the same mistake. And unless I am sorely mistaken that is precisely where you are headed.'

Will shook his still-throbbing head from side to side, on his pillows. 'I'm not sure I see...'

'Put it this way, Will. Your letter has brought you the torment of knowledge, but it also leaves you with the torment of ignorance; for it was written so long ago, and all the dear lives it embraces have moved on in their own blind way, and god alone knows how they stand now.'

Thomas moved to sit on the chest by Will's bed, rewrapping his towel about him.

'What I mean is… If you truly pin your hopes on reconciliation with Alice, then what on earth are you doing here? The longer you leave her the less chance will it have of fulfilment, for she is human, as you are, and cannot live on tenuous hopes for an indefinite time and a more uncertain future – even supposing she has the same or similar hopes. She has her needs, Will, and there are many close at hand who, at any moment, might well seek to fulfil them. Has it not occurred to you that even in the space of time between her penning this letter to your sister and you reading it, she could be married, or lost to you in any number of possible ways? My advice – and you can take it or leave it, of course – is either to return at the first available opportunity or try and forge a life here which is constructed on the moments as they come, the days as they come, not on some far-off dream. If you do not, then life here will become endless torment Will, mark my words. We need, perhaps more than anything else, the security of a recognisable rhythm to our daily lives, predicated in large measure on repetitions of what is most familiar to us; if your sights are fixed on goals over which you have no control, and their attendant anxieties, then you'll settle to nothing here, for it will all seem so irrelevant. There is no future, Will, only the present. Only the present. So… carpe diem!… Seize the moment!'

And on that note, Thomas retreated, climbed shivering into his bed, and snuffed out the candle.

After some little while Will's voice came out of the darkness. 'Thomas, I thank you for your words of advice, and make no mistake, I can see the wisdom of them. Yet, I cannot go back, not yet, just as you cannot, because we should be returning to the shaming circumstances of our own failures. Here, I have the opportunity of making something of myself, of regaining my self-respect, of redeeming myself, perhaps making a career and achieving some standing, even accumulating a little wealth. To return without these things would be pointless, can you not see that?'

'I see it, Will, but then you should think only of these immediate things and divorce them entirely from any notions of a future with Alice. You must... school yourself to accept that Alice is the past, just as Joanna is for me. We cannot live our lives haunted by their ghosts, for they would cripple us. Besides, in living for the moment, by throwing yourself entirely into your endeavour, whatever it may be, you may well wake up one day and feel yourself whole again. Believe me, that is the only way.'

Will was silent for some little time, digesting this, and wondering if the two cases were so similar: Alice, after all, was still living.

But when his voice stirred the silence, gently, it was in relation to another question. 'Thomas, one thing perplexes me, if you'll allow... You say you and Joanna brought only essential things when you left Ireland, didn't you, to create your new lives together, here in Queensland? With space at a premium, tell me, why ever did you bring your cassock, and all the other accoutrements of your rejected calling, of your own... imprisonment? Why was *that* Thomas?'

But the question was left hanging between them for Thomas was already asleep.

XXIII

Will knew it was late when he woke for there was the bustle of people about their business just outside and he quickly rose and dressed, feeling much refreshed by his long slumber.

Thomas, he saw, had already departed, and as he stepped out into the sun's glare, he almost stumbled into the priest's steaming cassock hanging from a line slung between the two saplings which stood on either side of the tent.

At the water troughs he encountered the O'Rourke brothers. They had been set to mending one of them, which had sprung a leak, the solder and irons having been provided from Mr Ridley's store. 'As it happens – James spoke for the two of them, John never yet having been heard to utter a single word – Mr Ridley was hoping to catch you when he was around earlier, but forbore to wake you, having been apprised of your misadventure. He did ask us to mention it if we should see you.'

Deciding to leave them to their labours Will thanked him and went to draw water from one of the other troughs. He knew, of course, what Ridley wanted of him; and he washed slowly, deep in thought, aware of his reluctance to face the man.

When he was ready, however, he set out to look for him. On his way down towards the far end of the encampment he encountered Dr Mallon, just then emerging from the long hut in the centre of the condemned row, which now housed the worst cases of the pestilence. He caught sight of Will, shrugged demonstratively, then changed direction and came towards him.

'Good morning, Mr Crosby.' He looked back towards the hut. 'Ah, 'tis a hopeless task, confronting an illness whose nature we don't really understand. If only we had the key... Anyhow, how is that head of yours this morning?'

'Well', said Will, 'from the moment I woke, till this moment, I haven't even given it a thought. So, I suppose it's better, much better.' He moved his hand to his forehead, as if seeking confirmation, then smiled at his own seeming foolishness.

Dr Mallon caught the sense of his gesture and smiled too, briefly. 'I trust you slept well...? Good! It was plainly not the concussion I feared it might be. However, you must let me know if the pain recurs... And now, I must be away: others, I fear, are awaiting my... So... good-day, Sergeant Crosby.' And tipping his hat he hurried off, threading his way through the maze of tents.

Will too strode off but then, recalling his mission, slackened his pace. Yet all too soon, he found himself at the little clearing where Ridley's quarters were.

Barney was stacking bricks from a pile that had come in on the *Aurora*, whistling cheerily as he did so. At the sound of Will's approach he turned and wiped his brow with the back of his hand.

'Ah, Will... You find me trying to create a bit of order out of the chaos left for us yesterday by Callaghan and Stevens and whatever help they had from the *Aurora*!' He straightened up and wiped his brow yet again. 'But it'll be Joe you're here to see, I think. He said you might... be dropping by. He's just away at the trench but he'll be back in a minute or two – unless he's fallen in...'

Will laughed as Barney went back to his task. Then he offered to lend a hand... just to pass the time while he was waiting.

When Ridley joined them, several minutes later, it did not escape Will's notice that something like a scowl flitted across the man's face.

'So, Mr Crosby,' he began (and the lapse into formality since their last exchange was not lost on Will), 'you have lost our rifle. You must see how that places us. We have only two and, you see, if one is lost it halves our already meagre chances of defending ourselves, should the need arise – which pray God it will not, but of that we can't be certain. However,' he went on, his voice steely, 'the circumstances in which you lost it give us even greater cause for concern – if the priest's account is to be believed – for it seems there is a distinct possibility the weapon may now be in the hands of the savages. So, I should be grateful if you would please explain yourself so that I can be sure of the facts.' The scowl had resurfaced, filling his face as well as the tenor and tone of his speech.

Rattled, as well as embarrassed, Will related what had taken place during the storm the day before, pointing out that it was certainly not a question of any lack of a sense of responsibility on his part, that he had, in point of fact, been unconscious when the gun disappeared, that...

Ridley nodded in acknowledgement, yet his face remained darkly impassive. 'Yes. I see. The rifle might have fallen out of the holster when the horse reared, especially if it had not been replaced firmly enough, earlier... Are you quite sure you searched for it thoroughly when you regained consciousness?'

The innuendos were hardly subtle, but Will, though objecting to being spoken to as if he were a naughty child, let them pass, sensing from the general tone of his discourse that Ridley was barely containing his simmering anger. Nothing positive, however, would be served by adopting a similar belligerent tone and provoking him further.

'I believed so at the time,' he answered truthfully, calmly, 'but given the state I was in and the continuing chaos brought by the still unabated storm, I own now it is very possible I did not. If you like, I'll go back right away and make a more thorough search.'

'Yes, I'd be much obliged to you if you would do just that,' Ridley all but snapped back. 'Good day!' And on this note, the man turned his back and walked purposefully over to where Barney was still labouring at his task.

'I'll give you a hand with that, Barney,' he called, a shade too loudly.

'So be it!' Will shouted back at him. Yet he delayed his own departure a moment or two, in the forlorn hope that the other might once again offer him the loan of the horse. When no such offer was forthcoming, Will turned on his heel and, now scowling in his turn, muttered his own reluctant valediction, which probably neither would have heard, and marched off.

However, he stopped almost immediately and turned back. 'Oh, Mr Ridley,' he called, 'Mr Ridley, there was something else.'

Ridley turned his head just enough to be able to see his interlocutor. 'Yes?' he said, the note of impatience clouding the word.

'Someone suggested I talk to you about a freshwater lake that is hereabouts. As you were probably made aware yesterday, I had gone off in the direction of Amity in the hope of solving the bathing problem... you'll doubtless recall... for the women.'

Will knew he had in no way redeemed himself, yet he wanted Ridley to know that his previous day's journey had been undertaken for the public good. That it had not been just some frivolous jaunt...

Ridley turned to face him, but his mien was as stern as ever.

'Yes. If you go further down, roughly opposite the landing stage where the ship is tied up, you'll see the beginnings of a narrow path heading eastwards. If you follow that you'll come to the lake; it can't be much more than a mile.' He shrugged and made as if to turn away, yet again, then added: 'The path is quite overgrown in parts, so... it might need a bit of clearing, but, in my estimation, it could serve your purpose right enough.' And he turned back to assisting Barney, this time withholding any form of valediction.

Will nodded curtly and went on his way.

It occurred to him he ought to let someone know what he was intending, and to that end he went in search of Thomas, finding him eventually in earnest discourse with Wilfred Farmer outside the hospital tent.

'Excuse the interruption, Mr Farmer,' he said, drawing level with them, 'but... Father Sheehan, I just wanted to let you know I'm going back to the scene of my yesterday's tumble.' He grimaced. 'Mr Ridley is much aggrieved at the loss of the rifle and insists I go back at once to make a more careful search for it. He is afraid it may have got into the wrong hands and could well be used against us... If I'm not back in a couple of hours I should be very grateful if you could send out a search party... No, I'm not really joking,' he added, seeing Thomas raising a quizzical eyebrow. 'I had the distinct impression from Mr Ridley that the natives, if encountered, are likely to be... well, anything but friendly. So, I should be very much obliged to you.'

Thomas nodded. 'Yes, of course, though let us hope this... caution, proves unnecessary. Maybe you ought not to go alone, and surely not unarmed.'

Will shrugged. 'Well, yes, but... in the circumstances... Mr Ridley made no offer of either gun or horse, and as far as I am aware, we have no other weapons in the camp.'

'Hm. I think Captain Kemp may well be able to provide you with something, at least a pistol, possibly even an escort. His men hardly seem overburdened with their duties from what I have seen. How far is it, anyway?'

'Oh, not much more than a half hour's brisk walk, I should say.' Will began to move away. 'Look, thanks for your advice, but I'll chance it. Thinking about what happened to me yesterday... perhaps the dangers are rather less than Mr Ridley would have us believe.' And with that he raised his hand in salutation, then bethought himself, 'Oh, and my apologies once again, Mr Farmer.'

Farmer shook his head. 'No call for it, Mr Crosby. Indeed, I was... if you want company, I'll gladly go with ye. It'll be... a relief to get away from this place, even if for only a short while.' And he made as if to catch Will up.

Remembering his previous encounters with the man, Will cast about in his mind for some way of politely rejecting the offer. But, before he could think of anything, Thomas was applauding Farmer's 'kindness' and commending him wholeheartedly to Will, who inwardly cursed him for it, for it left him with no choice but to acquiesce.

'I am much obliged to you, Mr Farmer, though I'm sure you have more pressing things to attend to... Really, I don't mind going alone...'

'...Hell no. To tell ye the honest truth of it, Ned, I'm tired o'... you know what I mean. Back in the nick there were nothing else for it... but now we're out... or as good as... there must be something better to be had...' Stevens was clearly in earnest.

'Aye... well... if your needs are... special, like... that's not so easy. There's that young matron, she might...'

'Can't see it, meself... Comely enough, I'll warrant you that, but out o' my class, I shouldn't wonder. Besides, she's probably getting all she needs from the doctors... and that Crosby... and the priest, I shouldn't wonder...' and his face cracked into a prolonged snigger. 'Anyways, a bit... too old for my tastes...'

'Too old?' says Callaghan, 'But she can't be above twenty-one or two...'

Stevens grimaced. 'You're not the only one with... special needs, Ned, not by a long shot!'

Callaghan looked perplexed. 'What... what special needs would that be, John-o?'

Stevens wagged his finger, smirking. 'Now that would be telling, Ned... but I'll be on the look-out, that I will...'

Callaghan folded away his clasp knife and put it in his pocket, then looked down at the strewn shavings from the stick he had been whittling. He looked at the stick – what little was left of it – then threw it away into the bushes behind them.

'So, what was all that in aid of...? I thought you were...'

'In aid of...? Passing the time, that's all... Getting through...'

Stevens grunted, none too sure he had understood the answer to his question. 'Well... there are better ways of passing the time... as I was saying... Anyways, just leave it to your uncle John-o. I'll be fixing you up afore not too long, mark my words, Ned.' And he winked, then gestured obscenely.

Callaghan looked away.

Stevens stood up from the sawn log where he had perched when they arrived there, maybe half an hour earlier. 'Best be getting on with this fucking grave, Ned, otherwise that high and mighty bloody priest'll be shooting his mouth off.'

Callaghan also rose to his feet and Stevens thrust a spade into his hands. 'There y'are Ned, pass the time with that…,' and he guffawed loudly, seemingly proud of his wit, and he kept on laughing and his unshaven chin glistened with saliva.

Callaghan plunged the spade into the soft, sandy earth.

XXIV

Will's last-ditch attempt to free himself from the unwanted attachment had failed, so he deliberately forced a brisk pace as the two of them set out side by side. Neither spoke for several minutes but then, as they left the camp behind, Farmer broke the silence.

'Mr Crosby, I owe you an apology – for my conduct, the day my poor wife died...'

Will cut short what he believed to be a wheedling attempt at ingratiation. 'No, no. You were overwrought. Anyone in your circumstances would have reacted in much the same way, I do not doubt; I, and indeed Father Sheehan, understood that. It was just that, in our desperation to do *something* to alleviate our grievous plight here, we felt we could brook no objection. Especially from the first person we approached on this decided course of action... who, as chance would have it, happened to be...'

'Aye,' the other agreed, lowering his eyes, 'that encounter was unfortunate... in all respects. Might I not... explain myself? So you'll understand... better?'

'Mr Farmer...' Will felt himself running short of patience. Nevertheless, he stopped and turned towards him. 'Really, there is no need...'

Farmer put a hand on his arm, and then promptly withdrew it, letting it fall limply to his side.

They walked on in silence for a while, Will's mood gradually lightening as he caught the scent of the sea and the forest wafting in on the gentle breeze, coming from their left. It was warm, too, and he unfastened the kerchief about his neck and pushed it into his pocket.

Just as they were about to enter the trees, Farmer came to a halt. 'My wife is… no more, Mr Crosby… No…' he corrected, as Will began to speak, 'it's not just that she is no more; it's that there is none here who knows why she died… What it was, I mean, that brought us so low, and so far away from all we had ever known and cared for.'

Sensing the deep desperation in the man, and suddenly mindful of his own, recent, similar unburdening and the relief it had brought, Will nodded, gently. 'Then tell me.' And he waited, in a more charitable frame of mind than he had been at their outset.

'Our story is far from uncommon in England now,' Farmer began.

'…Only in degree, and in one particular detail, does it differ from that of many others, others even in our sad encampment, I have lately discovered.' He shook his head as if in disbelief at his own words.

After a pause, the two men continued along the uneven track, Will now matching his step to Farmer's more measured pace.

'Back home, Mr Crosby, I was tenant to a big landowner in Leicestershire, a man who, in the scheme of things, appeared as reasonable and fair as could be expected. Our small, mixed farm prospered, by dint of our labours, so much so that I was able, after a while, to take on seasonal labour and then, eventually, to employ a man full time to tend our steadily expanding herd of cattle. My wife and I – and his voice wavered, noticeably – had already discussed the possibility of leasing yet more land and I had casually broached the subject with our landlord when he came one day, with his elder son and his bailiff, to supervise the division of our crop of wheat. That would be three summers ago. Well, he said neither yea nor nay, in the moment, but that he would give the matter his consideration.'

Farmer stopped again, distracted, it seemed, by some private recollection. He looked about him, his eyes fixed on the path ahead, arrested, Will surmised, by the unaccustomed silence – possibly the first time he had encountered it since leaving England. He appeared to be particularly taken by the immensity of the trees all about them. And still without speaking, he pointed to the shimmering sea, glimpsed through the undergrowth, away to their left. Then, bethinking himself, he shook his head, and smiled sheepishly.

'Well, it was on that same occasion that Sir Richard's elder son first set eyes on our only child, Margaret – Meg, as we called her – a fine, happy, yet modest lass, just gone sixteen, and well contented with her life and lot. But then Edward, the son, apparently took to visiting her, especially when she was working away in the fields – though quite unbeknownst to us. He was a fine-looking young man, no doubt about it, and this doubtless turned the girl's head.'

'But did you not question...?' Will began.

'We did, yes... That is, yes... and no. We were... not unaware of his interest in her but had no idea just how far matters had run in such a short time. Yet what little we did know bothered us, for we plainly saw it was very unlikely that a man who had been educated at Eton and at Oxford and who stood to inherit enormous wealth would have any serious interest in our daughter, and we did not wish to see her hurt. So yes, his *intentions* worried us very greatly...'

'And did you caution the girl?'

'Oh yes. We warned Meg not to encourage any advances he might make, but she insisted that we were worrying unnecessarily, that he was always most civil and courteous in his behaviour towards her.'

Will nodded grimly, already guessing the likely outcome of Farmer's story.

'But then,' Farmer continued, 'almost overnight, she became morose, silent, and took herself off to her room immediately supper was over. After a few days or so of this state of affairs my wife tried to talk to her. But this only brought on floods of tears, yet no explanation; indeed, it seemed to drive her completely within herself. So worried were we that I spoke with Sir Richard about the matter, the following morning, politely asking him to forbid his son any further contact with her.'

'And what did he say to that?'

'Oh, he readily agreed – said it was "quite unseemly", and he even apologised... profusely... for the young man's "thoughtless conduct." But... What was that?'

Farmer stood looking and listening; then he wandered off a few paces, looking all about him. After a moment or two away, he came back, smiling, apologetic. 'Forgive me, Mr Crosby, but this... all this... it's a new world. Back there, among the tents... so many people... and the feeling of ever-present, lurking danger. All it takes is to walk out of it and... I'm sorry, please...'

'Mr Farmer, you are right... and right to wonder at it. I have been twice away from the encampment, alone, and, well, I know exactly what you mean...'

At Farmer's prompting they resumed their walk, though at a slower pace. And his face was still lit by a smile – the first time he had lost his scowl, in Will's presence. 'But... what was I saying?' And immediately the man's gravity returned.

'Yes, Meg... Well, one morning, late in autumn, Joseph, our hired help, came banging at our door just as I was making up the kitchen fire and Hester, my wife, was preparing breakfast. He was white as a sheet and shaking violently. My first thought was that he had the ague and I asked him to step inside, but he shook his head wildly and took hold of my arm, pulling me out of the house and across the yard towards the byre. "Good God, lad, what ails thee?" I demanded, but he was beside himself. His eyes were wide with terror, and he was quite unable to speak. When we reached the barn, he thrust open the door and... pushed me inside.'

Will waited, his heart pounding, dreading what he knew he was about to hear.

Farmer closed his eyes. He was plainly fighting back the emotions welling up, yet again, at his recounting of the circumstances. And Will watched and pitied the struggle going on inside the man.

'At first, all was dark, for I had come in from the bright light outside, but as my eyes gradually adjusted, I saw what I took to be a sack hanging from one of the cross beams.... A sack, yes...'

And clearly, the vision was there, and all too present, before him, as terrifying now as it had been then.

'I turned towards Joseph and I demanded he explain himself at once. But the lad... No words came from him. Instead, he pointed frantically, and he dragged me towards the sack, and as we drew near it was... oh, god, it all became clear.

Farmer was gasping, choking almost, and Will's eyes closed upon this tragedy, so vividly painted.

'I broke free, Mr Crosby. And I rushed towards her, and I... But she was cold, quite cold, and there was nothing, nothing... we could do for her. The two of us, we... cut her down, let her down gently, so as not to...'

Farmer broke down completely, leaning his head against the trunk of a tree, and Will, deeply shocked by the horrific turn the man's story had taken, was at a loss what to say. He realised that for such grief there could be no easy comfort and he stood helplessly by until Farmer had once again managed a measure of control.

As they continued along the narrow track, with the ferns and towering eucalyptus pressing in, and down, upon them, Farmer touched Will's arm, his voice barely a whisper. 'So... when the doctor eventually came to examine her poor body, he told us that she had been with child. And, Mr Crosby, it would have been her sure knowledge of that fact that had driven my poor girl to her last, desperate act.'

Of course it would, Will acknowledged to himself, fully aware of how heavily the fear of her community's censure would weigh upon one so young and inexperienced. Had not Alice suffered something of those same fears before he had finally asked her to marry him? And he too... during almost all of their time together, after he had allayed those fears in her? But for Farmer and his wife the tragedy had suddenly been redoubled.

'Well... in that moment of blinding revelation, Mr Crosby, all my grief turned to rage, and I rushed off at once to Sir Richard's house. I pushed past the footman who had opened the door, and I stormed into the morning room, where the family were assembled. Without stopping to explain or excuse myself I threw myself upon the young man, seizing him by the throat, and had him half dead before Sir Richard and the servants he had called in his panic could haul me off him. They dragged me outside and held me fast until the constables arrived. I was then manacled and led off to the cells in Harborough, to be detained there until the local magistrates would hear my case.'

Farmer's chest was heaving, and only gradually did he overcome the emotions fuelled by the memory of these painful events.

'Having derived some little gratification from the injuries I had dealt the young man, my rage soon transformed itself back into grief, all the greater now because I knew I should be at home, comforting my wife, helping her to bear our terrible loss. And instead, I was...'

'What did you do then?' Will's mind flashed back to an occasion, by no means dissimilar, in his own woeful history.

'I asked to speak with the superintendent, Mr Crosby. And when he finally deigned to see me, some hours later, he listened with growing sympathy to my plight and said he would acquaint Sir Richard with the circumstances. For without his agreement I could not be released, even temporarily, and in his opinion such agreement was unlikely since I might well be thought a continuing threat to the young gentleman I had already assaulted.'

Farmer shook his head.

'In the event, Sir Richard himself came to see me. He had in the meantime learned of our tragedy, and he expressed his condolences, sincerely enough, I believed. But in no way would he admit either the justice of my actions or the guilt of his son. Indeed, he affirmed his intention of prosecuting me for grievous bodily harm, and at the same time gave us notice to quit the farm – "with great reluctance," he said. He later grandly consented for me to attend our daughter's funeral, though only on condition I remained in chains and was guarded the whole of the time. This latter action of his, when I was finally brought to trial, was interpreted as a mark of the man's humanity and great civility, of course, and was contrasted with my own "barbaric act". Farmer's voice was loaded with sarcasm.

'Yes, I recognise the signs...'

If Farmer was perplexed by Will's comment, he gave no sign of it.

'It was deemed that I had no case against Sir Richard's son, a gentleman of "exemplary character," and that the culprit in my daughter's fatal pregnancy should be sought elsewhere.' His face twisted in hatred in this further moment of painful recollection. 'Indeed, without being quite named, the finger of suspicion was pointed at poor young Joseph who, in addition to losing his livelihood, lost his good name as well.'

He exhaled, noisily, his disgust almost palpable. 'My "brutal attack" was judged to be entirely unprovoked... naturally!'

'Naturally!' Will entered easily into the man's outrage at the sham of English justice. 'And so you were duly sentenced...?'

'Yes. And though it was grudgingly admitted that I had become "deranged by grief" and was given a lighter sentence – it was still one year's hard labour, to be served at the Lincoln County Gaol!' Again he shook his head, his face drawn, white with anger. 'Twisting the knife just a little further, Sir Richard stood up in open court after sentence had been pronounced upon me and "generously" gave my wife a month, instead of the normal week, to make alternative arrangements before our eviction came into effect.'

Just then, however, they arrived at a point where the spring, which had detained Will so mysteriously on his previous visits, came into view, though still some distance off.

'Is that... water? Farmer asked, shielding his eyes.

'You'll see. Just a little further.'

Will could not but sympathise with the man. The process he described had brought back aching memories of his own rough handling by the forces of law and order. 'I too have experienced these shows of so-called magnanimity, which nevertheless ended in a sentence that gave them the lie.'

'But I thought...' Farmer looked at him, in bewilderment. 'I thought you belonged on the other side of the court room...'

'Hm! Well... perhaps you jumped to the wrong conclusion, Mr Farmer – several times, in fact.' Will's tone was sharper than he had intended. 'But no matter, just now,' he added, in a consciously, more gentle tone. 'Please... go on, if indeed there is more to tell...'

'Oh yes, Mr Crosby, there most certainly is. You see...'

Will became aware of the man's sudden, though barely perceptible, smile.

'...Prior to these events I'd never had any dealings with the law. I was widely respected, even beyond the confines of our small, village community, and I'd always believed every man was equal before the law; that all were presumed innocent until proven otherwise. What a booby I was!'

Will smiled bitterly, his own experience ghosting through the man's words. 'I expect you found an unspoken assumption that it was unthinkable the son of a land-owning, titled gentleman could be guilty of any such crime?'

'Aye, that was it, right enough! The status of "gentleman" towered like a fortress between Sir Richard's son and the crime, and, you know, there were really two matters of which I stood accused, not one: the crime of assault and the crime of daring even to suggest that Edward, Sir Richard's son, could be guilty of any sort of un-gentlemanly conduct!'

'Oh yes... yes... so you had to prove both your innocence and his unworthiness of the class he belonged to. Sounds like a lost cause from the start...'

'It was. And, of course, what really wrapped everything up so neatly for them was that Sir Richard was chairman of the magistrates' bench for the whole county!'

Will snorted his disgust. 'Oh yes, they have it all nicely sewn up between them, that they do!'

Farmer clearly appreciated Will's approval. 'And there was nothing I could prove. The only witness to whatever had transpired had... departed this life... I hope and pray, for a better. But Sergeant Crosby – a fiery glint entered his eye – the injustices, you know, they... didn't end there. Not by a long shot! In prison, indignity was heaped on indignity as a matter of course, cruelty heaped on cruelty. The warders were hard, sadistic men... men of our own class, mind... but they gloried in the power they had over us poor, defenceless inmates...'

Will smiled in recognition of this fact also.

… Always seeking to rub your face in the dirt, whoever you were, whatever you were there for… Oh yes, Will had seen this harsh regime for himself, and he said so.

'I tell you, Sergeant Cr… May I call you Will…? These… titles, they seem so meaningless, with all this… pestilence about, it sort of…'

His words tailed off as his forming thought lost. But Will fancied he had understood well enough.

'That's fine by me… Wilfred. Or is it Wilf?'

'To my friends I was ever Wilf. But I tell you truly, in the time I was there five of my fellow prisoners died, some – indeed all, according to the Authorities – by their own hand, as if… as if that mortal sin somehow confirmed their… natural criminality. But some of them, maybe all, were beaten or tortured to death by their keepers.'

After due pause, Will quickened his pace. Time was passing, and now that he had the essentials of the man's story, he wanted to get on with their search, even if for a gun they were unlikely to find.

Farmer kept pace, nothing deterred.

'If one of the warders took a dislike to you, life could become unbearable. They were every bit as criminal in their inclinations as the men they were set over. In that respect, though, I fared none too badly. You see, I realised early on that any sort of defiance would lead to more misery. So I did everything according to the regulations, while despising them, nonetheless. Mind you, not even absolute conformity guaranteed a trouble-free existence. The sadism was often random, and it didn't matter who the victim was.'

'Aye, I know; I've witnessed such goings-on, though I suppose I was fortunate… As a prison, Carlisle must have been almost civilised, in comparison.'

Farmer stopped dead, as shocked by the casual revelation as Will had expected him to be, and clearly had difficulty marshalling his next words. 'I've… I've never been afraid of hard work, being used to toiling long hours on the farm. But, honest to God, it was the intent of some of those warders to work us to death. At the end of each day you were often too exhausted to eat even, and you… you welcomed the oblivion sleep brought you for a few hours. Sometimes, though, I couldn't sleep. I'd lie endless hours, trying to fathom the past, to get a grasp on our tragedy, or worrying, you know, about how Hester was managing to make ends meet, being thrown on the charity of her sister and her husband.'

'It must have been hard, thinking about... everything... and what you were going through. Were they kind to her?'

'Oh, yes, they couldn't have been kinder,' Farmer answered, walking on. 'Yet she was ever aware of the burden on them. They were not nearly as well-off as we had been. George was just a farm labourer, you see, even if his master did refer to him as "my stockman"! But – his face hardened – those injustices fired a simmering hatred in me, and I took to calculating the future... for when I was released.'

'Aye, you do, I remember; it was all a part of the Hell of prison. I'd devise a plan, become convinced it would work... and then, of course, remember where I was... In gaol! In a place where you can decide and plan all you liked but could take control of nothing. The frustration of that realisation used to drive me mad...'

'But... what were you in for...?'

'Oh, that's a long story...'

Farmer sought no further explanation. 'In my case – and I decided this early on – I was not going to stay long in a country that was at war with most of its citizens. I had to get away from that so-called, "commonweal" that had destroyed our lives. I thought of America... or Canada, where my practical knowledge of running a farm, of rearing livestock, of growing wheat, barley and oats should mean I would never want for an occupation. America or Canada. It little mattered which. But then a ... an interesting piece of intelligence came my way – through my wife, as it happened.'

'Yes?' Will's attention had been flagging, but now he frowned and cocked his head to one side. Where was all this leading?

'Aye... In one of her letters, shortly before my release, Hester told me she'd learned from one of the maids at the big house that whatever his stance had been throughout my trial, Sir Richard's true attitude towards his son, once it was all over and done with, was very different. In fact, he *clearly* held him responsible for the whole tragic business!'

'Really...! His son?' Will whistled.

'Yes. It appears that he disinherited him – insisting that he go to one of the colonies and apply himself either to a profession or to planting...'

'Go for good, you mean?'

'Well, no. But he was not to return until he had saved sufficient capital to establish himself in his chosen occupation back in England. Oh, it seems the young man pleaded with his father, as did his mother – incredulous, she was! She and his two sisters! But to no avail: Sir Richard was adamant. So, with great reluctance and heavy heart, as the storybooks put it, our young, murdering philanderer set sail for... the Australian colonies, yes! Within six weeks of me beginning my sentence, apparently. I believe he is articled to a firm of lawyers – what else! Yonder, over the water, in Brisbane...'

They reached the spring, in that moment, and Will, taking off his hat, bent down and swilled its cool waters over his face and his brow. Then bending once more, he cupped his hands and drank.

XXV

If, several minutes before, Will had been moved by the depth of the man's grief and by the tale of the law's all-too-familiar distortions and lack of compassion, he now had the awful suspicion that Farmer had wanted him to know these things merely as a justification for whatever harm he intended his as yet unwitting victim. Was that it? And while part of Will understood well enough the powerful passions that would have been smouldering in the man to finally drive him across the world to exact his own justice, the other part baulked at the idea of a killing in cold blood – if that was what Farmer intended.

'So… when you finally get to Brisbane. What then?' he asked, trying to maintain a neutral tone, still hoping he was mistaken in his surmise.

Farmer seemed to consider carefully before offering a reply. Then, very quietly, it came in an icy whisper. 'An eye for an eye, Mr Crosby.'

Will's whole being revolted. 'And is that the only way?' he asked, hoarsely.

'It is my duty, yes… now that Providence has seen fit to take from me the only person who might have stayed my hand – and seeing that now I'm responsible for no one but myself. Nothing else matters. My soul is choked and will be until it is done. And when it is done, well, who knows, maybe I shall still find no peace, but at least I'll have the satisfaction of knowing that my murdered daughter and wife are avenged.' He was talking rapidly now, almost devouring his own words. 'I'm tempted to believe that God has delivered him into my hands for this sole purpose, Will. There is no father here to protect him from justice; and he's very far away from the fortress of class that meant the law couldn't touch him. Here, it'll be just him and me.' A contemptuous smile passed over his face. 'But now I hold all the trumps.'

Will shook his head. 'If you do execute him, as you say you intend, you will be a fugitive for the rest of your life.'

Farmer looked at him squarely. 'I'm a fugitive now, Mr Crosby.'

Will pondered this for a moment or two. 'Tell me, Mr Farmer... Wilfred, have you ever had the experience of killing a man... killing a man in cold blood, I mean? Because, if you have not, let me tell you, it is... far from easy. And the closer you come to him, the more you are aware that he too is a human being, no matter what he has done or what he represents for you; the enormity of his crime is quite dwarfed by the enormity of summarily ending a life. You will find your whole being revolts against it. Mark my words.'

But Farmer's eyes had glazed over. 'I am the instrument of true justice,' he intoned. 'I cannot see how I can avoid my duty: my duty to truth, to my poor daughter, to my long-suffering wife, even to poor, harmless, young Joseph...'

Will was forcefully reminded of the dead judge's attitude to his victims, and he felt that same total rejection, the same revulsion.

'And what will killing this man change?' Will caught hold of the man's wrist. 'Your daughter will still be dead; injustice will still continue to be meted out in the name of justice; the poor will remain the exploited, and the rich the exploiters. I very much suspect that the sweetness of such revenge fades in the moment of its fulfilment.'

'So – Farmer's voice, still quiet, nevertheless had an almost hysterical edge to it – you would have him go scot-free, would you? To laugh up his sleeve, smug at having flouted the law, and to do so again and again, if he is so minded? No, Will, I'm sorry, there has to be... a just retribution.'

A Whistling Kite hovered briefly above them, drawing Will's gaze. 'How can you be sure – he asked, having weighted his words carefully – that the attitudes you attribute to him are real, and not just the invention of your own torment? It would, of course, be convenient for your hatred if he *were* an out-and-out scoundrel, but can you be sure? How do you know *for sure* that in the time you were being made to suffer so cruelly he too was not also suffering? I mean… suffering the torments of guilt, perhaps even of personal loss, of love, even, and is maybe doing so still? Obviously,' he added, feeling Farmer stiffen, 'I do not know this man from Adam, but I hope you will at least investigate him thoroughly before you… pull the trigger or whatever it is you have in store for him.'

The man made no response, sullen at the rebuff he had received.

Will, however, had not expected words so contrary to the man's bitter feelings to bear any fruit, and he let the silence grow between them.

But after a moment or two he stopped and pointed. 'This is the place.'

Farmer seemed relieved at the distraction. 'Right then,' he said, rubbing his hands together, 'how shall we do it?'

Walking along slowly, now, Will scanned the ground for signs of the horse's hooves. Yet apart from the odd mark in the sparse, sandy grass on either side of the path, the deluge appeared to have washed all away. He said as much to his companion. 'I suggest we search a fair stretch of the scrub, one on each side of the path, then change over and work through it again. Does that sound sensible?'

Farmer nodded and moved over to the further side.

Glancing in his direction, a few moments later, Will saw him pick up a slender branch and use it to poke about under bushes and in the thicker clumps of undergrowth, presumably afraid of snakes and whatever else might be lurking there. He smiled to himself at the obvious nervousness, wondering whether the same caution would overtake Farmer when he finally confronted the man whom he accounted responsible for his daughter's death.

Their separation in this task further served to calm the antagonism Will felt had grown between them.

Eventually, when each had covered one side of the path they

crossed over, as agreed, but still they found nothing. After half an hour or so Will declared, testily: 'Well, we're clearly wasting our time out here! Shall we be getting back?'

He looked up and saw that Farmer had spotted the clearing and the coloured poles.

'Look, Will!' he called, in some excitement, 'Over there! What do you reckon those are?'

'What they are or what purpose they serve I do not know,' Will said, quietly, 'but... well... I suspect they have some religious significance. They are doubtless the work of the native people for I have never seen anything like them in Europe or, for that matter, when I was in India.' He turned and began to head back to the main path but after a few paces, stopped, sensing that his companion had failed to come along with him.

Farmer was halfway to the coloured poles, still flailing his stick from side to side as he went. Will watched him cross the clearing, curious now to see the outcome of the man's impetuousness, spurred on, quite possibly, by a still smouldering anger.

He saw him stop abruptly, hesitate a moment or two, then slowly draw back.

And Will smiled to himself, reassured that his own reaction in those same circumstances had not been the result of some sudden access of... what? Superstitious fear? He was pleased now he had not restrained or forewarned his companion; yes, he would be interested to hear the man's explanation of what he too had apparently felt so strongly that it had stopped him dead in his tracks.

'Well?' he said, as Farmer reached him, 'What did you see? Was it what you expected?'

Farmer seemed confused and mumbled something Will did not quite catch. Then, when he had regained some composure, he began fumbling for words: 'I don't know... I didn't see... there was, well.... there was something... I don't know. I felt fear, of that I'm certain... but I saw nothing.'

'I had the same sensation, yesterday,' Will said. Quietly, almost casually.

And the two men stood contemplating each other, the empty clearing, and the poles.

At length, Will broke the silence. 'No point in staying any longer.' And he set off purposefully, back down the track towards the encampment.

XXVI

The desultory conversation during their walk back was dominated by wild speculation – on Farmer's part – centring on the possibility of there being Blackfellows on the island, right now. In quick succession, he mentioned cannibalism, black magic, sexual depravity, and without seemingly pausing to breathe added, as if it were proof of all that had gone before: 'That clearing looks too recent, too maintained, for it to be otherwise, wouldn't you say?'

'I had the same thought yesterday,' Will responded, though quite what "otherwise" Farmer had in mind escaped him. 'An island is maybe a good place for them... particularly if they happen to eat fish!'

Farmer chuckled, though looking about him uneasily, Will noted.

Heading further into the shallows, Will added: 'I've heard it said that there are other creatures here too, such as the strange kangaroos, so they would not want for food – You, Wilfred, would probably be a last resort! Bit too stringy – if you don't mind me saying so.'

This time, Farmer urged on a half laugh, though still none too certain of his footing.

'And, from what little I know of them it seems they never stay in one place for long; they don't plant things, it seems...'

'Yes. They sound very primitive and very ignorant,' Farmer added, feeling once more to be on firmer ground.

Reaching the camp, Will wondered whether their common experience of the uncanny had been enough to heal the breach between them, as there was still much about the man that irked him.

Their arrival back at the encampment coincided with yet another crisis. There had been two more deaths in the short time they had been away, and preparations were being made for burial that same evening.

Will found Ballow and Mallon, both clearly cast down by their inability to contain the epidemic, and further preoccupied by the open rebelliousness of some of the families; several of whom were refusing to co-operate any further with regulations and orders which, they had argued, merely heaped inconvenience on the hopeless, ineffectual struggle against the disease.

Captain Kemp had been summoned, and Will saw him arrive in the centre of the camp, accompanied by a couple of his crewmen, both of them conspicuously armed with rifles.

A heated argument ensued about the whole idea of quarantine which, one of the passengers asserted, was nothing less than a death sentence imposed on all of them. Wearily, Dr Ballow intervened, trying to explain, as simply and reasonably as he could, why it was necessary, but his explanation was angrily shouted down. His face black as thunder, he was left threatening the previously agreed sanctions if regulations were flouted; whereupon several of the most vociferous among the menfolk stormed off together, in a wholly uncompromising mood.

The captain, his two men and the two doctors fell into intense, earnest discussion, presumably about how best to counter this insubordination. And Will hoped they would then tackle the question of how to regain the confidence and respect of the sorely tried passengers.

Farmer muttered something that sounded like thanks, but Will's attention was fixed on the parleying group at the centre of the camp. Farmer said something else, then sloped off in the direction of his tent. Will lifted a hand in salutation but did not turn round.

After a while, as the group seemed unlikely to dissolve for some time yet, Will decided he had best go and face his own impending crisis, so he set off down through the compound to seek out Ridley.

Finding him at once he reported his lack of success and, much to his surprise, met with no rebuke.

'Well, it was worth the try, I think,' the man said quietly, 'But we shall need to be vigilant, for there can be no other explanation than that the rifle is now in the hands of the enemy. Let us hope they have no more cartridges than the two that were in the breach when you lost it.'

Will turned away, pondering this fear and its still-resentful expression, for a few moments, then, his curiosity aroused, he asked pointedly: 'But if they are as primitive as they are said to be, is it likely they would know how to make use of such a weapon, Joe?'

Ridley laughed, a touch scathingly. 'Oh, they know right enough. There have been instances, in these parts, of our people being slaughtered by them, gunned down with their own weapons, at that. They are very much an unknown quantity, Will. Temperamental. Sometimes, they appear friendly enough, but then can cut up rough for no apparent reason. Always to do with the land – nobody can make out what all the fuss is about... as they never seem to do anything with it, except walk over it or dig out fat, grey grubs they eat alive – and raw, at that, would you believe it!' He shuddered theatrically and grimaced. 'Anyhow, I don't suppose they're likely to bother us here; certainly, I've never seen any on this side of the island.'

These snippets gleaned from Ridley's dismissal of the Aboriginals only served to fuel Will's curiosity the more. 'But... you've had direct dealings with them elsewhere, then?' he probed, tentatively – Ridley's 'this side of the island' seeming to imply such encounters.

'No. No. None whatsoever! In fact, I've never yet set eyes on one of the murdering bastards...'

'How then do you know so much about them?'

'Common knowledge... Things you pick up in the bars from people who've survived brushes with 'em. I've heard tales of cannibalism too...'

Will recalled Farmer's speculations on that self-same theme. 'Has anyone you know of ever spent any time among them, parleying with them, finding out what they're really like?' He forbore to add 'or been eaten by them.'

'I expect some fools have,' Ridley retorted, 'missionaries and such like, but nothing good seems to have come of it. You can't pin 'em down to anything. Parleying's out anyway because they jabber away like monkeys and you can't tell what the hell they're on about. Utterly ignorant! One man I know, who had a narrow escape from them a while back up on Tambourine, says you should treat them like rats. Shoot 'em on sight!'

Will realised he was out of his depth, wading through ignorance, his own, certainly, and Ridley's too, he surmised, cocksure though he seemed to be about the Aborigines' attitudes and habits. And yet, just as the thought of Farmer cutting down the unsuspecting young man he believed responsible for his daughter's suicide, had appalled him, so too did Ridley's general brutalisation and glibly proposed extermination, grounded as they were in little more than hearsay and speculation. 'Have we not, well... stolen their land from them?' he ventured, conscious even as he spoke that he was laying himself open to further ridicule.

Ridley laughed out loud, insultingly. 'What! Clearly – and no offence meant – you've only just got here... But tell me, have you any idea... any idea at all just how vast this land is? Most of the interior remains totally unexplored. We have no notion of what we'll eventually find there. But the bit we do know is already bigger than the United Kingdom and France and much else all rolled together. And it's all empty – and this is the point I'm making – utterly untouched; it's never seen a ploughshare or a fence. In fact, it's probably the nearest you'll ever come to knowing what the Land of Canaan was like. But, dotted about it, here and there, we come across these bogeymen from the Stone Age, barely managing to keep alive on bits of berries and bark and worms and the like; and yet, for God knows how long, they've had all this richness – and when you eventually see it, you'll have to agree – but they've done bugger all with it! Well, now they've missed their chance, for good and all! But – he jerked his head back – enough of this; because the die was cast long before you or I got here, and they'll just have to like it or lump it.'

And for Ridley, Will realised, the matter was closed.

'But listen,' said Ridley, his tone suddenly calmer: 'I was going to suggest we take a look at Brown Lake and see whether it will do as a watering hole for these fussy women of yours. From what I gather, Ballow seems anxious to get something sorted out as soon as possible. Have you the time? As I said, it's not far.'

'Now would be fine,' Will agreed. 'In fact, the sooner the better, for there was some sort of argument flaring as I came through the camp, just now... We've got to maintain discipline, at all costs, and my own feeling is that the more purposeful activities we can create, the better. People are restless, broody, sitting about the camp with nothing much to do... terrorised seeing their neighbours dying around them. What they need is... some sort of diversion, involvement in something that at least looks as though it will alleviate the general situation. In my view, whether frequent washing of bodies and clothes has any effect or not in containing the disease, hardly matters – though it would be wonderful if it did – the important thing is a change of scene, and the sense that you are doing something that might just alter things for the better. So, yes... by all means...'

He looked at Ridley and felt he might just have redeemed himself in the man's eyes.

XXVII

It seemed like a destiny. On and on it went, with no end in sight, this continuous procession into darkness.

Thomas watched Dr Mitchell's white, haggard face, recalling the macabre Triumph of Death that had marched relentlessly across the seminary walls in his innocent youth. And he imagined the doctor... soon now... joining that throng, heading into the endless dark. And his whole being revolted against it. The man was too young, still had so much living to do.

But then, what had he himself experienced of the world? And he was almost twenty years older than the poor doctor! An orphan, he had grown up among nuns and priests in the *hortus conclusus*, the cloistered garden the Church in Ireland maintained for its own – a 'refuge', which seemed a web of intrigue, woven with the warp of ignorance and the weft of privilege, looking back on it, once he had got out beyond its walls. The appalling conditions and waste of his parishioners' lives, magnified to monstrous proportions during the years of the Hunger, had set him adrift from all but that sense of duty the Church had instilled in him, and even this he came to see as a part of the fraudulent manipulation of a life that had never been his own. 'We can choose Good or we can choose Evil', the Holy Brothers had preached (with the Bible in one hand and the flail in the other). But in truth there was no choice at all.

The world was bigger, more complex, more compelling, and yet as a young priest in his first country parish, for all his religious knowledge, his Latin and his Greek, he was as ignorant as his peasant flock. Worse still, the Church had moulded him to aid and abet the gross injustices their landlords daily heaped upon them – by teaching them fortitude in adversity, peaceable acceptance of their lot, the promise of eternal rewards to come in Heaven. Yet his eventual hatred of the Church had not been his only loss. How could a God of Love countenance such suffering and injustice, the continuous slaughter of the innocents?

And for several years he had lived in bitterness, anger, and confusion.

Joanna had saved him. Joanna had re-made him, and by her gentle example shown him not only how to look upon the world but to take appropriate action to try and set it to rights. He had lost Love but found, in love, a driving power that might yet move mountains.

In these few stagnant days since her death, he realised he was continuing her quiet, secret ministry whose most tangible purpose was to awaken purpose in others. Whether as priest or as schoolteacher hardly mattered, though here, now, his magic robe lent him the necessary authority this present crisis had need of.

It was a fine line he trod between the Church's obscurities and the authority of a Cincinnatus. But once this tempest had receded, he would discard the mantle and resume the more liberal path he and she had marked out together. He was determined not to falter. For her sake he must not. And he thought of Will, and he reflected on his good fortune that in this most unlikely spot he should encounter another whose experience of adversity, though unlike his own in the particular, had played its part in bringing him to a stance – political… in its ramifications, he supposed – not dissimilar to his own. In one vital detail Will's experience had replicated his own exactly – in its continuing, quiet, spiritual presence of a *Liebfrau*.

Prior to Joanna's coming, the only real happy time he had ever known had been that period in Dublin, when through the good offices of a friend, he had read freely, for two or three hours each day, in Marsh's Library, seeking in particular those books he knew figured in the *Index Librorum Prohibitorum*. That time had been all too brief, and soon after, the incipient scholar-priest had been overwhelmed by the world's events, the poverty and sorrows of his ignorant parishioners, and the fruitless drudgery of his duties towards them.

But now this man, Will, suddenly turns up in his life, with a trunk full of books! Even a priest needed to withdraw from the breach, from time to time, he mused. For without attending to his own inner peace, the ceaseless cares of, and care for others would grind him into dust. And saintliness, much less martyrdom, had long since ceased to fascinate him.

His thoughts raced on. It wasn't just the randomness of seeming universal misery which gnawed at him. When such suffering came upon an individual or a family the randomness seemed more or less acceptable, it was just bad luck. No, not just the randomness, rather its tendency to settle, concentrate, then press hard down upon whole communities. As here, and now... or in Ireland during the past seven or so years. What sort of a god condoned or even, perhaps, required so much suffering?

'God', though, was always 'mediated', interpreted. And the Catholic Church had been interpreting so long that the very longevity of its interpretations gave it a terrible authority, a *gravitas* its flock (a precise metaphor!) never dared to question, for with questioning came the threat of apostasy. Hermetically sealed. The longest-running confidence trick in the history of the world, he shouldn't wonder: the sacraments, the Latin, the Index, the confessional, the intercession of the saints and the Mother of God... a huge spider's web of intrigue whose effects – and maybe intention – were to maintain the *status quo*, the ease of the few at the expense of the misery of the many. The poetry of deception and betrayal.

After all, anyone with a mind to think with could interpret... god. But what was certain for Thomas was the deadness of the Church's god, its very idea of god... Yet if reason had brought him to this point, his life-long habit of belief – which meant dependence – made him now doubt the validity of his doubts, even as he rehearsed them.

The habit of belief, itself – in what, hardly mattered – was a kind of paralysis, the worm at the centre of the apple. There had to be belief, though... even if only in tomorrow, for without it there could be no courage and if there were no courage to go on there could only be the downward spiral into the abyss; and yes, that was Hell, Dante's vision precisely, the emblem of all earthly despair.

Wrestle as he may with the problem, he could think of no adequate resolution.

The salt breeze through the open doorway of the tent caught his nostrils and he stood up, in instinctive response, knowing that the sea, the shoreline, and their open promise were what his spirit craved in place of this stagnant cycle that imprisoned him and his fellows. He stepped outside and caught the flash of ibis, rising up from the unseen sands, and momentarily his spirits soared with them.

Belief was dependence, and dependence was – oh yes, how clearly he saw it now – enchainment of will, of multitudinous, endless wills, the impossibility of freedom *to be*. You looked out through the bars of your cage at a better world, but the key to it had been hidden or lost. Was it not the case that he had been made dependent, and deliberately so, since before his memories began? Holy Mother Church took on more and more the guise of the wicked stepmother in the fairy tale. And yet, at the centre of her doctrine, comfortably cocooned, was the notion of Free Will! Ugh!

We all had it, the freedom to choose, as he had been schooled to accept. Yet in his case, it had been a barefaced lie and because he still found himself in limbo, between two contrary worlds, it continued so.

XXVIII

Ridley threw a saddle over one of the tethered horses and invited Will to saddle up the other. When they were ready, he grinned. 'Maybe you should take this smaller one since you seem to have found it difficult staying on Bluebell. What do you say?'

Ridley must be continually pricking and provoking, even if in jest, but Will refused to take the bait. 'Well, thank you,' he said, matter-of-fact, 'but I believe that "the devil you know…" Besides, it wasn't me Bluebell was trying to be rid of but the lightning. She and I had got along fine, till then.'

'As you please,' Ridley muttered, perhaps disappointed at Will's side-stepping, muted reaction.

Whatever it was, they rode for some little while in silence, Will noting the differences in the terrain and vegetation from that he had observed on his ride northwards the previous day. Here the ground was sandy and there was a preponderance of ghostly white trees ('snow gums', Ridley called them), many of them seeming dead, certainly bereft of leaves. But here and there was also a scattering of those odd, low-growing trees that had a sort of long, coarse grass sprouting from the tops of their trunks instead of leaves.

What the area did have in common with that traversed the previous day was the almost oppressive silence, broken only occasionally by snapping twigs and startled, brightly coloured parakeets, but apart from these there were no signs of other creatures, just the occasional tiny bird, half glimpsed, flitting through the undergrowth or among the higher branches.

Contrary to what Ridley had told him earlier, the going was none too difficult. In parts there was the semblance of a path, but where it seemed to be lost the undergrowth was rarely so thick it could not be negotiated with comparative ease. It took them no time at all to reach the lake which, at that end at least, had broad sandy shores and Will noted, keeping in mind the purpose of their visit, ample cover for dressing and undressing. And in his imagination, he saw lines of washing strung out between trees and the women and children swimming about and chatting together while they waited for it to dry: the possibility of temporary escape and maybe even enjoyment... Yes, it might just help to raise morale enough for people to keep going a bit longer...

'I take it there's no likelihood of crocodiles in there?' he asked, heading down to the water's edge. 'Or any other horrors that would make this pleasant-seeming spot dangerous?'

'Nah! The crocs don't get this far down. Or at least, I've never heard tell of any. There's always snakes, of course, and the goannas, but they tend to get out of the way, particularly if there's a fair number of people about, and plenty of noise – as there certainly will be, as it's women we're talking about!'

Will dismounted and let his horse amble down to the water's edge to drink, while he wandered off along the shoreline. Ridley, also out of the saddle but leading his own mount along with him, caught him up. 'If you like, to set your mind at rest, we could ride right round. It shouldn't take more than an hour at most.'

Will nodded. 'I'll just fetch Bluebell.'

A little above the lake there was a broad sandy ridge that seemed to run parallel to it and they followed this for about a quarter of a mile before it sank down again to the lakeside, at its northern extremity. The sandy shores had continued intermittently, sometimes lost to deep inlets but visibly present under the surface of the water. However, at this end the snow gums gave way abruptly to scrub and thorn bush, and for the first time, they had to make a wide detour to find a way round it. But that took them into swampy ground and being unwilling to risk the horses in what might prove a dangerous or foolhardy venture, they turned back. After all, they had satisfactorily established the safety of at least the western side of the lake, and Will was keen to report their success, and maybe even suggest a first expedition of bathers for the morrow.

Once again, he experienced that curious sense of elation he had felt only yesterday, fancying he was perhaps seeing the place much as God had created it, before the intrusion of men. He even said as much to Ridley as he drew level with him towards the southern tip of the lake.

The thought should have remained private. As if the stage had been set to disabuse him of his romantic notion – truly, foolish, he later owned – Ridley pointed laconically towards something white, hanging from a low branch over to their left. 'I think you may be mistaken, Mr Crosby.' And with this he spurred his horse over to the bush, bent down and, flourishing his riding crop, delicately retrieved what were, indisputably, a pair of lady's drawers. 'Not Aboriginal attire, that's for sure!' he announced with mock seriousness. 'Though they might just have been here since the Fall… or a fall! One can't help wondering how it was the lady came to leave here without them – or how she explained their absence once she arrived back…!'

For the rest of the short ride back to Dunwich, Will lagged some way behind his companion, having lost all appetite for conversation. There was something about Ridley he didn't rightly comprehend – a seeming delight, was it, in putting people down? Perhaps that was expressing it too simplistically; whatever it was, it came out of an apparent world-weariness, a mechanical scepticism that manifested itself in speech as sharply dismissive or cuttingly sarcastic, a verbal lashing that told you the man didn't suffer fools gladly. With Ridley, plainly, you were automatically a fool until you proved yourself otherwise, and had to be forever on your mettle.

But there was more than just this underlying Will's sudden moroseness, something he could not quite frame in thought, in those moments. Ridley's frivolous, disparaging, remarks about the item of female underwear had made a deeper impression and in a different way from what had most likely been intended.

After his midday repast, taken alone beneath the awning beside the quite empty, newly-sited cookhouse tent, Will came somewhere near the cause of his own vague disquiet: Ridley's acerbic wit had sullied something, a half-recalled occasion in a leafy glade when he and Alice were new to their love... maybe it was that; or maybe that was just a part of it. The truth was, he realised yet again, he needed this journey to the far side of the world to give him access to an abundance of places of innocence and his own total immersion in them; for that was the price of his return. His own, necessary re-making depended on getting beyond the reach of all venality, envy, depravity, of all chaotic, enslaving desires. Of course, his remark to Ridley about the unspoilt nature of that particular spot had been naïve, but that did not negate the sincerity of the aspirations that lay behind it – something that was perhaps outside Joe Ridley's powers of perception, much less appreciation.

These splinters of thought persisted all through the afternoon and it was only much later, when Will returned to his quarters and lay down awhile, that he made what he thought were significant connections and began to understand his reaction against Ridley's words.

It was linked to something he had read in the Judge's diary, about betrayal – by the man's wife and his brother. The cause of the betrayal, however, was not known, and would never be known, although the questions it begged were obvious enough. Had Rosper-Sandys' wife sought and found solace in the brother's gentler arms? The catalogue of bitterness that filled page after page of the diary certainly revealed a mind given to cruelty. Was the Judge's evident loathing of his fellow men really nothing more than self-loathing? More importantly, had a kind of innocence... or honesty... been restored for the poor woman as a result of that betrayal? Will realised he wanted to read more of the diary to get the true measure of the man.

And was not Wilfred Farmer's case of the same order, the betrayals it contained? And what of Thomas's? Or, for that matter, his own? Perhaps 'betrayal', whatever guise it took, was, after all, a fundamental condition of life anywhere, having its roots in prohibitions that often, especially in the heat of the living moment, made no sense at all.

XXIX

Will found Thomas and Dr Ballow in the hospital tent, ministering to a patient who had been newly brought there, the day before. Seated near the bed was a small boy of six or seven years, who was clearly deeply distressed.

Thomas shook his head, and with a particular look communicated the hopelessness of the case to Will; then taking him by the arm, he led him outside.

'Ah, Will, of all the tragedies we have witnessed in this damned place this is the worst. The little lad's father died on the voyage out, and his mother, in there, will soon have breathed her last. Ballow tells me there isn't an orphanage in or anywhere near Brisbane, and that in the normal run of events the boy would have to be shipped off to Sydney. However, his close proximity to the disease and two of its deaths rules out that course of action. For the time being, at least, he will have to stay here. Yes, poor little lad, it'll be a show of love he needs, and consolation, not just some impersonal provision of food and shelter. And can you see anyone rushing to provide those precious commodities? Of course not! Everyone has more than enough to contend with.' He paused. 'It's been bothering me, Will, these two hours past, so it has.'

'Well, what you're really telling me is that it's our problem. Is that not so?' Will's response came at once. 'Not just yours and mine, I mean… but, well, the doctors' and the matron's… all of us. And, in these… ghastly conditions, we'll all have to do the best we can for the child, won't we?'

Thomas looked at him. 'Aye… that's the top and bottom of it, I suppose. Though the plain fact is, Will, the medical people are so stretched I fear the practicalities, his day-to-day care, is most likely to fall to us, you and me. Wouldn't you see it that way, now?'

But Will did not. He recoiled instinctively from Thomas's stark reading of the situation, and the complications it would doubtless entail. It would restrict him in all sorts of ways he didn't want to even begin thinking about.

'That's a heavy burden, Thomas,' and he looked pained, 'and, if I'm honest, not one I'm inclined to assume. It's hardly a dog or a cat we're talking about here but a vulnerable human being.' He tried to keep his words light, non-committal. 'Attachments form and breed expectations. You can't just hand him over, later, to some faceless authority once this phase has been lived through. Well, you can't! It would be a further, cruel betrayal, and God knows what effect that might have on him – when added to all the rest.'

Thomas groaned. 'You're right, yes… of course you are. Once taken on, whoever takes him on, it has to be a long-term commitment, that it does! Nature would require that it be a woman, and ideally one who is married but childless… Well, that's crying for the moon here, Will. What shall I do? Ask around in the hope of a miracle?'

'You can, of course, but…' and Will's mind was now fully in revolt against itself. 'Don't you see?' he said gruffly. '*Already* he's become our problem – and I haven't even spoken to him yet! We can't fob him off on… just anybody, because they agree to take him on, can we? We'd have to be sure they were offering him the chance of a decent life, but also, especially, the love and compassion he needs now. These people here… their poverty, their general ignorance of things, things other than, well, just getting on with their lives, and… I know these are trying circumstances, but if they survive, what then? What of their new futures on the mainland? What if this would be condemning the boy to a life of, well, drudgery and misery? It looks to me as if he's had more than enough of a raw deal from life already.…'

Will stopped, suddenly aghast at what he was saying, at the

enormity of it, aware, if only vaguely, that behind it all ghosted his own little Lilian, his failings, his guilt....

'It is... undeniably so.' Thomas shook his head. 'But I no more want this than you do, Will. So... I will ask around. Then we'll decide... bearing in mind the things you've just said. Are we agreed?'

Will shrugged. 'I suppose so... but, damn it all, he's going to need someone now, isn't he? To see him through all that's going to happen to him now, things that a little boy should never have to face alone... Oh, come on!'

Will re-entered the tent. And after a moment or two the priest followed.

Yet even as Will stepped back inside, he hesitated. Was not this – it flashed through his mind – already a further betrayal of his little daughter on the other side of the world? Poor Lilian! No, it must in no way prove an obstacle to his return.

Ballow was just then bending over his patient, helping her take a few sips of water in her semi-conscious state, but he nodded over towards the prostrate Dr Mitchell. 'Oh, Thomas, could you see to the doctor? He stirred just now and said something I didn't catch. He may even be awake. Could you give him some water too?'

Thomas went over to the other side of the tent to do his bidding and Will glanced at the little boy now sitting in the corner, slumped forward on the edge of his chair. He had obviously been crying, for his face was streaked with grime. Will took hold of another chair and placed it backwards way round, in front of the boy's, and sat down, his chin resting on his arms on the back of the chair – something, he now recalls, he had been in the habit of doing whenever he and Lilian had had one of their 'serious' talks together. Something that had always made Alice laugh.

Pushing the memory aside, and attempting a cheerful tone, he asked, 'So, what's your name, young fellow?'

'My name is William Tawbridge, sir, but my mammy – and my daddy before he died and was put in the sea – always called me Billy, sir.'

Did Will imagine it or had the lad stressed the 'he' in mentioning his father, and had he said 'called' and not 'call'? Will could not be sure.

'Well, that is a coincidence,' he said quietly, 'because my name is William too, though my friends call *me* Will – which is a good thing, for that way, even though we have the same real name, we won't get confused whenever somebody says "Oh, Billy, would you...?" or, "Will, could you...?" or "Don't you think, Billy...?"'

The little boy chuckled briefly. Then, his face resuming its former look of anxiety, and with a sudden catch in his voice, he whispered: 'Is my mammy going to die too?'

Unconsciously perhaps, Will had prepared himself for this overwhelming question. 'She is very poorly, Billy. The doctors are doing all they can to make her better, but we have to realise that for all their trying they might not succeed. You will need to be very brave...'

Billy began to cry in earnest, not loudly but without any attempt at restraint.

'But, Billy, Billy... if the worst did come to the worst, you would not be on your own. You have some real friends here, friends you don't yet know about – Father Sheehan for one...'

And at the mention of his name Thomas looked up, grinned at the boy, and waved. 'You'll always be able to count on me, Billy, that you will.'

'So, you see', Will resumed, trying his best to seem easy. 'And busy though he is, Dr Ballow there for another.'

And though the latter did not turn away from attending to the boy's mother, he said quietly: 'That's for sure, Billy, you can count me in too!'

'...So that's two, Billy, and I'm sure Dr Mallon and matron will make a third and a fourth... then, if you'll have me, I could certainly be a fifth...'

The boy rose, looking entirely lost, and groped his way through the mist of newly welling tears to lay his head against Will's shoulder.

Will, taken aback by the suddenness of this reaction, hesitated for only a brief moment before encircling the boy's back with his left arm and pulling him more tightly towards him. He looked helplessly back at Thomas, who smiled, shook his head, but said nothing, as he tried, with little success, to coax some water down Dr Mitchell's throat. Will saw the look of desperation on Ballow's face and, realising the battle had been as good as lost, exchanged another glance with Thomas, who would need to find the ticket-of-leave men, have them prepare a grave for her...

Billy's small frame shook with the force of his tears, and all the while Will held him firm. Eventually, the tears subsided, and he became calmer, yet he made no attempt to free himself from Will's grasp.

Dr Ballow left the bed and came to sit in the chair that Billy had vacated. After a moment or two, he cleared his throat and, with some obvious difficulty, Will realised, addressed the boy.

'Billy. I'm very sorry but I do not think I can do anything more to help your mammy. I wish I could. Really I do.'

Billy lifted his head then and turned to face him, perplexed, still holding on to Will's arm. 'Why can't you?'

'Because I don't know how to. I... we, the medical profession... doctors, I mean... don't know enough about the disease. We don't even know what causes it, so we can't even take steps to prevent it. We know when it can occur and what sorts of things are connected with it but that's not nearly enough...'

'But why?' the boy pleaded. 'Why do some people not die of it and others do die?'

'It's hard to say, Billy. It affects different people in different ways but, again, we can only guess why, and we may be guessing wrongly. Now... what would you wish to do. Do you want to stay here until, until... it's all over, to be with your mammy to... the last...?'

At that, the little boy broke free and ran and threw himself on his mother's bed, wrapping his arms about her recumbent knees as if expecting to be dragged away at any moment. So violent was his movement that the dying woman stirred, half opening her eyes, and stretched out a hand and placed it on the boy's head, weakly tousling his hair. 'Hush, now,' she whispered, 'don't take on so. Be a good boy always, Billy, for your mammy's sake...'

'I will. Oh, I will. But don't go. Please don't go mammy...' the child whimpered.

Exhausted, the woman slowly shook her head and smiled, her fingers still entwined in his hair. 'I'm not going far, Billy,' she said, 'just popping out to see...' and her voice trailed off into a murmur, her long, final exhaling.

Not long after this, Billy felt his mammy's arm go limp, her hand slip gently down his face, like a caress. Her head tipped slightly sideways, and sensing she had gone, despite his desperate pleading, the child buried his head in the bedclothes. And then he sobbed and howled and beat his fists against the bed, in anger and in sorrow, expressing – though he did not know it – that same frustration and helplessness that each of the others felt in that moment.

And at the moment of every other death they had witnessed, and those deaths still to come.

XXX

Stevens and Callaghan were not in any of the places one might have expected to find them – the hospital hut, the loading bays, or indeed the joinery, which had been sited away from the passengers' compound, beyond even Mr Ridley's tents, so that the preparation of the coffins by the *Emigrant*'s carpenter, Mr Jones, would go unheeded by their potential occupants. Jones ('Davy' as he was grimly nicknamed) was not there either, but after checking that there were coffins already made, Thomas resumed his search back inside the encampment. And, still perplexed as to the men's whereabouts, he headed for the hospital hut.

Dr Mallon was tending some of the worst cases, assisted by the ashen-faced matron. The stench was overpowering, and the priest felt himself admiring their dedication, toiling away hour after hour in largely fruitless labour, in such atrocious conditions. And he stood in the open doorway, watching, until Mallon looked up.

'You haven't, by any chance, seen anything of Callaghan or Stevens, have you?'

The doctor shook his head. 'They were here a while ago, asking if there was anything at all I needed them to do, and since there wasn't, in that moment, they went off again.' He turned back to his patient, but then added, without looking up, 'I'm sorry. I didn't pay any attention to what direction they took.'

Thomas waved aside his apology, and left him to his unenviable, ministering tasks.

As he entered the cemetery gate, his mind returned to those

questions that had earlier occupied it, and now with a vengeance, given this latest example of life's... nature's... fundamental injustices, its utter indifference. What was the point of it all...?

Nearing the top corner of the burial ground, where the *Emigrant*'s ever-lengthening line of graves were located, he was suddenly bundled back into the sentient world, hearing a gasping, choking sound, and then... what was it? He stopped in his tracks to listen more intently, but now all was silent again. Having waited several minutes for the sound to be repeated, but hearing nothing, he went forward, and quickly reaching the embankment that led to the seashore, jumped down onto the still wet sand; curious still, sure that he had not imagined the noise, faint though it had been.

Not a yard from where he landed, the startled Callaghan and Stevens cowered beneath a half shelf of the overhanging banking, obviously trying to keep their presence secret. They were not alone. Seated just behind them was a young girl whom Thomas vaguely remembered having seen about the camp. He judged she would be about thirteen, certainly no more than fourteen years of age. She was blushing scarlet and kept her eyes averted, fixed on the sands before her. Immediately, he understood the meaning of the sounds he had heard not five minutes ago, incredible though it seemed in the moment: neither gasping nor choking but the lost cries of mounting sexual pleasure which, all too obviously, his approach had curtailed. And he fought to contain his anger, knowing full well he could prove nothing even though he knew all.

'By whose leave do you idle your time away here when there is work to be done? Eh, Mr Callaghan? Mr Stevens?' he began, desperately, trying to measure his words, to warn, even to threaten, though obliquely, so as to convey his complete understanding of the situation.

The two men shot a glance at each other, then away again.

Neither responded.

'Well?' the priest insisted.

Stevens was the first to recover his wits. 'Begging your Reverence's pardon, but the young doctor, sir, he said we was to take our ease a little since he had no immediate task to occupy us.'

'And we did look about for Dr Ballow... and, indeed, your good self... sir,' Callaghan added, opportunely... 'but finding neither, we took the young doctor at his word... sir.'

'That was certainly not the impression I had from Dr Mallon,' Thomas barked. 'And another thing, how does this girl come to be with you in this... concealed place?'

'Ah, well,' Stevens blustered, 'we come upon her playing here, didn't we Lizzie? And she was just telling us about the games she likes to play... weren't you, my dear?'

The girl mumbled something inaudible, and nodded, but did not look up.

Her obvious discomfiture prompted Thomas to bear down hard upon her in the hope she might give something away that would enable him to ensnare these two lying conspirators. 'Do your parents know where you are? And what you are doing?'

The child offered no answer, nor did she raise her head.

'Look at me, Lizzie... is it Lizzie, your name? And answer my questions.' Thomas's voice assumed an even harsher tone.

'Please sir, I don't 'ave no parents.'

'Then who cares for you? Who are you with?' Thomas was shaken by her answer, suddenly more acutely aware of her vulnerability.

'Please sir, I ain't wiv nobody,' the girl answered.

'But how old are you? How did you get here, if...?' And he was at a loss how to go on. Had he misjudged, somehow? Surely not.

'When I come out of the 'formatory back in London, sir, they said I could get a place as a maid... in a big 'ouse, over 'ere. So I come 'ere, 'cause there weren't noffin' for me, back there.'

'How old are you, Lizzie?'

The girl hesitated, her hands fiddling with the hem of her dress. She glanced at Stevens who, Thomas observed, nodded at her, encouragingly.

'Mr Stevens says I'm eighteen; leastways, that's what it says on me birf stificate, ain't it, Mr Stevens? I ain't never learned to read nor write, you see, sir, so meself, I can't rightly say.'

'Where is your birth certificate? I should like to see it.'

'It's wiv me fings, back at the tent, sir.'

Stevens winced.

'I see. So, tell me, how did Mr Stevens come to read your birth certificate if he and Mr Callaghan came across you here, just now, by chance?'

The girl was visibly flustered by the snare she had stepped into, and the priest pressed home his advantage.

'I think you are not being very truthful with me Lizzie, are you?'

Before she could think of an answer, however, Stevens cut in: 'Ah, sir, but that were a few days ago... when I was a-working near her tent. She comes out waving her birth certificate and asks me what it says, so I tells her it all, didn't I Lizzie?'

Thomas gave her no time to answer. 'Is that so? And why, in that moment, a few days ago, did you want to know what your birth certificate said? Why then?'

Again the girl was at a loss. 'I dunno, sir,' she pouted, 'I just did.'

Thomas then fixed his gaze on Stevens who quickly averted his eyes. 'And what games does this... eighteen-year-old... like to play, then, Mr Stevens?'

The man smiled foolishly but had no answer to give.

After an awkward silence, which Thomas deliberately let lie among them, he again turned his attention on the girl.

'Well, Lizzie, you and I are going back to your tent right now and you can show it to me... this birth certificate of yours...'

'Begging your Reverence's pardon... for the interruption, sir, I mean... but there's a matter I would like your opinion about.' Stevens' face attempted an innocent, perplexed look. 'Something as has been a-botherin' me, an' I've been meaning to ask you for a day or two now. It's about that judge what disappeared from your ship on the way out.'

Thomas stepped back, startled by the seeming irrelevancy of a question that had been far from his own mind.

'What would you do, sir,' Stevens was saying, 'if you knew he was helped overboard, sir, and you knew who it was what give him that assistance? I mean, I know what a priest would do, sir, but I heard tell you weren't a priest… not until you come here, leastways, that's what some people, people what were on the boat, are a-saying…'

'What are you saying, Stevens?' Thomas said sharply. 'I'm not following you. And besides…'

'Well, it's like this, sir, as it's been put to me. What a priest hears in confession can't be told to no man, whatever it is, so anyone what confesses a crime knows he is safe. That's right, ain't it… sir?'

'Yes. Yes. But I…'

'But… sir. Begging Your Reverence's pardon… sir. If someone confesses to what he believes to be a priest but who turns out not to be one, then he has reason to worry, wouldn't you say? And if the crime is a big one, like helping a judge miss his footing then I'd say anyone what knowed about that, other than a priest, that is, would have reason to worry. I thought I would mention that sir.'

'Did you, now.' Confused and irritated, realising this pseudo-hypothesis was meant to unnerve him, Thomas stood his ground.

'Yes… sir. And I happen to know, sir, there are three or four such worried men on this island, and it wouldn't take very much, in my view, to make them desperate – if you take my meaning.'

It was indeed a threat – of blackmail or worse. But Thomas, having regained his wits sufficiently, said simply: 'Well, Stevens, if the case you outline were to arise, then yes, your friends would indeed have cause for worry. But since the only priest hearing the last confessions of the dying on this island is myself, it plainly doesn't arise, for I am many years a priest…'

'Begging your pardon sir, you know that, and I do too. But it seems there is some doubt in… some people's minds… And if that doubt became any stronger, for whatever reason… Well, it's a very delicate situation, sir… that it is, that's all I'm a-saying…' And Stevens rose to his feet, beckoning to Callaghan. 'But we can't be idling here any longer, sir… Father… we had best be off attending to the needs of others. Maybe the doctors will have some task for us by this time…'

Thomas, relieved at this diversionary ploy, fell in – apparently in all innocence – with Steven's sense of public duty. 'Yes, indeed. It was precisely because there is an urgent task to be carried out that I was seeking you in the first place!'

'Oh, sir,' his adversary answered, brightly. 'So you were actually *looking* for us, and *didn't* just come upon us by chance?' He barely bothered to conceal his mocking tone. 'Our humble apologies, sir! Whatever we can do to help, you only have to... say the word.'

Full of contempt, but also of dark anger, Thomas all but spat out his orders regarding the swift preparation of the grave, for the interment he must perform at five o'clock.

Stevens touched his forelock in mock solicitude and smiled, then in the tones of a reasonable man declared: 'Then there's not a moment to lose, sir, but rest assured, all will be ready in time.'

Thomas started to walk away, conspicuously without insisting that the girl accompany him. But his anger boiled deep within. How could he have allowed himself to be panicked and browbeaten into silence over the matter of the child?

After a few steps, he turned, unwilling to concede total victory to villainy, and shouted back: 'Lizzie! I will see you later; now, don't you forget.'

The girl did not move from where she was sitting. She looked up at the sound of her name but made no reply. And Thomas walked on, quivering with rage and despondency – his pace quickening – to finalise arrangements for Mrs Tawbridge's funeral.

Once away from that scene, however, he began to think more clearly.

The first confession he had heard – the Limerick man, wasn't it? – late that same day Joanna had died, had in reality no more than hinted at the judge's murder; and the man had named no names. Yet what Stevens had as good as divulged in his eagerness to cut short his investigation into the age and condition of the girl, Lizzie, was that murder *had* been committed. Yes, certainly that... Unless – and Thomas came to a halt just past the line of graves, floundering amid new doubts – unless Stevens had fabricated the whole story. But could he have, on the spur of the moment? Was Stevens quick-witted enough, clever enough? And the more he thought about it the less likely it seemed.

Exhaling his frustration, Thomas had to conclude that he was probably a marked man. And yet – and he twisted round to the shore to glance back at where he'd come across the two rogues – in the weeks they had been on the island there had been no hint of it, even though opportunities to do him harm must surely have arisen for any man seriously intent upon it.

Thomas walked on, leaving the graves behind, then soon past the first tents.

Truth was he didn't even know himself what his present status would be with the Church, given his defection and the manner of it, and that was something quite apart from his own decision to quit the priesthood, of which no man here, who wished him ill, could have any inkling. So what, then? Was it that dire necessity had merely delayed the fulfilment of that intention but had by no means revoked it? Yet no one else (with the exception of Will) could possibly know that, and its day would most surely dawn.

'That put a flea in the bastard's ear now, and no mistake! Did you see him squirm, John-o?' And Callaghan chortled.

'That I did! Prying bastard priest, poking his nose where it don't belong!' added Stevens. 'He'll do it once too often, mark my words he will! Anyhow, talking of poking... Come on Lizzie, open wide, and let's take my little pleasure afore we go off to our bloody grave digging', he said, smiling and not quite commanding.

'Oh, Mr Stevens, I don't feel like it no more...'

'Ah, maybe you don't Lizzie, girl', Stevens cut her short, his tone sharper now, 'but there's them that does, Lizzie. Ain't that right, Mr Callaghan?'

'That's just about the top and bottom of it, Mr Stevens, leastways, as I see it.'

'But that man, the priest, he might come back...' the girl protested.

'No, he won't my dear, on account of what I said to him, see. So, no more ifs and buts about it. Let's have your frock off now – and I mean now! So we can have our bit of fun. Mustn't be selfish, must we?'

The girl knelt up and complied, though clearly unwilling. 'You hurt my bum last time, Mr Callaghan, so be more...'

'What did I say now, Lizzie?' Stevens' voice was harsh, menacing. 'You wouldn't like Mr and Mrs Parry to find out what games you *really* play when they think you're off playing dollies, would you? They could do... so easily, you know.'

The girl was still shaking her head when Callaghan pulled her roughly towards him.

'I'll leave you to it, then, Ned,' said Stevens, 'while I go over and make a start on the sodding grave. But don't be too long afore you come – if you take my drift – then I'll slip back for my own overlong dues. That way Sheehan's not likely to smell a rat.' And away he went.

XXXI

As he re-entered the encampment, Thomas changed his mind. He did not go back to the hospital immediately, wanting a little more time on his own to reflect further upon Stevens' words, the better to arrive at a decisive plan of action. But entering the tent he realised at once that that was not to be.

Pushing aside the tent-flap, he found Will inside, sorting through the judge's books, which were strewn all over the three beds.

'Ah, there you are!' Will said cheerily, barely looking up. 'Sorry... I'm trying to find something for young Billy to learn to read from. I promised I would teach him. Rash of me, I know, but... anything to distract him from this bleak moment, which has... Thomas...?'

'No... yes, you're right,' Thomas mumbled, still preoccupied. 'Where is the lad now?'

'With matron, but' – Will tossed another book aside – 'he keeps going back to his mother's bed where he sits and stares at her... willing her to open her eyes, I suspect. Trouble is, the women will be coming soon to prepare the body for burial, so I thought I would bring him here out of the way... as soon as I've found something suitable...' Will shook his head and grimaced. 'My guess is he's likely to fly into a fit of hysterical grief once he realises what's happening to her.'

Thomas cleared a space and sat down on his littered bed, watching as Will continued his hunt.

'I would hardly think Spinoza's *Ethics* is likely to give him a thirst for reading,' Will snorted. 'Or Monteskew's *Spirit of the Laws*.' And the two volumes joined the growing heap of rejections.

Thomas made no comment, and Will glanced over at him, slumped forward on his bed, his hand covering his eyes. 'Sorry,' he murmured. 'You must be very tired.' He began gathering up the books besieging his friend. 'There. You can stretch out, now.'

Thomas took off his boots. 'It's Montesquieu,' he muttered, breaking in on the growing silence, his eyes half closed.

Will looked up. 'Pardon? What did you say?'

'It's Mon-tes-quieu: *quieu*, not *kew*.' Thomas repeated the author's name. 'French. Eighteenth century.'

'Oh, right. Thanks...' Will said, repeating the word a couple of times – tolerably well, he thought.

'It was an important book. A pity the high and mighty don't read it, now – if they ever did... But what were you saying about it?'

'I said it was no use...'

'No use? No use! Excuse my impertinence Will, but... what the hell would you be knowing about it?'

Will sat down on his own bed, pushing some of the discarded books aside. 'Well, nothing at all. Indeed, I never heard of it or him, until...'

'So how can you say it's no use? No use for what?' Thomas didn't even try to conceal his irritation.

'For Billy...!' Will almost shouted. 'For Billy to learn to read from!' Laughing, he looked across at his friend's confusion. 'Thomas, have you heard anything I've said since you came in... apart from that... French name? I said it's far too hard... Incomprehensible to a six-year-old, let alone...'

'Ah!' Thomas exclaimed, twisting round then sitting up with a jerk. 'Cross purposes, Will... My apologies. I *wasn't* paying attention, you're right. You see, I've just had a very odd and, I think you'll agree, worrying experience.'

And he recounted what he had seen and heard on the seashore and the words he had had with the ticket-of-leave men. 'I'm sure enough in my own mind that they're molesting the girl... And that she is still only a child – despite a lot of rigmarole about a birth certificate.'

'Hm! I must say from the few dealings I've had with them they seem a shifty pair: I wouldn't let them anywhere near my... any young girl. We'll have to keep an eye on them, and on the child too... But tell me', Will added, after a moment, '*have* you heard anything, during any final... confession, or whatever you call it, that might make these men worried – if they exist at all?'

'Nothing specific, no. Although there was one poor man – the first to die on the island; he was hinting in that direction, and his own part in it. But he did not elaborate, or mention what part any others played, nor did it occur to me to ask him, it not being part of *his* absolution. Now, of course, I'm wondering if...' Thomas shook his head, in confusion. 'Well, if he was hinting at what he knew, rather than telling me what he'd done himself...'

'Have you any inkling as to who they might be, these "worried men", and... how many they are?'

'Well, assuming they are Irish, Will – which would not be unreasonable given the location of the judge's crimes against his fellow men – there are a dozen or so who, in my estimation, might well be capable of such an act; but of course, I have no proof, just occasional observation of character, and surmise.'

'Then you'll have to watch your step, no mistake, because if there is anything in it... Well, you just can't afford to ignore it, whatever Stevens' motives – though I strongly suspect it's all a fabrication.'

'Aye, I know, but I can't just let the uncertainty paralyse me. That would be unthinkable in our present plight. I have to be free to... ply my trade, peddle my illusions to those who need them, and there are still plenty who do.'

Will nodded. He was silent awhile, then asked: 'How would it be if I were to question Stevens, and maybe the girl herself for that matter? Many here presume I'm already a policeman, and I could certainly leave Stevens, Callaghan too, in no doubt that the report on their activities here would be unlikely to lead to any early release from custody. What do you think?'

'Hm... it might work.' Thomas pondered the matter a moment. 'But I think we would need to let Ballow know what we were about, and why, because I suppose he is the one most likely to be responsible for such a report. I'll have a word with him. Those two are surely up to no good and the sooner they're stopped, the better.' He lay back on his pillow, his hands folded behind his head. 'Sod 'em and Begorrah!... as we used to say in the seminary – don't we have enough problems without their shenanigans?' And he closed his eyes.

Will went back to his sorting, on Billy's potential bed, now rapidly rejecting one book after another. 'Ah, now, that's more like it!' he said, reaching deep into the trunk and pulling out a stout book. 'This should suit him better.' And he waved Anderson's *Fairy Tales* triumphantly in Thomas's direction.

The latter reached out a hand and took it from him. His eyes barely open, he examined it and agreed. 'Yes, the illustrations! What a joy they are!' he said, handing it back. and shutting his eyes once more.

Will read the inscription, then turned the pages, slowly.

'Strange though,' Thomas half-murmured, 'truly strange!'

'What's strange?' Will asked. 'Or are you now talking in your sleep?'

'Chance would be a fine thing! No, it just strikes me as odd that among the magistrate's books there should be that one, considering the... lofty nature of the other tomes you've been pulling out.'

'Well, whatever the reason, I'm much obliged to him. I'll go and fetch the lad now.' Will stood up. 'But I'll leave you in peace, find somewhere else.'

'No, no.' Thomas yawned noisily. 'I shall have to be moving, Will, for there's plenty to do before the funeral. Indeed, I'd better go and make sure those two fly-by-nights are actually digging the grave. Oh and, after the funeral, you won't forget about the girl and those two charlatans – keeping an eye on them – will you?'

'I shan't forget, don't worry.'

I'll have a word with Ballow, as I should be grateful for any headway you can make there... before they cause any more trouble.'

XXXII

What could explain the book's presence in what was, in all other respects, a thinking man's library?

The inscription proclaimed it to be a seventh-birthday gift to a 'beloved son', from 'your dear mamma', or something like that – he would check its precise wording, later. On the face of it, though, such sentimentalism seemed an unlikely reason for its inclusion, given the tenor of every word of the judge's he had read hitherto. If not that, then what else would account for it in the company of so much philosophical, political and... ponderous writing?

And Will found himself wondering who could possibly say what a man was, or what the judge might have been before he became the greatly-to-be-feared man-of-law – something his diary and Thomas affirmed. Had the judge – and here Will was conscious of venturing further into the misty marshes of surmise – like Thomas, like Farmer, like Will himself, not to mention so many of his own hapless victims, been tumbled by some mischance into the harsh adversities of a ravenous world of disillusionment?

If there were some truth in this line of thought, Will reasoned, then somewhere, deep within him the man had nursed the memory of a kinder world than the one he administered. Was he still keening after that loss, whether of a warmly cocooned, rosy childhood or – and the further possibility came to him only now – that of a lost child, as well as of a lost wife? Could it be that he and others judged this man of harsh judgements prematurely, unjustly? Or is it only one's deeds that count for anything?

Yet – and here he checked himself – in dealing with one's fellow men it was actions and their results that counted, not the emotional tangle that was motivation, which lay behind them, however much sympathy one might accord them. Thomas, in his theologian's robes, might well agree that this was what sin was – actions rather than un-translated thoughts.

Will paused outside the large tent, trying to focus…

So yes… if one admitted that humanity could include even a hanging judge, who could also quite justifiably plead for pity, for mercy, how would that weigh in the balance if set against his own misdeeds regarding Alice and his daughter?

And herein lay the problem. The judge's pretext for his gross misuse of the powers vested in him – his wife's infidelity, his brother's betrayal – was maybe only that, a pretext, for hadn't he been a 'hanging judge' long before that affair came to light? But whatever the truth of it, Thomas was right. Only power mattered.

Will exhaled his frustration. If there was *ever* to be a better world, then its present hierarchies and their vicious systems would have to be dismantled; but more than that, men would need to learn how to become worthier than they had ever been before. And if education, universal education, was the only answer, who would be the teachers and who the pupils? For already that seemed to imply a new sort of hierarchy, of authority, of power, and then – he shrugged – the same old merry-go-round as before. Oh, the problem was too great to fathom, for him certainly; and yet the sorrows of the world were guaranteed their unending cycles if the many, such as he, failed to address them…

Reluctantly, though relieved he had got this far in his head, Will took the few remaining steps that separated him from that philosophised world of suffering and the immediate one the hospital tent encompassed.

He found Billy still tearful and much agitated by the many comings and goings that plainly concerned his dead mother, even though he had no real understanding of how. Still holding her cold hand he turned his head as Will came in. The matron stood behind the child, her hands gently gripping his shoulders.

'Are they going to put my mammy in the sea like they did with my daddy?' he asked in fearful earnestness.

'No, Billy, they are not.' Will could thankfully answer, in all truthfulness, while yet fearing the further questions which must surely follow. But the child seemed to brighten at Will's reassurance.

'Oh, I thought they might do that, but I don't think she would like it. I'm glad that she is not going in the sea. She's always been frightened of the sea. She can't swim, you see; but my daddy, he can, and...'

Will took advantage of this momentary lightening of the child's anxieties. 'Come Billy, let me show you the tent that Father Thomas and I – and now you – will share. I've got something there I'm sure you will like. It's a book... A book full of pictures, as well as words.'

'A book?' The boy looked quite bewildered. 'I don't know what that is, sir. What is a... book?' His lip quivered, even as he felt his way around the new word.

'Well, if you don't know, the best way of finding out is to come and have a look. So, shall we?' He held out his hand, and the matron loosened her hold on him.

The child stood up; his curiosity aroused. But then he looked towards his dead mother – as if seeking her permission.

Will waited patiently, his hand still outstretched.

'I think she won't mind,' the child decided, looking searchingly up into Will's face.

'I think you are right, Billy.' Will smiled, reassuringly. And as they left the tent, he finally took hold of the boy's hand.

That the child did not know what a book was had taken Will aback, for though his own family were not great readers there had always been books at home: the family Bible, prayer books, and several others of a practical nature.

'The Bible is a book, Billy. I'm sure you know what that is...' he said encouragingly.

The child nodded, though none too convincingly. 'You had a Bible at your house in London, didn't you?'

'I think we did. It was... on a high shelf, a big black thing. But I didn't ever really see it, I don't think. What is it for?'

Will had not bargained for this and found he had no ready answer, owing not least to his own ambivalent attitude to the Bible and the uses to which it was put in the different parts of the world he had passed through. But an answer was certainly needed. 'Well, do you know about Jesus?'

'I know he lives up in the sky.'

Will smiled. 'That's right... or at least, many people think so. But yes... Well, the Bible is the special book in which the story of Jesus is told... though it has hundreds and hundreds of other stories too.'

'I like stories,' Billy said, with a sudden smile. 'My mammy... she telled me them sometimes when I was in bed and couldn't go to sleep.'

Will nodded. 'Well, Billy, sometimes people are good at remembering stories,' he said, 'or even at making them up. But most people are not. So they are written down in books, and that means that they're not forgotten, and everyone can go and read them there – provided, of course, they know how to read.' Will looked at the child. 'And... I'm going to teach you to read, Billy. So that when you have learned, you will be able to read stories for yourself, and become a clever boy – because there are lots and lots of important things written down in books. But I tell you, it will be difficult at first, for you will have to remember all sorts of things – like the letters – that seem... well, not very exciting at first, but when they are all connected together in special ways, they make words. And lots of words together make a story.' Will was rather proud of this explanation he had devised on the spur of the moment.

'I like stories', the boy repeated. 'But why can't *you* tell me stories, like my mammy did? My mammy...' The suddenly distraught child sought to pull free.

'No... no... Billy, she needs to.... rest, now. Anyhow, here we are, at our tent. Shall we go in?' And Will pulled back the flap.

XXXIII

'Ah, there you both are!' Thomas exclaimed, as they entered. 'Schoolmaster and pupil. You're a lucky boy, Billy, to be sure. If you work hard and learn to read, it'll be like… having lots and lots of windows to look through to discover all sorts of new and exciting things about the world.'

He patted the boy on the head, then turned to Will. 'I shall see you later, Will… maybe for a bite of supper with this wee fellow here? As you know, I have… things to do elsewhere, right now.'

And so saying, away he went to bury the boy's mother.

'Nunc et in hora mortis nostris. Amen.' And thus, following a brief, reflective pause in which some of those present (though not Thomas Sheehan himself) fancied they heard whispers of heavenly death, the priest brought to a close the short, sad chapter of Mary Tawbridge's earthly life.

Dr Ballow replaced his hat, glanced at Thomas, who was just then distracted, exchanging words with one of the ticket-of-leave men, and so set off alone in the direction of the tents. He had gone but a few steps, however, when the priest fell in with him.

'Dr Ballow, a word, if you please; it concerns those two back there.'

And Ballow heard of the priest's earlier encounter with Callaghan and Stevens and the young girl and of the strong suspicions it had aroused in him; of Stevens' intimidating response to his interrogation of the girl; and finally, the ploy he had then agreed with Will.

'The fact is,' Thomas concluded, 'there is no real authority here to enforce the law, much less interfere in situations such as this in which one strongly suspects a serious contravention is taking place. But… would I be right in thinking that, as far as those two are concerned, it would be you who made a report on their conduct here… to the parole board… or whatever Authority it is they are answerable to?'

Ballow shook his head. 'If it is so, no one has mentioned it to me. And frankly, I would doubt it, for my dealings with the law extend only as far as medical matters dictate.'

'Ah! Then what is to be done?'

'Things are all awry. As you probably know,' Ballow explained, 'we had thought that Mr Weatherall, the Government Immigration Agent, and two of the constables attached to him, would accompany us when we returned here from Brisbane, but by the time we arrived on the mainland, he had already departed for Sydney, apparently precisely to clarify the extent and nature of his authority with regard to Stradbroke and the peculiar conditions it necessarily encompasses as a place of quarantine… which leaves *us* in a limbo.' He shrugged, helplessly. 'He had left orders that no constables were to be deployed here in his absence, since they would have no clear idea of what their duties or their powers were.'

Thomas remained silent for a moment, as if not accepting this. 'Then we must be inventive,' he said, as they strolled along the already well-beaten path just behind the foreshore. 'Well, no one here, doctor, other than ourselves, can be aware of the true state of affairs. And they all fear the law, even if many of them do not respect it. Indeed, many here have had cause to feel it keenly and, as a consequence, have fled half-way across the world to escape its further ministrations… That habit of fear, though, is deeply ingrained and…' Thomas exhaled audibly and placed a hand on the doctor's arm. 'And therefore, reluctant though I am to do so, I think we must feed that fear, wherever the necessity arises – wouldn't you agree? Not just in this particular instance, with the girl, but also with the rebelliousness of that hard core of discontent among the menfolk – not forgetting the possible perpetrators of a heinous crime on the voyage out…'

'What, then, do you propose?' Ballow inquired, wondering where the priest's words were leading.

'In this moment, little more than what Will and I are proposing – that he approach the girl, and Stevens, using his policeman's "authority" *only* if that proves necessary… And that we all keep our eye on her and, indeed, on Callaghan and Stevens – as far as our different comings and goings allow. This should not prove too difficult. And though we have no powers to prevent people leaving the camp, I think we do need to know where those particular people go, whom they associate with, and what else they get up to…'

Ballow nodded his agreement.

'Obviously,' the priest went on, 'we want to avoid any sort of confrontation. But that doesn't prevent us from collecting evidence that will… might… become useful once some kind of normality returns – hopefully speedily, in the shape of Mr Weatherall and whatever legitimate force he can muster.' He stopped, turned, and faced the doctor squarely.

'Certainly, we should try and avoid confrontation,' Ballow answered, 'and trust Mr Weatherall will not long delay his return from Sydney. The earliest we can hope to see him here, I would guess, would be in something approaching three weeks, and a lot can happen in that time. But yes, I think we must keep the situation under review, and… maybe even think of some further step, in case these measures you are suggesting prove insufficient.'

Thomas made no comment, for he and the doctor were obviously in substantial agreement. The two men walked on, the hospital tent now in view, each absorbed in his own thoughts.

Inside the tent, an anxious Dr Mallon sat beside Dr Mitchell, watching the sick man's laboured breathing.

Mallon looked up as they came in. 'It may be my imagination… but the doctor's breathing seems somewhat worse than it was only a few hours ago.'

Ballow advanced towards his sick colleague's bed and took out his stethoscope, placing it against the patient's chest, then, with Mallon's help in turning him, against his back. 'Yes, I fear you are right,' he concluded, 'and that augurs badly for him, poor man.'

Mallon nodded but said nothing more.

Ballow pursed his lips. 'But are you all right yourself, Patrick? You look very red about your neck and cheeks.'

'Yes... or maybe... I'm not sure, to tell you the truth. Certainly, I feel very tired, hot, a bit listless... I'd like to think that was owing to the little sleep I've had since arriving here, but I'm not certain it is the cause.' Mallon placed his hand against his brow. 'It's an odd feeling,' he said, slowly. And closing his eyes, he sank forward so that his forehead was resting on Mitchell's bed.

Thomas glanced quickly across at Ballow and received the answer he had expected and feared.

Ballow walked over to where Mallon sat and put his hands on both his shoulders: 'I think you are just over-tired; you must get some rest, Patrick. Maybe you should climb into the bed here – it's newly made up – and shut your eyes for an hour or two. We can manage without you... for a while, anyway.'

Dr Mallon rose to his feet, a little unsteadily, but in trying to remove his outer clothing pitched sideways against the bed that had lately seen the death of Mary Tawbridge.

Both men leapt to his aid, and then helped him undress, but this sudden show of weakness made Thomas realise that a second doctor had almost certainly fallen victim to the pestilence. 'Poor, unfortunate soul,' he murmured.

Once Mallon was safely in bed, Ballow went off to call the matron, whom he found in her tent preparing a hasty meal before returning to her duties.

Oddly, in that moment, he realised for the first time, how young she was to be carrying such responsibilities. He smiled and insisted that she eat before coming to her vigil, though she was more than ready to abandon her food when she heard that the young doctor had also probably succumbed to the fever.

'It is a bad business! Indeed it is,' she said. 'What we need is more help, not less, and now this comes upon us. Whatever are we to do?'

'We must go on as best we can, the two of us, with whatever help Father Thomas can give us. I shall get a message to the hospital in Brisbane when the *Aurora* returns, appealing for more volunteers, but alas! I cannot insist that anyone puts his life in danger by coming here. Well, take your victuals in peace, Miss Labone, then come and relieve me so I can go over to the huts to see how things are turning out there.' Then his curiosity got the better of him. 'How did you come to be a ship's matron, so young, that is? It is most unusual.'

'Indeed it is,' she replied. 'But my dear mother died on the way out here, of the pestilence... We were coming here to settle.'

'Oh, I'm sorry... What a sadness for you...'

'Yes. It is. Mamma... she had been to Brisbane once before and it had taken her fancy – mine too, listening to her accounts of it. But it was not to be. Not for her...' She began to cut into the salted beef on her plate. 'She was the indentured matron on board, you see, having plied that trade ever since my father passed away. I was just nine then; he was a ship's surgeon, and she'd often assisted him...'

Miss Labone put down her knife and fork. 'I simply fell into her place, that's all,' she said, quietly. 'Poor George – Dr Mitchell, that is – he couldn't possibly have managed alone... although there was one kind passenger, Wilf, who helped a great deal, regardless of the dangers; Mrs Kemp too: she was unstinting, until the captain...' She shrugged. 'I'd learned my mother's skills almost incidentally, from an early age, so it was the only thing to do in the circumstances. Carry on.'

The doctor nodded: 'You have been... are... invaluable.' He turned then and left, just a moment too soon to note her blushes.

When he re-entered the hospital tent, Thomas was still sitting beside Dr Mallon, and said he would stay there until the matron came, if the doctor needed to attend to matters elsewhere.

'When I come back,' Ballow declared, 'I shall examine Mallon; though from the way he looks now, I rather fear the worst.'

He set out at a measured pace, glad of the cool evening air. He knew there was little he or anyone could do to help the young doctor: his illness must take its course. But the other business to which Thomas had alerted him was a different matter, even though, in the strictest terms, it should hardly have concerned him at all.

An idealist, with a strong belief in the forward march of science and its patient, systematic analyses of facts and the understanding they released, Ballow detested the makeshift, floundering, moment-by-moment responses he was obliged to make to questions of which he had but little grasp, which circumstance had thrust upon him. These failures, over which he now presided, had their roots in a whole series of missed opportunities, of misplaced priorities, of greed over reason, back in Brisbane. Perhaps if he had been more forceful in his dealings with his fellow townsmen, had insisted rather than deferring to other seeming priorities, they would now all have been better prepared to face the crisis that had come so suddenly upon them. Perhaps.

The trouble was – and he was all too aware of it – he was an educated man, with a clear vision of what their fledgling society could be, isolated among many who were brasher, more outspoken, without wider vision or ideals, intent only upon exploiting opportunity to get rich quickly and establish themselves as important, envied men, whose hands were ever upon the levers of power. Thus, the Chamber of Commerce had taken precedence over the hospital, as had the two banks, the law courts and the town gaol. He groaned at the folly of it. Even in Brisbane only the first stage of the hospital plan had been completed, and was by now well behind schedule, whilst here on Stradbroke, in spite of a project first mooted three years ago, nothing had been done until the very last minute to begin to realise it. There were those, sitting in the Council, who had even openly opposed the construction of a school there and the search for a schoolmaster, and certainly not out of any respect for quasi-Rousseauian notions about the preservation of innocence!

Truth was Brisbane needed more learned, professional people. And yet all it was like to receive by way of immigration was well represented by these unfortunate passengers from the *Emigrant*. Tradesmen, farmers, the odd builder or carpenter or plumber, but in the main people who brought no skills at all, agricultural or city labourers who could neither read nor write. Often, they seemed little better than the convicts who, until lately, had regularly been dumped in these colonies by a Mother Country anxious to rid itself of its own feared, troublesome underclass.

Ballow crossed the clearing, cutting through the rows of tents, scenting that peculiar damp sweetness the forest exhaled at dusk. And he knew in his heart of hearts he wanted to be free of it all – of other men's follies and his own feeble complicity in them.

Many coming here dreamed of a new life in a new unsullied land yet for the most part it was they, by their very natures and condition, who would vaporise the dream. It was already happening – indeed, in Sydney, had already happened some time ago, and it was that fact alone that had prompted him to move up to Brisbane, in the hope that the new colony might somehow have enough prescience to avoid the errors of the old. But, he acknowledged, he had been here long enough to recognise that his desire for a new kind of community, which was conscious of its own self-perfecting aspirations, seemed as far from realisation here as it had in the capital. This enforced levelling that Britain somehow foisted upon them was a far cry from his own notions of a new, open society. The levelling was ever downward, so that even this newest colonial venture would end up losing its way in the same shabby old cul-de-sacs, a penal colony yet, in all but name. Yes, he thought, already this new State totters.

Maybe, when all of this misery on Stradbroke was over it might be time to think of moving on again, so as to keep ahead always of the death of aspiration. Yet, if mankind itself were the world's real epidemic... where was there to go?

The silence in the main hut and a cursory inspection of its four inhabitants, three of whom were far gone in fevered sleep, offered the prospect of further respite, however brief. The doctor took out his kerchief and mopped his brow, sitting down on the steps outside.

It was all but dark now and he welcomed the refuge this provided.

If, in his student days back in Edinburgh anyone had told him that in a little more than twenty years' time he would find himself in such a place as this, fighting for the lives of a group of people whom chance had thrown together and with whom he felt few affinities, and in circumstances that would negate almost all he had ever learned there, would he have wished to go on with his studies to follow his desired profession?

In truth, he suspected he would not.

He could not escape the feeling that all his lifetime's best endeavour was rapidly running to waste, in this hell hole, for with fifteen burials recorded since the ship's arrival he had proved no more useful than the most illiterate man among them.

New South Wales had been his positive choice, but ever since his arrival in Sydney, what, seventeen… eighteen years ago now, it had seemed to impose ever-narrowing, always negative options upon him, hustling him further and further northwards in that moment, wherever he happened to be, when he became aware that the plagues of the old world had once again taken root, become endemic. What use would he be to anyone, he mused – himself included – if he finally stepped off the edge, out into the wilderness?

He leant his head back against the door jamb, musing that what had started out as a pioneering mission for scientific progress – and the inevitably better world it guaranteed – had soon degenerated into a seemingly endless struggle for adequate funds, adequate facilities, the strength, the will even to convince his fellow men of what to him was always so blindingly obvious. But few of them would be convinced, too few anywhere to make any noticeable difference. Short-term gains, too little trust in their fellows, and an insatiable rapaciousness characterised the bulk of humanity.

The raw material had been all wrong, of course, the great majority morally and spiritually alienated even before they had been compelled to quit their native shores, their only stock being poverty, ignorance, guilt, and resentment. His own overlong persistence had ignored these realities, founded as it was on an unshakeable faith in progress, sirened along by the pristine beauties of this vast, empty land, those beauties he experienced whenever he took horse and, for a little while, rode out alone. How childish it all seemed now. The real world was all of this squalor and madness, prelude to the long fall into meaningless oblivion.

A scream, followed immediately by a hurried whimpering, coming from inside the hut, tore him out of his hopeless reverie. He rose, wiping his hand across his brow, and stepped back into the other darkness.

XXXIV

Billy had shown a startling aptitude, a commendable eagerness, for what Will had tried to impart, in his amateurish way. Both, he felt, had derived some satisfaction from their efforts. But now the little boy was sleeping, in the third bed that had briefly belonged to Dr Mitchell but which he had occupied only once, as far as Will could remember, before the fever had struck him down.

Before he had sunk into sleep, Billy had come back to the question of what was to happen to his mammy if she was not to be put in the sea. They couldn't leave her there in the hospital tent for everybody to see, could they? Will had tried to reassure him that a solution would be found and that they would talk about it again in the morning.

They had read only a couple of paragraphs, at first mainly to get the boy to recognise the different sounds certain letters represented, as well as a few simple words. The choice of story had been entirely arbitrary, Will being unacquainted with the book's contents. He had opened it at random and so lighted on the tale of 'The Snow Queen'. Its opening lines were full of three- and four-letter words and these, he had reasoned, would be more easily memorised.

Not surprisingly, Billy had almost at once been taken over by the story itself, his face lighting up at the notion of a magician's mirror that could make whatever was good and beautiful shrink almost to nothing, while making whatever was ugly and useless appear ten times bigger than before. He continually interrupted the lesson to ask: 'and what happens next?' – so much so that Will, in part embarrassed by his own ignorance, in part irritated at the child's divided attention, had promised to read him the story on the following day, on condition that the questions stopped there and then, and Billy paid full attention to the letters and the words. The boy eagerly nodded his assent, though that didn't quite put a stop to his questioning. Nevertheless, Will judged, the lesson had in the end yielded some profit and seemed to augur well for the future.

Yet reading stories was decidedly not what he had seen himself embarking on, especially children's stories, for it had been Alice who read to Lilian, as she had read to her pupils during her teacher-training days.

He picked up the book again, now, and started to read 'The Snow Queen' from the beginning. He soon realised that the 'fairy tale' seemed also to be telling another story beyond itself, and he frowned. It appeared to be telling him that a purely mechanical way of thinking – which was being passed off as 'natural', encompassing all realities – was enough to stifle any instinctive response to the world around. Or was this just his imagination...? Reading too much into it? Anyway, it had set him thinking again: it had been such elaborate systems, whose values one was never allowed to question, which had forced him to seek refuge on this far side of the world, dragging his unhappiness and regrets behind him. He glanced across at the sleeping child, and smiled again, wistfully.

And now here was a story about a girl who was determined to force a new beginning on another child, Kay, who had lost the right way because of the distorting mirror's enchantments. This girl, Gerda, had a truer, instinctive vision of the happiness the world might afford, of life's best purposes. And out of love that would not even contemplate rejection, she persisted – in spite of the huge obstacles she encountered – until her mission was fulfilled. Hm! Well, an adult might see that. But a child?

Will had had little experience of such writing, even as a child, it being (according to his stern father) the domain of well-to-do ladies and their pampered offspring. So he remained sceptical, even a little impatient with it. He leaned back and closed his eyes.

But almost immediately, he was distracted by Thomas ducking into the tent.

'Thomas,' he almost growled, sitting up again. And then, in a hoarse kind of whisper: 'You're an educated man, and I'd be mightily grateful if you could help me sort something out...' And he waved the book in front of the priest's face.

'Oh, that,' said the other, imitating the whisper. 'And how did the boy make out, then?'

'Fine... fine. No, it's me that's having the difficulties.'

'You? How do you mean?' Thomas threw his head back and chuckled softly.

'Shhh...' Will glanced in Billy's direction. 'Well, to start with... can a fairy story be more than just a story... for children, I mean? And if not, can it have a... well, a serious meaning... for grown-ups?'

Thomas stared at him. 'Are you serious, Will...?'

'Well, I wouldn't be wasting your time if I wasn't,' he responded gruffly, conscious of a mounting embarrassment.

'Well, why shouldn't it? Agh! Give it here!' Thomas commanded. He proceeded to scan two or three pages before handing the book back to Will. 'So, now, I take it to mean something like this...' – and in a few words he confirmed more or less what Will had surmised.

'So, it is a means for conveying... what? Morals? Common sense? I don't know – how would you put it?' Will was aware that he was, not least, seeking to arm himself against Billy's inevitable, searching broadsides.

'Yes, those things and more besides. That's one of literature's greatest gifts, I would say; the entertainment is a bonus, a kind of... packaging; at least, with the romances and poems that are worth giving time to.'

'Well I'll be damned... And there was me thinking that if you wanted to read something serious... I'd always avoided this other stuff, and to tell you the truth, it never came my way as a child. My father saw to that!'

Thomas shook his head in disbelief and began to laugh again, then checked himself, remembering the sleeping child. 'Oh, Will,

I'm sure you're not in the minority in thinking that way. Maybe the greatest wisdom has always come through such books. But...' Yet he shrugged his shoulders, suppressing the polemic rising within him.

Will, however, was leafing, back and forth, through the book, seeking further confirmation of this sudden revelation, in other stories. But soon he began to yawn, and his heavy eyelids defied, then defeated, the newly awakened curiosity that had at first impelled him. He was on the point of entering sleep when he remembered he had failed – for understandable reasons – to apprise either Thomas or Ballow of the success of his excursion to Brown Lake.

Then there was still the hanging question of Thomas's robes...

He is standing in a river and a strange, impenetrable mist has come down and the blinding snow keeps on falling. The water is already above his knees, while the snow drives into his eyes and mouth and ears. He does not know where to make his next move, for he cannot tell which is the way forward, or which the way back. He tries to see which way the river is flowing but it is impossible to tell, for perversely it swirls and eddies round and round him. Either he must stand and wait for sight to return or take a step which, in order that it shall not lose its meaning – its rejection of the other choice, that is – must needs be followed by another and another, until he reaches dry land. Or drowns.

Contemplating this problem, he realises that in this moment (which is all time) he has no other being outside this one dilemma – neither the past, which he can no longer see, nor any intended future, which he can no longer see, nor the river's future nor the river's past. He has lost all sense and motive of action. The river is dammed within him, no longer mingling with that which is all about him; he is but is no longer; suspended between then and after, there and yonder, in an eternal now.

In this time, which is no time, nothing he has ever known can help him. To take one step would be to step outside reason into fear; reason tells him to stand still and not enter the fear which is all around him – yet if he follows the counsel of reason, what is his reason if he stands there forever?

Then suddenly he senses he is wrong; the river he supposed pent-up within him, his only being, is fast dissolving into the shrouding, the blinding, and the empty waters. Forever. Forever. And forever. But he is wrong again. With unseen cause and fathomless motive the unending is suddenly ended.

The mist eddies and tears, the snowfall weakens; rents, like jagged windows, are opening all about him and he peers through them into pallid sunlight. On the one hand, a sleigh moving slowly away from the river into a white wasteland, going away backward, when his instinct and his desire tell him it should be approaching, and he shouts and waves frantically, through the distorting, ever-fraying window, but no one looks back; and on the other hand, a curious, almost familiar archway, decked with roses filled with snow, through which he sees another identical archway, also covered in snow-filled roses, then another and another until they merge into mist and snow falling steadily upon distant trees.

And Alice is shaking him gently. 'Will. Will. You cried out in your sleep!' Yet even as he rouses, her face is shading away into that of Thomas…

'Several times, you cried out, distressed about something or other. I had not yet closed my eyes, fortunately… and I couldn't leave you to suffer there any longer… wherever it was…' The priest returned to his own bed and snuffed out the candle. 'Are you all right, Will? All right, now?' he whispered into the dark.

Will mumbled that he was. Yet his eyes were wet. The dream sleigh had been bearing her away, and the child; and with them was his…

He turned over on his side, but sleep would not claim him again, not fully, not yet. It was only a dream, he told himself, yet he was losing… losing what? His own sustaining dream of reconciliation? He trembled, unable to shake off the sense of foreboding it had forced upon him. He, too, a victim of the splintered mirror, he thought bitterly. 'Oh, Alice! Alice!' he cried silently, into the darkness.

XXXV

A SUITABLE BATHING PLACE HAS NOW BEEN LOCATED AT BROWN LAKE, ABOUT 25 MINUTES' PLEASANT WALK FROM THE ENCAMPMENT.

AN ESCORTED BATHING EXPEDITION FOR FEMALES, AND THEIR CHILDREN, FROM SECTIONS 1 AND 2 OF THE CAMP, HAS BEEN ORGANISED FOR TOMORROW AFTERNOON AT TWO O'CLOCK PROMPT. MEET FOR ROLL CALL AT THE SOUTHERN GATE.

ONLY THOSE WOMEN WITH MORE PRESSING DUTIES WILL BE EXEMPTED, BUT ALL MUST REPORT TO HAVE THEIR REASONS CONSIDERED.

THANK YOU.

DR DAVID BALLOW

Ballow himself was uneasy, had been from the start, about the 'military' tone of the notice. Almost as soon as the message was posted, at four different locations, a noticeable tension filled the air and by noon the situation was turning sour.

As he left the store huts to begin his rounds of the sick, he saw that a seemingly spontaneous meeting of several of the more outspoken men was taking place, not far from the huts. Passing the clearly disgruntled men (who were even then being joined by some of the women), he changed direction, and headed for the hospital tent, where he found Thomas talking to the still feverish, though clearly conscious Mallon.

'Oh, Patrick... This is indeed a very welcome sight!' Ballow's face beamed in pleasure. But then it was quickly transformed into something darker as he turned his attention to the priest. 'I think trouble is brewing, Father Sheehan,' he said, 'doubtless as a reaction to the notices about tomorrow's bathing expedition...' He sat down heavily on one of the upright chairs. 'There's a growing crowd of people over by the huts, and their words were both loud and heated as I came by just now. One or two jeered openly as I passed.'

Thomas grimaced. 'Trouble... you say? Well, maybe best to let them hammer it out among themselves rather than try and argue them into submission right now. To be sure, sooner or later, they'll simmer down, and someone will come and tell us what they've decided. It'll surely be easier to make whoever it is see sense than try and win over a whole crowd, wouldn't you say?'

Ballow signalled his agreement. 'I certainly wouldn't like to take the risk of exposing ourselves to that lot in their present mood. Let's just hope there are some among them who can calm them down a bit.'

Seeing that Mallon was stirring, he rose and went over to him, sitting down on the end of the bed. 'How are you feeling, Patrick? I must say, although you don't look at all well, it is good you are conscious and talking. Last night's delirium seemed all too familiar... I confess, you had me worried...'

Mallon nodded, then smiled grimly. 'I'm not too sure now it is the fever, or if it is... maybe a milder form of it than we have seen here hitherto – if such a thing is possible. He pulled himself a little higher. It could be the Dengue. Though it's hardly the right season for that. I feel pretty wretched but not so bad as to think I shall sink any further.'

'That's something anyway... But we must wait and see,' his superior said quietly. 'Certainly, you have not followed the downhill course of poor Dr Mitchell here.' He tip-toed over for a brief glance at the doctor, far gone in sleep. 'I wonder how much longer he can last in this comatose state. If only we could get him to take some food, give him some strength. I think the fluid we are managing to get into him is hardly sufficient. If he doesn't emerge from the coma soon then he'll certainly die of starvation and de-hydration, if other features of the pestilence don't claim him first.'

Thomas, who had been waiting for an opportunity to speak, cut in on their conversation: 'Hm. Don't you think, Dr Ballow, we should perhaps have Mr Crosby here with us, I mean... in case we are called to account for our decision about the bathing expedition? After all, he's the only one among us who has actually been to Brown Lake, and it's more than likely that anyone sent from the meeting will have questions to ask about it, and...'

'Yes, indeed, good idea. Do you happen to know where he might be at this moment?'

'Yes. I think I do.' Thomas smiled. 'He's teaching young Billy Tawbridge his letters, over in our tent. I'll away and fetch him – and check on the mood and the progress of the palaver, en route, though not from too close quarters!' He rose and left the tent.

Although his route led diagonally away from the gathering, Thomas could see it was still in session and that many men, and womenfolk, were now in attendance. Occasionally, voices were raised, and it appeared that some disagreement was being expressed, back and forth.

There were still quite a number of people going about their various chores, and other business, in the area he passed through – precisely those two sections of the camp immediately affected by the order – and he couldn't help but notice how they melted away at his approach, either into their tents or off in some other direction, so that not one of them waited or turned to greet him. This fact, rather more than the meeting, whatever its eventual outcome, greatly disturbed him.

Of course, he was the main perpetrator of the bathing idea – and he would not have denied it – but the rift his sudden 'invisibility' implied augured badly for the future of the camp and its purposes, and these same people who now withheld their greeting would be the prime sufferers. Not that he saw his own role as being of much value or importance for the living, but that of the doctors was crucial, and if, as he surmised, the rift was along traditional, hardened, class lines then they too, perforce, would be regarded as complicit.

Dislocation and disintegration into total chaos, he thought, would rapidly follow and for sure, nothing good will come of it.

Thomas was all too familiar with the signs and workings of that apocalyptic process, born of desperation, as communities collapsed into accusations, hatreds, lawlessness, and savagery in the Irish countryside, so that no one could feel safe or even hope, anymore.

That he rejected the label undoubtedly fixed on him, and the fault lines that now apparently set him and the doctors apart from the rest, was of no practical use whatever. The true division, he knew well enough, lay between knowledge (however little he and the others possessed in the prevailing circumstances) and utter ignorance. The real problem was medical, not political. Yet, given the great disparity in numbers, coercion was not a viable option, even if he and the others had any stomach for it. Only reason, patience, and persuasion – words, of course – could help avert catastrophe. But how that was to be accomplished... well, as yet he was quite unsure.

Nearing the tent, he heard Will's voice, and stopped to listen.

'*The Snow Queen... always sat in the centre of this lake; she used to say that she was sitting on the Mirror of Reason, and that hers was the best – indeed, the only one – in the world...*'

'*...Little Kay was quite blue with cold...*' But here, Will's voice faded, and Thomas stood still, straining to hear; then, to his pleasure it picked up again:

'*... was busied among the sharp icy fragments, laying and joining them together, in every possible way, just as people... what are known as Chinese Puzzles. Kay could form the most curious and complete...*'

Realising the story had some way yet to run, and given the more urgent matters at hand, Thomas pushed through the closed flap into the tent.

'My sincere apologies, Billy,' he began. 'But Will...' And he outlined the reason for his intrusion. He then turned to the boy.

'Agh, Billy, even though I too was enjoying the story as I stood listening outside, so I did, Mr Crosby and I must try and explain some important things to a lot of unhappy, angry people who are – he glanced at Will – just about to come and find us. But, Billy, I'm sure your storyteller will come back as soon as he can and finish the reading; is that not so, Mr Crosby? And, what's more, I'd like to be here when he does, for it seemed to me it was a very grand... a very gripping sort of story.'

'Indeed it is...' Will stood up and stretched. 'And I'm learning from it, with every line I read...' He winked at the priest.

Billy, for his part, only nodded and looked hungrily down at the page. Just as the two men were leaving, he asked: 'What is a "mirror of reason", Mr Crosby?'

Will, caught off-guard, for his mind had already leapt to the present threat at which Thomas had intimated, looked hopefully at Thomas. 'I'm not really sure – but maybe Father Thomas can help you.'

Thomas clicked his tongue in mock indignation. 'Thank you very much, Mr Crosby!' He stepped back inside the tent and looked at Billy. 'The "Mirror of Reason"? Well now, it is surely anything that tells you honestly how things really are. It doesn't have to be a real mirror, of course. It can be anything that... reflects the true nature of things.' Yet even as he finished speaking, he realised his explanation was likely to be far above the little boy's head.

The child's look told him he was not mistaken. 'Anyways, Billy, you... just be looking at the grand pictures, there, and I'll think some more about it... and then try and explain it better.' And, without risking further questions from Billy, he slipped outside, and the two men fled.

XXXVI

As they neared the hospital tent, they could hear two male and one, strident, female voices inveighing against poor Dr Ballow, who was quite unable to get a word in edgewise as they spelt out the 'demands' of their fellows.

'... and all them what is showin' no sign of having the pestilence demand that they be taken to Brisbane as soon as the *Aurora* comes back 'ere...' a voice was saying. 'There's no sense or justice in them having to wait here until they too are struck down by the disease.'

'...And then again, all this unnecessary business about going bathing,' the woman's voice piped up, 'it just ain't natural. It don't have nothing to do with the disease. It's just a way of making us suffer more indignities, just another way of showing us poor folk who the bosses are...' And she, in her turn, was interrupted by the younger of the two male delegates.

'Just like what they do in the army, making poor soldiers march up and down for hours on end then having them go off and polish buttons and boots they only polished the day afore and the day afore that...'

Thomas, having paused a moment, now strode in. 'Well, my son, I think you may well be right about the way they do things in the army...'

'Not "may," Father Sheehan, I assure you – for I have suffered it all too often myself!' Will interjected, making his presence felt. 'Our friend here is quite right. It is a way of making soldiers toe the officers' line. And it has to be said that without this... and other kinds of discipline… it's doubtful soldiers could function efficiently as a fighting unit when the need arose… Still…' And he shrugged, smiling at the young man.

The man himself looked bewildered. 'Are you saying, Sergeant Crosby, that… that you're agreeing with me?'

'Indeed he is, my friend,' Thomas answered, before Will could give his answer. 'But he's also saying that what, at first glance, looks like oppression has another, much more important purpose, as important for every soldier as it is for the officers: that of turning a lot of individual men into an army, into a united, fighting force…'

The young man looked even more confused.

'But that's only partly relevant in this matter of the bathing,' Thomas declared, charging on. 'Although, like an army, I suppose, we should all be of one mind… and purpose. Now, tell me – he looked sternly at each of them in turn – who among you has had medical training?'

Each looked at the others, frowning, uncertain, before the first man spoke again, a note of truculence in his voice.

'None of us, as you well know! But… what's that got to do with anything?'

'Just this,' Thomas said emphatically. 'One of you said, just a moment or two ago, that bathing has nothing to do with the disease. And for all I know you could be right, because I don't have any medical knowledge either.' He paused. 'But I'll tell you this: when three doctors, whose learned opinions I respect, suggest to me that there is a strong likelihood that dirty hair, skin, clothes, living conditions… all have a connection with the spread of this killer disease, then I listen to them carefully. They are more likely to be right than just anyone, now… that's for sure! And then my own experience of this self-same disease, back in Ireland, also tells me they may well be right…'

'Well, if that is so,' sneered the woman, 'why have those two – and she nodded at Mitchell and Mallon – not been able to escape the fever, for all their fancy washing?'

Her companions nodded in shocked admiration of the point

made, while the obstreperous woman glared at Thomas, savouring her moment of glory, her arms akimbo.

'I'll tell you why it is, good lady,' Dr Mallon said suddenly, raising himself with some difficulty onto his elbow and surprising everyone. 'It's because we have been constantly in contact with the filth and squalor, which conditions on the cramped boat, but also now in our small, closely clustered living quarters, have imposed upon us all. No one is saying that bathing the body and the washing of clothes is a cure, but it may be a preventative measure. If the plague owes its existence and spread to bad air, then we must take steps to rid ourselves of that bad air. Surely, that is reasonable, is it not? It's only common sense, after all.' And he fell back upon his pillows, exhausted, though his eyes burned bright.

No one spoke for a moment or two, then Thomas took a step towards the petitioners. 'The only man among us... I can almost guarantee it... who will not be struck down by the disease, is Sergeant Crosby here.'

Will shuffles uncomfortably, as first Thomas's, then three more heads turn in his direction, as if he has suddenly become a prize exhibit.

'Remember how he chose not to remain below decks on the voyage out, living under a lifeboat instead?' the priest goes on. 'And how we all laughed at him, washing his bedding every week, forever stripped to the waist in all weathers, at it with his soap and water and comb. Remember all that? Well, I'd say he's had the last laugh, that I would. And unlike the doctors, he doesn't have to go into your crowded tents or touch you or your filthy clothes. And look at him! The picture of health itself.'

In spite of his embarrassment, Will can only admire his friend's acuity, his audacity, and most of all, his silken tongue.

The three delegates find themselves at a loss for words, each looking to the other to resume the statement of their cause, but none seems minded to speak.

Recovering somewhat, Will takes up the mantle. 'It's true, I think, though I may well be tempting Fate by saying so. One of the few useful things my too-many years in Her Majesty's Service taught me was that "cleanliness is indeed next to godliness". And it is a lesson that needs to be more widely learned still, among our fellow citizens, both here and back home.'

'Indeed, it does,' Dr Ballow declares roundly, pressing home their advantage. 'Why do you think it is that whenever an outbreak of any kind of pestilence strikes, anywhere in the world, it is, and always has been, the poor who are struck down in huge numbers?' And he looks challengingly at each delegate in turn. 'Dirt and too close proximity to their fellows are the reasons, I'm convinced of it, and so should you and your neighbours be. Eliminate the dirt and the proximity ceases to be a problem!'

It is clear that the resolve of the delegation is crumbling.

'Friends,' Father Thomas declares, his gaze fixed on the three shuffling tribunes, 'there is nothing more to be said on the matter, that I can think of. Perhaps, then – he holds up a silencing hand – it would be to everyone's advantage if we were to return with you now to the meeting that delegated you… to explain this to all those gathered there. What do you say to that?'

Oh, the nimbleness of Thomas's mind! The words… like magic… that never seemed to fail him.

After a moment or two's whispered discussion, the older man explains that while he has not agreed with everything, some things do make sense; the younger man even half-apologises for their initial rudeness; and even the woman nods her reluctant acquiescence. All of them nonplussed, battered by the salvo of words…

It is thus with some trepidation that six individuals, walking in two groups of three, approach the waiting crowd.

XXXVII

Their reception is nowhere near as hostile as Ballow had feared. Only in a few quarters is there jeering and shaking of fists.

The older male delegate – Harry Turnbull – takes the stand, slowly gaining confidence as he explains to the gathering that, following the conversations at the hospital tent, there are some further matters which all must now consider.

'These three men here – Turnbull's arm sweeps over the doctor, priest and sergeant – have come to explain. So will you listen now, all of you, so we can agree on the best course of action? For these are life and death matters…'

As he is speaking, three or four men, Will notes, push their way back through the crowd to walk away, making no secret of their anger and disgust.

Thomas, too, has noticed their departures, and touching Turnbull on the arm, he points to them and signals with his eyes that he should try and persuade them to stay.

'Hey! You might at least hear what is to be said, before you decide it is not worth the hearing,' Turnbull shouts after them, to general murmurs of agreement from among the crowd.

Two of the men turn round, and one comes back several paces.

'Huh! You, Turnbull, have betrayed us! These men have duped you, as the bosses always do! They plainly have you eating out of their hand – you should be ashamed of yourself!' And he spits vehemently.

Turnbull looks abashed. But then Thomas leaps up onto one of the three barrels that had been set there for the meeting's earlier speakers.

'There have been no betrayals, by God there have not!' he thunders, not quite checking his anger. 'And there are no bosses here, either, I'll have you know – if you are referring to the doctors, Mr Crosby and me! But in a crisis, such as the one we are all facing here, someone has to make decisions, do they not, about vital concerns that affect us all? Because unfortunately, you see,' he continues, calmly but forcefully, 'the settlement in Brisbane was not yet ready in its organisation or its knowledge to cope with the misfortune we have brought to its very doorstep. And its lack of experience has left us all sadly without proper, competent leadership…

'Won't you see? Come on! None of us three, or indeed the other two doctors who now lie gravely ill because of their dedication, had or have any ambition to control or oppress the rest of you. Yet because certain decisions were needed, well… we took them! Rightly or wrongly we took them! But we took them in conditions of dire necessity, for the good of us all. And that – he glares at the sneering speaker at the back of the crowd – also includes you. Common sense should tell you that unless things are organised, then anarchy will quickly follow, and that would augur badly for the weakest among us. Believe you me, just as soon as this wretched business is behind us, you will not hear of me again! To be sure you won't!' And, somewhat flushed in the face, Thomas steps down.

The men, although muttering under their breath, show no sign of leaving a second time, and Thomas, noting this, nods towards them in due acknowledgement.

Taking advantage of the ensuing lull, and wasting no time on preliminaries, Dr Ballow takes over.

'I accept that there are risks to all who are thus compelled to remain together,' he explains, 'and my duty is to seek to offset these risks. Our medical knowledge of the disease may be extremely limited, but we do know a lot about the circumstances in which it occurs – and flourishes. And it is this knowledge that urges us to beg you… yes, *beg* you… to conform with our request regarding cleanliness – the hygienic measures that are at the root of this present dispute. But this is for your good, and the good of those about you. It is a question of medical common sense and certainly not one of imposed authority.'

'You say that now, doctor,' Turnbull interposes, perhaps seeking to regain the credibility he senses he has lost among some of his fellows, 'but it was different when the bathing idea was first raised. All that business of making us sign our agreement, with threats of withholding our grub if we didn't… Was that not coercion… Was that not the voice of Authority?'

A buzz runs through the crowd, and the man smirks in satisfaction.

'That, Mr Turnbull, was… rather badly handled, I agree' Thomas responds, stepping forward, 'and to my shame I admit that I was the instigator of it. But in our defence, I must say two things. Firstly, Dr Mitchell – whose very sensible idea it was – had just collapsed; Dr Ballow was away in Brisbane; and – in desperation… yes, desperation – Mr Crosby and I felt, rightly or wrongly, that we had to take some measures to combat the menace all around us, to show you all that something positive could be done. Secondly, we knew there would be opposition, chiefly because people always resent change to their normal routines. And yet, this particular change seemed absolutely essential and needed to become habit itself, and quickly. Do you not see?' Thomas scanned the crowd. 'We were left, in that moment, without any medical authority to explain the principle to you, and, as I say, we were desperate. I apologise, truly I do, for the offence given. And I implore you all, in all good faith, to accept that what we are proposing is for the good of us all.'

'And will you be bathing, too, Father, seeing… like… it's *absolutely essential*…?' And the man smirks as a gale of jeering laughter starts up.

Thomas leaps up onto the barrel again and pulls up his cassock as far as his knees. Dangling a leg before their eyes, he announces:

'As you can see, neighbours, I already have… I already do. Every single day!'

After a snigger or two, a loud cheer greets the priest's audacity.

With a bow, Thomas lowers his cassock. And then, before Turnbull or anyone else can speak, he continues, changing both tone and pitch: 'There is one other thing which, in my view, makes the matter even more urgent, and it is this, my friends. Dr Mallon, who arrived only a few days ago to assist Dr Ballow, has now also fallen ill.' And he turns towards the three delegates, who offer their confirmation, with peremptory – and sad – nods.

There are many gasps from among the crowd. And for a moment or two, until the priest raises his hand to resume his speech, a further round of anxious murmuring ensues.

'My friends,' Thomas says eventually, 'we are uncertain whether he has succumbed to the pestilence or whether it is some other illness that shows similar symptoms; but whatever it is, it means that for the time being at least, Dr Ballow is working alone – except for our courageous young matron. In these desperate circumstances it is surely the duty of all of us to do, well, whatever we can to help them, and in helping them help ourselves.' And with this he steps down yet again from his rostrum.

He looks inquiringly at Will, then at Dr Ballow, but before either can react, two or three people begin to clap. And from these ragged beginnings a loud cheer breaks out, with prolonged applause.

'Well spoke, Father!'

'God bless you, Dr Ballow!'

'Hear, hear!'

Taking advantage of this unexpected change in mood, Dr Ballow quickly re-mounts the makeshift rostrum. And when the clamour abates, he thanks all present, then gives practical details about the following day's expedition to the lake. 'Bring whatever garments and bedding you have to wash. And something to carry them in. Oh, and you'll need towels too,' he reminds them. 'But we have soap a-plenty, and this we'll distribute before we all leave. Thank you all. That is enough for now.'

The crowd begins to disperse peaceably, people going in their different directions. Two or three make a point of coming to speak briefly with the doctor, so Will moves away slowly in the direction of their tent. 'Best see what young Billy is up to, if he's still there...' he says.

Thomas falls into step, but after a moment he lays a restraining hand on Wills' arm and points ahead of them. 'Look! That's her – the girl. And she seems to be in a mighty hurry, wherever she's going, wouldn't you say?'

Yet even as Thomas is speaking, a woman coming in the other direction accosts the girl, takes firm hold of her arm and begins shaking it roughly, clearly upbraiding her. Then she raises her free hand as if to administer a slap, but after waving it around, continues her onslaught.

As Thomas and Will draw nearer, the girl pulls away.

'I'm going, then...'

'Now, don't you be more than half an hour, or your supper'll be cold, mind you!'

'Course I won't, Mrs Parry...'

Exchanging a glance, the two men enter their tent.

Billy is not there, the book still where Will had left it. 'So where's he gone, then?' he murmurs, tying back the flap so they may observe the girl's direction. 'And... what was all that about? Do you think this might be an appropriate moment to confront her, Thomas – the girl?'

'Oh, Will, on what pretext? You can hardly do so without her giving you reason, I would say. So... perhaps not.'

'I was thinking of following her. You never know, she might lead me to a situation like that you found her in.' Will puts his head out of the tent. 'Damn it! I can't see her anywhere, now...'

'Well, she's only got half an hour before she has to be back – you heard that, I take it...? Then she can't get up to too much mischief, can she? No, let it be for now, Will. But it's odd, don't you think? When I asked the girl who was responsible for her she said "no one." Yet we've just seen her with that woman... Mrs Parry, wasn't it? Maybe we should try and talk to her, first, and find out what the relationship is between them. The girl definitely said she was on her own...'

'Well, now we know who she is I'll watch out for opportunities... like the one we've just passed over.'

Will sits down on his bed but then springs up again, immediately. 'Just now, though, we'd better look for Billy.'

'To be sure we should! But where…?'

'The hospital tent, I imagine. He was asking again about his mammy, what was going to happen to her. I think we should tell him how things are…'

'Well, I'll go, and I'll talk to him.' He casts a smile in Will's direction. 'I'd best be getting back there myself… after what I told all those people.'

XXXVIII

These days it was a rare event if Will found himself alone, and there were times he truly craved solitude. He immediately began rummaging in his trunk and soon located what he had set his heart on: his pipe, tinder, and tobacco boxes; he could not remember the last time he had smoked.

Slowly and methodically he loaded the pipe, set a light to it when it was ready, and sat down on his bed to enjoy it. Then, bethinking himself, he got to his feet again and went to the door of the tent. It was hardly likely he would be left alone there for long, maybe not long enough to smoke it to the end. He stepped outside, looked around, then wandered off along the path that led out of the encampment then northwards, along the Amity track.

Once he was away from the camp, and unlikely to encounter anyone, he relaxed a little, and before he had gone a hundred paces settled down with his back against the bole of a giant of a tree, a Moreton Bay Fig, he seemed to remember Ridley calling them.

He smoked for several minutes, enraptured almost by the unaccustomed aroma of the tobacco, and the stillness, the space. And then, perhaps as he'd known they would, his thoughts turned to home, to Alice, and his little daughter.

A walk they'd once taken, indeed more than once, was through the woods at Tithe Barn, he smoking at first, as now. They were heading, though idly and contentedly, for a particular point from which they could look down on the sea, to show Lilian, who was on his shoulders, the minute fishing smacks or colliers as they moved up and down the Firth. Little did he know then, in that interlude in his life, which was all-too-brief, that those simple pleasures and their attendant feelings of completeness were soon to become the distinct object of an endless longing, and regret…

What would they be doing now, and where, and how was their life without him? Did he hope – selfishly – that it would be as his own, tinged ever with sadness, a sense of irremediable loss, a sense of having already lived the best there was to live?

And yet, he also feared it might be so.

But… someone was coming along the path, singing jauntily. As the voice drew nearer Will recognised the song as a bawdy barrack-room ballad he had known years before, one that left nothing much to the imagination. And suddenly, standing there before him, was the odious Stevens, grinning from ear to ear.

'Ah, Sergeant Crosby, so I find you taking your ease and indulging in solitary pleasures. To be sure, there is nothing like a nice pipeful of baccy for putting a man to rights… well, unless, of course, he has a yearning for other sorts of pleasures…'

Will regarded the man intently, from behind a cloud of upwardly drifting smoke, conscious not only of his resentment at being thus accosted in an intensely private moment, but beyond that, of his real loathing for the man. He would give him short shrift and send him on his way.

'If you would *please*…' he began, curtly.

'…And if it *is* other pleasures you have a mind for, then I'm your man, Mr Crosby.'

'Now then…' Will stood up, annoyed at the man's rude insistence, fully inclined to strike him across his smirking face.

'…There's not much in the way of opportunity, given the plight we're in here. But, as I say, I could fix you up – at the right price, of course.'

Stevens smiled benignly, like a parson opening a church bazaar, and Will froze, remembering the girl, for it was doubtless she who was being offered him right now…

'I just thought I'd mention it, for there's little to relieve a man's sense of boredom, or his manly needs, in this godforsaken place.'

...And if to him then why not also to others?

Restraining himself, however, Will feigned interest, and probed further. 'So... can you offer us a choice, Mr Stevens, or do you have, well, just the one filly in your stable?'

'Ah sir, these is hard times, so they are. For the moment, it's just the one, but I'm hopeful soon to be able to widen the choice. Not everyone who sailed on *The Emigrant* was a lady... that's for sure, and some will be looking to resume their old trade again, once they get to Brisbane, so – Stevens winked, grotesquely – a little practice here, in the meantime, wouldn't come amiss. And I'm... well, I'm working on it. Oh, but you'd be far from disappointed, even now, Mr Crosby sir, I can vouch for that. A filly that bucks at no fences...' He gestured crudely and guffawed out loud, spittle glistening on his unshaven chin.

Driven now by his overwhelming urge to smash the man's face, Will sprang forward. Stevens, unsure what his intentions were, took a step back. And there was a moment in which Will had the deep satisfaction of seeing real fear sweep over the pimp's face. Then he dispersed the tension as quickly as his sudden movement had occasioned it.

'Look, Mr Stevens, my pipe has gone out... before its time, and that... negates all the pleasures one previously had from it. Sufficient unto the day, eh, Mr Stevens!' And he pushed past the man, taking the spent pipe from his mouth, tapping it against the tree as he passed.

'She's in great demand, sir,' Stevens shouted after Will's retreating figure, clearly as bewildered as he was meant to be. 'So the sooner you make your bid the sooner...'

Neither slowing nor turning, Will merely raised his pipe in a vague gesture, which could have signified anything.

Will knew he had acted rightly. The simmering, if tightly controlled anger he had felt in Stevens' presence was real enough. Even so, as he headed off without any particular destination in mind, he found himself wondering about his own motives and, indeed, his own most private feelings and – as Stevens had put it – 'yearnings'; for without doubt he had them, and constantly. He grimaced. What would be his true response, he wondered, if Stevens were one of these days to offer him someone older, even if only by a few years, than the child Lizzie?

In all the long journey out, and now here too, he had thought of his own sexual deprivation as just one more burden, and by no means the greatest, for in that respect the privacy his lifeboat sanctuary afforded had enabled him to shed it whenever it became unbearable. And he could dream of Alice, feeling closer to her than at any other times since they had last been together in reality. But here, on Stradbroke, it was a different story, with everyone being compelled by circumstance to live in such close proximity with everyone else. Privacy was well-nigh impossible and thus, he wondered, had his apparently flippant inquiry about 'choice' been two-edged? Probing the true meaning of Stevens' offer to confirm his surmise about the girl – yes, for sure – but perhaps with a further element of…what? Curiosity… stemming precisely from his 'yearnings'? Hope, perhaps, that something a mite less distasteful than procuring a child was possible should he choose to avail himself of it?

For the moment Will did not need to insist on any response from his innermost self, for Stevens had made it clear that such an option did not presently exist. Yet he more than half-feared what that response might be; and the doubt was sufficient in itself to set him pondering his own likely hypocrisy in this matter and thus, more importantly, his assumed right to sit in judgement on Stevens. After all, as a soldier, he had at various times been no stranger to the brothel… And thus, was he the right person to don the shining armour, to take up the sword in young Lizzie's defence? to rescue her from the prostitution into which she had been lured? How could he be?

Will's life, hitherto, had been no preparation for such moral heroism and, recognising the tenuous nature of his own proclivities in this matter, he now doubted his ability to see it through. Even his title, 'Sergeant Crosby', and the presumed moral authority it bestowed upon him, felt intensely uncomfortable. Too much had happened in recent weeks, and he was by no means sure his originally intended role was the right one for him. And given these doubts, Thomas must be alerted to their implications, and the sooner the better, since his own turning away from this delicate task must surely thrust it back upon the priest. There was no one else.

Neither Thomas nor Billy was to be found in the hospital tent.

The Matron, barely pausing in her ministrations, told Will they had gone off together, some little time before. Thus, feeling he had idled away enough time, and suspecting Thomas might have sought peace and quiet in their tent, Will made his way directly there.

The tent was empty.

Will sat down on his bed and pondered yet again this situation in which he, and indeed all the rest were struggling to survive, each individual seeking to believe in a future over the water if for no better reason than to justify to his loved ones back home, and even more to himself, perhaps, the many sacrifices his odyssey had demanded.

He looked around the tent and was suddenly aware of its makeshift nature, its air of temporariness, of precariousness.

If Brisbane was about to establish its brothels, he reflected (always assuming they were not already in existence), then even by the standards of the old life, the new life was cankered in the bud; and this fact somehow made a nonsense of that journey and the deprivations it had entailed. Of course it did. It was like having come full circle, effectively to arrive back at the point from which you had started. There had to be some lessons learned from past errors, otherwise... what was the point of anything?

Will stood up and walked to the opening to peer out, though focusing on nothing in particular, lost still, to his troublesome thoughts.

Truth was, this new word 'democracy' he had heard on so many lips here of late – the ship's officers, Thomas, even Farmer, once – and in which so many appeared to place their hope and trust, would merely describe just another way of organising and controlling people, if everything remained the same in men's hearts. All of them yearned for a new start, he was sure of that. But not only had they all to want something better, but they also had to purge themselves of those aspects of their own inner being that had contributed to the doleful conditions of their past lives. All of them wanted equality, freedom, and a new start, but to what purpose, if it was merely a re-shuffling of the cards to acquire a better hand? No, he snorted, dismissively, all it would amount to was the chance to establish a new system in which they, and not others, came out on top.

He frowned, gloomily, half rejecting his own logic, then turned back inside and sat down on Thomas's bed, as if hoping for a new slant, somehow, on the matter. But instead he closed his eyes. Appreciable change in the direction of something nearer perfect could only come about, he suspected, if honest self-searching, a willingness to strive after the common good took root and flourished. Hm... Stevens, he reflected, indeed all the Stevenses, though they stood at the opposite pole from the deceased judge, had much in common with him; the former occupying the obverse side of the coin, all right, yet desiring the crown on the other, the face that represented the power the judge (and those of his class) wielded over them. They wanted the freedom to become the masters on their own terms.

Such notions were disheartening enough. But what dogged Will especially, in this moment, was the certain knowledge that once the brothels were up and running, he would be unlikely to spurn the pleasures they offered, in the absence of better. Was it this kind of knowledge of self that at odd times made him feel tarnished, hypocritical even? All too aware of their reality, how could he laud it over the likes of Stevens, let alone set about redeeming himself?

He stood, yet again, and lifted the tent flap. The freshness, the piercing light and the cloudless sky were all at variance with his thoughts and the ways they reflected. This tangled skein enmeshed him, and he must find a way out of it.

Already, Will realised, reading to know and to connect could lead at best only to awareness – of how things had been, were now, or could be. At worst, it led to frustration, anger, to this heavy inwardness which weighed on him now. He shrugged helplessly. It was perhaps the inevitable fate of the well-read, thinking man to suffer constantly the complacency, the ignorance of the huge majority of his fellow men. Oh, it wasn't that he could not live and acquiesce with them and their blindness, he could; but that was not the point. Rather, having had his eyes opened, albeit as yet not very wide, he could not close them again, knowing that better was possible... if a way could be found to convince even a minority that it was indeed so.

He resumed his original position on his own bed, his mind still churning away. Then, on a whim, he reached over to the late judge's trunk and picked up the diary, intending to make some brief record of these thoughts to which he knew he must sooner or later return. But the book fell open at a page that was densely written, and curiosity nudged his half-formed purpose aside.

In XX, M's examination of the singular importance of fortresses in different hypothetical circumstances seems to be based on the sound premise that underpins the whole treatise, namely that it is a faithless world, and one would be foolish indeed not to take cognisance of this fact in every critical moment. My own experience certainly endorses this view. The two people on whom I should have been able to depend absolutely were the very ones to betray me and, if that, then the rest can safely be assumed guilty, even in advance of any test of their faith or honesty.

In XVIII, he also discusses the need for P to know how to be evil when circumstances leave him no option, and he speaks there of the dual nature of fox and lion that must thus govern P's thinking and his actions. I would have thought that in a world where few, if any, ever keep faith beyond the dictates of their own self-interests P would never have any alternative but to employ either guile or force to maintain his polity, whatever the circumstances!

My experience leaves me in no doubt whatever that the only person one can count on is one's self, and that that self must be protected at all costs; it must, in M's terms, reside at all times behind the walls of an impregnable citadel, for only there will it find the right conditions for a blameless, fulfilling (I do not say happy – no, never that) existence. Outside those walls (like the notion of Dublin's pale, no less!) one must expect only barbarity and deal with it harshly, not with any expectation of improving but merely to contain and quell. And I would go further – and mercifully, the powers vested in me will permit it – there is nothing to be gained from crouching behind the walls awaiting the assault. Vigilance demands continual harassment of the enemy, by whatever means are at one's disposal. The district of Queensland will thus have a large, powerful, highly mobile force of men whose sole purpose will be that of detecting and nipping in the bud any hint of insubordination, while its courts will mete out a justice that in addition to what the law demands for any given crime will strike at men's evil natures.

In this, as in so much else, I find M's observations so apt.

The dead hand of the ill-fated judge was immediately recognisable in the general tenor of these comments; but 'M' and 'P', who were they?

It was all but dark now and Will realised he must seek out Billy, and Thomas, wherever they were. Queues would be forming at the mess tent, and one always ran the risk of arriving too late to fill one's platter, as the amount of food prepared was not always sufficient to go round... To be fair, the cooks had no way of knowing, any evening, how many families would be cooking for themselves and how many would be hoping to find their victuals at the tent. And that too was a problem, a practical one, that needed to be addressed – but by whom?

XXXIX

The two figures stood in silence, side by side, looking down at the newly turned earth of the little boy's mother's grave.

They had been there a while, Thomas gripping the boy's frail shoulders as he wept quietly, occasionally wiping away the tears with the back of his hand; but then more had come, and there had been no staunching them. The priest had made no attempt to console him, or to hurry him away, for long experience had taught him what the boy could not know – that tears were a necessary washing away of initial grief and shock, the rending prelude to a new beginning.

After what seemed an interminable time, the child turned his tear-stained face upwards to look at his protector.

'Father Thomas,' he faltered, the tears filling his eyes yet again, 'what is to become of me now that I have no mammy and no daddy? How can I live without them?'

Thomas nodded his comprehension, then whispered: 'Billy, come with me. I want to show you something.' And he took hold of the little boy's hand and led him along the line of graves to the first one, Joanna's. 'Not many weeks ago, Billy, I stood crying beside *this* grave, for the first time, and asked myself the self-same question.'

The child looked up at him, incredulously.

'Oh yes, I did too, Billy. And sometimes, whenever I can, I come back here and I cry all over again, and maybe I always will, I don't know. You see, I too lost someone whom I loved very dearly, the very same day we all arrived on this island, and for the self-same reasons that you lost your mammy and your daddy.'

The child half-turned his head and looked up at him, a question in his eyes.

'Oh, yes, Billy,' Thomas reassured him. 'And because of this I know *exactly* the fears you feel, for they were – and truly, still are – fears I suffer myself, even though I am very much older than you are. And yet, here I am, living on without her, though in a very real sense I shall never be without her, just as you will never be without your mammy and daddy, because these people are inside us, Billy, they are a part of us, and we'll never forget them. Even if we live to be a hundred.' He led the boy slowly back to his mother's grave. 'In one sense, Billy, you've been luckier than I have. You see, I never knew my parents. They died when I was too young to remember them, so I don't know what part of me comes from them because I have no idea what they were like; to this day, I don't know their names even.'

Billy frowned, evidently thinking about Thomas's words, and after a little while asked, 'Do big people cry as well when they are hurt? You said you do.'

'Oh yes, nearly everyone does; age really has nothing to do with it. Believe it or not, Billy, but crying, when you are very, very sad, as you and I are, is actually good for us and is nothing to be ashamed of, ever.'

A long silence followed in which the boy circled his mother's grave, stopping at different points, occasionally. He picked up a short, dead branch that had fallen – probably as a result of the night winds and rain coming in off the sea – and poked desultorily at the soil. He then turned to face the priest again.

'Does my mammy know she is under the ground?'

Taken off-guard, Thomas walked round to the other side of the grave. 'Hm. Billy... I need to think about that one... But the real, at least, short answer, Billy, is that your *mammy* is *not* under the ground.'

The child looked utterly bewildered.

'I know, I know,' Thomas began again. 'I just said she was. But really, your real mammy, well, she wasn't what is under the ground.

She was all the love she gave you and all the things she did for you, the things she told you, the sense of safety she gave you – all those things you fear you no longer have – and all the lovely memories you will always have of her. What is under the ground is not those things, just the…the…wrapping, the… parcel all those good things came in.' He paused, looking at the child to see whether he was understanding his words. 'The trouble is, Billy, we all tend to think that the things we see with our eyes and touch with our fingers are all-important, but it isn't so, it very often isn't so.' He looked kindly into the child's face. 'If you think about it, you'll realise that what was so important to you about your mammy – and your daddy too – was not how they looked but what they were.'

Thomas had resisted slipping off down the convenient road of the body being the temple of the Holy Spirit, for he no longer knew what he felt about that, and yet he was conscious of having given an explanation that traversed a parallel road. What he dreaded, however, was the next logical question, not just because he could not answer it, even for himself, but because, more than anything else, right now the little boy had need of certainties, having been cast so cruelly adrift.

The question was not long in coming.

'Well,' Billy mumbled, 'if my mammy is not under the ground and my daddy is not under the sea, where are they, then?'

'I don't know, Billy. Nobody does.' All Thomas could do was settle for the simple truth, because he reckoned it was more important to retain the boy's trust than to satisfy his need of the moment with a honeyed fancy. 'But they are somewhere, and it isn't where the bodies they no longer need are. There are so many things we do not know, and what happens when we die is one of them, maybe the most important of them. We just don't know, and we have to learn to live with that not-knowing. The best we can do, as I see it, though others may tell you differently, is to hope that they are somewhere where we shall also eventually be... together. But in the meantime, we have to get on living the lives we have here, today, tomorrow and for years to come, because there are so many things... good as well as bad things... that await us along our lives' different paths... But of one thing you can be sure: neither your mammy nor your daddy would wish you to be so sad at their going that you never took another step into your very own special future.'

The child nodded his half-understanding, drying his eyes yet again. 'But where will I live and who will look after me?'

'None of us knows where we will live eventually, when we leave this island, Billy, but for the time being, at least, Mr Crosby and I would be so pleased if, for now, at least, you would continue to share our tent with us.'

Billy's face lit up in an unexpected smile. 'Do you really mean it?'

'Of course I do,' Thomas replied. 'There would have been no point saying so otherwise.' He remained silent for several moments, so the child could begin to take stock of his new situation in the world and in the hope that the fears that had been plaguing him since his mother's death might begin to recede.

But at length it was he who broke the silence, seeing Billy's glum face near to tears again. 'Billy, there will be times when the sadness comes back to you,' he said gently. 'I know because, as I've said, mine comes back to me. And I find that at those times it is a great comfort to come here and sit by her grave and talk to her in my mind. I always feel better when I have done that. It might work that way for you too.'

So there they had stood, by the graves, contemplating the strange repercussions and ramifications of their personal, yet somehow shared, loss.

After his careful expression of these thoughts, realising the sun was already quite low in the sky, Thomas now prompted the child gently. 'You'd best be saying 'goodnight' to your mammy, then we'll be getting back, because there will be supper soon, and I must...'

He stopped, suddenly, and turned the boy round to face him. 'Now, Billy, there is one thing you must promise me, and it is this. You must not ever go outside the encampment unless Mr Crosby or I or one of the doctors or matron is with you. Do you understand? While there are no fierce animals here, as far as we know, there are poisonous snakes and spiders whose bite can kill... Yes, indeed, there are... So you must always be very careful where you tread, especially when you are going through long or thick grass or going anywhere in the dark. It's always best to make a bit of noise, Billy – which I'm sure you're really quite good at!' And Thomas was relieved to see the boy's sad, serious face break into a broad grin. 'Because that'll frighten them off. Do you understand me, now?'

'Yes. I know. My mammy told me that. She said there might be deep holes I could fall down, and she said I shouldn't go in the sea either.'

'Well, she was quite right and I'm glad you remember her warnings. But listen now. Tomorrow there is going to be a trip to a lake that is not far from here, and a lot of the ladies and children will be going, and it might be possible for you to go along with them too, if you wish. In any case, Mr Crosby will certainly be going. It might be quite exciting. What do you think?'

The child nodded enthusiastically. 'Oh yes, I should like that, 'cos when I grow up, I'm going to be an explorer. I bet you didn't know *that* did you Father Thomas?'

'I did not,' Thomas answered, 'but that being the case, it seems to me tomorrow will see you take the first step along your new life's way – don't you agree?'

Billy's face beamed. 'Oh, yes. I do... but it doesn't mean I will forget my mammy and my daddy, not even one teeny-weeny bit...'

By the time they re-entered the tented area, the sun was rapidly westering, and though a fair number of folk were still moving about, Thomas realised he'd been away from his duties for too long and, for a start, should look in on Dr Mitchell.

'Well, Billy, you run off and play for a while, or read your story book, because there are some things I must do before we go to eat.' And he smiled, noticing how the child turned his nose up at the reading suggestion. 'Do you have any friends... among the other children?'

'Oh yes, lots. There's John and George... and their sister, Margaretta. I'll see if I can play with them... if I can find them.'

'Yes, you do that. But it will be quite dark soon, so when it is, come and look for me at the hospital tent, or if you don't see me there, go to the huts over there. Or failing that, back to our tent and wait there until I come… or Mr Crosby does. And we'll go and find something to eat together. Now then, does that sound like a good plan?'

Billy nodded, seemingly taking it all in, and less burdened than he had been an hour before, and away he skipped, down the roadway.

A heartening sight greeted the priest as he pushed through the flap into the hospital tent, for there was Dr Mallon, in his nightshirt, kneeling on Dr Mitchell's bed, propping him up while the matron coaxed some water down his throat. Mitchell was barely conscious and was muttering incoherently, and Thomas noticed how thin and emaciated he had become through lack of food. His breathing too was laboured, and in an attempt to make it easier, Mallon suggested they find more pillows to try and wedge him into a sitting position.

'Give me those from my bed, Father Sheehan. I can get some more, I should think – is that not the case, matron?'

She nodded. 'Yes. Over in the long hut, there should be some.'

When Dr Mitchell was settled as comfortably as his lamentable condition would allow, Thomas observed, brightly: 'You must be feeling somewhat restored, yourself, Patrick, given what you've just done to help Dr Mitchell.'

'Aye, it is so, though I must lie down again, for I feel a little light-headed with the exertion of it.'

Thomas moved quickly to his side and took his arm, leading him slowly back to his bed. 'I'll go over to the store now and get you some pillows… or a bolster…'

'No, *Father* Thomas, you will not – the matron checked him, placing a peculiar emphasis on the title – '*I'll* go, for it's almost dark and you'd be unlikely to find them…Or else you'll very likely set the place on fire striking a light to see by.'

Thomas chuckled. 'You clearly know a clumsy fool when you meet one.'

Miss Labone shrugged haughtily and tossed her head in mock disgust. 'I never yet found a man who was not so, and I don't think your privileged position with the Almighty is likely to make any difference in your case!'

Thomas roared with laughter. 'Ah! That's me exposed, sure enough. And put in my place!'

The young woman turned and smiled mockingly.

When he judged she was out of earshot, Thomas turned to Mallon, who was lying rather awkwardly on one elbow. 'Well, that's the first time I've heard her utter more than three words together! Clearly, she has her opinions, as well as a nice line in caustic humour, I'll be bound! I don't know whether 'tis my imagination, but I sense her wholehearted disapproval... of me, I mean. I think she sees me as the proverbial wolf in sheep's clothing! And in that she would not be entirely mistaken, I do confess...'

He stood there a moment or two, head tilted to one side, and murmured: 'A pity though... So it is.'

But Dr Mallon, in spite of his uncomfortable-seeming posture, had already slipped away into sleep.

A few moments later, in walked Will, an open book in his hand, and perplexity on his face.

'Ah, you are here! So Billy was right... I wonder, would you take a look at this for me...?' And Will showed Thomas the page in the judge's diary, which the priest squinted at, in the failing light.

'So... what is the problem, Will? Seems clear enough to me...'

'I'm relieved to hear it. So... you'll be able to enlighten *me* about the mysterious "M" and "P", then?'

'Hah! M's the divil incarnate – or so many have argued since his little book of common-sensicles first saw the light of day! Old Machevil himself, so it is!'

'Sorry... who would that be, Thomas?' Will shrugged his shoulders, impatiently.

'Niccolò Machiavelli: he's your man,' Thomas chuckled. And "P" is the *Prince*, the subject of the book he wrote – for a sixteenth-century Florentine tyrant, as a sort of *vademecum*. It's long been on the papal index of prohibited books, and that's how I came to read it: Marsh's library has a rare, early edition!' And he chuckled again, relishing the memory of his youthful rebellion. 'Yes, yes... And if I'm not mistaken, it's part of your Prosper-Sandy's legacy... Isn't it?'

'Is it? I'll go back and check – are you coming? Billy was fast asleep...'

'No. I'll see you at the mess tent, Will. But don't be long.'

Billy was still asleep, so Will quickly and noiselessly searched out the volume in the judge's chest, sat down, and opened it, first at chapter XX, then at chapter XVIII. In both cases he found that parts of the text had been heavily underscored in thick black ink, as well as being commented on in the margins in a neat, minute hand; and skimming through the rest of the text he found this to be the case generally, which made it difficult to read the print at all, especially now the light was all but gone.

So, what did it all mean, for the judge?

He took the diary to the tent opening, where the light was marginally better, and re-reading the entry he quickly realised that the question the judge had been addressing was more or less that which had been preoccupying him over the past few days.

Yet how different – and how repugnant – were the judge's reasoning, language, and conclusions, from his own. No, he would not accept the dismissal of all human beings as faithless and entirely self-centred... in spite of his own shortcomings, and his many negative experiences at the hands of his fellow men. Well-disposed, intelligent men could always establish and live by laws designed to curb their own worst excesses, couldn't they? It was surely only a matter of finding the right people, and then of creating a community whose aims, and values, were radically different from those which all here in the camp had fled from in the Mother Country. Yes, indeed!

'Billy', he called softly. 'Wake up! Come on. Time to eat!'

'I'm ready to...' said Billy, yawning, and rubbing his tummy quite comically. 'I'm really, really empty, Mr Crosby...' And out he went, ahead of Will.

'Wait for me!' Will shook his head, smiling as he stepped outside, tying the tent flap securely behind him. And as he hurried after the child, he found himself wondering whether this writer, this Machiavelli, had been as dark in his assessment of human nature as the judge had painted him.

When time and opportunity allowed, he would read the chapters properly. But tonight their priority must be to work out the final details for the bathing expedition, for the following afternoon.

XL

To Will's mind, there was something quite strange about the whole expedition to Brown Lake… and not just in its outcome.

The previous day's meeting had, in the end, given the impression that everything would run smoothly. But it was evident from the outset that some, at least, were still disgruntled at the whole idea and the inconveniences it brought them.

A number of women – especially the older ones – arrived at the meeting point armed with all kinds of excuses ranging from sick husbands or children to care for, to physical disabilities, sudden rashes that had made their appearance overnight – not to mention moral and religious scruples and, in one case, a mortal fear of water.

Dr Ballow, on whose decision these excuses were upheld or dismissed, was quite at a loss, being as taken aback by the size and vehemence of the newly kindled revolt, as was Will himself. And once he had begun to accept one or two of the proffered excuses as legitimate, a fair number of those women who had initially seemingly resigned themselves to going, began to defect to the queue of dissenters. It soon became obvious that the party would never leave at all if each case were heard and argued.

The doctor conferred hastily with Captain Kemp.

Kemp signalled to his two, armed officers who, with Will, were to accompany the expedition, and without more ado they began herding all the women out towards the path, pushing the more recalcitrant none too gently, with the flat of their raised muskets.

There were howls of anger and derision from the women so treated, exacerbated by the curses of a small group of men who had gathered to witness the departure. Yet none of the women dared disobey and none of the men tried to intervene.

It had been an inauspicious-enough beginning, but matters were soon to get worse.

Once it became clear that neither Ballow nor Kemp had left the camp, the taunts and jeering increased. And after a clod of muddy earth had struck him on the cheek, one of the armed officers lost his temper – to the point at which he raised his musket to his shoulder and swung it around threateningly in a wide arc – though instantly restrained by his companion.

For a time, however, this hasty gesture had the effect of subduing the more unruly elements, and the party moved slowly and sullenly along the path.

The women then gradually split into three or four different groups, some moving more quickly than others, and as the gaps between them began to lengthen the problem of protection (should it prove necessary) and supervision (should there be any defectors) rapidly became insurmountable, given that only three men had been assigned to escort them. Will's shouted request that they should all keep together – because of the possible dangers – went unheeded, indeed, was cause of further jeering from the group nearest to him. And the two shipmen met with no more success in *their* endeavours.

The expedition was in a state of chaos, which, at least in part, seemed to have been deliberately orchestrated.

Yet, when Will, who was bringing up the rear, eventually arrived at the lake, some of the women from the two forward groups – noticeably a preponderance with young children – were at the water's edge, with their skirts tucked up, already up to their knees in, or preparing to enter, the water.

Not so the last comers, most of whom were sitting on the banking above the lake shore, with their arms folded – an obvious gesture of defiance. The older, mainly married women sat apart from the younger, single women, yet all displayed the same truculence. The officers tried to persuade the women, cajoling, threatening, even joking with some individuals, but largely without success. Will forbore adding his voice to theirs, dismayed and disgusted by the foolishness, the sheer pig-headedness being displayed.

After surveying the scene for a few moments he went over to the two officers, one of whom raised his eyebrows in a gesture of despair – or was it contempt? – at the conduct of the women.

'Well, gentlemen,' he said, 'we've done our best. We've got them here, but there is no way we can get them into the water if they refuse to go. I suggest we leave them to it now and come back for them in a couple of hours, when...'

'I think not,' the second man cut in. 'Our orders, Mr Crosby, were to protect the women from any possible dangers. After all, we don't know what...'

'Yes... you are right, of course,' Will said, curbing his anger. 'Though given their attitude you do feel like leaving 'em to their own devices... to see how they make out then!'

'My feelings exactly!' said the younger of the two men, lifting his hand to his cheek. ''Twas a good thing you restrained me, Frederick. For two pins I could have...'

'Aye, it's a thankless task, right enough,' Frederick agreed, as first he, then his companion, sat down on a knoll close to the water's edge.

Will, who remained standing, suddenly moved down to the water. 'Look!' he called back, without turning. 'Over there! What do you make of that?'

The other two sprang up again and were quickly at his side.

'I saw something – over on the other side. There was movement, I'm sure there was.'

The two sailors fixed their gaze in the direction of Will's extended, pointing arm.

Vision was hampered, however, by the glare of the sun onto and off the water, and at first none of them could be sure whether there was anything to see or not. The three of them shifted away to their right, some twenty yards or so, to try and peer round the intense light that was centred on the middle of the lake. Will went on a little further, stopping to stare intently, every ten paces or so, until eventually he ceased moving altogether and beckoned to the other two.

'Yes, there, look! Something white, and another... thing, moving about in the rushes, near the water's edge... Do you see them?'

The older officer, Frederick, took a small telescope out of the pouch at his side, and setting it against his right eye, he proceeded to adjust the lens, to focus finally on the far shore. After a little while, he passed the eyeglass to Will. 'And what do you make of that, Mr Crosby?'

Re-focusing, Will could clearly make out three, no four, then another, and... six figures, in all, men cavorting about, all completely naked. Even as he watched, two of them slid into the water and began swimming towards the centre of the lake. Soon, they were lost in the dazzling glare, while Will and his two companions waited for what seemed forever for them to emerge from the light at the point their initial direction had suggested. But they failed to do so.

The three watchers hastened back along the shoreline towards where the women were washing themselves or their children or clothes in the shallows, or just sitting gossiping higher up the bank, where a sizeable clutch was still steadfastly refusing to enter the water. One or two had stood up and were ambling along the top of the embankment that Will had traversed with Ridley, all of which he noted at a glance though too intent on catching sight again of the swimmers to pay much attention to what was happening on the slope behind him.

'Maybe they turned back', Frederick suggested.

'Perhaps,' Will responded. 'But what concerns me is who they are and what they are up to.'

'Surely, they can only be from the camp,' Edward, the younger man, volunteered. 'They must be... some of our people, though their being here today of all days suggests they're up to no good.'

Will admitted his bewilderment. 'That is certainly the most likely explanation, but I'm a bit uneasy about it. I suppose you too have heard the rumour that there are some of the native peoples on this island...'

'Well yes,' the older officer cut in, 'but they are black – as the ace of spades, apparently – whereas the people we saw were definitely white, weren't they?'

The two officers went on to hazard further guesses. And when Will glanced away for a moment, he saw that there were two women walking determinedly towards them.

Prompted by Will, the two men also turned to face them.

'Yes, what is it?' Will asked, doubtfully, surprised at their apparent wish to communicate *anything* after so much abuse.

'Not all of us was against the idea of coming 'ere, sir,' the smaller of the women ventured as they joined the men.

'I'd say a big majority of us… in fact,' the other said. 'The objectors are very loud, and vulgar with it, and we didn't want you to go thinking we was all tarred with the same brush, or that it'd all been a waste of time… That doctor, we saw the sense in what he were sayin'...'

The two officers smiled, evidently gratified. 'Thank you for taking the trouble to say so,' said Frederick, 'for up to now, our impression has been quite the opposite...'

Then the smaller woman spoke again. 'I hope you gentlemen don't mind us mentioning it but… well… some of us are a bit shy about exposing ourselves with you gentlemen being so close, like; so we was wondering if… well, if you could maybes go just a bit further off – if you wouldn't mind, that is?' And she looked plaintively at Will, and then from one to the other of the officers, as if half expecting some objection or even a rebuke for her outspokenness.

'Oh, but… how thoughtless of us!' Will responded. 'Of course we will. However – and he drew back a little – the more concerned among you can simply go further along the shore. I know for certain that there are clumps of bushes at intervals, there, right down to the water's edge, and these could provide separate, quite private bathing areas. We shan't disturb you… though we mustn't go too far away in case any emergency arises. But we can go a bit further off; of course we can...'

A quick glance passed between the two women.

'Yes?' Will inquired, scrutinising each in turn. Were they party to something he and his two companions knew nothing about? 'Is there some difficulty...?'

And once again the women exchanged a swift glance before the taller one spoke. 'No, not really, only... it's what you just said, like. We wouldn't want to go too far along the lake side, not too far away from you men... It could be dangerous... though some of the younger women don't seem to mind the risk...'

And Will realised she was right, for where there had previously been maybe a dozen of the more loud-mouthed, more troublesome women sitting well up the banking, only a couple now remained. The woman's reply struck him as odd, though, a bit strained, certainly inconclusive. But he was at a loss to say why exactly.

It was the younger of the two officers, also clearly perplexed, who filled the ensuing silence. 'Well, there's surely safety in numbers.' And he smiled awkwardly. 'As far as we know, you would only have to be wary of snakes but any noise at all and they would be off – or so we are led to believe...'

'I for one will be taking no chances... I can't abide even the thought of snakes!' the smaller woman cut in, her face twisting in disgust. Then as they were leaving, she turned her head and over her shoulder threw back the comment: 'And besides, there are snakes and then there are... snakes, as I see it.' And she flounced off, leaving the impression of a fleeting smile behind her.

'And what, do you suppose, she meant by that?' Will asked when the women were out of earshot.

The older officer shrugged. 'I have the distinct feeling we are not fully in the picture; something's maybe going on that we don't know about... that we're not meant to know about.'

'First, all the lip we had to take...'

'...Then those men who seemed to disappear into the sunlight ...'

'...And the women who sat down there, as if for the duration, then suddenly are nowhere to be seen...'

Will listened as the two men aired their suspicions aloud, then added his own. 'Yes, and now the request that we move further off...'

He was pensive for a while, then bethinking himself, concluded: 'Well, whatever it is – assuming it is – they're adults and must decide for themselves. It's one thing protecting them from physical dangers, quite another interfering in their private business... or their stupidity. Anyway, it's probably nothing; we're perhaps letting our imaginations get ahead of us. As it is, we *can't* patrol the whole area, given the state of undress some of the women are likely to be in – much as I'm sure we would like to....' And his comment elicited the intended guffaw.

There was a brief silence before one of the two officers observed: 'In any case, with so many young children present, I can't really think that...'

'You're right,' said Will, turning to look at the nearest group of women, most of whom – to his mild surprise – seemed to be standing looking in their direction.

Seeing him now facing them, several of the women began waving, shooing him away and he, suddenly understanding their gestures, waved back to them, and reminded his companions of their as yet unfulfilled promise about the distancing.

The three of them strolled slowly away, back towards the end of the lake and as they went Will glanced more than once over to the other side, to where the naked men had been. The light at the centre was now rather less intense and vision was easier, but there was no sign of them.

Once they reached the end of the lake they stopped and looked back towards the bathers before settling down beside a clump of silvery eucalyptus.

Their conversation was desultory, and Will, who barely knew the two officers, felt increasingly uneasy in their company. At length he rose to his feet.

'I think I'll just wander over there to satisfy my curiosity. There may be something to indicate who they were... the men...'

'Fine. We'll keep an eye on things from here.' Frederick, the older man, took out his chronometer. 'Let's say we'll give them another half hour or so before the first whistle – will that be enough?'

'Yes,' said Will, 'that sounds about right. I'll set off back here when I hear it.' And away he went at a brisk pace.

XLI

It felt good to be alone again.

Will breathed in the smells of damp earth and rotting vegetation and felt strangely elated by their ever-present reminders that he was here, in a new world, on the threshold of a new life.

Traversing the bottom end of the lake, past the bush where Ridley had made his strange discovery, was easy enough, and over to his right he could see the track along which they had all come, snaking away back to the encampment. Once he reached the opposite corner, however, the going became distinctly more difficult; the thorn bush thickened, and the grass was taller and denser than he had hitherto encountered in his acquaintance with the island's vegetation. He drew the heavy machete from its sheath at his side and began to hack a way through until he reached a point where his path became easier.

It was an area in which the curious grass trees grew in profusion, a place of tall ferns, unusual antler-like ferns too, growing from the crooks of giant trees from which thick, rope-like lianas fell and looped. And though the soil was still sandy, the place had a cloying dankness about it quite unlike the more pleasant airiness of the other, familiar side. It occurred to him, even as he was swinging the knife, that no one had come by this route in a long time, so that the men they had seen must have reached this side of the lake from some other direction. They must have done.

After a hundred or so yards of relatively easy passage Will was faced with yet another thick thorn brake, but instead of trying to cut his way through it he veered off to his right, away from the lake, hoping to skirt around it. To a point it proved to be the right decision though he still had to use the knife on occasions. He was conscious, however, of perhaps now moving too far away from his intended destination and that sooner rather than later he must begin to correct his direction or return the way he had come, resigning himself to another bout of strenuous cutting. Would he have enough time?

While still in this trough of indecision, to his dismay he heard the first faint, yet distinct sound of the officer's whistle, warning the women they had only another half hour before they must be ready to muster again for the return journey. Here was a dilemma. Either he must give up on his attempt to reach the point where the men had been and return at once to his companions or hope that within the next ten minutes or so he could find a way through. He opted for the latter course and once again began hacking away at the undergrowth.

It was while thus occupied that young Billy strayed into his mind, from nowhere, and he realised, only now, that the child had not been at the muster point at the outset, even though he should have been there. The women's unexpected unruliness had squatted so stubbornly in his mind that it had driven all else from it, and now he felt both guilty at having let the boy down and uneasy that something untoward had prevented him being there. Why had he not come? It was too late now, but he must make a point of finding him the moment he got back to the encampment.

It was having arrived at this decision that, obscurely, persuaded him to abandon his present task and so, sheathing the knife, he retraced his steps.

The nearer he came to the gathering crowd the louder their chatter and cries became – quite the reverse of the situation during the outward journey – and arriving once again within sight of the corner of the lake he saw that some of the women and their offspring were already strung out along the return path. Indeed, one small group was quite far off, disappearing round a distant bend. Drawing yet nearer, he saw that another group – a mixture of the older and the younger ones – was just then leaving the lake and several of them waved to him, seemingly quite exhilarated. What could have brought about this apparent change of mood?

Walking quickly from the corner, back along the lakeside, he went in search of the two officers. He caught sight of them up on the steep area of banking just as Frederick sounded the second whistle. And all the while women and children, in small groups, were passing by him, cheerful and smiling for the most part, and an amicable banter, sometimes even flirtatious, had replaced the earlier abuse.

He climbed up to where the two men were standing watching the straggling groups sauntering along the path. The women were laughing and joking or deep in conversation, many of them carrying bags full of freshly laundered clothes. Their children darted back and forth in all directions. The younger officer was obviously counting them as they went by, thus Will did not speak so as not to break his concentration. To the other, older man, he remarked, 'Well, there seems to have been a change of heart among them now their ordeal by water is over!'

'Aye, t'would appear so; maybe a bit of misery washed off with the grime. I wager we shall not have quite the difficulties persuading them the next time as we had herding them to this baptism!'

Their laughter was cut short, however, by the teller informing them that all but three of the women were now accounted for, and on hearing this the other took out his whistle and blew a long, shrill blast. 'It's obvious they've enjoyed their anointing so much they're reluctant to leave' he said. 'We'll give them another five minutes and if they're not here by then someone will have to go and put a boot up their pretty little arses.' He grinned lecherously. 'Thinking about it, that's a task I don't mind undertaking myself!'

As the already departed women moved further away, the habitual silence of the place gradually reasserted itself among the trees and over the surface of the lake. The winter sun was already low in the sky, indeed so low it was no longer visible to them, and deepening shadows crowded in with the intensifying silence. Will marvelled at the sudden transformation, while experiencing an inexplicable sense of uneasiness in this now abandoned place. They were facing the direction from which they expected the three stragglers to appear, but there was neither sight nor sound of them.

'We'd best go and see what's holding them up,' Will suggested, at length.

The two sailors agreed, and, after a moment's discussion, it was decided that Will and the younger officer – Edward – should make the search while the older man would hurry after the last group of women and accompany them back to the tents.

Will and his young companion set off, walking along the ridge so as to command a better view of the lakeside and its path ahead. They went on for another ten minutes or so, hardly speaking, before they arrived at the point where the ridge began to slope down towards the end of the lake.

'Try another blast or two on your whistle,' said Will, 'for if they've wandered away from the lake and got themselves lost that should give them a direction to aim for.'

The officer did as he was bade, startling a flock of white, sulphur-crested cockatoos that had already begun to settle on their night perches, high up in the eucalyptus, but when all the flapping, screeching commotion had died down the silence again drowned all. They listened intently but heard nothing.

'Shall I try again?' Edward asked, clearly anxious.

'Indeed yes; maybe you should do so at regular intervals.'

Yet the end result was ever the same total silence. So they began to shout, pausing to listen after each salvo, but the all-enveloping silence invariably rushed back in.

Dropping down to the level of the lake they made their way back along the sandy track, stopping every now and then to inspect the cane brakes or bushes or intermittent clearings, but they found nothing.

'Do we know who they are – who we're looking for?' Will inquired, but the young man shook his head.

'Unfortunately, there was no opportunity to make a list of names because of the… irregularities, Mr Crosby… before we set off.'

Despite the failing light, it was clear that some sort of vigorous physical activity had taken place at one spot because the sandy beach was all churned up; there were a number of footprints still visible and as they were inspecting them, the officer called out to Will:

'Here, come and look at this!'

There were two clear prints that were much larger than the rest.

'These were never made by a woman, and that's for sure. What do you reckon?'

Will bent down to inspect them more closely, in the fading light. 'My experience in other lands tells me...' he said, glancing back up, 'that these two prints belong to a man, for sure... and one who's used to wearing shoes. Look, the toes are not at all splayed, just the opposite, in fact. So... I'd say that definitely rules out the natives, even if there are any of them hereabouts...'

'Then,' the young man declared, 'it's quite certain the men we saw over on the far side were from the camp. There can be no other explanation.'

'Yes, or...' Will was half remembering something that had struck him when he had been over there... 'Unless... something not beyond the realms of possibility... they came across from the mainland.' He stroked his chin. 'Makes you wonder, doesn't it?'

'Well, whoever they were, Mr Crosby, they were certainly here with something in mind, either with or without the collusion of some of the women.' He paused for a while, pondering the dilemma. 'What did you find on the other side, by the way?'

Will had to admit his failure to detect anything significant. 'But look,' he said at length, 'I think we are wasting our time, now. It will be dark in another fifteen minutes or so, and I for one don't fancy trying to find our way back in pitch blackness.'

'Aye, you're right! Those women aren't here... More than likely they're back at the camp themselves, by now. And maybe I just miscounted... though I don't think so.'

They moved off at a brisk pace and reached the encampment just as the last wisps of light vanished from the now grey, winter sky.

XLII

Just a few hours earlier, on the other side of the world, events had been occurring that would necessitate a further upheaval in the lives of Alice Fallowfield and her child.

Retiring to her room at around nine o'clock, Alice lights the candle at her bedside, undresses quickly and, once in bed, takes up again this strange romance by Ellis Bell, a writer previously unknown to her, for the few minutes before her day's accumulated weariness finally overcomes her.

Snuffing the candle, she settles down to sleep, but sleep will not claim her. This is something that happens but rarely, but whenever it does her thoughts turn to memories, flickering to life in the darkness, and these, in turn, eventually to tears, in spite of her continually renewed resolve to be stronger and to cut loose her emotional ties to the man who had so wantonly betrayed her. And this occasion proves no different, so that in a matter of minutes she is sobbing in the dark, yet trying hard, so hard, to control herself for fear of waking the child.

At some point in her distress, she becomes vaguely aware of Mr Hewitt's footfall on the stairs, his reaching the first landing, then opening the bedroom door to look in on his daughters, as was his custom each night before retiring. However, she does not hear his own bedroom door either open or close; and despite her emotional turmoil this omission perplexes her so much that she now finds herself distracted, listening intently for any hint of movement below.

What on earth can the man be doing?

After a seemingly endless interlude of silence, Alice hears the loose floorboard creak on her own – top – landing. She tenses, for what seems another age, but all is silent.

Suddenly, she feels a cold draught, which confirms to her that her door has been opened. And she freezes: not afraid, but uncertain, still caught up in the turbulent seas of regret.

'What is it, Mr Hewitt?' she says quietly. 'Is there something amiss… with one of the girls?'

But there is no answer, or rather, for answer she senses the man's nearness.

The fears and uncertainties of a few moments before turn to panic, as she feels him climbing in… his hands stretching out…

'Mr Hewitt!' Alice sits bolt upright. 'Mr Hewitt,' she cries, 'whatever do you think you are doing? You are making a terrible mistake. Please stop!'

Yet still he does not speak.

'Mr Hewitt! I have given you neither encouragement nor…'

Alice feels the man's hot, rough hand covering her mouth, his other hand pulling frenziedly at her night-dress, and she struggles ferociously, bucking and heaving and punching to prevent the man's intended rape.

Though small in stature, Mr Hewitt is no weakling, and for two or three minutes they wrestle thus, in the darkness.

Almost overcome, Alice finally manages to bite the hand that still covers her mouth. And she starts to scream, and this wakes Lilian, and a door opens, on the landing below.

'What is it mummy, are you hurting?'

At Lilian's sleepy cry, not two feet away, the man moves swiftly. And he flees the room leaving the door wide open. Alice hears him descending the stairs, then speaking testily to his daughters, in the room below.

'Ssh! It is nothing; just a bad dream,' Alice tells her little daughter. 'I'm all right now. Off you go to sleep again.'

She hears the child mutter something, which fades away into an incoherent murmur as she slips back, easily, into sleep.

Not so her mother. Her heart still pounding, Alice listens intently for sounds or any further movement downstairs. Evidently the man's daughter – whichever of them has been awakened by the commotion – is pacified by whatever explanation she has been given.

At length, she hears his tread on the stairs, but now receding, going right down, into the parlour, and the stairway door thuds shut.

After waiting a minute or two, Alice re-lights her candle, climbs out of bed and closes the door, wedging a chair firmly against the knob as a precaution against any further incursion, should the man feel emboldened by the liquor he might now be returning to, before the fire, alone.

She waits a few more minutes, until she is sure he is no longer prowling about. Then she snuffs her candle, once more.

How long Alice lies awake after this is impossible to say. But when she wakes, finally, with a start, it is already light.

She listens out for any sign of movement downstairs. Sometime between sleep and waking she had decided she must quit the place in the morning… even though it would mean returning to her parents' home, and the new and old torments that this would undoubtedly bring her…

Satisfied there is no sound, she leaps from the bed and begins throwing her own clothes and Lilian's into the two portmanteaux she had brought with her, all those weeks before. The child sleeps on as Alice busies herself with these preparations, so when all is more or less ready, she goes cautiously down into the parlour then through into the kitchen.

There is nobody there.

The girls will still be upstairs, and their father out, probably, attending to the animals as he normally does at this time in the morning.

Then she catches sight of the envelope propped up against the large blue-and-white-striped milk jug, in the centre of the table. It is addressed to her, as she has immediately surmised it must be. She slits it open with the bread knife and reads its few, scrawled lines.

Dear Miss Fallowfield,

I apologise for the foolish misunderstanding and I beg of you not to leave us. I'm sure we can continue as before. I do assure you that nothing untoward will occur again. I don't know what came over me and am so embarrassed at my conduct.

However, I will quite understand if you decide it would all feel too uncomfortable for you. If that indeed proves to be the case then please take the enclosed wages (for this and next month) and please, do not think too badly of me.

Yours very regretfully,

Tom Hewitt.

She reads it twice over, then slowly replaces it in the envelope, finding herself feeling sorry for Mr Hewitt... and for herself. She knows him to be a man of few words, and as coarse as his business makes him, but until last night he has been both civil and just, even kind, in his dealings with her and her daughter.

As she sits pondering a while, one by one the Hewitt children appear. Alice attends to their needs, to get them off to school on time, and as she does so, she weighs up the advantages and disadvantages of staying on.

'Isn't laal Lilan gayin to school theday?' inquires Susanna, helping her two younger sisters on with their coats.

'No. Not today,' Alice replies, softly. 'She wasn't well in the night, so I'm leaving her to sleep a while yet.'

'Aye. All reight then,' the girl says, on the point of leaving, 'that's what our dad said, in the middle of the night... that she wasn't well.'

Once alone again, Alice sits down at the kitchen table. Really, her decision turns on only one important question, which would arise sooner or later: could she spend the rest of her life here, with Tom Hewitt? And she knows the answer even as she starts to consider it.

In her heart of hearts she knows she is far from ready even to contemplate life with any other man than Will Crosby, and until such time comes, if it ever does, she must avoid situations like... like that which... had arisen in the night. And that was an end of it.

With no further hesitation, she goes back upstairs and, smiling, wakens Lilian. 'We're going to go and see grandpa today. You'll like that won't you?'

And within half an hour Alice has left Kirkby Stephen for good and all.

XLIII

'So what happened to you, Billy?' Will asks, when, at last, he finds the boy, sitting close to the hospital tent, looking out over the water towards the mainland. 'I thought you were coming to the lake with us this afternoon.'

'I wanted to come, Mr Crosby, but I went to talk to my mammy. And we were talking for such a long time, and then I remembered, and I ran, and I ran, but... Did you manage all right without me?'

'Oh, we managed well enough, I suppose.' Will smiles, appreciatively, at the boy's innocent self-aggrandisement. 'But it wasn't quite the same without you.'

Billy gets slowly to his feet and admits that it hadn't been too good for him either. 'Can I go next time do you think, Mr Crosby?'

'Of course you can,' Will assures him. 'But just now, I've got to help Father Thomas, so I'll see you a bit later. Maybe we can have a reading lesson before bedtime. What do you think?'

Billy makes a wry face. 'Oh, all right then... if you can't think of anything better...'

Will laughs and ruffles the child's hair. 'Till later then, Billy.'

Inside the hospital tent Will found a brief message asking him to go and see Captain Kemp about the 'peculiar goings-on at Brown Lake.'

As soon as he nears Kemp's quarters, it is obvious the captain – who is standing there with Dr Ballow and Father Thomas, as if waiting for him – is annoyed. From the start their conversation bears almost entirely on the intrusion of the unidentified male swimmers on the women's ablutions – whether by accident or design – and the disappearance of the three women. The two officers, standing, with hangdog looks, to one side, have evidently already met with some sort of reprimand; so... is it his turn, now?

'Well, there is nothing we can do about it tonight,' the captain says, curtly. 'But certainly, first thing in the morning you had better muster a roll call and make sure that all are safely accounted for.' He looks hard at Will. 'If everyone is accounted for, it is unlikely we shall learn any more, and – he shrugs – perhaps that is no great matter. What worries me more, *obviously*, is what is to be done if anyone is missing. And we must now plan for that contingency.'

Several moments of fruitless debate ensue, and then Kemp, still looking grave, presents his own views.

'If the women colluded in their own disappearance, that is their own affair,' he declares. 'However, if they have also left the island, they will be deemed to have broken the quarantine restrictions, and thus be liable to prosecution under due process of the law. But, if they have been kidnapped, or worse, there is a real danger of generating such panic here that the whole bathing programme will be put in jeopardy... and much else besides! And... as I'm sure you have already realised... the three men who accompanied the expedition may very well, and with some justification, be held responsible. Had you considered that?' he finishes, glowering at each in turn.

Will's hackles rise at this – and the arrogance behind it. Responsible for what, exactly? 'With all due respect,' he argues testily, 'without actually wandering about freely among the women, in their various states of undress, I do not see how we three men could have done any other than we did. Maintaining decorum meant maintaining a certain distance; indeed, we were politely requested to move further off, which we duly did.'

'Aye, that's right, captain,' the more senior of Will's erstwhile companions confirms, boldly.

Kemp makes to answer him, but Will raises his hand, unwilling to be deprived of his full justification.

'By your leave, captain, you were not there,' he says, struggling to keep his tone even. 'The trees and undergrowth around the lake were at times very thick and there was nowhere that would give us a view of the whole area; nor, indeed, was there any way in which we could prevent the women from roaming wheresoever they pleased, once they were out of sight. So, I for one would resist most strenuously any suggestion that we three were negligent in any way, or at all responsible for what did or did not take place. Indeed, begging your pardon, the idea is ludicrous – as anyone would agree if they were to go and take a look at the area and the well-nigh impossible task we were assigned!'

Will is flushed, and for a moment he wonders if he has gone too far. But the captain has riled him with his glib assumption and... no, he does not regret speaking out. He stands his ground and looks at the captain squarely.

Kemp's face registers his displeasure, but he holds his tongue. And it is the hitherto silent Father Thomas who attempts to smooth the plainly ruffled feathers.

'I think, gentlemen, we have to accept Mr Crosby's explanation. Quite apart from the delicate question of decorum stands the fact that there were clearly both limiting and possibly extraneous factors none of us could have predicted, and the three men assigned to the task cannot be blamed for those... and their consequences.'

Dr Ballow murmurs his assent, then Kemp adds coolly: 'No such accusation is likely to arise – and rest assured, I am not making it. But let us pray to God that all the women can be accounted for tomorrow and that that will be an end of it.'

Early the following morning, Will and the two officers visited that part of the camp – roughly a quarter of the whole – from which the women had been drawn.

They were there almost as soon as people had begun to stir, taking names, and asking questions; yet with every minute that passed, the task became more and more difficult, since individuals went off on their different errands and their whereabouts could not accurately be checked.

The word of a husband or a mother or of someone else who claimed to have seen such and such a person but a moment or two before, had to suffice, making Will uneasy, for only a fool would accept that everyone there was trustworthy. He quietly suggested they place some mark against the names of those who could not be accounted for in person, with the intention of returning later on in the day.

After half an hour or so, according to their ragged survey, the women were all deemed to be present. Will was heartened, while aware that, as they had strongly suspected yesterday, they might still be being hoodwinked in some way.

The two officers said they would report back to Captain Kemp, while Will was to speak to Dr Ballow, the three of them agreeing to make their second 'raid' on the sector at four o'clock, just as people were emerging to prepare their evening meals. That, surely, would settle the matter once and for all.

Ballow had just finished attending to a woman in a tent close to the hospital, so Will accosted him and apprised him of the results of the survey. Ballow nodded as Will spoke, but then seemed to contradict that seeming assurance: 'Still, I am concerned the quarantine regulations may have been breached, Mr Crosby. So I'd be obliged if you would check a second time... even though your census may prove just as inconclusive...'

Will shrugged. What else could they do?

'But surely,' the doctor said, brightening in that moment, 'surely, if somebody's daughter or wife or young companion was missing, their absence would be reported to us, would it not?'

Will nodded, seeing the sense in this, particularly with regard to wives and daughters. 'But that still leaves a fair number of mainly younger women, who have no such attachments.'

'In that case, would it not make sense, and save your time, if you were to focus only on those, since we have our records that locate them in specific tents?'

'Yes, of course.' Will brightened. 'If you would lend me the allocation records, I'll try and identify those women in their lodgings and not bother the rest. It'll certainly save us time, as you say – and spare us much likely abuse.'

The two of them walked across to the hut at the back of the encampment where Ballow had his makeshift office, but within moments of opening the two unlocked drawers of his table it became apparent that the list was not there.

'This is most certainly where it was,' Ballow exclaimed, in some consternation, 'for there was no other place I could put it. These two drawers are the only such facilities at my disposal.'

'Are you suggesting someone has removed them? Stolen them?'

'I can come to no other conclusion, Mr Crosby. But if it is so, then it surely lends weight to the suspicion that whatever occurred yesterday was planned in advance, and that something illegal is afoot.' He closed the drawers noisily, venting his anger. 'Which, perhaps, brings us by a rather curious route to the matter Father Sheehan raised with me the other day – the likelihood of Callaghan's and Stevens' pimping.'

Will's brow puckered. 'In what way? I didn't see either of them yesterday. Are you suggesting…?'

'I don't wish to imply that they were *directly* involved in yesterday's "occurrence". Indeed – the doctor added – I'm almost certain I saw Callaghan working up at the cemetery, late in the afternoon… Or rather, I can't think who else it might have been since, so far as I am aware, only he and his unsavoury companion have that dismal duty… No, what I'm surmising, and no more than that, is that if any of the *younger* women have disappeared, it can only be to the mainland – which could well be for the purposes of prostitution. And if that *were* the case, then it would seem too much of a coincidence for our sextons *not* to be involved, one way or another – if we discount the possibility of kidnap by Aborigines…'

He sat down on the steps of the hut and stretched his arms, yawning involuntarily. 'The truth of the matter is, Dr Ballow, that although we know *something* happened yesterday, we don't know what, and so, any conclusions we may come to are pure speculation.'

He looked up at the other man. 'We really are groping in the dark.'

'Well,' the doctor countered, 'only my medical colleagues know where I keep my few papers, and they, certainly, are above suspicion. And it's unlikely that any of the immigrants would have that information.' He paused, clearly racking his brains. 'No, to the best of my knowledge, none of them would have had occasion to set foot in this room... And yet, now I think of it... yes, on one, maybe two occasions I have spoken to Stevens in here, and who knows, maybe even to others that have slipped my memory. Hm... But can you think of any other reason why anyone would wish to steal the passengers' allocation list, if not to assist in a disappearance? What other possible uses could it have?'

But Will could come up with no satisfactory answers to the doctor's questions. And even if the doctor was right, it did not prove that the missing women (if indeed any were missing) had colluded in their own disappearance; forcible abduction was just as likely.

'It's difficult to know what to do,' he admitted. 'We have evidence of nothing substantial... nothing...'

'No, indeed.' The doctor pondered the matter, then suggested they postpone the return visit until early the next morning. 'In that way you can treat it as a military operation, involving all of Captain Kemp's officers, yourself, Father Sheehan. And me too... if you think it... Anyway, we should first cordon off the area to prevent anyone who had a mind to leave, and then interrogate everyone in turn. Perhaps someone will be so scared as to give us the information we're seeking.'

Will stood up. 'Possibly. But to treat these people as if they are criminals or, at least, are suspected of having committed a crime, could have bad repercussions on what is already a difficult situation. By which I mean, obviously, the reason why we are all locked down on this island.'

Ballow nodded and smiled. 'Well then,' he said, 'perhaps you *should* go back this afternoon, after all, and frankly confess our concern that one or more of the women has been abducted. It might just stir consciences if there is some conspiracy of silence.'

'Yes. That seems a far safer approach,' Will murmured, relieved. 'And, thinking about it, it might be better if I went alone. If the three of us turned up yet again it would certainly smack of coercion and likely as not get us nowhere.'

'Well, maybe, Will. Try it anyway.'

'So we're agreed. I'll go and tell the others they are absolved from that duty, and I'll let you know what happens, if anything, this evening.'

XLIV

The more Will thought about it the more convinced he was that there must be a link between the disappearance of the list and the skulduggeries of Callaghan and Stevens. The coincidences were too great: hadn't Stevens as good as told him he was soon hoping to extend the choice of his 'wares'? And mightn't whatever had transpired yesterday have had something to do with fulfilling that 'hope'?

Will found himself wishing he had paid more attention to Stevens' words, on that occasion, than to his own indignation, for he could not now remember enough of the detail to be sure of what had been in the other's mind. It occurred to him also that the child, Lizzie, might be in some further danger, and he knew, as a matter of urgency, that he must seek out Mrs Parry to find out what he could about the child and that lady's relationship with her. However, his first tasks were to find the two officers – and Billy.

Strolling back through the camp, still mulling over the diverse strands of the web being spun about them, Will realised he needed Thomas's opinion now, to help him decide what action they ought to take. The two officers had simply wished him 'Good luck!', both much relieved that they were no longer required to participate in a second visit. He turned in the direction of his own tent and, on nearing it, saw the priest standing outside, in conversation with James, their neighbour.

'Ah, Thomas, I was hoping... And good day to you, too, James. I hope things fare well with you and John.'

'For the time being, we cannot grumble... Well, Father, I must be getting along,' and, backing away, O'Rourke touched his brow in salutation.

'Ah Will, I've been out hearing the confession of another poor soul about to quit this earthly life, giving her absolution... And it gets you down, truly it does, no matter how many times you've been through it before.'

Will grimaced. 'You, more than any of us, must feel you live on the very edge of that precipice that separates this world from the next... It cannot be easy...'

Thomas's smile, in truth little more than a rictus, seemed to suggest disdain, or revulsion, even.

You know, Will,' he managed, at length, 'it is a very strange thing urging such unfortunate people towards a hope, presented as unquestionable certainty, that... well, that you no longer see that way yourself... Yet, you know, I would steadfastly refute any suggestion of hypocrisy on my part, that I would!' And his eyes flashed defiance. 'For what one feels and believes, in that moment, when crossing the threshold into the darkness, is more important than anything you have ever believed or thought or hoped or done in your entire life, because, in that moment, all but the moment has become utterly irrelevant... No, really, it must be so, Will. If you take that final step convinced that there is an intense, immense light forming out of the darkness, then even a faithless priest like myself can believe he has done something of real significance towards lightening the burden of dying.'

'I see that readily enough, Thomas. Of course I do. But...'

'And yet, you know, Will, for me, 'tis like becoming an actor, being both my knowing self and my created self at one and the same time, or rather, the self of now accompanied by the ghost of a former, believing self...' Thomas extended his arms, palms outwards, then retracted them, to emphasise the rational contradictions in the point. '...And when I see the threshold has indeed been crossed and I look upon the dead face of the person I have thus deceived, I realise that now, eternally, it does not matter one way or the other. For nothing matters once we are no more. Nothing at all. And in all truth... Oh, but 'tis no matter, so let it be. But, as I say, it gets you down at times...'

He fell silent, head bowed. And Will waited, understanding... and yet not quite understanding.

'But Will, I'm sorry... Doubtless you have more pressing matters to discuss than the conscience of... a disenchanted priest performing at the footlights of eternity!'

Will laughed aloud at this last piece of self-deprecation. Yet he felt uneasy at thrusting aside his friend's preoccupations too soon, for clearly, they troubled him, and set beside them, his own matters of the moment were maybe trivial in comparison. Therefore, he stood there, unwilling to be the one to dismiss those preoccupations, noticing yet again how deeply blue his friend's eyes were, beneath those heavy eyebrows, and that great shock of black hair, hinting towards grey at the temples. But it was his eyes, piercing yet impenetrable, that drew him now, and held him...

Thomas's verbal onslaught, originating in a train of thought so different from his own, had quite taken the wind out of Will's sails. And whether to make some comment on the matter, or whether to let it pass, he was uncertain – the horns of a dilemma. Yet, illusions or not, that these things mattered, and perhaps not solely to Thomas... of that he was in no doubt.

'I wonder, my friend – he began, hesitantly – and I am far from sure about any of this... but it seems to me that without these rituals, these ritual endings to our lives, death would be full of terror... especially here, away from all that is familiar, and lost to us... Everyone has to be able to cleave to something, don't they, as what we have is so very little. And if that something is beyond us, bigger than us.... well, perhaps that helps. And I suppose that for most people, if all that lay before you were akin to, well... nothingness, it would negate the value of anything you ever did... did or said... regardless of how you felt about it in the moment. And yet – here he paused – unlike you, perhaps, I have enough doubts about my doubts to enable me to go forward with something like... optimism! Or not quite optimism, but.... Anyway, there you have it. But yes, you are right, there are several matters... about which I would greatly appreciate your opinion...if you have the time.'

Thomas chuckled. And looking up, Will saw only a warm compassion, now, in those deep eyes. 'The matters are probably linked,' he continued. 'Shall we walk... down to the sea, maybe?'

'Yes, of course! Let's head for those rocks.' And he pointed into the middle distance as he was speaking. Thomas took his arm, but neither moved a step. And, laughing at himself, the would-be ex-priest reiterated his suspicion that his own preoccupations, though perennial, were really quite inconsequential. 'Our major concerns must always be with the living,' he declared. He exhaled loudly. 'So yes, let me hear about the latest conundrum our neighbours have laid before us.'

Will nodded, released his arm, and rapidly outlined the morning's events.

'From what you're telling me, and if there is indeed a connection between the women's disappearances – assuming they are real – and Callaghan and Stevens, then Lizzie may well need rescuing. Bad enough the antics of those two rogues on the island, but if the girl were to be... spirited away... then...' And Thomas shrugged, in helpless acknowledgement of the all-too-possible scenario. 'But what about...?'

This probing of possibilities went back and forth a while, then Thomas stooped to refasten his sandal.

'Come on. A good start might well be Mrs Parry – if we can find her, for I'm none-too-sure I would recognise her again. Would you? The rocks, I think, must wait another time. Now, which way is it?'

Will led Thomas to the part of the camp Mrs Parry lived in, suggesting that if they weren't able to find her tent, they could always ask around. And in fact the first woman they encountered pointed them directly to the Parry's tent.

Mrs Parry, just then returning from drawing water at the troughs, was somewhat bemused to learn that the two gentlemen were there to speak with her. However, once she had understood the reason for their visit, whatever reticence she had been inclined to in those first few moments, quickly disappeared.

'Oh, that girl!' she snorted, setting down her pail. 'She has proved to be the bane of our lives since we arrived here! Many are the times my poor husband and I have rued the day we ever agreed to chaperone and protect her until she was finally settled in some suitable employment at our destination.' Her eyes flashed, but there was no mistaking her heartfelt frustration.

Casting cautionary glances in the direction of her tent, she motioned to the two men to move a little further off with her. 'Though not – God be thanked! – a victim of the fever,' she whispered, 'my husband has been far from well since we came here. It is the continuing damp, I think, that does not agree with him, and he has become very listless and is continually downcast. And that girl's wilful, headstrong ways have without a shadow of doubt played a large part in his continuing poorly condition.'

Thomas, by his gestures and demeanour, made it plain how much he sympathised. 'I take it, Mrs Parry, the girl is not here now...? Have you any idea where she might be?'

'No, Father, she is not here, and seldom is – often not bothering to come for her meals, even though I have begged her to be a little more considerate towards us. As to where she goes, I have no idea. She says she is away playing with others or exploring, but I have to say that in my comings and goings within this tented area I never see her.' She shook her head in obvious despair, looking at Thomas, then, briefly, at Will... 'But what is it, gentlemen, that brings you to this questioning?'

Thomas, however, ignored her query. 'Have you any idea how old the girl is? Does she have any documentary proof of her age?'

Mrs Parry looked perplexed at this apparent leap from the priest's interest in Lizzie's whereabouts. 'Well, we were given very few documents relating to the girl, nor do we know, for certain, what age she is. Indeed, I think Lizzie herself would be unable to answer that question accurately... I should say maybe thirteen or maybe fourteen years... no more. I do not think more for she has not yet become... a woman... if you take my meaning?' And she paused, scrutinising the priest's face, until she had some sign – from Will, as it happened – that her 'meaning' had indeed been 'taken'. 'But what is it? Is she in some sort of trouble?' And again she looked from one to the other.

Thomas nodded. 'We fear she is, Mrs Parry. 'In trouble,' that is. Indeed we are well-nigh certain of it and are worried for her sake. Some days ago, I myself found her in a rather... compromising... situation with two men of unsavoury character, and we fear she is being misused... in the worst *possible* way.' He looked directly at the lady to be sure she had understood the full import of his words. 'Indeed, the matter may have gone even further.' His face registered his complete distaste. 'It seems likely that she is being prepared for a life of... of ill-repute... for when she gets to Brisbane.'

The colour all but drained from Mrs Parry's face and her hands were trembling. 'O Lord above, how can this be? Have we not tribulations enough here without this additional shame being thrust upon us? She is but a child. Who can be so wicked as to...?' And her words trailed off into bewildered silence.

'Mrs Parry, there are, sadly, not a few men, presently on this island, who would not scruple at a girl's age – if she were offered them,' Will responded, as gently as he could, recognising in her a woman of no great experience of the wiles of the world. 'And especially in a time and place in which the – and he cast about in his mind for the appropriate word – in which the... conveniences... of city life are withdrawn.'

There were tears in the woman's eyes. 'Such wickedness! We had no idea, for these are matters that are quite beyond anything my husband and I... And to think that child is a part of it. What, oh what, is to become of us?'

'But we're here to help, Mrs Parry,' Thomas said. 'Now, tell me... in good faith... would the girl obey you if you forbade her certain things?'

The poor woman shook her head, looking quite helpless. 'No, Father. I don't think so. Not anymore. At first, early in the voyage, she was as good as gold: respectful, considerate, and clearly grateful that we had undertaken to look after her. You see, she is an orphan... we believe... and we were told it had been thought best for her welfare that she seek a new life in the colony. Perhaps we were too trusting... I don't know...' And she shrugged her shoulders. 'I suppose she was grateful then... at being the centre of our attention, not being used to special treatment of any sort. But as time went on and she became acquainted with other people, especially the younger, single women, here, she gradually became more... rebellious... I suppose. At first it was in little things – like not helping with our family chores, leaving them all to me – but then, more openly, ignoring our pleas... Since our arrival here, she has lived a life more and more apart from us, being hardly civil, though taking from us in whatever way she pleases if it suits her.' Her aggrieved tone, verged on self-pity, escaped neither of the men. 'But authority over her? No, I have none. None at all.' She shook her head again in despair, perhaps too at an incomprehensible world.

'Is that her tent there?' asked Will, nodding at the one next to the Parry's.

'Yes, it is, but – as I say – where she is right now, I can't say.'

'Do you mind if we take a look inside?'

Mrs Parry hesitated. 'I don't think... I don't know that... I can give you permission. I would not even think of entering it myself. Not now, not since things became so strained between us.'

'I understand,' said Will. 'It doesn't matter. I don't suppose there is anything there anyway that would add to what we know already. It's just that... well, she mentioned a birth certificate – which she said she was unable to read, being illiterate...'

'Oh, I think it unlikely she would have such a document, sir,' the woman said quickly. 'The few papers she has were entrusted to us before we left Plymouth. And there was certainly no birth certificate – indeed, my husband and I did remark upon the strangeness of it when we first looked through them.'

'Is the girl illiterate, then, as she claims?' Thomas inquired.

'Yes, to all intents and purposes. She can make out one or two simple words, and she recognises her own name, but that's about all,

I would say. My husband offered more than once to teach her her letters, but she hadn't the patience or the interest. It seemed she could not concentrate for long enough. So, well... he gave up trying.'

'Mrs Parry – Thomas spoke firmly – it would make it much easier for all concerned if, in fact, we could determine the girl's true age. If she is a juvenile, as we strongly suspect, then legally we could take steps towards her protection from... from these predators. If she turned out to be legally an adult, then what she does is her own choice, and however foolish we may think it we cannot prevent her. If you would like to busy yourself elsewhere, I think Sergeant Crosby and I might just... if you... don't mind...'

Mrs Parry hesitated for a moment then nodded her head. Clearly perturbed by the priest's suggestion, she turned away, retrieved her pail, and entered her own tent where she could be heard speaking agitatedly to her husband.

Will moved quickly. He undid the ties and pulled back the tent flaps. And then stepped back at once, holding his breath. 'My God!' he exclaimed, when the first moment was past.

'Would you look at that! What an unholy mess! Ugh, sorry....' Thomas backed into Will in his haste to retreat.

It was impossible to know where the bed was, let alone any other features. There were discarded clothes and rags and bags and remnants of food everywhere and the stench...

'God's blood!' the priest croaked, a handkerchief pressed to his nostrils.' Then, after several long seconds, he nudged Will. 'Well, Sergeant Crosby, what are you waiting for? As chief representative... the only representative... of Her Majesty's forces of law and order on this island...'

Will pulled a face. 'Oh no. I'd say that lot required a higher authority... such as that vested in you, Your Holiness...'

'Agh, no...!'

'...Though, on second thoughts, we might just give it a miss, don't you think?' And, laughing, he reached in to quickly retie the tent flaps. 'Let's just presume she is a child and treat her accordingly. We can always demand she produce the certificate she claimed she had, in your hearing, Thomas...'

'That we can! For our health's sake... we can.'

'And now...?'

'And now, let's try and find the girl herself. I suggest we start...'

'...Where you found her on that first occasion...?'

And side by side, the two men hurried off over towards the sea, taking in long draughts of the wholesome, salt sea air.

XLV

As they approach the ever-lengthening line of graves, on their way down to the shore, they find young Billy buzzing about his mother's plot. He comes skipping towards them, his face spattered with soil.

'So what are you up to, Billy?' Thomas asks, 'Are you busy telling your mammy all your latest news?'

'No. Well... I was at first but that didn't take very long really. I'm making a garden for her, all round her. Come and look.' And indeed, in a manner of speaking, that was what he was doing, picking flowers and leafy twigs from the bushes, and sticking them in the loose soil around the grave mound.

'That's nice, Billy,' Will begins, relieved to have come across the boy, 'and I'm sure your mammy will like it, but... the way you are doing it means the things won't last very long. You see...'

'Oh, that's all right, Mr Crosby, because I can put some new different things in every day, can't I?'

'And so you can, my son,' Father Thomas acknowledges, stepping forward. "But tell me, what was it gave you the idea of making her a garden?'

And Will realises his own answer would only have disillusioned the boy, with reference to another order of reality that – as the child has ably demonstrated – is quite without relevance.

'Oh, sir, it wasn't my idea at all. It was hers. She always used to say she would like to live in a house that had a garden, so I'm making that wish come true for her, now. And I have, nearly, haven't I?'

'You certainly have,' says Will, making amends, 'and very pretty it looks too.'

The boy falls silent for a moment. Then in a burst of childish generosity he offers to make a garden for them too – if they would like one. 'All around our tent, it could be. Shall I, Mr Crosby?'

'That is truly a kind thought, Billy,' Thomas answers, gently nudging Will, 'and we should like it very much. Only... well, we should prefer our garden to be around a proper house, not a tent. And so, when we move away from here over to the mainland – and he points over the water to the barely discernible coastline – then maybe you can make one for us, there – just like this one. It would be better so... would you not agree, Mr Crosby?'

'I think it's a capital idea,' Will replies, falling in with Thomas's gentle subterfuge, 'and I am sure Billy will make an excellent job of it.' He bends down and strokes the boy's hair.

Billy, flushed with pride at the appreciation expressed, doesn't seem to notice the refusal it contains.

'You could be right, Father Thomas,' he says, twisting round to look up at the priest. 'And just now I have a lot of other things to do, anyway... just like you do.'

'Of course, Billy! Of course!' Thomas says, his eyes twinkling. 'So we'll be bidding you goodbye. And I *do* like your garden.'

Exchanging a smile, the two men quickly cover the ground to the shoreline; and, stepping down onto the sands, their minds turn once again to Lizzie, and her corrupters.

But they are none of them to be found.

''Tis an odd thing, is it not,' Thomas remarked, musing upon Billy's sensitivity, as they strolled back towards the camp, 'that we so often think of gardens as places of comfort? Or maybe we don't always even think it; we feel it, rather, almost instinctually. You know, I was brought up in a garden – more or less, anyway: a sizeable cloister with a garden at the centre of it. As a young child I was convinced it was the Garden of Eden, which the Fathers so often spoke about to us orphans, and it was... well, my security, Will. I played there;

and later read and prayed there in all weathers, though admittedly retreating into the cloister itself when the rain became incessant – as it is wont to do, at any time, all over Ireland.' He looked at Will and laughed. 'Oh, it is so, I do assure you!'

'...And I believe you, Thomas. The Isle of Man was bad enough!' Will motioned with his hand. 'So... do go on... with your garden reminiscences!'

'But looking back on it, Will – Thomas threw him a quizzical look – I realise it was really my prison, my delightful prison. For until I went beyond it, I was not at liberty to question its real value, having nothing at all to compare it with. Yet, more than that – and here I tip-toe into the flowerbed of philosophy – the idea of the Earthly Paradise, the lost Garden of Eden, has it not always been, and does it not even now continue to be, one of the poet's "mind-forged manacles"? For whilst ever we are captivated by its allure, its nostalgia for a perfect "time before", whose re-creation depends on a re-establishment of the rules and context of that time before, there can be no real mental or spiritual progress. That place of innocence and delight is but a millstone about our necks. That, at any rate, is the way I have come to see it.'

He stopped in his tracks and looked at Will. 'But you are smiling: don't you ever have such thoughts? Or is it just this unruly head of mine that loses itself in these... I suppose, meaningless mazes?'

Will grinned. 'I'm sorry, Thomas, just something you said that hit me... something I had never thought of, before... But just fancy: where Alice came from, there was a river Eden... The river... the Garden... Silly, really...'

Will stood silent, going back over the priest's argument, approving its logical progression yet unable, quite, to accept its conclusion. Not able, he realised, because the garden as 'delight' and, more importantly, as 'safe haven', had always had a future life in the all-too-brief past life he had shared with Alice... It was she, not he, who had often brought the topic into their lives, as they moved from one place to another.

'It would make this place even more pleasant if we could tidy up the garden and I could plant flowers for all seasons...' Speculative.

'When we have a home of our own, promise me it will have a garden that will be as much a part of the house as the house is of the garden...' Wistful.

'I shall wrap the house round with wisteria and climbing roses, and we shall fall on grassy banks, ensnared in a profusion of flowers of every description... and there make endless, delicious love...' Wickedly...

'The fruit trees and bushes and vegetable patches will pour their goodness into our bodies. But more than that, Will, it will be our place of respite, of fruitful solitude, our constant renewal...'

Dear, gentle, Alice...

Will shakes his head at the memories. And all of that had been for him a revelation, with its own magic, its poetry – thoughts such as could never have come from him, gardens being entirely outside his experience. Queen Street, Whitehaven, was an ever-upward-climbing terrace towards the church at the top, and only there did one encounter trees and clipped lawns among the gravestones. The houses had their back yards that held the washhouse, the coalhouse, the ash bins, and privies, all of them slate black.

Yet Alice had grown up in the country. Her father had lived for his garden, and she had early caught the infection, which, as idea at least, he too had caught, from her. And at Appleby – and only there – they had had the hire of a garden that was, potentially, what she'd always dreamed of. 'If this garden were mine, I should...' And so vividly had she dismantled and re-created it in his mind that by the time they had left that idyllic place, he too was a believer in their future garden...

No, in all truth, he couldn't subscribe to the thoughts Thomas had expressed.

And in that moment, Will realised his life's quest henceforth must be that garden; for when it was complete his yearning would have given way to his happiness, its hedges encompassing all that he had lost before... through his own, one original sin.

He raised his head and looked towards Thomas, his face the picture of dejection. But Thomas's concerned, questioning eyes were already fixed on him. But what could he say?

At last, he spoke, hesitantly. 'I see the logic of... what you say, about the garden you grew up with, and about the Garden of Eden... I see all that well enough...'

'But...?'

Will's face contorted into a look of bewilderment, was it? 'Yes... but, you see, gardens have always figured in my life with Alice... that is, as something we always dreamed of having; and I cleave to the notion of what a garden can be, mostly because of what a garden meant to her. And yes... I can see it may have owed much to thoughts – however fleeting or... obscure – of the biblical Eden. But it also seemed wholly achievable at the right time, in the right place, and what's more, wholly desirable... for one's inner peace. And God knows, I have need of that commodity, and have had these three years past!' He reflected for a moment. 'Maybe, I could have shared your view, Thomas – had my experience been yours, I mean. But, coming at the garden idea from where I started, I crave... for the future, that is... its magic, its attraction, and its enclosure... provided I have my own Eve with me. Do you understand... from *my* point of view?'

'Agh! But of course I understand, man. And what's more, I confess that though my rational stance is as I have stated it, that in no way precludes my own emotional attachment to the idea, in practice – only a fool would reject such a haven, especially in times of great stress or of...'

A moment or two's reflective silence, then the shrill cry of a bird, in the forest behind the encampment, startled the two men; but then it ceased as abruptly as it had begun.

'Goodness, but that's a sound I've not heard before,' Will said, breaking the all-enveloping silence, which had come upon them like a breath of air. 'But you were saying, Thomas...?'

'Yes, yes... In times of sorrow,' Thomas said, slowly. 'But chiefly – and an irony it is, to be sure – but this is how I see it. The cloistered life... as a permanent condition of life, that is... excludes much of the infinite richness of our human condition on this Earth. And thus, if I were still a believer, I would see all forms of religious enclosure as being, paradoxically... an insult, yes, precisely that... to my Maker.'

Will laughed, recognising the paradox. 'Well, the enclosure doesn't have to be religious to be stunting, does it? We are living an imposed kind of monasticism here, are we not, with all of its negations? Not least of which is its celibacy... One can understand the frustrations that are leading some of our "monks" here into temptation and then into corruption...' And before he could take the thought any further, they had set off again, back towards the tents.

'Aye,' Thomas said, 'and I suppose I am rather intolerant of that particular kind of temptation, being trained – beaten would be a more accurate description – to reject it and live with the rejection... which, incidentally, is yet another instance of the "stunting" you just alluded to! My Joanna... she strove continuously to eliminate its baleful effects, that she did, bless her soul... But I hope you who did not have the benefits of my beatings are not suffering too greatly in that respect... Are you?' And he arched his eyebrows, knowingly.

Will smiled. 'Well, not unduly, I suppose. Though just occasionally it almost smothers everything else...' Then the smile turned into laughter, 'but to tell you the honest truth, if we ever do leave this prison island alive, in addition to the pint of beer and the pint of milk I have promised myself I may yet go in search of a good woman... a bad woman, that is; but it'll depend very much on the feelings of the day, I shouldn't wonder!'

Thomas laughed with him. 'Well, Will Crosby – he declared, after a short but serious-seeming reflection, hand on forehead, eyes closed – I might just come along with you! Though you can have my share of the milk... and the beer too, for that matter...'

And all too soon their thoughts about gardens were abandoned since their words had brought them back more or less to the point of their original search.

XLVI

Back along the lake shore, among the bushes where some of yesterday's women and children had modestly prepared themselves to bathe (then dressed again with equal modesty), the child Lizzie, completely naked, is begging the man Stevens to give her back her clothes.

'Please, sir...'

'First you tell me the truth,' he says. 'Then we'll see about your clothes.'

'I am telling you the troof, sir, I am. The man give me only nine pence, even though I says what 'e wanted cost a shilling. That you 'ad said so.'

'But still you let him, for nine pence?'

'No, I didn't. 'E said, 'All right then, forget it,' them was 'is words, sir, and I thought 'e meant 'e wouldn't do it, but then 'e did after all, and I couldn't stop him...'

'Lying little strumpet!' Stevens snarls in his exasperation, and he silences her with a heavy swipe across her mouth. 'So where's the rest of the money he give you? Where've you hidden it?'

Whimpering now, the child continues to protest that it had been as she said, but Stevens will have none of it. Or, perhaps, he feigns a continuing front of disbelief.

'Right then,' he says decisively, 'you know what now.'

And the child nods, clearly fearful, watching her tormentor unbutton himself, and when he is ready, she bends to do his bidding.

Dr Ballow stood over Dr Mitchell, his patient, noting again how emaciated he had become in such a short space of time.

In his brief spells of lucidity, they had tried to feed him but had never really succeeded. In the water they gave him they had introduced cane sugar, or as an alternative, sugared lime juice, but though the liquid undoubtedly helped keep him alive the other morsels had had little or no visible effect. Ballow knew that Mitchell's only hope lay in his regaining full consciousness so that he could be treated and fed properly. Yet his growing familiarity with the course of the disease told him there was little likelihood of that happening and that, however long it took, short of a miracle, the brave young doctor was doomed. He shook his head, sadly, and made sure the poor young man was as comfortable as could be. Then he turned to his other patient, his colleague, Dr Mallon.

'How are you feeling, Patrick? Have you noticed any signs of the fever abating?'

Mallon yawned. 'I still have the headache and occasionally am given to an almost uncontrollable state of shivering. But at least I can keep up my strength by taking food and drink more or less normally. My own view – and I don't know whether you would concur – is that whatever I am suffering from, it bears little resemblance to the typhus. Indeed, its symptoms are more akin to those I have encountered in patients suffering from malaria, or Dengue fever – as I suggested before. If we had quinine, I should be tempted to take it, even though my ailment has not developed quite as malaria does.'

'Well, I wouldn't argue with that. But my – our – ignorance about all of this does depress me very greatly. We are continually floundering, and in the end, it is Father Thomas who generally brings more comfort to our patients than we do… albeit, in many cases, the last comfort they will have in this life.'

'Yes, he does…' The young man made a wry face, smiling a little, despite his pounding head. 'He is a quite remarkable man. Have you noticed how he… he never insists on the rites laid down by the Church of Rome?' Mallon heaved himself up onto his pillows, the better to see, and converse with his colleague. 'I called him on my second day here, to comfort a patient who was near to his end, and on seeing the priest enter, poor Mr Ball looked quite dismayed. "But I am not of your faith, sir," he says. And Father Thomas – do you know what he answered? He said, "Well then, my friend, that makes the two of us." And he proceeded to talk to the man as though they had just met casually, like in the street or the ale house, and he even had my poor patient laughing a little... before death finally overwhelmed him.'

'Well, Patrick, although I have no belief in these things myself... 'tis a pity there are not many more clerics like our friend. There would be a damned sight less trouble in the world if there were, don't you think? All the squabbling about whether a bit of bread and a drop of wine become something else – which they clearly cannot – and the strife that bit of can't has always caused, putting people to death in the most hideous ways because of it, when it's all mumbo-jumbo anyway... Well, it says a great deal about our human gullibility... and sadism. How could they preach the love of God and at the same time burn people to death – after mangling their poor bodies in all kinds of ingenious ways? I despise them all! And then... then, in a God-forsaken place like this, you come across someone like our friend, Father Thomas, and you realise how much at variance he must be with all of that. He has to be, to do the kinds of things I've witnessed in the short time I've known him... What part of Ireland would you say he was from? Half the man's charm, I swear, is that accent of his, his manner of speaking, his tone...'

'What part? That I cannot say.' Mallon shrugged. 'But on this other matter you raise... Well, I would not go as far as you do, about the spiritual side of things. But I'm wholly in agreement about the various churches' management of faith, and of the faithful...'

'Management? Manipulation, rather!' Ballow snorted. 'Just another form of politicking, to preserve all the privileges and power you've ground out over the centuries – at immense cost to ordinary humanity. You know, when I first came here, I thought maybe I would be able to leave all that behind. But no... Sadly, as I've come to understand, it travels with virtually every being who reaches these shores – like the lice and the fleas.'

'So it is, no doubt,' Mallon consented. 'And yet, for all that, people like you and me keep on hoping we can somehow get ahead of it all, and help build a decent, humane society out of the tabula rasa that this new country presents us with in...'

'*Tabula rasa*, you say...? Well, you're right enough about the hope. But it's precisely because there is no *tabula rasa* that we are doomed to fail. Think about it! The people coming here are much of a muchness... they bring the poison with them, don't they?'

'They're the worst affected, generally among the most ignorant sections of their respective societies...'

'They're victims, that's for sure – of the priests, of whatever persuasion...'

Back and forth they went, conversing in a way their official duties in Brisbane had never allowed them to do before – despite seeing each other more or less every day, for two years...

Having failed to locate the child at the shore, or in all of the likely, nearer places in the vicinity of the encampment, Will and Thomas, after hurriedly taking some vegetable soup from what the cook had left over from lunchtime, took the path out towards the lake.

On reaching its nearer, southernmost tip, Thomas turned to his companion. 'So, what now, Sergeant Crosby, since you know the place...'

'Well, Your Grace...' Will began, in mock humility, then proposed that Thomas search the western side whilst he went off to resume his aborted exploration of the further shore.

He stood for a while, watching, as the priest set off at a leisurely pace along the sandy shoreline. Then, remembering the route he had taken last time, which had almost immediately led him into difficulties, Will followed a less likely-seeming path nearer to the lake shore, over on the other – eastern – side. After an initial patch of thorn, it opened out to permit more rapid progress and soon he reached the spot where they fancied they had seen the men on the previous day. Sure enough, the grass was trampled; there was even a discarded ale flagon planted in the top of one of the grass trees.

And then Will spotted a path leading away at right angles to the lake shore. After a moment or two's hesitation, he elected to follow it, at least for a little way, hoping it might throw some light on the previous day's mysteries... even that it might lead him to the child they were now desperately seeking.

He had not gone far, before he realised that he was on a well-used track, which soon rounded back on itself and ran in a straight line as far as the eye could see, in what he judged must be a southerly direction. It passed through swathes of eucalyptus and the occasional gigantic fig and other towering trees whose names he did not know. Bending down at two or three different points, Will examined the many footprints in the dusty sand, but nowhere could he find any that might have signalled the recent presence of the girl.

He straightened up and considered the implications of his observations. The most pressing task was to find the girl, and this track, it would seem, was not going to help him do so. Besides, the footprints were almost certainly all yesterday's, and curious though he was to know precisely where the sandy pathway led, he surmised it must come out at some other landing stage or inlet on the western side of the island, though further south than Dunwich; and, perhaps, neither visible nor attainable – other than by boat – from there.

Arriving back at the lake shore he picked his way through the undergrowth for maybe a hundred yards or so, moving northwards, further up the lake. The trampled grass and churned sand told him that others had been there recently, and once or twice he spotted what might conceivably be footprints along the always narrow margin between the sandy shore and the line of vegetation.

Every now and again Will cast a glance over to the other side thinking he might catch a glimpse of his friend, but he didn't – which was not particularly surprising, since, as he recalled, the priest's passage along the farther shore would be quite untrammelled by obstacles such as this wilder side abounded in. And Thomas would almost certainly have made swift progress towards the lake's northernmost extremity.

Deciding that his present course was unlikely to serve their immediate purpose, Will turned and retraced his steps along the shore, determined to reach the other side as quickly as possible, now.

It was then he heard what he thought might well be a human cry. Or was it merely the call of some exotic bird? He stopped and listened for it again. But all was as silent as before, so away he went, expecting to encounter Thomas near the point at which they had parted more than half an hour ago.

Father Thomas, though mindful of the task which presently occupied him, was exulting in the unaccustomed sense of freedom that his parting from Will afforded, realising that ever since their arrival on the island there had been few moments that he could call his own. Furthermore, he realised, this was the very first time he had been out of sight of the encampment. And he began humming to himself, though only in his head, exhilarated, yet unwilling to break the silent peace.

Looking about him, he decided he liked the feel of the place in which he found himself: its open aspect, the whiteness of the sand along the narrow lake shore, recalling many a strand on Ireland's Atlantic coast. But most of all its almost soundless tranquillity. And these realisations, as much felt as thought, caused him, quite unconsciously, to slacken his pace to a saunter. He remained vigilant, nevertheless, carefully scrutinising each bush-lined alcove leading to a narrow beach or inlet, but increasingly disposed to believe that his search would be unyielding, though far from unrewarding. It was more self-indulgence than moral imperative – if he were honest with himself – that propelled him towards the top end of the lake.

And it was in this relaxed, carefree frame of mind that he suddenly came upon the very thing he was searching for.

So unprepared was he that It took him a moment or two to realise the meaning of the scene before him. He stood there transfixed, first in horror, then by an overwhelming anger.

There was Lizzie, kneeling naked with her back towards her tormentor who, though facing away from the priest, was easily recognisable from the faded grey sailcloth jacket he always wore. The girl was whimpering and begging something of Stevens which, in his fury, Thomas could not make out.

And all at once, he was hurtling uncontrollably down towards the shore.

The man, sensing his approach, half-turned in his direction – conveniently as it happened – just in time to receive the massive blow to his jaw that sent him reeling sideways halfway into the water.

Taken utterly by surprise, Stevens, attempting to rise to his knees, had no time to gather his wits together before the priest's boot caught him fully in the groin. Groaning with the pain of it, he sank face downwards into the sand, his feet still in the water.

Thomas's anger was by no means yet abated. He bent down and hauled the man to his knees. And, holding him steady with his right hand, crashed his left fist into the side of his head, felling him yet again. This time Stevens did not move at all, having either lost consciousness, or – with the burly priest standing over him – decided that complete immobility was his surest form of self-defence.

Thomas prodded the inert Stevens with his foot, eliciting another groan, then, seeing that the man was too injured or dazed to cause him any immediate trouble, he turned his attention to the girl, who had not moved, or ceased her whimpering. He knelt down to help her, but she cowered away, trying to cover her nakedness with her hands.

'Come child, I am not going to hurt you. Tell me, where are your clothes?'

'I don't know, sir. Mr Stevens took 'em and won't give 'em back to me.'

Thomas twisted round towards Stevens and saw that although he had moved his position, he was making no attempt to stand. 'Well, you filthy blackguard, where are the child's clothes?'

The man made no reply but continued his moaning.

Thomas got to his feet and went over to him. Then, rather more gently than might have been expected, he rolled him over onto his back. Stevens opened his eyes and stared fearfully up into the priest's still red, angry face.

'Stevens, man. Will you be telling me where the child's clothes are, or do I have to beat it out of you? The choice is yours, but don't delay!'

Sorely pummelled as he was, Stevens' voice was barely a whisper. 'Along the shore, there – he gestured weakly with his right hand – there's a broken tree; her things are up in its top.'

Thomas nodded. 'Now, don't you move from there, you little rat, and don't you dare utter a word to that child. Do you understand?' He said, menacingly, then he turned to Lizzie. 'And you, girl, wait here!'

Stevens indicated that he understood well enough. Lizzie gave no sign of having heard or understood, but she made no move, so Thomas set off, almost at a canter, in search of the tree.

He found it almost at once, but it was somewhat higher than he had imagined, and he would not be able to reach the garments – which he could see well enough – without climbing some ten feet or so. 'Ah, for God's sake!' he complained as he circled the tree, while yet realising there were probably just sufficient hand- and footholds to scale it. But in his clerical garb?

He looked back to make sure he was not visible from the place whence he had come, then removed his cassock, and, with surprising alacrity, he shinned up the tree in his pants. Reaching out, he retrieved the girl's clothes, and then, since they kept snagging on twigs and broken branches, he tossed them down onto the sandy earth beneath. His own descent was a good deal slower, for the footholds had to be felt for carefully with his booted feet. Finally down, he pulled on his cassock, bundled the garments together, and hastened back to where he had left Stevens and the girl.

'Well, I'll be damned…!'

They were gone. Dropping the bundle, and cursing yet again, under his breath, he scrambled back up to the main path – and he saw them at once, maybe two hundred yards away, heading in the direction of the encampment. The limping Stevens appeared to be pulling the naked girl along by her hair.

'God damn the evil little bastard…!' he growled; and he set off in hot pursuit.

But after a moment or two, he saw them freeze, Stevens clearly hesitating, before setting off again in a changed direction, pulling Lizzie higher up the banking towards the thick screen of trees behind.

'What in the divil's…?' But then he immediately saw the reason for it… Will was hurrying along the path towards them! And it was obvious he had seen them and understood the meaning of what he saw, for he too diverged up the banking to head them off. And Thomas smiled his immense satisfaction.

Stevens, panicking now, dragged the girl right round, clearly intending to go back the way they had come. But seeing Thomas also closing in on him from that direction, he had no choice but to stand his ground and await events.

As his pursuers drew nearer, however, they could see plainly enough that he was holding a knife to the child's throat.

'She gets it if you come any closer,' Stevens shouted, 'I swear to God she will!' He was almost screaming in his desperation.

Thomas stopped four or five paces short of the man. 'Stevens, you are already up to your neck in trouble as it is,' he bellowed, trying not to look at the naked girl, who was trembling in her captor's grasp. 'Adding murder to your list of crimes will do for you, once and for all, and so it will.' He drew his extended forefinger across his own throat and moved a step nearer. 'Hurting this child, whom you have already harmed so very badly, will gain you no advantage, for we shall still be here to tear you limb from limb when you have done your worst.' Another step nearer. 'And certainly, whatever your threats, you will not be moving from here!'

Before the panicking Stevens could begin to answer, Will moved in and stunned him with a well-aimed pebble. The pimp went reeling into the bushes behind him. Will was on him at once, holding him face downwards, his knee in the small of his back, twisting his arm upwards until, squealing with the pain of it, Stevens released the knife.

The sobbing, distraught girl made as if to run off. But Thomas caught her arm. 'Oh no, you don't!' he roared, grasping her tightly. 'From now on *you* are going to start behaving like a civilised human being, Lizzie. To begin with you'll need your clothes, which are… Come with me.' And, so saying, he marched her back down to the bushes by the water's edge and commanded her to dress quickly.

Will got to his feet, then hauled Stevens up into a sitting position, noticing as he did so the blue bruise spreading across the man's jaw and the blood dripping from the wound above his right ear where the pebble had struck him.

'That little devil has been the undoing of me with her taunting and flaunting…', Stevens groaned, his face contorted in hatred.

'How dare you, Stevens! She is a *child*,' Will barked. 'And however misguided she has been you were happy enough to take advantage of her for your own grubby ends, and that is going to put you back behind bars for quite some time, I shouldn't wonder. But at least you won't hang – which is something you may one day thank us for… although I can't ever see you mending your ways. You're a natural jailbird, if ever there was one!'

Thomas and the girl reappeared, the latter continually trying to pull away, and still snivelling.

'Father Sheehan,' crooned Will, in mock politeness, 'would you mind giving me the loan of your rope? Off your cassock, I mean.' And he nodded at the priest's waist. Then, smiling, he jerked Stevens to his feet, secured his hands in front of him, swung him round and began marching him towards the camp, a prisoner.

Thomas followed behind, still holding the girl firmly by her arm, in no mood for any further shows of disobedience.

And as they went along, the four of them in procession, with Thomas hitching up his cassock with his free hand every third or fourth step, Will started to wonder what they would do with their prisoner, once back at the camp.

The whole situation… it could now rebound on them. For whatever the moral rightness of their action, there was no force of law to underpin it. There was no provision of any sort – for all he knew, not even one building whose door would lock…

He sighed, heavily. And those men they could count on for support were likely fewer in number than those who might come to their prisoner's aid – Stevens undoubtedly had his friends, men who might not take kindly to seeing him treated in this way...

These doubts were real enough, and, perhaps unconsciously, Will slackened his pace. He looked back at his comrade, to seek, through some sign, perhaps, his views on the matter. Yet as he looked, seeing him holding the girl, half in anger, half with tenderness, a counter image flashed upon his inward eye... An occasion when he had held his own daughter Lilian just so, angered at her defiance, her refusal to budge from the spot, when her mother had repeatedly asked her to put away her scattered toys...

The sudden memory blinded him with tears.

XLVII

When the camp came into view, Will turned to his friend, who had doubtless been mulling over the same difficulties.

'Follow me, Thomas,' he whispered, 'and quickly.' Surprise might work to their advantage, but only for a limited time.

The priest nodded, looking relieved. And none too gently, Will yanked Stevens on. 'If you utter so much as one word to anyone, anyone at all, then I promise you, I'll break your neck on the spot.' And to emphasise his determination he yanked upwards on the rope that held his captive. Stevens yelped with the pain of it.

Instead of passing in among the tents, Will led the procession stealthily along the backs of those which were closest to the trees and undergrowth, at times having to squeeze past ropes and pegs that had been set close to or even within that verdure. His objective was clear enough in his mind: to reach Captain Kemp and his officers so that an armed cordon could be placed between Stevens and any who might take it upon themselves to come to his rescue.

Some five or six people observed their irregular route and perhaps even noticed the rope that clearly signified Stevens' plight, but none made any attempt to raise the alarm, even if one man did point and mutter some comment to his neighbour.

Luck was with them. No one sought to impede their passage and they were soon enough through the gate at the far end of the compound and into the area occupied by the ship's officers and crew.

Captain Kemp was in his tent talking heatedly with two of his officers, but, hearing approaching footsteps, he came quickly outside. The officers also emerged, their eyes widening at the sight of the strange group.

'So what have we here, gentlemen?' the captain began. 'A case of in flagrante, could it be?' And he smiled, far from jovially.

'Precisely that, Captain,' Thomas acknowledged, 'Caught red-handed he was, violating this child.' He pointed to Lizzie who, for her part, tossed her head to one side and looked resolutely away.

'Indeed! And what do you say to that?' the captain asked, looking directly into Stevens' eyes.

'If anyone's been violated, Captain... sir, 'tis me. By these two men here.' He lifted his swollen jaw and turned to show the cut on the side of his head, and then added, plaintively: 'It may have been a misunderstanding on their part, sir; I can't say for sure. But I assure you, what the reverend gentleman is saying is not true, not true at all.' And he smiled fondly at the girl.

Will scowled at him, unable to believe his ears.

'Tell him, Lizzie dear,' Stevens coaxed. 'Tell the good captain that what they are saying is not true, that there was nothing like that.'

Lizzie did not turn her head, nor did she look at anyone. But what she said was clear to all present.

'Of course it ain't true. I were playing and Mr Stevens come... a-looking for me.'

'And what were you playing at, Lizzie *dear*?' Thomas asked, fighting hard to curb his anger. 'Without a stitch on, and your clothes a hundred yards away *at the top of a tree*?'

Smiles and sniggers followed his words, and for a moment, it all looked quite simple.

'Why sir,' the child said, turning to face the priest, without so much as a blush. 'I'd been a-bathin'... in the water... like what I 'eard the ladies was a-doin' the day afore.'

Thomas raised his eyes heavenwards, and shook his head; though, observing him closely, Will saw that he could not quite hold back the shadow of a smile.

'I see,' the priest said, his voice heavy with irony, 'and your clothes at the top of the tree?'

'I put 'em there for safety, sir.' The girl's reply came back pat. 'So's nobody would run off wiv 'em.' And she smiled, wanly.

'Oh, *really!*' Thomas said, in mock astonishment. 'But why so far away from where I found you... together with this man here?'

'Well, they was not far away when I first went in the water. They was only far away when... when I come out on it.'

Thomas shook his head in disbelief at the child's ingenuity, then changed tack. 'So, Lizzie... dear, why were you kneeling naked, weeping, with Stevens kneeling just behind you, when I came on the scene?'

The child thought for a moment. Then, hanging her head as if in shame at the memory of it, replied, 'Cos I were ashamed at him seeing me like that wiv no clothes on an' all. I were askin' him to turn away so as I could go get my fings...'

'I see,' said Thomas, drily. 'And what did he say to that, Lizzie... dear?'

'Well, he didn't really have no chance to say aught, 'cos it were... it were then you set on him, an' hurt him so bad he were nearly dead of it.'

Thomas looked at the ship's gentlemen, raising his hands, palms turned outwards, to express his utter frustration. The captain nodded and smiled weakly back, but there was little encouragement in these gestures.

Thomas then turned to Stevens. 'Nearly dead of it, were you? Nearly dead of it, indeed! So how was it that when I came back with the child's clothes you and she had... felt unable to wait? Were, in fact, already a good two hundred yards away... and going at speed... Oh, and by the way, if you *had* just happened on the child, how was it you were able to tell me precisely where her clothes were?'

Stevens smirked and shook his head, as if in disbelief, 'As to the last point, begging your reverence's pardon, I think you are mistaken. 'Twas the girl herself as told you where she had stowed her garments.'

Thomas glared at him but, realising a wrangle about this point would in no way further the cause of essential truth, pressed him hard, instead, on the first matter.

Stevens, however, appeared quite unflustered. 'Well sir,' he began, but then turned to Kemp, addressing his reply half to the captain, half to the priest. 'I was at my wit's end. I had already had a flaying at… at your hands, Father, and I was not to know but what you would dole out some more such medicine… when he come back, sir. And besides… I thought this poor innocent child had already seen enough violence… and my first thought was to get her away, as quick as I could – though I was still very weak and very shaken from… your assault…'

Captain Kemp shook his head, dumbfounded, while the priest roared with laughter.

Will, who had witnessed none of the events to which Thomas alluded, nor yet heard about them from Thomas's lips, till now, could only surmise what had really taken place. Yet, listening to Stevens' quite plausible, but far too glib account, and watching Thomas's reactions, he understood well enough that the reality had been entirely otherwise. And, in a flash, he remembered… Hadn't he seen Stevens more or less dragging the completely naked child, by her hair, and then quickly veering off away from *him*, towards the forest?

'Look, Stevens. I can well understand you wishing to escape Father Thomas's fury, given the injuries he had already inflicted upon you…' Will began. And Stevens' eyes opened wide, at this apparent support of his claims. 'But tell me, why did you also try to run away from *me*? Answer me that!' Will's eyes blazed. '*I* who could have been your protector, *I* who have never given you cause for offence… And why, incidentally, were you dragging that poor, naked child, along with you…?'

Kemp was now looking hard at Stevens.

Stevens blinked, hesitating for a moment, then explained: 'Ah, Sergeant Crosby sir, my mind was all confused, what with… the beating and all that I had lately suffered, sir… And besides, I was only too aware of the need to protect young Lizzie here, in her nakedness…'

'Oh aye? Why then, if you were seeking to *protect* her, were you *dragging* her by her *hair*…?'

Again gales of laughter escaped the ship's officers, and even Kemp's face flickered into a brief smile. Thomas shook his head, exasperated.

Will now fixed the man with a steely glare. 'We've had enough of your lying, Stevens, unless you'd like more of this!' And he thrust a clenched fist under the man's nose.

Stevens stepped back, his face white with fear, or rage, and he looked at the captain, perhaps seeking sympathy, even protection. The captain stared at him but said not one word. Stevens, clearly realising he was entirely isolated, quickly screwed up his eyes. 'To answer your question, Sergeant Crosby... Because she was very... hesitant, quite unsure, said we should stop. But I knew, sir, that there was not a moment to lose if... well, if her modesty was to be preserved...'

Will could hold back no longer, joining the officers and Thomas in their unrestrained laughter at the man's effrontery, at his consummate deftness with the warps and wefts of a job-lot of possible truths.

'Stevens,' Thomas interjected, finally, "tis a pity you chose pimping rather than the stage as your trade, for in the latter, I'm convinced, you would have made your mark – and steered clear of the ever-renewing, soon-to-be-deepening misery that you choose as your lot. The stage, man... for that's what you *should* have chosen. But it's too late now!'

Stevens squinted, in apparent disbelief: 'I do not know what your reverence can mean by that, sir, I...'

'Be that as it may...' Will cut him off. 'So, how then do you explain the knife at the "poor innocent child's" throat, when you realised that you couldn't escape me or, indeed, Father Thomas, who was fast closing on you from behind? Explain that if you can!'

Stevens, for the first time in this whole exchange, appeared nonplussed. 'Well, sir...' he faltered, 'like I said, sir, I was all confused and... and... well, I panicked... sir.'

Yet even though he plainly now saw himself at bay, his quick wit soon had the tables somehow turned again. And one might have thought it was his accusers who struggled to make their case; that, if anything, his being at bay was a sort of tactical triumph.

'You panicked?' Captain Kemp said at length. 'Panicked, you may have, Stevens, but what did you hope to gain by threatening the girl with a knife?'

'It was like this. I figured, sir, that if I could somehow convince Mr Crosby and Father Sheehan, here, that I meant business – with the knife, I mean – then they would let us go. But sure, I meant the child no harm, as I did explain to her even as I was taking out my knife...'

Captain Kemp had heard enough. 'Is *any* of this true, Lizzie?' he barked.

The child mumbled something in response.

'I cannot hear you,' the captain said, none too kindly. 'Speak more clearly, girl, so that we *all* may hear you!'

The child's eyes were now fixed on the ground as she shuffled nervously from one foot to the other.

'You have nothing to fear now, child,' the captain persisted, a touch more gently, 'for we shall protect you. Speak the truth, therefore.'

The child seemed to sense that, despite his tone, the captain was fast losing all patience with her. Suddenly, she blurted it out: ''E did, sir, I swear 'e did... He did say that to me...'

The captain closed his eyes, quite unable to believe the girl's complicity in her own undoing. 'You have her well-schooled, Mr Stevens,' he said, not troubling to hide his contempt. 'I wonder. What is the nature of the hold you have over her?'

Stevens shook his head, his face a mask of pained innocence. But his left eye twitched, and his hands trembled. 'Hold... sir?' he said quietly. 'I know not what you can mean, sir.'

The captain clicked his tongue and turned to his two officers. 'We'll accommodate him aboard the *Emigrant*. Clap him in irons and stow him securely below decks... till we get to the bottom of this whole distasteful affair!'

XLVIII

The sun was already well down the sky, over the mainland, and Will, who'd been running, paused in his search for young Billy, allowing his eyes to stray towards its bluish haze, so near, yet in these present circumstances, so far away, in its comforts and security.

To him – and, he surmised, to many others presently stranded in this claustrophobic margin of a bay – it little mattered what was already established over yonder. What was much more compelling were the possibilities it afforded for the realisation of every man's dream, of that world each one of his fellow-travellers had doubtless brought with him in his head, to be found somewhere in the vast emptiness that lay beyond Brisbane or, indeed, within the new township itself. But whatever the substance of each dream, what they all must have in common was that sense of a new beginning, the effective rejection of whatever their lives had been up to their point of departure. And again his eye settled on the gradually intensifying blue line of the horizon, a threshold which, even from here, some yet were destined never to cross.

For him, however, it was not so clear cut. Oh, yes, how thrilling it would be if he were to find himself immersed in a new sense of innocence, of setting out all over again unburdened of that wariness of his fellow men, that knowledge of them and of the world they tainted, which prudence demanded for one's very survival. Yet, even were he to find it, or something like it, such a society would be for him but a partial context, merely a means to an end which itself lay back in that older, certainly more corrupted world to which, nevertheless, his heart and soul were riveted.

How could it not be so?

Will bent down, and sent a small, flat stone skimming into the shimmering waters, feeling the intense pull of that empty horizon with its dimly discerned mountain shapes towering away behind the as yet invisible township.

If only Alice and the child had been with him here – oh how ardently he desired that they should be – he could embrace it all and mould it to their every wish. Instead, he must be in it but never quite of it; a divided soul striving for respect, for self-respect, in the one world, in the hope that, once gained, its currency would hold good back in that other.

The horizon was taking on a misty, turquoise hue, and he sighed, deeply. In that moment of realisation, with that vision set out before him, the seven years he must stay apart from Alice seemed even more of an eternity; and, as Thomas had hinted, the vision itself was, in all probability, wildly, romantically doomed.

And now there was this other complication: his guardianship, or at least, joint tutelage, of a small boy; and this bound him in ways he would not wish to be bound – not only to the child but, seemingly, to this man who, whatever he might say and believe about himself, was still a Catholic priest.

The irony was cruel and crippling.

Of course – he reasoned – these obligations to the child could well be revised once they were able to engage with whatever competent authorities there were in Brisbane. Billy could simply be handed over to them. Handed over. Not abandoned. No, for he and Thomas would see the boy, frequently even, but without having the day-to-day responsibility for him. He would then be able to detach himself and…

But could he *really*? Could he *really* do all that and… detach himself?

It wasn't just Billy's dependence, compelling though that was, but more, if he was honest, something in himself. Billy had quickly defined himself and become a 'somebody'; a unique little somebody he had told himself he didn't need… though not of late. No… thinking about it, now… not of late.

Will turned his back on the sea, on the distant mountains, the invisible township. So where was the boy? Back at their tent now, perhaps? And he strode back purposefully, to reconnect with the world of duty.

The child was there, right enough. As Will entered, he appeared absorbed in the latest Anderson story they had begun the previous night, his head down, trying to fathom the words, mouthing them, even aloud. But when he looked up, it was obvious he had been crying.

Will decided to ignore the tears. 'Are you managing to understand the words, Billy?'

'Oh, I can read it all the way, all the way as far as… this word here,' Billy said, a little boastfully. He indicated a fair stretch of text down to the ninth or tenth line of the page. 'But I don't know what this is,' and he pointed to the word 'island'.

Will chuckled. 'I'm not surprised. When I was your age, I wouldn't have known, either. Our language is full of all sorts of words that seem to ask you to say them one way when, in fact, you have to say them a different way. And don't, for goodness sake, ask me why, because I don't know! I dare say Father Thomas could give you an answer, though, so save your question for him… if you were going to ask it!'

Billy grinned. 'I was,' he said. Then he applied himself once more to his learning, once again murmuring to himself as though Will had vanished from the scene.

'Well, do you want to know how to pronounce it or don't you?'

'What?' said Billy, reading on.

'The word you asked me about – don't you want to know what it is?'

'Yes…' Billy dragged his eyes, but not his finger, from the page.

'Well you pronounce it 'i: land'… Have you got that Billy…?'

But now Will's attention was distracted – by a scrap of paper lying on his bed. Picking it up, he read the few words written on it, scrawled in a childish, or unpractised hand.

'Sara Jayn Dunikan and Buny Brisen is gon for strumpits.'

Frowning, he turned it over, but there was nothing more. 'Billy... have you any idea how this bit of paper came to be here? Billy...?'

'No...' Billy did not look up until he reached a full stop. 'I didn't even know it was there... And the Ugly Duckling doesn't know either, Mr Crosby. So don't bother asking him... if you were going to...'

Will grinned at the cheek, or whatever one might call it, of this mere six-year-old.

The boy went back to his reading, obviously pleased with himself.

Will sat down and looked at the names again. Had Thomas perhaps dropped it? Or had someone entered the tent when all its occupants were away? Someone afraid to speak out, who wished to remain anonymous...?

'Mr Crosby...' Billy whispered, suddenly. 'Can I tell you something?'

'Of course you can, Billy... What is it?' Will asked, his mind still half-engaged with the conundrum posed by the piece of paper.

'When I was out before, talking to my mammy about the garden I was making, and asking her if she liked it, and what colour flowers she liked best, a man came. He said he'd helped put my mammy in the ground...'

'What?' Will twisted round, all ears. 'What did he say?'

'He said my garden was nice, and he wanted to show me something. And he...'

'And... did you go with him?'

'I hadn't finished my garden, so I...' The child hesitated. 'He had a bad smell, Mr Crosby. Like fish. And I didn't like it. I didn't like him either.'

Will reached over and took hold of Billy's arm. 'Did he try to make you go with him?'

'I didn't want to. But he kept saying it wasn't far, and I would like what he wanted to show me...'

'And then, Billy?'

'I ran away. And I went looking for you. But I couldn't find you, and I came back here and hid from him... in case he was still looking for me. I didn't like that smelly man. I... I...'

Billy was again close to tears.

'And you are right not to like him,' Will said, gently, rubbing the boy's shoulder. 'He is not a good man, Billy. Was that the reason for your crying... before?'

'Yes, 'cos I was frightened of him. And I couldn't find you, or Father Thomas. And I didn't know what to do, and I...' Billy pushed hard against Will, as if to stifle the sobs that now rocked his small body. 'And I couldn't...'

'Shush, now, Billy, shush...'

Inching away, Will got to his feet, and held his arms out. Billy wriggled off the bed and nestled against him, not looking up. And they stood there a moment, in mutual, quiet comfort, Will finally experiencing something like a release from his own tension.

'You're safe here, Billy. And I'll make sure this man doesn't bother you anymore. Believe me, I will...'

So, he thought, as Billy turned back to his book... while Stevens was messing about with the girl, Callaghan was on the lookout for some other poor, unwary child. And perhaps Callaghan would understand the kind of wisdom Thomas and he had dealt Stevens. Oh yes. And far more readily than any words of warning...

And, suddenly smouldering with rage, Will found himself more than ready to provide it.

Deciding there and then to take action Will all but crashed into Thomas just outside the tent.

'Now, steady on, man! What is it? You look as though you're being pursued by all the banshees in Hell, so you do!'

Will drew him aside, and quickly told him about Callaghan, and poor Billy's encounter with him.

'Then there's no time to lose, is there? So off you go.' Thomas was almost pushing Will. 'And I... Just a minute.' The priest stepped back to peer round the tent flap. 'The boy seems busy enough, so I'll... I'll come along; give you some... moral support, is it?'

Will smiled.

'And I'll tell you this,' Thomas went on, now leading the way. 'The feeling of satisfaction that came from the "moral lesson" I gave Stevens has not left me yet, Will. And I'm sure I could feel the same about Callaghan's mouthful of dust if we were so lucky as to find him.'

Was his friend in earnest? Will felt oddly uneasy. Certainly, he'd not been aware of any propensity for violence in the priest's past. The anger that had unleashed the storm on Stevens was one thing, but he could not imagine Thomas acting so, in premeditated, cold blood…

There was no discussion about where their steps should lead them; it had become almost axiomatic that the top end of the cemetery was Callaghan-Stevens territory. And thus, yet again, Will found himself approaching the seashore at the northern-most edge of the encampment. His thoughts about Thomas, however, had served to put a break upon his own anger, at least.

Passing the line of graves on their right they walked rapidly on to the point at which the banking down to the shore was less steep. Yet whilst it was still some twenty or thirty yards ahead of them Thomas suddenly placed a restraining hand on Will's arm, bringing them to a halt.

'Listen!' he urged in a stage-whisper, 'can you hear it?'

Will looked puzzled. 'But what…? What can you hear?'

'Whisht!' the priest commanded, 'just use your ears man!'

Will strained to hear whatever it was that had evidently so startled his companion. At first, there was only the soughing of the breeze through the wispy leaves of the casuarinas – Ballow's name for them – which enclosed three sides, almost, of that little corner of the burial ground. But all at once, there it was, clearly differentiated from that sound: the voice of a man singing.

'Whoever can it be?' he wondered, aloud.

Thomas shook his head. 'Whoever it is, is singing in the Gaelic, and that's a fact! But a strange Gaelic such as I never heard in my parts of the country; something from the extreme west, or the south-west, at a guess.' And he urged Will on, increasing their pace.

And Will found himself driven by a similar curiosity, and because the lilting song was expressed in such a softly melodious baritone voice.

Clambering quickly down onto the foreshore, they spotted a figure seated on a large rock, some forty, or fifty yards away, seawards from them. And they stopped again, uncertain, not wishing to interrupt the dirge – for so it now seemed – in all its sad and heart-rending beauty.

XLIX

Dr Mitchell had seemed to rally a little mid-morning, and for an hour or two the matron's spirits had soared. Come midday, however, he was once again prostrate, his breathing irregular, and by mid-afternoon his condition was worse than it had ever been.

For the past three hours or so the young matron, sitting alone beside him, has sponged his forehead and arms, and talked to him in whispers to try and rouse him from his coma. And now she leans forward and kisses his brow, then his lips.

The thought has come to her that he may well die without ever knowing how she loves him... It had started on board the *Emigrant*, although she had never dared to so much as hint at these feelings in their daily work together, for fear of being rebuffed, or of damaging their working relationship in circumstances in which so many depended upon it for their very lives.

There would always be time, she had thought.

'Please, George, please, oh please, don't go any further into the darkness... you have to know... you and I, if you will have me... you see...'

And Miss Labone falls to her knees, her hands clasp together, her eyes shut tight. 'Oh just and merciful Father, most loving God...' And she pleads his case, believing implicitly that goodness – of which dear George Mitchell possesses a superabundance – will be rewarded. But even as she prays, she admits to herself she knows nothing; and is helpless before this immense dark figure looming over the good doctor's bed.

They recognised the singer at once, though his back was still turned towards them.

'I'll be damned!' Thomas whispered.

'No… Surely not! I don't believe it!' And Will moved forward a little, the better to see, with each step feeling less sure of their purpose. Thomas followed, and as they drew near, Ned Callaghan half-turned towards them, but then swivelled back to face the sea, as if they were of no account, and went on with his singing.

Veering diagonally out, one on each side, they rounded the rock and came face to face with him, placing themselves between his gaze and the sea.

If he was at all startled by their presence, he did not show it. 'Ah, Father Thomas is it, and Sergeant Crosby? An honour… indeed, a double honour, to be sure!'

'Callaghan,' Will began unceremoniously, 'I'll come straight to the point. An hour or two ago you tried to persuade little Billy Tawbridge to go for a walk with you. Why did you do that?'

'Ah, yes, Mr Crosby. Well, so I did, I was that excited myself!'

As he spoke, Will caught the unmistakable stink of fish about him that had so alienated the little boy; but it was mingled also with the stench of rum, and Will backed away a couple of paces, out of reach of their combined effect. 'Excited?' he questioned drily. 'About what, precisely?'

'Why, about the tiny blue crabs, hundreds of them all running about at the sea's edge. Something I had never seen in my life afore, such… such a… wonder! And I wanted to bring him where they were, you see. I was sure the little chap would take such delight in a marvel of that sort… I know I did at his age… Tiny blue crabs, hundreds of them…!'

Thomas took a step or two closer, he too having evidently caught the whiff of rum.

'Tiny blue crabs be damned!' he almost shouted. 'No such thing, except in your rum-soaked, addled brain, Callaghan!'

Will scrutinised the man's face keenly, uneasy at the priest's angry rebuttal, and remembering... those little blue, spider-like crabs at Amity Point, scuttling about at the water's edge... And so, reluctantly, he found himself coming to the rogue's aid.

'No, Father Sheehan,' he began, ''tis not so fanciful, for I too have seen these tiny crabs, up at the northern tip of the island.'

'I had never seen their like afore, sir,' Callaghan exclaimed to Thomas, beaming in his excitement. 'And I was just dying to show somebody, before they... they kept disappearing, into the sea... And that boy was just the one, because he seems to spend a lot of his time beside his mammy's grave, always alone, he is... And I thought this might draw him away and out of the grief I know he must be suffering. For I too have suffered that self-same grief, and worse, for I never knew when my own mother died nor where she was laid to rest, if rest she could. But the child ran off, so...'

And once again, as if his two inquisitors had ceased to exist, he looked beyond them, to the far horizon, and took up his song again.

Thomas and Will exchanged puzzled glances.

After listening for a moment, Thomas began speaking to the man in words that Will could not understand – in Gaelic, he presumed – though haltingly, as though he were not too confident or competent. Yet he spoke on until Callaghan interrupted him, in the same tongue, and he too with longish pauses, which drifted into silence.

'Father Thomas...' Callaghan murmured, 'I have not spoken my native tongue for upward of... thirty years. Shall we not use the language we are... more versed in?'

Thomas looked abashed, maybe even a little put out. 'It was just that hearing you sing in Gaelic, I presumed...'

'But speaking, Father, 'tis more difficult than singing songs... songs you learned at your mother's knee and heard her sing day in and day out as you were growing... so that's the fact of it.' And Callaghan resumed his humming, rocking rhythmically back and forth.

'And where was that Callaghan?' Thomas asked. 'Where was the place you learned not only the song, but how to sing it so... beautifully, and so... feelingly?'

And Will smiled, soothed by the song, and not minding this curiosity, which was further delaying their purpose, if it was easing, as he suspected, his friend's stung pride.

Tears came into Callaghan's eyes, and Will found himself marvelling that such a man... a monster... could be capable of tears and, indeed, of the kinds of sentiment that would compel them. Or was it just the maudlin sentiments of the drunk?

'Inishmaan,' Callaghan answered, and he looked intently at the priest, before resuming his humming.

Thomas nodded. 'Ah, then that explains the strangeness I thought I detected in some of the words of the song. Inishmaan,' he said, turning towards Will, 'is one of the small group of islands, the Aran Isles, that lie outside Galway Bay, almost the most westerly fringe of what we call Britain. But – he turned back to Callaghan – 'tis a long way from Inishmaan to Stradbroke Island, is it not?'

Callaghan broke off his humming. 'So, how did I come to be here, is that it?' He laughed bitterly. 'Certainly not by the grace of God, and that's for sure!'

Thomas looked uncomfortable. 'I'm sorry' he said. 'It was not my intention to... scratch away at old wounds.'

'Old wounds! Old wounds?' the other repeated, his almost childlike forthrightness turning to anger. 'There's nothing "old" about 'em. They're the same every day, fresh every day, the way they have been these thirty years past, and ever will be, I suppose, to my dying day. They are an ever-present torment, something I never understood and never will understand, however much I go round and round it. I sit here sometimes, as you found me just now, looking over to the mainland, just as I did when I was a young child on Inishmaan, and I'm thinking there is something important I should know... over there, where I am looking, and not here where I am, and yet the vastness terrifies me, just as it did then, when I was a young child... Yet they tell me the vastness of the mainland here dwarfs the whole of Ireland out of existence. I wouldn't know, nor would it matter, for the terror is only in part to do with the vastness.'

Callaghan stretched his arm out and swung it slowly round in a wide arc. 'On that mainland, over there, I have known only suffering. In my body, in my heart, in my head. Like a lead weight that presses down on you, but for no particular purpose, pressed… I don't know… casually, by no particular person… so that you get to thinking it is the normal condition of life. Only, I know it isn't, because long ago I knew something very much better, cleaner, simpler – Inishmaan – from which I was torn like the stones from the fields and cast into a wilderness that is called the World, and…'

Thomas went on with his questioning, and as Callaghan's replies came back, Will became aware – although his every instinct told him they should not continue to indulge this man – that it was more than idle curiosity, on Thomas's part. It was his humanity and his compassion that were being engaged… and causing some confusion.

'Torn? Cast?' Thomas was repeating. 'Whatever can you mean?'

Callaghan took a long pull from the flagon that squatted on the rock beside him then looked at the priest. 'Do you really want an answer… Father?' he said, with clear, heavy irony laid upon his last word.

Thomas nodded and looked down.

'So be it, then. It was like this. I would be all of… five, or six, year-old when the soldiers came. We were still mourning the loss of my da' and my uncle – my mother's younger brother, himself no more than sixteen – drowned in a sudden swell that overturned their currach. My uncle's battered body was washed up three days later and we waited and waited for my da', but he never came home. Every day, two and three times a day sometimes, my poor mammy and me would go over to the cliffs on the western side and peer down into the swirling seas, but he never came home. So we buried my uncle and waited. My mammy told me that the good Lord God had taken my da' for a sea-angel and we stopped going to the cliffs to seek him, though I went over there many times alone, until I gradually became convinced by my mammy's words.'

Will found himself sharply reminded of young Billy – not just the man's words, but the same story of loss at such a tender age. Then his thoughts leapt to Lilian, and he closed his eyes… Someday, for certain, he must ask his child's forgiveness. So much young loss, so much...

With a conscious effort, Will tore himself away from these painful thoughts and back to the matter at hand.

'...Then, one day,' he heard Callaghan say, 'the soldiers came over from Doolin way, and nobody knew why they were there, searching all over the island, it seemed.'

He broke off suddenly, gasping, as if fighting for breath, and almost a minute went by before he had composed himself enough to continue.

'It was on the third day that four of them came by our cottage in the morning. I was inside but my mammy was out at the front, beating the rugs she was. I saw them go by through the open door, and I dashed over to it and stood there to marvel at their beautiful red coats and their silver buttons. It seemed, in that moment, I had never seen anything so fine, so beautiful as those red coats.' The man shook his head. 'How these fripperies can deceive us when we are young!'

And again he stopped.

And again, that same sad lament beneath his breath almost.

Then just as suddenly, he resumed his story. 'Yes. They had not gone more than a hundred paces before they came back. They spoke not a word, but one of them took hold of my mammy, so roughly she cried out at the pain of it, and he pushed her inside the house. Another took hold of me and flung me out of the door onto the path, where I fell to my knees. Then he turned away, laughing at my tears, and followed the other three inside.'

Will shook his head, recognising a truth that the behaviour of fellow soldiers towards Indian women had imprinted on his memory during his time in the East.

'I tried to go back in, at once, but they had dropped the bar across the door. I waited outside for an endless time. I could hear my mammy crying out and crying tears, and I became frightened, but there was nothing I could do. I went away down the street to Mrs O'Flaherty and told her what had happened. She took me into her house and barred her door. She gave me some milk, which she heated... in a soot-blackened pan it was... I remember, and she said I was not to fret.' And he repeated it. 'Not to fret! Not to fret!' Callaghan laughed scornfully.

'A long time after that, my mammy came a-knocking at Mrs O'Flaherty's door and that lady let her in. She was all bruised in her face, with cuts there and streaks of blood, and she could not stop her keening. Mrs O'Flaherty took her into another part of her cottage, and I could hear them talking, then water splashing, and gradually less and less sobbing from my mammy.'

Seeing the tears welling in Callaghan's eyes, half-hearing him murmur something under his breath, Will glanced at Thomas. But neither of them spoke.

Callaghan jerked the flagon up to his lips, as before, and flung his head back, his throat working rhythmically as he sucked in the liquor. Then he wiped his mouth with the back of his hand.

'The next day the soldiers left Inishmaan... But worse was soon to follow. In less than a week they were back. More of them than before. And they stayed much longer. And all the time they were there, first one then another would come to our cottage, sometimes even in twos and threes, and they used my mammy as though she was less than nothing...'

Callaghan fell silent, his eyes riveted on the horizon. And Will realised what a Herculean task this recounting was for him. A minute went by. And another. Then suddenly, he resumed his tale.

And still it was driven by anger; yet ice-cold.

'And then there came a day when two of the soldiers took hold of me and marched me to a part of the island away from the houses and each of them buggered me, then left me there, crying and bleeding, so badly torn was I. But my mammy...' Callaghan let out a pitiful cry. 'My mammy – he whispered hoarsely – was in a worse state. She never laughed any more after that. She spoke no words. She sat and stared out at the sea and we hardly ate, and I had to tend our cow; though it was a neighbour who, taking pity on us, milked her each day...'

'Oh, the callous, casual brutality of it...' Thomas shook his head. 'So, what became of you... Ned?' he asked, gently.

Callaghan stared fixedly out to sea, his chest heaving.

'When I told my mammy what the soldiers had done – not straightaway, mind – she took me off, one stormy night, and begged Mrs O'Flaherty to hide me, shelter me for a bit. That lady did not want to do it... she was frightened... But in the end, she did... though it served little purpose. Those two soldiers soon came looking for me, and for all the days they were there till they left I received the same treatment from them.'

Tears gushed from Callaghan's eyes and meandered slowly down his pockmarked face, to be drowned in his bushy red beard. It was like a child crying. Disconsolate, inconsolable. And time seemed to stand still.

Eventually, Thomas sat down on the rock beside the weeping man and laid a hand on his shoulder.

Callaghan, still staring at the far horizon, roughly scored out the tears with the back of his hand. 'Then there came a day when, arriving home after one of my solitary escapes over to the far cliffs, to get away from... you see... and I found the door barred; and I thought that there must be soldiers inside, tormenting my mammy in whatever way it was... for I did not then know the nature of it for her. I banged on the door and cried out for someone to open, but no one came. So I wandered off again down the lane.'

His face contorted at the memory of it.

'There were two or three women talking in a group, but they turned away as though I was not there. Once past them, I noticed how silent it all was, strangely silent because, I realised in that moment, there were no soldiers about... not anywhere. I remember, I stood listening for some minutes, trying to catch the familiar sounds of them...'

'And then?' Thomas prompted.

'Then one of the women came from behind me and, taking my hand, brought me to Mrs O'Flaherty's door. She banged upon it without a word of explanation to me until that lady, trembling I saw, opened it just a crack. "'Tis all right, Mother, the soldiers have all gone," the woman said, pointing away towards the horizon, which the soldiers' corvette was fast approaching, "but they have taken away two of our neighbours, this wee mite's mammy for one…"

'And then, of course, I knew. And I had this feeling, young though I was, that I would never see her again. And so it has proved. Oh, my poor mammy…' And Callaghan sat rocking back and forth, his arms wrapped about his shoulders, convulsed by his sobbing. 'The two women took me inside and they… gave me something to eat… and…

…But how she died or where she is buried, I cannot say, but it has plagued me all my life, and will to my dying day. Sometimes, it drives me mad, and the only way to escape that madness is down the neck of a bottle… My celestial liquor, this is…' And he patted his flagon, gently, affectionately, then slopped more of its contents into his mouth. 'And today, Father Sheehan, is… one of those days.'

His head fell forward till his chin was resting on his chest and he spoke no more.

Will motioned to Thomas to come away, realising that this strange, wholly unexpected interview was at an end. All thoughts of punishment were dissolved in the man's tears; and, tiptoeing away, almost, they left him to deal as best he could with the life-sentence that had been bestowed on him as a child, no older than young Billy.

L

'Oh, Will, are you not cut to the quick!' Thomas said, once they were out of earshot. 'Whatever misdemeanours Callaghan has been guilty of in his life, he had a blighted beginning, to be sure. How could such tragedy not shape the man that was to come?'

'It would be a hard man indeed who could not extend some kindness to such suffering and torment,' Will acknowledged. And he found himself wondering what else Callaghan had lived through; for he had clearly been in this continent for quite a while to have served out the prison sentence that was supposedly now in its final stages. 'How old would you say he is?'

'Late thirties, early forties, maybe? But what I *cannot* understand now – hearing the man's story – is why he is associated at all with Stevens. That one, I would say, has not a drop of honesty or decency or feeling in him whatsoever!'

'Who can say? But strange circumstances make strange bedfellows, and there can be fewer circumstances stranger than these in which we all find ourselves, right now... Though, of course,' Will added, 'we do not know whether they were acquainted afore coming here, do we?' And he smiled, suddenly aware that the adage he had just voiced might equally apply – certainly in his own mind – to his own relations with an Irish priest! 'I don't know what you feel about it, Thomas, but it was a shock to me to find him more... '

'...more complex than you had expected?'

'Aye, maybe that is the word; although in his way, still a simple, almost innocent, almost childlike man, wouldn't you say?'

'Indeed, yes,' said Thomas, at the extreme edge of his exhaling breath. But "judge not", he mused, more to himself than to Will, "that ye be not judged..." How often does that line catch us out? Yes, yes, childlike, if you take away the bottle and the beard...'

'And such a child as we must not let Billy become.'

'No. And the dangers are all too close. But Callaghan, Will. Maybe he's still a victim – of Stevens, I mean. And maybe also of misfortune and other injustices we know not of, heaped upon him by those that launched him into this cruel world. Yes, indeed. Hitherto, we had all too readily seen him as another thing of darkness, a fitting counterpart to Stevens; my doing, really, since I found them together on that first occasion, with the child Lizzie. It seemed a reasonable assumption... I'll try and be wiser, hereafter!'

'Well, yes,' Will said, a note of caution in his voice. 'But even so, if we are now a bit wiser about the causes, that still doesn't mean we can turn a blind eye to their effects on others. Especially in this matter of the corruption of the girl – and, indeed, whatever else the man may have done. Are you convinced by his explanation about Billy and the little blue crabs? I'm sorry if I did seem to back his story so quickly, by the way, but it was because of my own experience at Amity Point... Though I have not seen them hereabouts, myself.'

'Hm. I think we'll need to talk to him again, find out more about the things that give us concern. Yes, and get him to fill out the rest of his story, the better to assess his complicity in Stevens' likely crimes...'

But Will's mind had moved on. 'Thomas... a couple of things, from what you just said. The first is to tell you, before I forget, that when I was over the other side of the lake, earlier, I found a well-used track leading to the water's edge at the point we saw the intruders, yesterday afternoon. It struck away in a clearly south-westerly direction and my guess is it leads to a jetty, or bay, that might be used by people coming over from the mainland... which would certainly lend plausibility to the notion of the women having been taken off the island...'

'Ah, but we must remember, Will, we don't yet know whether any such abduction has taken place.'

'No, we don't. But – Will felt in his jacket pocket – this brings me to my second point.' And he handed the torn piece of envelope to his companion. 'Look. I found it on my bed, when I went back to the tent, before we began our search for Callaghan. What young Billy told me – about Callaghan – put it clean out of my head.'

'"Sara-Jayn Dunikan and Buny Brisen is gon for strumpits." Oh, are they now!' Thomas laughed out loud. 'So what do you make of it?', he asked, reading it again. 'Do we know these women?'

'No. And we don't know who left the note either: someone who was afraid to speak out, perhaps, when we were round among the tents this morning. But if two women have left the island, whether by abduction or complicity, then the quarantine rules have been broken. And that would certainly be of concern to Dr Ballow and the Authorities over in Brisbane, don't you think? Always assuming that's where they've been taken.'

'Doubtless. And we should try and find out who was responsible for this.' Thomas waved the torn fragment back and forth. 'Or go and interrogate Stevens.'

'Oh yes, after his last performance…?' Will tossed his head back, scornfully.

'Ah but we should, Will. And whilst we are on this subject, I'm also curious to find out why Lizzie, whom we both saw clearly being ill-treated by Stevens, should have come so readily to his defence, when we thought we had him netted. I don't know… I wonder if there is something Mrs Parry hasn't told us… But where do we start?'

Will considered a moment. 'Why don't you go and talk to the girl? And I'll do what I was intending to do anyway – ask again around that part of the camp I was in first thing this morning. It's just possible one, or both of us might get somewhere. And *then* we can move on to Stevens.'

'Yes, that seems… logical.'

The two parted company. But a moment later Will had re-joined Thomas, caught in an after-thought.

'You know, Thomas,' he said, ruefully. 'Callaghan's right: Billy does spend far too much time alone – it's something we should try and rectify… But, come on, one thing at a time!'

And, newly resolved, the two headed off towards their different objectives.

LI

Alice had never before felt how isolated Redhills was. Although not much more than a couple of miles into Penrith and a bit more, over the fields, to Dacre, there was little in either place to hold her, now. Perhaps she had outgrown these rural places for larger, more active towns out in the wider world. Whatever the reason, her urge was ever outwards, and thus it was that she and Lilian would accompany her father to the church at Dacre each Sunday morning, though turning back well short of the lych-gate. She felt acutely embarrassed at the thought even of entering upon the scene of her false marriage, and into the presence of those parishioners who had witnessed it and so warmly congratulated her at the outset of her new life as an army bride – with their smiles and their handshakes.

Once a week, she would walk into Penrith to buy the newspapers, sometimes taking the child with her. At other times she would leave her to play with her sister Mary's little girl, also called Lillian – 'with two lahs', as the little girl always reminded – depending, however, on how relations stood with her mother on that particular day...

Experiencing constant anxiety, and especially in her mother's presence, Alice was ever groping towards the future; straining to be away, longing to establish some kind of independent life for herself. The child was a burden, in this respect. But not one she regretted, not for one minute; for Lilian was, apart from who she was, a constant reminder of a happy time, her one tie, still, to Will Crosby... wherever he was.

And once again, Alice found herself wondering where, and whether she would ever see him again.

It was this not knowing, eddying round always in her mind, that was hardest to bear, lost as she was – as she freely admitted to herself – in his total absence. Time and again she went over her own immediate reactions and conduct in the wake of her discovery of his terrible deception. Knowing herself, as she was then, could she have acted any differently…? And yet her pride and her scramble for some remnants of dignity had produced only misery, exacerbated continually by the child's persistent questioning, even now, about her daddy's whereabouts and why he never came home – which led always to self-condemnation.

Knowing what she did now, at this distance in time, would she still have placed those doubtful, salvaged assets above the deep love she bore him, then and now, if the chance were to come again? Was being seen and judged to be beyond recrimination by people whom she hardly knew or cared about sufficient reward for her stubborn refusal even to see him?

Some days, when the depression had her by the throat, the very questions themselves seemed ridiculous, not worth the asking. She had given him no hearing. On two occasions, when he had tried to see them, she had barred the door against him. If he was foolishly guilty of… on the face of it… a prodigiously dishonest action, she was guiltily foolish in her conventional reaction, and it was she, not he, who had condemned herself, her child and, who knows, him too, to long years – maybe a whole lifetime – of regret.

And so it all went round and round in her mind.

For weeks on end the 'positions vacant' columns yielded nothing Alice felt she could respond to with any enthusiasm, and in those weeks, she knew she was entirely at the mercy of chance, waiting for someone to seize upon her need as their own, while being entirely unaware of her need because for them she did not as yet even exist. All she could do, after each disappointing scan of the advertisements, was to resign herself, let another week go by; and in that creeping time desultorily pull weeds in her father's well-nigh immaculate garden, sweep leaves, prune bushes, and wash roses free of greenfly, thus playing a small part in maintaining a perfection that was not her own.

And then there was Lilian. Lilian, who seemed to slip all too easily into one ailment after another, nothing grave, but perhaps symptomatic of the child's own deep sense of loss, her incompleteness, she too lacklustre, even in her play, and certainly about her lessons and school itself. She moped around the house and the garden, settling to nothing for long.

Then came a day when suddenly everything changed.

Alice's father arrived home at four in the afternoon, being on early shift in the signal box that week. One of the drivers, down from the coast, had given him his West Cumberland newspaper and glancing quickly through the 'Vacancies' column he had noticed a likely looking position as housekeeper to a well-to-do family – ship-owners, in fact – at Netherton, near Maryport. And he thrust the paper into her hands, desperate to help his favourite daughter, ever trying to make up for his wife's persistent coldness towards her.

It was still only a housekeeper's situation and her one experience of that had made her wary, seeming less grateful to her father than she might otherwise have been. She had hoped to aspire to governess, for she still bitterly resented losing her trainee teacher's status and would have liked to continue teaching, even within a family setting. Yet she realised such posts would be few and far between in their part of the country. And besides, would the two years' experience she had had in supervised teaching be deemed sufficient by families seeking a governess for even their children's early education?

After much soul-searching, self-doubt, and lack of any conviction, Alice sat down and composed a letter.

Her experience of 'housekeeping' had been brief, and although Tom Hewitt had not mentioned references in the note he had left for her begging her to stay in spite of his gross misconduct, she was sure that now, many weeks after her flight, he would see the whole episode in a different light, no doubt finding some way of blaming her. So a reference from him, even if forthcoming, might not be a recommendation. Nevertheless, she cited that brief experience but explained that she had left reluctantly, though necessarily, because of her employer's clear but unsolicited, certainly unwanted, attentions towards her. Then she worried that this information would little support her case, in the end posting the letter convinced that nothing at all would come of it.

The next day, determined to put it out of her mind, she sought to busy herself with tasks about the house and the garden... Safety measures, she told herself, whenever the application drifted back into her mind, to plague her.

Then, on the following Friday, as she was getting Lilian ready for school, she heard the snap of the letterbox. A brief note in a clearly once neat but now wavering hand invited her – quaintly – to 'a conversation' at Ghyll Mont House, Netherton, on the Wednesday of the following week. Elated, but then immediately full of trepidation, she wrote back to confirm her intention of presenting herself for the 'conversation', then dashed out to post it, calling in on her father at the signal box on the way back. Her mother had merely sneered when she heard the news.

Her father was content, however, declaring his intention of accompanying her, since the journey, by train and coach, would take all of three to four hours. Without someone to talk to on the way, growing anxiety might easily sap her confidence by the time she got there. Alice smiled; she would be glad of his presence.

That evening, her mother eventually said she 'supposed' she would look after the child on the day in question, though 'could see no sense' in her husband wasting the time, 'not to mention the loss of a day's pay,' in making the journey as well.

'No, I don't suppose you can,' he had countered quietly, his tone measured, 'but I shall be going none the less. And you will be looking after Lilian.'

No, he did not raise his voice, her father, even when roused to anger, but her mother, and indeed the rest of his family knew from the manner of his speaking on such occasions, never to cross him.

LII

A policeman. Him?

The more Will Crosby was involved in these investigations the more certain he became of how temperamentally unsuited he was to be one – which was a problem, since it was this precise role that was intended to occupy him during whatever time he spent in Queensland.

His attempts to elicit more information about 'Sarah-Jane Dunikan' and 'Buny Brisen' had drawn only blank stares or vigorous head shakings, and yet he felt sure, from the averted or blinking eyes, that several of those he questioned were lying. And, knowing his only real hope of success lay in yet another anonymous note, which, given the barely literate nature of the first one and the effort it must have cost its author, seemed unlikely, he could only hope Thomas had fared better with the girl…

Prison, back home, had proved to be a watershed for Will, though he had not understood quite to what extent until he found himself in this new prison, whose restrictions, albeit different, reminded him of those he had experienced in Carlisle.

As a younger man, having been brought up in a small house in a large family, then later in the army in which every space was public, he had never given solitude and silence a passing thought. And at first, when they were forced upon him, by the many hours he spent in his prison cell, he had not had the inner resources to combat the total absence of freedom those hours represented. When, eventually, the prison library had begun to furnish him with the only means of defence his gaol sentence allowed him against that torment of isolation, a slow, gradual, eventually antithetical readjustment of his priorities had come about. And he had come to resent the fact that roll call, or mealtimes, or recreation times forced him to leave his book before he had grown tired of it, or had finished a chapter, or a paragraph, even.

Will's appetite for reading was much more compelling than the trivial alternatives that prison discipline and its timetable demanded of him. And even while chatting with fellow prisoners or spooning his food he had often found his thoughts wandering back to what he had been reading, reconstructing the arguments in his mind, questioning them, applying them where appropriate to situations he had known from his own experience and testing them there. Looking back on the experience now, he knew full well that without those books and their probing he might not have survived. Not in the way that he eventually wanted to.

Early on in this transformative process he had been perplexed by his mind's fixations on remote, abstract, or fictional questions in preference to those with which his immediate surroundings confronted him, the kinds of experience his life hitherto had presented as the whole of reality. It had taken him quite some time to batten onto the plain fact that his mind was demanding its own expansion into new, until now never-dreamed-of areas of outer and inner engagement, which somehow afforded him a more powerful awareness of who he was, and of how he might stand better in the world than his original destiny would have allowed.

At some point, between then and now, he had unconsciously begun to grade the different types of knowledge his expanding world brought before him. Whilst not turning his back on the ordinary (as being also, often, the necessary) he was aware that so much of it was scant and occupied more concern and energy than it was worth. It was the difference between accepting the world as it was – of others' making – and seeking ways to mould it to make it more palatable, and not only for himself.

But here, on this island, even minimal retreat into that world of inner reflection was all-but impossible; and, while glad of companionship, Will was growing impatient with all that kept him from the book road that had become its habitual precondition, that might open it up to him, anew.

Yes... and it was ironical that prison had afforded him the opportunity to appreciate what was traditionally the preserve of the privileged minority! And that now this other 'prison' was having the reverse effect, of snatching it all away again...

And even as Will became conscious of the thought, the raucous shouts coming from beyond the flimsy wall of the tent seemed to menace his very existence. No, not even this poor refuge could guarantee him time or space or silence enough to collect himself and know who he was. And he swore, vehemently, barely under his breath.

Yet were not the Stevenses, Callaghans and Lizzies of this present world his concern only because his conscience demanded it? Everything fuelled by his sense of obligation to the commonwealth, to friendship, if not to what amounted to some indefinable 'weakness' within him? Billy was away playing just now; but he too, Will acknowledged, was not exempt from his resentment, which at times even caused him to deny the affection he bore the child – that powerful 'trap' of the affections, if you will, that life so often set on self. But beyond that, were not the self-imposed limitations of his whole purpose in coming here – to find a way of returning, and resuming that life at its best – an identical trap...? Which brought Will back to his starting point: his initial aspiration towards being a policeman, the supposed key that was to unlock the door to this longed-for future...

He sighed in despair, unable to see a way forward, a way to escape, or reconcile the many contradictions of which his life was now composed. Its humdrum nature, as indeed that of any environment he had hitherto lived in... with the exception of those wonderful moments he had shared with Alice... could no longer suffice.

Will sat on, his thoughts ranging back and forth, seeking out a path and a purpose. He picked up the dead judge's books one by one, gazed at their titles, then set them back down in the chest once more, one by one.

Idly, he leafed through the diary he had so enthusiastically embraced that first day as the future chronicle of his new life. And he noted, yet again, that he had written not one single word in its beckoning, empty pages. And thus – the thought came to him – the book still reflected only the judge's black view of the world and the relationships of things and people within it... a view which somehow encompassed his own present circumstances much more readily than his initial optimism had seemed to promise.

He sighed, shaking his head. Where was there an end of it? Would crossing that brief stretch of water to the mainland miraculously change everything, if, indeed, he lived to see the day when that final release came? Would that sense of imprisonment fall away the moment he set foot on the shore of the continent proper? He somehow doubted it.

Throwing down the diary he once again picked up the last book that had come into his hands in his absent-minded telling of them, as though they were a rosary. Its spine bore the single word, 'Machiavelli,' and he remembered having consulted it, in connection with certain comments the judge had made in his diary. And as soon as he opened the volume, he saw all the underlining, and the small, cramped jottings at its margins, its ticks, and other markings. He saw too that it was really two books in one, and that the first one, entitled *The Prince*, was much the shorter. Its chapters were generally short and it might indeed prove a good starting point for his promised, systematic reading, when the day dawned... if it ever did... on which he could feel himself at liberty to indulge that wish. Or...?

Attempting to ignore the cries of children, nearby, Will flicked through its pages, dipping into a passage here, another there, quite at random. But then, guiltily almost, his curiosity flaring, he turned back to the first page, and began to read more slowly.

It was not so much an interview as a lengthy disquisition – of who was who in the family, what their interests and habits were, whose room was where, and what 'Miss Fallowfield' would be asked to do to maintain the smooth running of the household.

'It will be rather jolly having a little girl about the house once again,' Mrs Abbot concluded. 'It is such a *long* time now since William's youngest, Sabina – Bina, as we called her then – was skipping up and down these stairs. A young scamp she was, always. Yet, to tell you the truth, Miss Fallowfield, the house has been very gloomy since she went away. From schooling her dolls in the nursery to her leaving for London, last year, all seemed to happen in the twinkling of an eye. But I digress. We shall look forward to having you with us… a week from today, if that is convenient.'

And Alice left quite bewildered, her head spinning, but eager to tell her father all that had transpired.

The fog was lifting a little, and the way ahead seemed clearer than for many a long day past.

LIII

'**D**amn the girl!' he cried, fiercely.

Spurred on by a rush of adrenaline at the prospect of Lizzie's redemption, Thomas had not considered the possibility she might not be at her tent. 'Well, maybe not quite that…' he added, bethinking himself. And he turned to see whether the Parrys were in their tent, or somewhere in the vicinity.

It was Mr Parry who came stumbling out of the tent, looking quite as ill as his wife had earlier said he was.

'Ah, Father Sheehan, if it is that accursed child you are looking for, I'm afraid we can't help you. No, as far as we are concerned, she has ceased to exist. This morning, when she suddenly turned up here, all smiles, looking for a bite to eat, Florence – my wife, that is – attempted to reason with her, to persuade her she was well on the road to her own ruin. "Lizzie, child," she said, "what have you got yourself mixed up in?" – I heard her say that, distinctly. Kindly like. But the girl would have none of it and poured out such a torrent of foul-mouthed abuse that it was hard to believe we was in the company of a girl barely out of her infancy. We are plain-living people, Father, in no way used to such language and behaviour, and so I rose from my bed, come out here, and told her very straight that from now on she were no longer welcome here and must fend for herself. Florence were mortified…' He stopped then, suddenly aware of the priest's questioning eyes upon him.

''Tis indeed a pity it came to that…' Thomas murmured, vexed, 'though I can well understand your frustration and your anger.' He looked about him, at a loss. 'I don't suppose you have any idea where she might be right now?'

Parry shook his head. 'No, nor do I wish to know. I'm sorry, but that's the top and bottom of it.' He turned as if to re-enter the tent but was prevented from doing so by his wife rushing out. Contending with several deviant strands of her hair, she hustled him aside.

'Father Sheehan, I hope you will not think too badly of us, that we have failed... failed utterly with the girl, but neither of us is strong enough to put up with the worry and wickedness she heaps upon us.' And, panting a little, she struggled to control yet more unruly wisps and strands of hair. 'Where she is now, I have no idea, but... a while ago, now, I saw her on the point of leaving the encampment in the company of... of two men.'

Her cheeks flamed, at this, though whether from embarrassment or anger Thomas could not be sure.

'When she saw me, the wicked girl made as if to detach herself from them, to give the impression she was innocently going off alone in another direction, I suppose. But I had seen her first, I had.' She darted a glance at her shamefaced husband. 'I was in no doubt she was with them.'

'Did you watch where she went, after that?' Thomas asked, unsure quite what had flashed between them. 'For, to be sure, I have too long neglected speaking to her.'

'No... Truth to tell, I was glad to be shot of her. But... if it's of any help to you, one of the men was that burly, ignorant Irishman... oh, begging your pardon, Father. I didn't mean...'

Thomas waved his hand in a vague gesture of dismissal, recognising this all too common, almost instinctive, English prejudice against his fellow countrymen. But a ghost of a smile touched the corners of his mouth. 'Oh, now don't you go concerning yourself about that little... slip of the tongue! There are many worse things in this life. As we both know...'

'I mean the red-headed six-footer with the cleft chin,' Mrs Parry cut in, as if anxious to distance herself from her *faux pas*. 'He looks a nasty piece of work!'

'Ah, yes, I know well enough who you mean,' he said smiling, equally anxious to put her at her ease, while remembering his own earlier encounter with the man. 'McIlroy's his name.' No, it was hardly surprising that he should be involved in some part of this affair, if not even in the death of the venomous judge... 'Rest assured. I shall seek him out,' he added, turning to go.

But a kindly, warning hand was laid gently on his own. 'Oh, but go carefully now, Father Thomas, go carefully; for that man is a bad lot, through and through – 'tis common knowledge here.'

Thomas nodded. 'I thank you for the warning, Mrs Parry, that I do; and I know you are right, having already had one brush with him, at the cookhouse fire, weeks back... But I can't let that prevent me snatching the girl from his clutches.'

Slowly releasing his hand, Mrs Parry returned to cajoling, but never quite controlling her wilful, wayward hair.

Thomas hurried away, knowing precisely where the man had his dwelling – right against the perimeter fence at the southern end of the compound. As he approached, he saw that the tent flap was closed. But drawing nearer he heard sounds coming from within, then distinctly a girl – the girl – gabbling and giggling, though he could not catch any of her words.

He stood back from the tent, thought for a moment, then taking the bull by the horns called quietly: 'Mr McIlroy, a word, if you please.'

All fell abruptly silent within. Thomas waited for fully a minute but there was no response.

'Mr McIlroy, I'm waiting.'

More giggles. Abruptly suppressed.

Then a man's voice, clearly irritated, spoke some words, but again Thomas could not make them out.

There was some fiddling with the tent flap from inside until McIlroy's large, red head appeared through the loosened entrance, though taking obvious care not to allow the priest any glimpse inside.

'Ah, so 'tis youse is it, Father Sheehan? Well, maybes you'd best be on your way – if you know what's good for ye. I have nothing to say to youse.'

Thomas waved a hand in the air. 'Look, I'm here to speak with the child, Lizzie, whom I know to be in the tent with you.'

'What *child* are you talking of man? Lizzie is no child and, in any case, she's a-living here with me now. She has no wish to speak to youse… nor would I allow it. So, just… bugger off, while you still can, you meddling, papish bast…!'

Another giggle, becoming almost a shriek of laughter, from inside.

'Lizzie,' Thomas called, barely raising his voice, 'if you do not step outside immediately, I shall come in and drag you out. So out you come, now! At once!'

McIlroy's red face scowled up at him. Then, heaving himself up out of the tent the bulky man lurched towards the priest.

'Did you not fuckin' understand what I said to youse?' he bawled.

Although Thomas had sought not to draw attention to himself or the tent's occupants, McIlroy's loud, savage tones had been heard, and soon two or three men were standing there, a few steps away from the imminent confrontation, with still others arriving.

'Put the bugger in hospital, Seany,' a small, rat-faced youth exhorted.

Smirking in the direction from which the voice had come, McIlroy raised a fist above his head: 'Well now Mick, me boy, 'tis just the thing I have in mind.' And on he came.

Thomas stood his ground. He could see the man's right fist clenching and as it came hurtling towards him, he side-stepped deftly, in a dainty, tripping dance-step, almost, and McIlroy, connecting with nothing, was thrown off balance, falling all the while towards where Thomas had been or, rather, towards where Thomas's right knee was just then coming up hard to greet the man's face.

There was a loud crack and McIlroy grunted, sprawling his length at the priest's feet. He lay there gasping for fully half a minute before, urged on by his lusting cronies, he clambered to his feet, panting hard. Blood was streaming from his nose, channelled down through the cleft in his chin, and he was swaying unsteadily. Only then did Thomas realise he had supplanted some of McIlroy's teeth, for he spat bits of them from his mouth into his open palm, looking bewildered.

Suddenly, McIlroy's face contracted into a snarl and he lunged forward again, unfortunately, straight into a fist that caught him on his left ear, followed instantly by another one that connected squarely with his jaw, and down he went again.

Thomas stood looking at him, making no attempt to disguise his contempt. The man tried to crawl forward but then slumped back down, groaning.

After what seemed an age, he managed to get to his knees, his eyes goggling, not seeming to focus. Thomas moved forward and McIlroy covered his head and face with his arms, moaning his lamentations all the while. Thomas ignored his protective measures and, bending so that his mouth was level with the man's already swollen left ear, spoke quietly into it.

'Now then, Mr McIlroy, whenever you are minded to threaten violence again, in the future, I would advise you first make serious inquiries about your intended victim; he might just be someone who, despite all appearances and presumptions to the contrary, has some little skill in the art of pugilism. Would that not be sensible, now?'

Thomas stepped over the once again fully prostrate figure, threw back the flaps of the tent, and peering inside said quietly, but brusquely, 'Get your frock on, girl. You're coming with me.' And as soon as the by-now snivelling child had done what he asked, he reached inside and dragged her out by her left arm.

'We're going to have a serious talk, Lizzie, you and me,' he informed her, in a harsh whisper, 'and you are going to start behaving in a civilized manner.'

With that, he strode towards the small huddle of McIlroy's astonished partisans, dragging the unwilling, frightened girl behind him. And as he drew level with them, a pathway opened up for him, people backing readily away. Thomas, it seemed, through his slaying of their Goliath, had gained a kind of respect in their eyes, such as his cloth and his quiet role in the community had hitherto been unable to provide.

With not a word exchanged, he marched the child away in the direction of the tent she had earlier abandoned. But then, thinking better of it, not wishing to disturb the poor Parrys, who had already had more than enough of the girl's shenanigans, he headed for his own, hoping to find it free of occupants.

Nodding at those of the camp's inhabitants who mutely observed his passage through the camp, the priest had little time to reflect, other than to realise that the anger which had thus far governed his actions was no longer appropriate – the child was already scared out of her wits. He stole another glance at her. Whatever her misdemeanours, she'd as yet had little or no chance in life. Abandoned by, or bereft of parents, for whatever reasons, she was a frightening reminder of what young Billy might eventually have become, after that cruel moment when life had set him adrift, quite alone, on its choppy, uncertain sea. It was true, wasn't it? Lizzie was having to cope with too many of life's adult complexities when she was barely out her of own childhood. It was understanding and practical help she needed, not harshness, not recriminations.

'Come, now, Lizzie,' he murmured, consciously relaxing his grip on her arm.

LIV

Private citizens who become princes by good fortune alone do so with little effort; but then they must put a tremendous effort into maintaining their station...

As Will succumbed to the temptation the open book, the silence, and his present isolation seemed almost to urge upon him, two things struck him most forcibly. Firstly, that this Machiavelli was a man who had no doubts about the rightness of his opinions, expressing them directly and, more often than not, bringing forward a fistful of examples to demonstrate their truth. And secondly, that he was almost totally ignorant of the histories of the ancient and the Renaissance worlds whose events were being adduced to confirm these apparently unassailable truths.

And it was being continually reminded of this ignorance that almost caused him to abandon the book in despair, after only a few pages. Perhaps this was not to be the starting point, after all. And he laid the open book down on the bed...

But then he swore aloud, and roughly seized the book once more, refusing to be defeated so easily. And when he had considered the matter a little further, he realised that these histories of more than three centuries earlier were *not* the point of the book. *That*, if he had understood aright, was the importance of the *lessons* of history; lessons the author was passing on to a ruler so that he could make use of them in *his* time, in *his* pursuit of security and the establishment of an efficient state.

With this realisation, Will read on more quickly. And although his initial sense of frustration had not quite left him, little by little he became conscious of another factor. Yes, unmistakeably so! Ghosting alongside Machiavelli's narrative was another, of his own making: the translation of the author's lessons of history, ostensibly apposite only to the world of a prince of some three and a half centuries ago, to his own world, to the present. The book was about power and how to use it once it had been acquired; and it was about how to safeguard that power and avoid common pitfalls which could undermine and destroy it.

As Will read on, he was vaguely aware of sounds coming from another far-off world, yet they were not compelling enough to distract him from his immediate purpose. He eased himself into a more comfortable position, propping himself on one elbow, the book flat down on his bed. Of course, he would need to return to it, maybe on several occasions, for there was more in its message than he could possibly master in one headlong rush from first page to last.

Time could barely keep pace, however, and suddenly, very few pages remained to be read.

It was at this point that he was arrested by a chapter that seemed rather different in character from anything that had gone before it. It swerved away, suddenly, out of the realms of history, the presumed concreteness of the past, and into a discourse that was altogether more... more... wispy, insubstantial; a speculation on how Fortune controlled so much in life, but then on how, with careful forethought, its effects could often be headed off. And as he neared the end, Will began to understand why this chapter, perhaps more than all the rest, so captivated him.

And he thought again, back to that fatal moment in his own history, when chance had thrown together two men, brothers, who were in possession of two irreconcilable truths, and how one of those truths had prevailed and destroyed the other, entirely.

Well, of course it had...

Will read through the chapter again, his speed in reading belying the heaviness in his heart, weighing its message against those events that had sent everything awry for him. And yet... in all practical senses he *had* followed the kind of advice Machiavelli offered. He *had* taken precautions, *had* built his own '*dykes*' and '*embankments*', in nurturing a conspiracy of silence among the members of his family, about Nancy. And yet, in spite of his best endeavours, the deluge had raged, and submerged his whole world...

But he hadn't, had he? He'd *not* taken every possible precaution. Will rolled over to slump back down on his pillow. No, he had foolishly left too much of his precarious purpose to others, effectively, that is, to chance... to Fortune! And in an earlier chapter, this wise Machiavelli had made a telling distinction between the way things are and the way we would like them to be – and woe betide any fool who mistook the one for the other. And, Will acknowledged, glumly, he had been just such a fool.

The way things are and the way we would like them to be...

His folly, right enough, had been to fear truth at the outset, the truth of his own situation with Nancy, thus substituting the way he (and Alice, no doubt) wanted things to be for the way they were in reality. It had been a failure of courage, first and foremost, one which implied, also, a moral failure, and a consequential failure of trust... and then a conscience that nagged like a raging toothache until the day that immense tower of lies had come crashing down about them...

Much later, when settling down for the night, Will's thoughts would return to the book and the ways in which it read him.

And he would acknowledge, however reluctantly, that what he was lacking was a certain quality of mind that Machiavelli seemed to be calling 'virtue' – though it couldn't really be that, not as one commonly understood the sense of that word. No, it was something more like the ability to see things clearly... then to act decisively upon that perception. Did he lack such decisiveness? He couldn't be sure, yet the very possibility of it irked him...

And once again, he would return in his mind to the event that had shattered his life and Alice's. And he did not for one moment doubt that on many occasions he had seen clearly enough that the lie he was living could at some future time call him to account, for that amount of foresight he had certainly had. No, it was in the other part he had failed. Having seen the future possibilities and their likely consequences, he had failed to act, either by renouncing the lie and facing the maelstrom, or by maintaining it but taking much greater care over its preservation.

And now, when it was all far too late, it was glaringly obvious to him that that second option should never have been contemplated at all.

Will drifted into sleep, to wake only an hour or so later, however, in a panic. He had been on the point of confessing all to Alice.

Oh, Alice...

He was sure he must have cried out, yet all was quiet around him. In his dream he hadn't actually confessed, for his flight from the dream- to the waking-world had prevented it. But if he had in real life? If, some little time after setting their preparations in motion, he had gone to Alice, had hung his head in contrition, and... It would have availed him nothing, would it? For in its consequences, the outcome would have been much the same, and he would still be here, ruing his fate... Renunciation of the lie would have been little better than its preservation. The only way would have been not to stumble into it in the first place... And it was all too late to mend!

After that realisation, his mind would allow him no rest, and sleep abandoned him.

Life, however, moved on, inevitably so, imposing its distortions such as to make the originally unpalatable become bitter, stultifying, as it pervaded one's whole being... Whatever actions we took in any given moment, he saw clearly, would have their consequences, and we had to be sure we could live with them – not just in the moment but at any time beyond it... and that was one lesson of history he had not found anywhere in Machiavelli!

Yet – and the thought came upon him, apparently from nowhere – whichever way we turned, it seemed, we could not long evade crucifixion, which, apparently, was a pre-condition of our very existence...

For several days, Will's thoughts would meander in and out of the suggestions thrown up by this reading.

Day after day, he would be reminded of how brutally short life could be. The deaths that occurred were by no means only of the elderly. Billy's mother was almost certainly not yet out of her twenties, and Thomas's Joanna the same, and what had they seen of the possibilities and places that made the world so beautiful, and yet, so casually careless, and cruel? Scythed down so early, both of them, purely by chance of where they happened to be, as a result of choices they had made because of the forces of despair, suffocation, human greed, or indifference, or whatever it was, that had weighed them down in their former lives...

And he would be glad of the decision he had come to, that night.

Chance always assumed risk, didn't it? Yet we never quite believe that in our own case. We cleave to the notion that we will somehow (by chance?) slip through its net unnoticed...

Hitherto, Will had come through largely, he still believed, because he had taken the precaution of isolating himself, on board ship. He had attended tirelessly to his personal cleanliness – more of Machiavelli's 'dykes and embankments,' he told himself – simple things that the overcrowded conditions of the steerage, in particular, had made impossible for the great majority. And then here, on the island, he had contrived to remain physically aloof from all but Thomas... and now Billy. Thomas was in the thick of it day after day, constantly exposed and, sooner or later, would he not fall victim... as the two doctors had done? And Billy's parents... they had both succumbed to the fever, hadn't they...?

Will closed his eyes. It would be a miracle if the child were not harbouring the disease. But please God, no, not that. Not any of them... Please...

If there was a sense of fear in his motives, he was hardly aware of it, but Will was suddenly resolved to quit the camp, to breathe a purer air and find the solitude and the space he so much needed. Just for a day or two… He was merely setting out to explore the island again, as he had begun to do when they first arrived. And who knows, he told himself, already feeling a weight slipping from his shoulders, he might find things or places or… something that could be of benefit to the whole, sick community. Yes, that was really it – the greater good of the whole community…

But for the moment, he was not quite free. Not yet.

LV

Someone was inside… What infernal luck!

Thomas halted, straining to hear. Was it Billy, or…? Of course, if it were, he could ask the child to go and play outside for a short while: he certainly didn't want him being anywhere near Lizzie. But if it was Will…? Where else could the man go, to find a little peace and quiet?

His worries proved groundless, however. It was Will inside, straightening his bed covers, but making ready to leave… Perhaps he'd already caught sight of the girl, and understood Thomas's pressing need; but whatever the reason, Thomas was grateful.

'Ah, Father Thomas!' Will inclined his head, formally. 'And you have… Hello, Lizzie… Father Thomas, I'm just stepping out to look for Mr Ridley. I'll explain why, later…'

Thomas grinned and winked, mightily relieved his little problem had been resolved, without even being mentioned.

'Lizzie and I are going to have a little chat, aren't we, Lizzie?' He looked benignly at the girl. 'Oh, and… good luck,' he called, after Will, remembering Ridley's unpredictability. Then he sat down on his bed and motioned to the girl to sit down on Will's, directly opposite him.

'Now then, Lizzie…' And the priest folded his arms, resolved on an intimate, paternal sort of tete-a-tete. 'Let's see what we can make of this business, shall we?'

That man! Will was thinking, and laughing to himself, as he made his way down towards the gate in the fence. So, he had at last caught up with the child! Yet, from what they had seen of her so far, it would be nothing short of a miracle if she could be persuaded to mend her ways. It was almost certain the corrosion went much deeper than her recent escapades with Callaghan and Stevens; it was maybe even a predisposition, for who could say what she came from, back there in London, trying to fend for herself at too early an age? Thank God he was not undertaking that unenviable task himself.

But if Thomas were successful, would that mean they'd have another child on their hands...? Will chuckled – though with more irony than mirth – they might be gathering them up as they went, like the Pied Piper!

Noting he was now past the southern perimeter fence, Will's face assumed a more serious look, for he was nearing the hut Ridley and Barney shared.

The door was wide open, and he stood there, blinking in the sunlight, his eyes trying to penetrate the gloom. There didn't seem to be anyone inside, but then he heard voices from round the back of the dwelling. And sure enough, there they were, occupied with their two horses.

It was Barney who spotted him first. 'Ah, here's Mr Crosby come a-visiting,' he said cheerily.

Ridley, whose back was turned, swung round to face him, noticeably less enthusiastic in his welcome than his companion, though without his habitual scowl, at least.

'Mr Crosby?' he inquired, raising a questioning eyebrow.

Will stood his ground. 'Mr Ridley, I've come to ask a favour of you.'

Briefly, he explained his plan, omitting to mention any of his more personal motives – other than the would-be explorer's natural curiosity – those which, for him, made it more urgent than the telling suggested.

When he had finished explaining his request he looked, none too hopefully, from one to the other in the gathering silence – silence because, he realised, Ridley and Barney were also engaged in a prolonged exchange of glances of their own. So, what was going on?

At length, Barney nodded, and Ridley, evidently taking this as confirmation of his own thoughts, smiled broadly.

'Well, Mr Cros... Will,' he said emphatically, 'maybe we can do each other a favour.'

Will waited.

'It's like this, see. Barney and me should be going back to Brisbane to report on our progress... such as it is... with regard to the siting of the hospital and other buildings. The date for the report was set well before you people arrived, and since no one has thought to countermand it, we have a mind to take the opportunity of escaping to a bit of... well, comfort and congenial company, just as soon as the ketch gets back – which should be anytime in the next day or two.'

Ridley fiddled with the stirrup straps he was adjusting. 'In more normal times we would expect to be back within a week or so, but they might... since there's not much more we can do here, until *your* people leave the island... they might find something else for us to do, over there... And so we were wondering... as you are certainly no novice when it comes to horses...'

Ridley's stress on 'your people' was not lost on Will; nor was that clumsy attempt at flattery – given the man's previous, sneering remarks about his horsemanship, at the time of the gun affair.

'...So we can't say for sure what will happen... But *however* long or short the time, Will, the horses will need tending... And if you would take that task on for us, we'd be mightily obliged, wouldn't we Barney?'

So that was it.

Barney laughed. 'I'd say, Will, your dropping by in this moment, with your request about a horse to ride was nothing short of providential! So yes, we'd be grateful, right enough – and I dare say the horses would too, because they need a lot more exercise than we've been able to give them of late.' He looked at Ridley and grinned, conspiratorially. 'What you have in mind would suit them fine, no doubt about that, eh Joe?'

Ridley nodded. 'For sure, if he rides both horses – though not at the same time! So, what do you say, Will?'

Will knew he ought to be thankful, grateful in his turn, for the way things had turned out... providential indeed. Yet he had the nagging feeling that they had turned out rather too well – but not for him. To borrow a horse for a couple of days was one thing; to take on the responsibility for two animals, and for an indeterminate period was quite another. Did it not amount to yet another restriction, when the whole point of his expedition had been to free himself, temporarily, from all existing constraints? He had the sudden sensation of being assailed from all sides.

'I don't suppose you could take one of them over there with you?' Will asked, knowing he could not afford to refuse outright. Circumstances (and chiefly other people's) laid a moral obligation upon him. He could not refuse, and not just because of the appeal to his better nature, but also because such a refusal would doubtless be matched by Ridley's, with regard to his borrowing just one of the horses. 'And preferably not Bluebell...' he added.

Both men immediately shook their heads in an emphatic negative.

'Out of the question!' Ridley snapped, turning his palms outwards in a show of helpless futility. 'If we were absolutely certain we were not coming back, then yes. But, as I thought I'd made clear, that decision is entirely out of our hands.'

Will nodded, resigned, and agreed to take care of both horses. 'You'll have to show me where everything is,' he conceded, 'and explain about their feeding and mucking-out routines.'

'Naturally...'

And, evidently relieved, Ridley and Barney lost no time in leading Will off to the makeshift stable.

LVI

If Thomas had believed his friendly, patient approach would have the child eating out of his hand, he was to be swiftly disabused. Lizzie lapsed at once into the sullen stubbornness he had witnessed on other occasions and barely raised her eyes to acknowledge even his presence. It was like talking to a stone.

All too soon his patience ran thin. And, since reason was not even granted an audience, it required all the forbearance he could summon up not to strike her. Exasperated, he banged his fist down hard on the improvised table at his bedhead, knocking over a glass of water. And only then did he see a startled reaction, followed immediately by a glimmer of a smile on the girl's face.

'Lizzie, child!' he bellowed, 'I am trying my damnedest to offer you the way to a new life, a new beginning, don't you see? But in your obstinacy and ignorance you defy me, and in so doing you condemn yourself to untold miseries that will surely come from the likes of Stevens and McIlroy!'

The child sniffed her scorn and turned away.

'Can you not see, Lizzie, that what they have led you into can only bring you endless misery?' he pleaded.

Lizzie snorted. 'I like what they've led me into,' she said. 'I like the things they do to me. It's nice. It makes me feel better than anything else there is. So there...! And if they pay me for it as well, then how can it be misery?'

Thomas closed his eyes.

Encouraged, she went on. 'It's you what is evil. I saw what you done to poor Mr Stevens and then to poor Mr McIlroy, just because they was a-trying to protect me from you. They was lookin' after me, and you hurt 'em both bad. But that won't stop 'em none. They'll still want to look after me, spite what you done.'

And Thomas understood, finally, that in the girl's eyes he had no authority whatsoever, and thus his words bounced off her, unheeded. But… did she know anything at all about Stevens – and his past…?

'Lizzie,' he said quietly, 'Mr Stevens has been in prison, and he will soon be going back there. So how can he look after you? Even supposing he ever intended to do so.'

The girl tossed her head. 'You're a-tellin' me lies to try and frighten me,' she shouted. 'Mr Stevens is a-goin' to marry me and we're goin' to live in a big 'ouse he has in Bisbale; so there!' And she stuck out a defiant tongue – which brought a momentary smile to the priest's lips.

But that moment passed.

'Lizzie,' he began again, in near desperation, 'what these men are doing to you is wrong, and what they are making you do to them, is wrong. Not only that, but there is a strong risk of disease; or you could even – God forbid it! – become pregnant!' Did she know of such things? 'How on earth would you manage with a young child to look after when you are… little more than a child yourself?'

The girl laughed out loud, a forced laugh, nevertheless. 'Mr Stevens said you would be a-tellin' me lies about such things, an' he were right! You just have! He knows a lot does Mr Stevens.'

'Oh, but these are not lies, child, they are facts,' Thomas answered, cursing the man's malicious foresight. 'They are very real possibilities, I assure you. But listen…' And, on the spur of the moment, he decided to make a concession he would not have thought necessary, just a few minutes before. 'Listen! What you do with them is not wrong in itself, in its proper place, at the proper time. But because you are so young, well, this is not the proper time.'

Lizzie's face was a blank and she said nothing.

'At your age you should be knowing other things, not this. You've had a bad start in life, through no fault of your own, and these men are taking advantage of that. They are using you for their own selfish ends and filling your head with all sorts of nonsense about the future, things that most certainly will not come to pass. No, Lizzie, let me finish,' he said, as she started to protest again. 'These are men who have already been condemned by the law for their previous wrong-doings, and will be again, nothing is more certain! You *must* believe me. For your own good you must!'

The girl's only reply was a heavy, theatrical sigh.

A deepening – for the priest, exceedingly troubling – silence ensued, in which he scratched and scraped away at his mind, trying to find something there, anything, that would make inroads into the child's seemingly impervious faith in the promises she had been made and in those who had made them. He tried another tack: 'Did you ever know your mother and father, Lizzie?'

The child looked at him, puzzled; then she considered the question for a moment, only to come back at him with the same stonewalling defiance as before. 'And what's that to you?' she demanded.

'If I am to help you – and believe me, that is what I intend to do whether you wish it or not – then I need to know as much about you and your past life as I can,' he replied, battening down his anger. He waited a while, then prompted her again, 'Well, did you? Yes or no? I'd like to know.'

Again she sighed, as if it were all too much trouble. 'Never had none, as I knowed of.'

'Then who brought you up? Who fed you, put clothes on your back, made sure you had a roof over your head?'

'Parish,' she snorted. Then, 'bloody parish done them things. Fat Mr Beales who give you extra bread or soup an' things if you did certain things to him. An' more besides if you let him do things to you, like. Fat pig Beales. Bloody parish. Till they kicked you out on the street. Then nobody – till you got sent to prison.'

'Oh, child.' Thomas could hardly believe what he was hearing. He was appalled at the carelessness and depravity that had evidently dominated her life since her earliest memories.

Some words he had read somewhere, goodness knows how long

ago, slipped into his mind: 'Give me a child to the age of seven and he'll be a Catholic for life,' or something to that effect. Yes, he recalled. It was some high and mighty cardinal, wasn't it? Well, the converse could also be true, without the shadow of a doubt: if the devil or his disciples had a child during that same period…

But what was he thinking? The devil! His disciples! What pious cant! Yet evil, certainly, in whomsoever it was manifested…

Lizzie sat there, silent, watching him, rhythmically kicking her legs up and down.

But this wouldn't do. To accept the sense of the cardinal's dictum – whichever way it was applied – was to accept the defeat of all reason, and Lizzie's was a case in which defeat was unthinkable. He edged forward and held his hands out to her, hoping she would take them. She did not.

'But surely you can see that Mr Beales – all the Mr Beales, and Stevens and McIlroys – only use you and reward you if you do as they bid you, but not if you do as you want, especially if you deny them?'

The girl appeared to ponder the question awhile. 'Well – that's the way fings are, ain't it? They tries to get the fings they wants just like what you do.'

Thomas flinched.

'But it's nothing if it gets me what I want, is it? See mister, nobody never wanted me till I come here, and now everybody does. The world's a better place for me than I ever thought it was.'

Lowering his still extended hands Thomas shuffled back on his bed. No wonder he had failed. Questions of freedom and independence were as remote from the child's struggle with life as was the moon; abstractions, nothing but moonshine! And reason too – or at least, as much reason as he could call upon – that too was utterly remote. He shook his head, sadly. All these things were less than nothing when set against the needs and desires Lizzie recognised and, through long practice, evidently knew how to fulfil. And the thought passed through his labouring mind, that she really was lost, irretrievably, after all… Perhaps nothing could save her.

Suddenly, the girl stood up. 'I'm going home, now, to Mr McIlroy. I'm hungry.'

And as she pushed past him, Thomas could only nod helplessly. And so she left, barely bothering to conceal the smirk that just then possessed her entire face.

Thomas sat there, stunned by this failure of his – to which he was quite unaccustomed. Perhaps he had been fighting the wrong battle; or the right battle on the wrong battlefield. He had presumed certain unspoken, yet nevertheless common premises, and had learned all too late that the girl had never acquired them.

The revelation was as momentous as would have been the unhitching of the Universe.

He bowed his head, a moment; and then sprang to his feet.

'Damn and blast! Damn and blast... for the fool that you are, Thomas Sheehan!' And with that he flung back the tent flap and stalked outside.

Not caring to encounter people, whoever they were, Thomas turned right, into the path that led out of the encampment, and marched rather than walked, driven on by unremitting anger, and incapable of thought. He covered a fair distance, and then, unaccountably, swivelled round and stamped back the way he had come. Re-entering the tented area he veered off to the right, away into the cemetery; and there he flung himself down, finding his place. Joanna's place.

What had he said to the child? Or not said? Breathless, he waited... until his habitual, rational self could regain its grip; and he could consider evenly, and better comprehend, his failure.

At length, Thomas sat up. Oh, he could well understand the wisdom of the cardinal's statement, about having a child until the age of seven, and even more, its necessity in a world in which the forces of evil were every bit as likely to possess a young mind as were those of any presumed good. Years ago, the Church would doubtless have handed Lizzie over to the Inquisition, as one possessed by the Devil; and again, he recognised the wisdom of such un-wisdom, combating the irrational with the irrational. But fear and torment wouldn't do. No, Lizzie had to be educated in order to herself arrive at an appropriate knowledge of herself, and of the world that hedged about her. But how...?

All might be well, someday – he thought of Voltaire – but not now, alas; and that 'someday' was as remote now as it had been in Voltaire's time: in this sad case, of a child depraved, and in this whole, miserable experience of Stradbroke, following on from that hideous voyage, and the loss of Joanna, and so many others... And even before that, the Great Hunger... All this was nothing if not confirmation, was it not, that the evil that men do triumphed, seemingly always? And especially, in conditions of natural adversity? Oh, what a thing was man...

It was all very well for the likes of Voltaire to withdraw, in all humility, into their cocooned world to cultivate their own gardens. But, by Jesus! There were times when the urgency of a situation would not permit such leisurely paths to a far-off, though undoubtedly better, future; and that which confronted Thomas, now, was just such a case. '*Il faut cultiver notre jardin.*' He recalled the words, easily enough; but suddenly, found he was seeing them quite differently.

Thomas, his eyes bright, leapt to his feet like some latter-day Archimedes.

'Lizzie is my *jardin*, damnit!' he shouted. 'And cultivated is what she shall be, willing or no! Weeded, hoed, worked to a fertile tilth.... And I shall do it, by God I shall!'

LVII

A day or two later, Will had woken early, to find Thomas gone, and Billy still asleep; he had thus enjoyed a little thoughtful reading. But now the boy was stirring.

'Morning, Billy!', Will called softly.

'I had a dream, Mr Crosby…' Billy stretched noisily, still only half awake. Then he sighed deeply. 'A very *nice* dream, it was.'

'Did you, indeed! And can you remember any of it?' Will laid aside his book.

'I think I can.'

'All right, I'm listening.' Will got up and went to sit on Billy's bed.

'Well. I was sitting on that rock, the big one that's all greeny from the seaweed… the one you can always see, even when the water is right up to the bank. And the sea was all round me and I was watching it. And a long way off there was something moving, ever so slowly.' And Billy's two little forefingers slow-marched across the counterpane. 'But I couldn't see what it was at first.' He looked closely at Will, to check he was following.

Will nodded, encouraging him to go on.

'After a while, Mr Crosby, I saw it was a person, and he was walking out of the water and coming towards me. And when he got a lot closer, I saw it was my daddy! He said he'd been walking on the bottom of the sea, for *ever* such a long time, but then the sea went back, and I jumped off the rock and took hold of his hand. And he said, 'Where is your mammy, Billy?' So I took him and showed him, Mr Crosby. He said he liked the place where she was because if was close to the seashore, and he 'specially liked the garden I'd made for her. And then… And then he said he couldn't stop long, but he would be coming again… and I had to tell my mammy that.' Fully awake now, Billy was jigging about, in excitement.

Will could not help but be touched by the child's innocence, and a lump rose in his throat as he found himself wondering about his own daughter, and whether she, perhaps, ever had dreams about him. But such thoughts were not for now… if ever… 'So, what happened then, Billy?'

'Well, Mr Crosby, I can't say because, you see, I think I woke up. Maybe my daddy is still over there with my mammy. What do you think?' And with this thought, he bounded out of bed to the doorway of the tent. A moment or two later he was back.

'No, I couldn't see him. And he skipped about a little, in front of Will. 'He's probably gone back to the sea by now.'

Will looked at him steadily. What a tragedy the boy had suffered. It was clear to him from the things Billy said that, though undoubtedly poor, they had been a close family; and he admired the child's brave ways of dealing with the terrible adversity that life had heaped upon him.

'Billy,' he said, edging closer to the boy, 'I'm pretty certain your daddy will come back to you in dreams, your mammy too; and maybe they'll find a way of being together in their dreams as well.'

'Do you really think so, Mr Crosby? I want them to, to come back…' The boy fell silent; and then Will felt a pressure on his legs. 'Mr Crosby…?'

'Yes?' said Will, smiling down at him. 'What is it?'

'Some of the ladies are going to the lake, today, aren't they? And you said – his big blue eyes looked up into Will's – you said I could come too, the next time.'

'Oh, did I?'

'Yes, you did! Can I come? Please?'

Will smiled at the boy's persistent enthusiasm. But in truth, he had forgotten all about the bathing party, and Thomas hadn't thought to mention it, either, when he had told his friend, late last night, what he purposed, on this day. And now he could kick himself for his forgetfulness, which, if he shirked his escorting duties, made this excursion appear doubly selfish. Should he put it off? Would he have to?

'Mr Crosby?' the boy repeated, still waiting, almost patiently, for an answer.

But then… no one had actually approached *him* about accompanying the women, had they, so maybe other arrangements had been made without any intention of involving him at all. Yes, that would explain Thomas's silence on the matter – its irrelevance! And Will decided that the bathing party was no impediment, after all.

'Mr Crosby!'

'Oh… No, Billy, I'm afraid not,' he said. 'But… let me tell you why?'

The lightness in his tone went unnoticed. Billy shook his head from side to side, his lower lip trembled, and his eyes slowly filled with tears.

'But you said… But why not…?'

'Because, Billy,' Will said, desperate to retrieve the situation, not having expected so extreme a reaction from the child… 'I'd like you to come with me instead! We're going to explore another part of the island, and… but didn't you tell Father Thomas you were going to be an explorer when you grow up?'

Billy nodded, still dubious.

'And do you know what else, Billy?' Will continued. 'We are going to do it on a horse!'

'On a horse?' Suddenly, the child was beaming from ear to ear. 'Oh, but Mr Crosby, I can't ride a horse. I've never been on a horse. Not ever!' And he jumped up on his bed and started bouncing on it, making clip-clop sounds. 'Are you going to teach me?'

Will smiled. 'Oh, you can sit in front of me on my horse, and that way you'll see how easy it is, and you'll also see everything we pass, much more easily than if we were walking. So, what do you say? Lake or horse?'

'Oh, the horse! The horse! Yes, please!' And he leapt from his bed and, to the best of his ability, mimicked his imagined man galloping round on horseback.

Will nodded, content. And though he later wondered at his own conduct – hadn't he been intending to leave the camp, its worries and its people, all of them, behind... including Billy? – yet, thinking about it now the decision was made, he did not regret the impulse that had just then prompted it.

The imagination was as nothing compared with the reality, even though Billy's excitement was initially tempered by a certain caution, even fear, when he saw the size of the beast that was to transport them.

'Are you sure the horse wants to carry us, Mr Crosby? Because if it doesn't it's a long way for me to fall down. How do you know if it does?'

'Well,' Will said, amused at the child's ingenuousness. 'I've ridden her before, you see Billy. We're old friends – aren't we Bluebell? So I don't think she is likely to object.' But he refrained from mentioning that he knew only too well what a long way it was to fall.

Having checked that the rifle and cartridges were in place, he slung the water flasks over the horse's back, ahead of the pommel, and hoisted himself into the saddle. 'Come on, then!' And he reached down and held his arms out.

'Er... I don't think I should try and climb up there, Mr Crosby, so maybe I'll just walk alongside you. That might be best, mightn't it?'

Will laughed and swept the boy up into the saddle in front of him. 'Now, what was that you were saying, Billy? I'm afraid you wouldn't have been able to keep up with us on foot; we shall be going a lot faster than that.'

Billy chortled, but Will noticed his small knuckles were uncommonly white as he gripped the pommel with both hands. 'You'll soon get used to it, mark my words,' he assured him.

Will's plan was to ride quickly up to Amity Point then, gaining the north beach from there, to try and travel along the sands as far eastwards as they and the sea would allow. They set off, almost immediately into a canter, and Will felt the child stiffen.

'Billy, you're not going to fall because I won't let you! Remember, I've ridden horses hundreds of times. I used to be a soldier – did you know that? So just lean back against me and try to relax.'

The boy did as Will suggested, and before long was paying more attention to Will's stories about India, and to the terrain they passed through, than to maintaining his statuesque position on the horse's back.

'Oh, look at those big birds, Mr Crosby! Up there, look! They're like… like broken-off bits of rainbow!'

'Yes, they are… bits of rainbow!'

After a short while, they came to the stream and the clearing and Will, still curious about the painted poles and their purpose, slowed the horse to walking pace, though he did not attempt to leave the track. He had thought not to mention the poles or the mystery they represented, and merely glanced over to his right, but the sharp-eyed Billy spotted them at once.

'Oh, look, Mr Crosby, over there. What are they? Why are they there? Do they belong to anybody? I should really like one of those to put in my mammy's garden. Do you think I could? Can we stop?'

Will smiled at this deluge of questions: 'Not so fast, Billy! I don't know why they are there, and I don't know who they belong to. But I'm fairly certain they belong to somebody. And if that is the case then I'm afraid you can't have one because that would be stealing, wouldn't it?'

The boy sighed theatrically, his face puckering into a grimace. But then a moment later he was back to his theme. 'Well, whoever they belong to shouldn't leave them there! Not if they don't want to lose them. That's what I think.'

Will could see his point. 'Well Billy, in the world we come from, you could be right, but until we all arrived here, on this island, there probably wasn't anyone who would want to steal them. So whoever put them there probably didn't even give the matter a thought.'

Billy fell silent, and Will, taking furtive advantage of this lull, spurred the horse once more into a canter, along the sandy track.

'Mr Crosby', Billy said, thoughtfully, as Will slowed the horse to negotiate a fallen tree trunk, 'do you know what they remind me of, the bright colours on those poles?'

'No, Billy, tell me?' he said, his mind half elsewhere.

'They were a bit like the big snake I saw the other day.'

'A snake?' Startled, Will began to pay attention to what the boy was telling him.

'…It had so many colours it looked like a rainbow bending and then twisting and sliding over the grass.' And the child even took his hands off the pommel, for the first time, to present Will with a visual image of the snake's movements. 'It was ever so big. Bigger than a tree, even! But I wasn't frightened of it. In fact, Mr Crosby, when I shouted at it to tell it to stop, I think it was frightened of me and it went quickly away, all slippy and slidy, into the long grass, and I couldn't find it anymore.'

'Billy, did you really see a snake?' asked Will, starting to feel annoyed with himself for assuming that a six-year-old boy could be left to roam, even the familiar part of the island, unsupervised.

'I did so. It had such lovely colours, like those birds we saw back there.'

'But Billy, have you already forgotten what you were told only a few days ago, and what your mammy had also told you? You must not, not under any circumstances, go anywhere near the creatures you see on this island, especially snakes and spiders and other insects. Very many of them are so poisonous that you would… might die… if they were to bite you. Do you understand what I'm saying? And such creatures don't know any better than to bite, if they are at all frightened, and for sure, anyone chasing them *will* frighten them; so, if you went looking in the long grass for the snake, when it disappeared, you were probably in great danger. Please, Billy, promise me you will *never, never* do anything so foolishly dangerous again!'

The child looked at him, clearly quite startled. 'But Mr Crosby', he protested, 'I know those things, and I don't go anywhere near them. Only… only… this was different. The rainbow snake told me so, himself. He told me he knew a lot more things than I knew, and he said he wanted to tell me some of them, in secret…'

'Now, now, Billy,' Will interrupted, a note of impatience in his voice. 'Snakes don't talk. And there are no exceptions to the warning... and the rule about such creatures! You must keep away from them at all times. Do you understand?'

Billy hung his head, clearly chastened by Will's sharp tone. And he said nothing more for quite some time. Then cautiously testing his protector's mood, he ventured a tentative 'Mr Crosby...?'

'Yes, Billy, what is it?'

'I think you are – and the child hesitated, as if weighing up the wisdom of his thought before it was uttered – you are wrong about the snake.'

'Billy...' Will sounded a note of warning.

'...Because it did talk to me, sitting up on its big stone before it moved. It talked to me in my head.' He sat stiffly, stubbornly, looking straight ahead. 'I know it did.'

Will laughed. 'I think maybe you were dreaming again, Billy,' he said, patting the boy on his shoulder. 'But that's all right.'

LVIII

The arrival of the *Aurora*, the previous morning, had been anticipated with an almost tactile optimism, fuelled no doubt by the eager, easy chatter of Barney and the not infrequent laughter of the normally saturnine Ridley, who had hauled their packs down onto the quay almost as soon as the ketch had been spotted leaving the mouth of the Brisbane River.

For the great majority of the island's temporary inhabitants, the ship was concrete, visible evidence that the world had not forgotten them. And so the inside of the perimeter fence was soon crowded with onlookers, perhaps relishing a foretaste of the day when they too, God willing, would be packed and ready to re-join the rest of humanity.

Yet, riding through the silent forest, with Billy, now, Will recalled how quickly hearts had sunk, and the almost festive mood had been dissipated.

As soon as the gangplank was lowered, a tall, thin, almost spectral figure had appeared, hesitating at the top, a white handkerchief pressed to his nostrils, surveying the scene spread out below him. A hush had fallen over the crowd, and standing a little apart, Will had quickly realised that this must be Weatherall, the immigration agent. Long-awaited, and yet, until that moment, quite forgotten.

After a moment's hesitation, Dr Ballow – who was standing on the quayside with Captain Kemp and his First Officer – had stepped forward and raised a welcoming hand and hat, undoubtedly recognising the high-ranking official, despite the perhaps affected, ever-present kerchief. Weatherall, for his part, had advanced halfway down the plank, but then stopped; and as Ballow took another step towards him, the immigration officer had raised his right hand, not in a gesture of salutation but rather of warning, that he should come no nearer. A strange sort of parley had ensued, involving the three men who had met to welcome the ketch and the government official who, plainly, had made up his mind, whether on the spur of the moment, or sooner, not to set foot on the island.

Ridley and Barney had hovered within earshot. And it was from their sometimes voluble, reactions that the broad drift of the conversation had been conveyed to the quarantined majority.

This tense encounter had lasted ten, maybe fifteen minutes.

Then Weatherall had turned on his heel and retreated once more to the presumed safety of the *Aurora*'s quarter deck, from where he observed the rest of the summary proceedings. Provisions for the stricken inhabitants were hurriedly unloaded and dumped on the quayside by members of the ship's crew, and water was quickly pumped into the three large vats.

In less than two hours, the ketch had slipped its moorings and was once again crossing the bay, headed for Brisbane… *minus* Ridley and his colleague, who had stood there for a long time after the ship's departure, deep in conversation with the other three, all of them disconsolate, angry, perplexed.

In those long moments, played out as if in slow motion, Will had looked about him at his fellow-prisoners, aware of their shocked, utterly bewildered silence, and had felt something like admiration for their forbearance, or whatever it was that had prevented them from tearing down the fence and storming the ship in their frustration. Even before the small group on the quay had dispersed, the crowd of onlookers had begun to fragment, men or couples drifting away to their separate miseries, with yet another burden to bear. Although the details had yet to be conveyed to them, it was clear to all that they remained outcasts, and must continue to suffer and to fear, locked in close proximity with their own and their loved-ones' potential deaths.

Subsequently it would be made known that Weatherall's decision had had the full support of the Brisbane city council, acting on the unequivocal advice Weatherall himself had received in Sydney, to the effect that quarantine must be absolute. No one, not even the two doctors who had volunteered their services in the emergency, were exempt. Of course, the city council's failings, just as much as the arrival of *The Emigrant*, had been cause of the emergency, but that was waved away as a mitigating circumstance, not even acknowledged for what it truly was. The hapless Ridley and Barney, despite having had minimal contact with the ship's passengers – a fact vouchsafed by Ballow himself – were also regarded as potential carriers of the ship fever and were forbidden to return until the epidemic had fully abated. And for weeks afterwards, their particular dejection – and resentment – would be plain for all to see, that of freemen who had become prisoners, though they had committed no crime; citizens filled with a sense of gross injustice.

Yet, in practical terms, the greatest problem the *Aurora*'s summary departure had left was the continuing presence of Stevens. He had been locked away in one of the *Emigrant*'s upper cabins, for just over a week, and allowed out around the deck for only two fifteen-minute periods each day. There were clear signs, however, that his state of mind was deteriorating rapidly. It had been intended, of course, that he be transported back to the township to be dealt with by the city's magistrates, but even that concession had been refused.

Ballow had examined Stevens towards evening, the previous day, and declared that he must not continue much longer in the terribly cramped conditions in which he had hitherto been kept, for his morale and his grip on the realities around him were exceedingly weak. Some protests were raised, including by Thomas and Will, but in the absence of suitable facilities it was eventually agreed that he be returned to the community, albeit with certain provisos, among which an absolute embargo on his leaving the camp area, or passing through the perimeter fence to the passengers' part, or having any contact with the girl, Lizzie.

It had been these events and their consequences that had finally determined Will's departure, allowing him to cast off the qualms and scruples that had surfaced in his mind since the idea of a journey to the other side of the island had first come to him. And, though he commiserated with Ridley and Barney for the setback they had suffered, it had now relieved him of his supervision duties of the horses…

It had been a dream, only a dream; and Thomas kept telling himself this, as he emerged from its undergrowth and into rapidly dawning consciousness. Yet, finding his body clammy and his penis erect, even when fully awake, and one image persisting, refusing to be displaced… Oh, so deeply disturbing….

The child, Lizzie, kneeling naked in the sand, offering herself, her head turned sideways so that her leering, lascivious face was almost entirely visible, grinning grotesquely back at him. And a little beyond her, on a high rock, dressed in regal scarlet robes that were far too large for him, sat Stevens, his right arm outstretched, pointing a finger at the fallen priest, also on his knees, close behind the child…

Thomas sat up, silently, desperate not to waken his companions, and swung his legs over the side of the bed. After maybe half a minute he felt for his boots, picked up his cape and stole outside. All was hushed. The air was cool, verging on cold, and the sky was a vast archipelago of stars. Perhaps because he needed it so urgently in those moments, he felt, almost physically felt, their calming, pristine spring washing over him. And he stood there, face turned upwards, eyes closed, longing for the fear and disgust to be exorcised, the sense of disgrace and dishonour and infinite loss. Seeking to still his beating mind. Oh when, and how, could his will ever become truly upright, wholesome, and free of that shameful image and all he feared it signified within him?

Oh yes, mankind was in a fallen state all right, whether or not it had ever fallen away from any kind of grace. Yet grace was surely what was needed if the righteous mind were ever to connect with, and correct, the midnight stirrings of the stalking beast within; for he doubted that any human power could ever safely bring about such a state, the fruitful dawn.

362

Thomas would live with the shock of this self-revelation for many days to come, but he spoke of it with no man. And most consciously of all, he avoided any contact with the girl, unnerved, uncertain of where or whether he might find the moral strength to confront her and release her from her own imprisonment. And his.

A little more than a couple of hours later, after the first glimmers of dawn had eventually given way to silver sunlight, another tent flap was pushed aside, and Dr Patrick Mallon emerged for the first time in almost two weeks.

He stood, mesmerised – it might have seemed to any observer – by the shafting sunlight glinting on the sea-wave crests beyond the line of dark shadow cast by the forest behind him, and hot tears – released, he presumed, by his gratitude – suddenly blurred that vision, pricking at the corners of his eyes.

LIX

Sometime before they got to Amity, Will had decided that a halt would be wise once they reached the Point. For one thing, Billy might be glad to set his feet on the ground again, and Bluebell would certainly be grateful for some rest. But mainly, Will wanted Billy to see the tree-full of kingfishers and, if they were still there, the tiny blue crabs such as Callaghan had claimed he wanted to show the boy.

Once there, Will lowered the child to the ground, and even before he had dismounted himself Billy had run over to the water's edge and immediately discovered the crabs for himself.

'Oh, Mr Crosby, do come and look. I bet you've never seen anything like this before! What are they? Are they spiders?'

But by the time Will had caught up with the child the very last of the tiny crustaceans was just scuttling into the safety of the sea or down their sandy burrows.

'Oh… they've all gone, Mr Crosby. Why did they do that?' Disappointment was written all over his face.

'Just stand quite still and silent a moment or two and watch the sand by the water.' And he took hold of the boy's hand, and together, stock still, they scanned the wet beach before them. Sure enough, in less than half a minute, the 'spiders', to Billy's great delight, began to re-emerge.

'They are crabs, Billy, not spiders,' Will whispered. 'Tiny crabs. And it's true, I've never seen the likes of them before, except the once when I rode up as far as this; indeed, that's why we stopped – I was hoping to show them to you.'

Billy hopped down the sand, watching them, until the last had disappeared back into the sea, and he came skipping back. 'They're lovely, Mr Crosby!'

'Yes. And they are not the only beautiful things you'll see here. Look over there.' And Will pointed back at the silvery tree on which he had observed the colony of kingfishers on his previous excursion.

'Ohhhh! They are as pretty as my snake was, Mr Crosby! And those other big birds we saw back there,' he said gravely; then off he ran towards the kingfishers... which promptly scattered in all directions.

'Come back birds!' Billy cried, waving at them. 'Come back!'

But since they did not obey his command, but observed him from their new, more distant perches, he came slowly back himself.

'Why did they do that, Mr Crosby? Didn't they want to talk to me?'

'Oh, Billy,' laughed Will, charmed by the child's stubborn, yet intimate interpretation of the world about him. 'Billy, all birds are frightened by sudden movements – like the crabs were. They think they are being attacked, and so fly off to a safer place. Perhaps, if you had walked more slowly and not shouted at the top of your voice, they would still be there.'

Billy considered a moment, and then looked up. 'You *could* be right, Mr Crosby.' And then he turned away and walked with a slow, comical plod, back along the strand.

Smiling at the boy's precociousness, Will followed behind at some distance, leading the horse at her own pace. Billy, for his part, made off in the direction of the long creek, with its dark mangroves, and after a while flopped down in the white sand to watch the huge numbers of birds wading in its shallow waters. By the time Will caught up with him again he seemed lost in thought, and it was clear that another question was bubbling up, and its eruption was imminent.

'Mr Crosby...' The child looked suddenly troubled. 'Why is it that all of these birds and even the tiny blue crabs are alive, and my mammy and daddy are not? They aren't any good to anybody, are they, even if they are beautiful colours?'

The question was serious and, Will realised, vast, not only for Billy but for him too.

'Child, sometimes... just sometimes, you ask the most impossible questions! And I can't really give you an answer because... well... they... there are things I have never thought about before in my whole life. And this is one of them!'

Billy seemed taken aback, but then he sighed, dramatically. 'Oh, all right then, I'll ask Father Thomas. I bet he will know.' And he knelt down and dug his fingers deep into the wet sand, scooping it up, then letting it filter slowly between them.

Will, though relieved he was not to be pressed on the matter, nevertheless cast about in his mind to shape some sort of answer, even if just for himself. He ambled along slowly, leading the horse, reflecting on Billy's words.

But a minute later, the child was back, tugging at his arm. 'But why is it? And why does Father Thomas always know the answer to my questions, and you don't... sometimes...?'

Will let go of Bluebell's reins and stopped. 'All right, then.'

Billy sank down to the sand at his feet and waited, his face tilted upwards, his brow puckered.

'Because Father Thomas, Billy, is a very clever man. He has read lots and lots of books and thought about lots of things that have never even entered my head. I am... was... a soldier, remember, whereas he was... is, that is, a priest, and priests have to think about things much more than soldiers do. I'm sure he would give you a much better answer than I can. But I *will* try, none the less, and I will give you an answer – *if* you give me time to think about it, and don't fire a dozen more questions at me in the meantime! It is, after all, an important question, and you are right to ask it.'

Billy grinned. 'All right then,' he said, springing to his feet once more and skipping off still further along the sand spit, towards the point where the long creek reached the open sea. 'But Mr Crosby...' he called back over his shoulder, squinting into the fierce sunlight, 'I hope it won't be *too* long, because I just can't stop the questions coming into my head, and jumping out of my mouth...!'

'Cheeky little imp!' Will called after him, laughing.

So, why was it? Different circumstances, or just luck, maybe? Will went back to his ruminations, but despite recalling that the writer, Machiavelli, had said something on the matter, was unable to quite call it to mind. He contemplated the birds, the crabs, about them, and other creatures besides, and wondered how many of them would still be alive the next day, deciding it might be a question of how close to their natural state – the place they belonged to best – they were. Could it be that? After all, these creatures inhabited a world perhaps free of disease, where all danger was external, coming from other creatures; whereas human beings... they crowded together in their towns and cities and ships; and despite being generally safe from dangers from without, they could never be sure when dangers lurked within. Was that it?

But it didn't really seem much of an answer, when he thought about it, even if it perhaps contained some grains of truth. But space, he felt, adequate space to be in, individually – that was part of it; adequate control of that space around you, adequate knowledge of how to control it wisely... Human beings couldn't just fly off to the next tree or the next, or quit the land for the sea, at the approach of some perceived danger... He sighed. Thomas would surely have a better answer. And he half hoped the child would have forgotten his promise by the time he caught up with him.

The sun was now overhead and very warm and Will judged that, if they were to make any real headway into unknown territory, they had best be moving now onto the northern shore and trekking eastwards. He hailed Billy, who turned and came running back towards him.

'I like it here, Mr Crosby,' he confided, panting. 'Everything looks new, doesn't it? And look, the fisherers have flown back to their tree again, and look, the crabs have come back out of the sea. Do you think my daddy will see them in the sea sometimes, wherever he is...? So... if you are ready now, Mr Crosby... why are the crabs alive and safe when my mammy is not?'

Will swallowed hard, then hazarded his response. 'For the moment they are safe... as we can see... and, of course, alive. But many of them will most likely be dead by tomorrow. You see, Billy, on the land there are probably many animals and birds that will eat them, and when they get into the sea, probably many fish waiting to eat them too. They are not really very safe; not for long. Their lives will be much shorter than those of your mammy and daddy, that's for sure. Maybe even now the kingfishers are thinking about swooping on them and gobbling them up – as soon as we have gone.'

Billy screwed up his nose and closed his eyes.

Will thought for a moment. 'Just because we see them, now, apparently safe, that doesn't mean that's how they are always; far from it. In that little space between the water that covers them and the sand that reveals them, they are always... dodging back and forth between one danger and another. And sooner or later, their luck will run out...' He looked at Billy, conscious that his groping towards some sort of answer, an answer that made some sort of sense to him, had left the little boy behind. 'Truly Billy,' he confessed, 'I don't really know. I'm just trying – as we all have to do with life's difficult questions… Maybe you *had* better ask Father Thomas after all.' And on that note, he swung himself up into the saddle and pulled the child up after him. I'm glad you liked the place, though…'

But something, some movement was it? caught Will's eye, and, looking quickly around them, he instinctively felt for the reassuring rifle butt in its holster. But there was nothing he could see other than maybe the glint from a pile of tiny seashells just ahead of them at the water's edge, which, he was almost certain, had not been there the last time he had been here. It was some distance back from the tide line, and all the shells were the same type, some sort of periwinkle perhaps.

'What is it, Mr Crosby?'

'Ah, nothing. I was just looking at those shells.' Will spurred the horse forward, and before long they came round onto the much narrower northern shore where, eyes everywhere, he sensed a deepening silence. It became oppressive almost, and he broke it deliberately.

'Look Billy, over there. That island is called Moreton Island and...

you see those ruined huts near those rocks? They were built by the very first men who ever came to this island from the mainland, over twenty years ago. And...'

But he could think of nothing more to say about them. So he urged Bluebell into a canter and veered over to the sea's edge, keeping a wary eye on the forest over to their right.

LX

The Church, which could not be wrong about *everything*, would argue that an uncommitted sin was a contradiction in terms. A sin was malicious intention realised; but the thought itself, untranslated into action, that is, was as nothing – unless it was a heaven-sent warning, perhaps? But dreams... in which *intentional* thought was *not* present... were they like unrealised actions? A dream came from greater depths though, from some sort of volition formed out of instinct, was it? the very root, maybe, of our mortal corruption...?

But *if* the dream were a warning, about a... a... depravity whose existence his waking mind would... did... strenuously reject, what then? He did not desire the child, or he was not aware of doing so, just the opposite, in fact...

And yet those shadow-puppets had seemed so real...

Thomas's brow furrowed. And so bound up was he in his own tormented thoughts that he was barely aware of the matron's quiet grieving... What could it all mean? That his will was not his own to command, perhaps?

It was a terrifying thought, that this night he, Thomas, had been rehearsing indulgence in the very sin for which he had condemned both Stevens and McIlroy. Not just condemned, but savagely assaulted...

For God's sake! No, he could not accept that. He would not! But... what did it mean, then? Damned if he knew the answer...

But... just supposing she was *not* the child he believed her to be, but, as she and Stevens and McIlroy all claimed, a young *woman*, and one who was not in the habit of spurning such advances ('I like what they do to me', she had said), what would the dream signify *then*?

Thomas's fugitive thoughts scurried all over the place, searching for a right understanding – alas, one that refused to be found. And suddenly, he abandoned them, and looked up.

The matron is standing at the foot of Dr Mitchell's bed, her head in her hands, quietly sobbing.

Sensing her need for this private release, Thomas shifts his position on the hard chair, and looks over at the doctor's inert form, stretched out before them. Poor man, little more than twenty-five, twenty-six, though the disease ravaging his emaciated body these past weeks has piled the appearance of a more advanced age upon him. For that to happen, his own Joanna had not survived long enough, and had been spared that indignity. Even in death her beauty had bloomed regardless...

And what does the poor doctor's hopeless, unconscious struggle avail, or signify? Is this mocking travesty of human form into which he has metamorphosed the true image of God? Whatever it signifies, the arc of time has closed over this selfless, courageous man, forever. And Thomas growls, in despair, suppressing the howl his whole being aches for, and cheated humanity demands.

Again, he looks up at the young, grief-stricken matron, and is suddenly overwhelmed by such pity, and for all of them – Miss Labone, the lifeless doctor, himself, and for all who must yet suffer the trial and sentence that time invariably brings. Unthinkingly he rises, quickly covers the few feet that divide them, and throws his arms around her, drawing her to him. He finds no resistance, no tensing, in her trembling body.

Hot and dusty from their swift ride northwards into the increasing heat and humidity of the day, Will slows the horse first to a trot then to a walk, satisfied that for the time being, at least, nothing threatens them from the forest backdrop to the shoreline. Then, setting Billy down, he himself dismounts and all three, man, boy and beast, amble in the gently flushing waves that wash over their now bare feet.

And in proportion, as his sense of caution recedes, Will becomes aware of a feeling of elation spreading steadily through his entire being.

It is precisely for this, it comes to him, that he has undertaken this journey – for the simple pleasure of giving himself up to the unhurried swell, the listless breeze, the salt spray on his face – all cares washing or wafting away and evaporating into thin air.

How long is it since being alive has felt so right and positive? To answer truthfully, he knows he would need to travel backwards some considerable distance through time; years now separate him from a sense of well-being such as has just now stolen upon him in this remote, island paradise.

He glances at the boy, skipping through the water, back and forth, bending to pick up a shell or a stone or a piece of driftwood, then dropping it and searching (though hardly that) again, but with no objective other than what is there to satisfy careless, fleeting curiosity. The boy, like Will, is entirely absorbed by and in and for the moment. And just how essential the boy is to these moments, Will now understands; he cannot imagine them without him. And he watches, feels compelled to watch Billy, in his exploring, discovering, delving, ever questioning leap into life. Nor is he entirely unaware of what this realisation implies for both their futures, though he will not dwell on it here and now...

How long or how far they continued in this carefree way, Will could not later say, so absorbed was he in, and by the unfolding day.

But suddenly, Billy was running back towards him, stopping, and turning every now and again, and pointing in the direction he was coming from.

'Look, Mr Crosby! Look...! What do you think those moving things are?'

The shimmering light glancing dazzlingly off the sea makes it impossible to see clearly with the naked eye and at that distance what they might be, other than dark shapes. Will moves round to the other side of Bluebell and draws the eyeglass hurriedly out of its case, hoping he might see some of the creatures they have not yet encountered: a kangaroo, perhaps, or its smaller cousin, the wallaby. After all, it would be fitting if they were here too, in this earthly paradise.

As soon as he adjusts the viewfinder, however, he realises he is looking at human beings, mainly children – four or five of them – and a couple of female adults, one kneeling, the other stooping and apparently picking things up and dropping them in a sort of sack she has, fastened about her waist, all of them close to the water's edge.

'They're people, Billy, some children too…, the black people who live in these parts. Come on, let's go and meet them, shall we?'

Had he not been in the tender grip of that careless, utopian mood, he would have been much less bold – something Will realised only later, however, with hindsight. As it was, his earlier wariness had abandoned him completely. And irresistible curiosity, together with his overwhelming sense of the goodness of everything in these golden surroundings, propelled him forward, heedlessly, to make contact with these lives which must be so very different from his own.

He decided against remounting, fearing that a man raised high on a horse might frighten them off. Nor did he perceptibly quicken his pace, or neglect to indulge Billy's delight in what the sea and the sand offered up to them. They thus ambled at a leisurely pace towards this imminent encounter with a new world, as though it were an everyday occurrence.

It is obvious, long before they come up with the group, that they have been spotted, for the kneeling woman is calling out – though with no note of panic in her voice. And a moment later, two or three men come running from the edge of the forest, all of them carrying what prove to be spears, and other weapons the like of which Will has never seen before.

And if, in this moment, a shadow of doubt does cross his mind it is repressed, for he raises his hand in greeting and holds it aloft awhile, to show he is unarmed and means them no harm. And, watching him, looking for guidance in this wholly new experience, Billy copies his action.

Another two figures emerge from the forest, and the whole group, a dozen or so in number, are now strung out across the sands between the sea and the forest shade, all of them stock-still, observing their progress.

In spite of this sense of well-being, which he is reluctant to renounce, Will becomes aware of a growing tension within him, more anticipation than fear, or vague hopes. His mouth is suddenly dry, and he wonders whether he should mount after all, or maybe just loosen the rifle in its holster. Yet he does neither.

At a point still some fifty yards away from the inert, watching figures, they have to cross a stretch of water that encroaches much further upon the land than has been the case until now; and because the sun is over to their right and slightly behind them, both their shadows and their reflections show clearly in different places in the water.

Billy notices this at once.

'Oh, Mr Crosby, look! My shadow has found a friend, and so has yours, and Bluebell's!' And he dashes forward trying to jump onto his own reflection, but with every attempt, once the splash has settled back, the reflection remains steadfastly where it ever was, ahead of him. He shouts in glee and bounds forward again and again, and Will encourages him, sensing obscurely that this childish diversion may well prove useful in this tense moment.

'Go on, Billy, catch it!' he shouts, and claps his hands at each leap the boy makes, taking care to keep his hands visible the whole time.

And his instinct is right. The kneeling woman also claps her hands, and the men relax visibly, whereupon three of the black children of more or less Billy's stature dash forward and hurl themselves upon their own reflections; and the four children jump and dance and kick up the water, all laughing hysterically together.

Will, smiling broadly, goes past the children and towards the men who are even then converging on the two women by the water's edge. When he reaches them, he glances back at the still gambolling children, then turns to greet the group, smiling all the while. The adult members of the group are also grinning in appreciation of the children's playfulness, and one of the younger men begins jumping about in imitation of them; and everyone laughs at his antics.

Then, suddenly, a silence falls upon them and deepens, for a gradual awareness of the enormity of this meeting seems to gather in the minds and faces of all present. And Will surmises this is something far bigger than the moment in which these individual members of different races come face to face with each other... for the first time, can it be? Two worlds barely known to each other are suddenly touching, and no one can have any inkling of what the outcome will be. This silence is all they have in common to express the evident sense of awe that has descended upon them.

The children's laughter now seems far away.

Two different worlds... And it dawns on Will that all these people are virtually naked, and the Eden story he and Thomas had discussed some weeks before comes back to plant itself at the forefront of his mind. But unlike Adam and Eve, in the Genesis account, no one seems abashed. He steals a glance at the two women, both of whom have now joined the cluster, and his gaze, lighting on the firm naked breasts of the one with the gunny sack, causes him to avert his eyes guiltily, and there is no turning away from, nor mistaking, the stirrings within him. And he realises in the moment that he has not seen a woman naked since his time with Alice.

Of course, during his time in India Will had encountered people of a different race from his own. But there, the two races had been aware of each other's strange ways for upward of two centuries, even borrowing and adapting aspects of the other's way of life and language; here, on Stradbroke, however, a void was meeting a void. And, he would later think, that initial tension had perhaps been generated by both a fear and a hope: the fear of difference, the hope of being able to pour something of themselves into the other's vacuum, so as to reach out over the abyss that divided them.

Sensing this – although he would have been hard pressed to express anything like it in words – here, now, Will casts about in his mind for some way of breaking through, and out of, the tension and the silence.

His eye lights on a curious looking, but clearly carefully crafted, piece of wood one of the men is holding, and catching the man's eye, he cautiously reaches forward as if begging it of him. It is immediately proffered, and he takes hold of it, reverently almost, and examines it, running his hand along its highly polished surface, turning it and repeating his action on the other side.

When he judges he has paid sufficient, admiring attention to the object he hands it back, and with a theatrical raising of both hands and puckering of his brows he tries to indicate his bewilderment. What is it for?

The man nods, gravely almost, and stepping forward, cautiously takes Will by the arm, then after a couple more paces away from the group, moves slightly out of Will's reach, swings his right arm back behind him and hurls the thing away in the direction of the trees!

Momentarily stunned by such profligacy Will stares at the man with obvious alarm written in his face. The man smiles and points in the direction he has thrown it and, to Will's utter amazement, here it is, curving back towards its owner's hand like a well-trained hawk, such as he had sometimes seen the Moguls use for hunting in Rajasthan. Again, the man throws the heavy, curved blade, and this time Will watches its arching trajectory all the way and marvels yet again at its simple beauty and, he suddenly realises, the technical skill it represents. Yet, what purpose does this apparent toy fulfil for its owner? With exaggerated gestures he again questions him. And this time, beckoning Will to follow, the man strides away towards the forest's edge.

At a distance of some twenty yards from the trees, he stops and scans them carefully. Then he points at a group of blue and scarlet parakeets, in the topmost branches, pulls back his arm, holds it for a moment then swings it forward, his eye never leaving the birds. But something, perhaps even that sudden, backward jerking of his arm, has disturbed them and they scatter in panic, in time to escape the weapon which, Will is now in no doubt, would surely have killed or badly maimed any bird it had struck. And again, in a trice, the weapon is safely back in the hands that had launched it.

Will nods vigorously, expressing his amazed comprehension, then turns to hail Billy.

'Billy, come and see...'

But the invitation dies on his lips. Billy is now completely naked, running about among the Aborigine children, with his wet clothes strewn about on the sand. The boy is suddenly caught by a tall, pubescent girl, who immediately begins fingering his genitals, while with her other hand she pulls Billy's hand towards her own.

Then, seeing two younger girls just starting to demonstrate their own similar differences to the bewildered-looking boy, Will calls again. 'Billy, you must see this...'

LXI

Will glances at the men and women, whose eyes are fixed on the children, having followed the direction of his own gaze, perhaps, when he called out to the boy. Yet none of them appear anxious or perturbed.

Billy now breaks from the group and comes towards him, clearly in some embarrassment. Will affects not to notice this, or his nakedness, and instead makes great play in getting the Aborigine man to show the boy the wonderful wooden implement that had so captivated his own attention.

As the demonstration is unfolding, Will becomes aware that they have been joined by two more men, who have presumably also emerged from the forest, and with whom the other men and women are talking animatedly – 'jabbering like monkeys', was how Ridley had described it. One of the two – older, with grizzled grey beard and wiry, grey-streaked hair – appears to be a man of some standing, judging by the deference of his fellows, and Will, his attention divided, feels he should lose no time in paying him his respects. So he moves away from the display, which is obviously delighting Billy, and walks slowly up to the newcomers.

'They think you come down from moon, mister.'

Will gapes at the man, hardly believing he is hearing English, or a sort of English, for it takes him a moment or two to realise that that's what it is.

'From moon, mister,' he repeats, laughing.

And Will laughs too, feeling the tension draining away from

him. 'Ah, not quite so far as that, though from a long way off, yes indeed.'

'I say them that too,' the man answers. 'So where go now?'

'Nowhere... really; I am just... trying to see more of Stradbroke,' he explains, somewhat lamely, '... to see whether it is different over this side, from where all our people are.' And as he is speaking, it occurs to him, he should maybe warn the man, and his people, to keep away from the disease-ridden Dunwich area.

'It's... not good the other side. You should not...'

'Yes, mister, know 'bout big sickness... Not go there. Maybe soon go other island. But... this island not what you say it, mister. This island Minjerribah. Mean "mosquito place."'

'Min-jér-ri-bah,' Will repeats, sensing a rebuke. 'But I'm quite sure none of our people will come *here*,' he says. And he says the word again. 'Min-jér-ri-bah... Is that right?'

'So, why *you* come?' the man persists.

Will sighs inwardly, realising that any answer approaching the truth will be too complicated.

'To be alone,' he says at length... 'In a different place. To feel... the silence. To breathe clean air, and to see new things.' And he shrugs and smiles, at a loss for more, but hoping his words will be understood, and ring true.

There is a silence, and then the man begins to laugh quietly. 'No new thing here, mister, only old thing. Very old thing.'

'Well, I mean... new to me,' Will falters. 'And already, I've seen something... "new": this marvellous weapon you have here. I have never seen anything like it before. What do you call it?'

The man looks proud. 'Nunukul make ever since Dreamtime. Long long time back. Very long time back. We call "boomerang".'

Will half turns to watch the continuing demonstration, pulled by Billy's excited laughter. Then, after a pause, long enough to indicate his appreciation of the technology, he asks: 'But how is it you speak *our* language?'

'Work long time pilot boat.' He points back along the shore towards Amity. 'All gone now. Also Gnoorganpin lighthouse.' And he points again, in the direction of Moreton Island. 'Bit back help save people when boat go down.'

'You mean… a ship went down at… Amity Point…?'

'No mister, Gnoorganpin. Bit back. Lot men die. Now ship go different way.'

Nodding slowly, Will considers this information for a moment. Then, becoming conscious of the people milling around them, presumably fascinated by this 'man from the moon', he decides to move on, to ask about their life, here. But first, thinking it befitting, he introduces himself.

'My name Will,' he says, in self-conscious imitation of the Blackfellow's manner of speaking, and holds out his hand.

The hand is ignored, but the man grins as he says, 'Me Tompani.'

'Tum-pá-ni?' Will repeats, almost childlike, and looks inquiringly at the man to make sure he has pronounced it right. Tompani nods his approval. Then Will asks: 'Do you all live near here?'

Tompani smiles a knowing smile. 'Not like you Whities, always same place. Nunukul live always different place, many different place.'

Will tries to say more clearly what he means: 'Yes, but your homes… your houses… are they in the forest…?'

'No houses. Not need houses. Here now, tomorrow different place.'

'But always somewhere on…' About to say 'Stradbroke', Will stops himself in time. But he has forgotten the word. 'On… this island?' he ends, shamefacedly.

Again Tompani smiles, at the same time shaking his head in denial. 'Not always. Sometime Gnoorganpin. Sometime Minjerribah. Sometime other place.' And he sweeps his arm round, gesturing broadly.

Will realises that what is being described is a nomadic way of life among the many islands in Moreton Bay, and he remembers someone had already told him this about the native peoples, probably Ridley, yes Ridley.

Billy comes skipping towards him, full of amazement at the clever trick he has been shown. 'Are we going anywhere else, Mr Crosby,' he inquires, 'or are we staying here for a bit? I think maybe we should stay here… until my clothes are dry. I can't put them on when they are still wet, can I?'

Ignoring the question for the moment, Will thinks it only proper to introduce the boy to Tompani. 'Billy, this gentleman is Mr Tompani. He is, I think, the headman of these people, so you should make a bow and say, 'I'm pleased to meet you, sir.'

Billy smiles shyly at the Aborigine and does as Will bids, before plunging on with his curiosity. 'Can you do magic tricks like Mr Coonar?'

'Mr Coonar?' Tompani chuckles, bends forward, and shakes the boy's hand. 'Hello Billy.' He glances at Will. 'Billy is Will son?'

'No, but…' Will is at a loss once more, acutely aware that Billy is also waiting for his answer. 'Billy lost his father… and his mother… to the big sickness, and so we… I, that is, look after him.'

Tompani nods but makes no comment. Then turning back to Billy he smiles, a kindly smile.

'Tompani do many thing, know many thing. Oh yes, Billy!'

'Well… what can you do? Show me!' the boy shouts, in his excitement.

Will puts a restraining hand on the child's shoulder. 'Whoa, now! That's not very polite is it?'

Billy blushes and looks down at the ground, grinding the big toe of his left foot into the sand. Then, timidly, he looks up at the Aborigine, 'Sorry Mr Topmani,' he mutters softly, 'I didn't mean to be rude.'

Again Tompani chuckles. 'Then I tell you Billy. I can… tell story. Lots story. Make music. Call fish. I can… catch all animal, fish, and bird. I always know where water. Where witchety. Which plant good which not good… for eating… I know all Dreamtime story. Make boomerang. Make…'

Whether everything in his list impresses Billy equally, Will can't be sure, but on hearing this last-named object the child seizes upon it.

'Oh, Mr Top-mani, will you make one for me?'

'Billy…!' Will scolds.

But Tompani, far from affronted, seems delighted by the child's forthrightness.

'Sure I can, Billy. I make.'

'Ohhh…!' Billy cannot contain his excitement. 'Did you hear that, Mr Crosby?' Then, still jumping about he turns to Tompani. 'When will it be ready?'

'Billy…!'

Will shakes his head, shrugs and smiles in what he hopes is taken as complicity with a fellow sufferer.

Tompani looks at him, then makes a non-committal gesture. 'Need find right wood first.' And he nods, solemnly.

Will touches Billy's arm. 'Perhaps you should go off and play again, Billy. Oh... and see whether your clothes are dry yet.' And he winks at the boy, hoping he will understand the full intent of this last suggestion.

Billy speeds off, his naked body white, gleaming in the golden sunlight.

'Mr Will,' says Tompani, 'Come! I show you other thing you not see yet.' He turns and strides away over the sand.

'Is it far?' Will calls, nodding sideways at the horse, whose reins he is still holding.

Tompani stops and points at a huge outcrop of rock at which the beach apparently ends, for it juts some way out into the sea. 'Not far. We go there.' And his arm swings inland to a steep gully close to the trees: 'Not far. Bring horse.'

'Billy,' Will shouts 'I'll be back shortly!'

But Tompani shakes his head. 'No. Billy come. Him see too.'

'Billy, on second thoughts, come with us!' Will calls again. 'Come on… and don't forget your clothes. They should be dry enough to put on again by now.'

The boy races up, and starts to dress slowly, grumbling that his trousers are still damp. 'I think I'll just carry them, Mr Crosby', he says. And Will realises in that moment that the child has quickly adjusted to his naked state and that 'dampness' is simply another word for reluctance.

LXII

D r Mitchell had lasted only until midday.

Neither Ballow nor Mallon had really known their brave colleague, indeed the latter not at all, but ever mindful of the epidemic, both had determined he should be buried without delay. A grave was hurriedly prepared by Callaghan. And now, Thomas, the two doctors, the tearful matron clustered, disconsolately, around the closed coffin.

Just as the priest was about to begin the burial service, however, Wilfred Farmer came hurrying up. And, pointing back, he alerted them to many others hastening towards them from the encampment.

'Did you know,' Farmer said quietly to the priest, as they waited, 'I sometimes helped Dr Mitchell in the ship's hospital, on the way out. He was a good man. I could not let him pass from us without paying him my respects... All of these people, I imagine, will feel much the same. He was a light for many when all else seemed dark.'

There was a distinct catch in his voice, as he spoke. And Thomas reflected momentarily on how first impressions, determined by particular circumstances, were so often at such variance with the truth.

It was some fifteen minutes before the service got underway, by which time a hundred or more people had gathered about the grave. And, mindful now of his congregation and their undoubted mixture of faiths, Thomas tried to steer a simple course with his words and prayers.

Towards the end, he announced a silence, in which any who wished to do so could pray, each in his own way, for the soul of the much-revered doctor. But almost at once a lone voice struck up, close by him. 'Who would true valour see…,' it began, intoning a hymn the priest had never heard before. The one voice was soon joined by others, and yet others, and by the time the second verse was reached the hymn had swelled and a huge chorus sang out, from the heart.

Thomas stood in silence, overwhelmed, moved almost to tears by the release that this simple gesture of spiritual solidarity afforded. And from where he stood, his eyes moved instinctively in the direction of the first in that ever-lengthening line of cross-marked graves, with tears now welling fast and falling onto his cheeks.

Meanwhile, Stevens stood clinging to the cross-wired fence which separated him from the main encampment, oblivious to all but his obsession with the child Lizzie.

Sick in mind and body though he was, he would not let go of her… or the modest, yet for him, untold riches she had seemed to promise, by her prostitution…

'McIlroy, she's mine!' he whispered hoarsely, close enough to McIlroy's tent and knowing the pair inside could hear. 'Give her up! Give up what you've stolen from me!' No response came, so he took up a new litany. 'Lizzie! Lizzie! Remember my promise to wed thee! My house in Brisbane! The lady I could make thee…? Don't you play me false, now…!'

Yet the silence persisted, punctuated occasionally by the giggles and snorts coming from the girl within.

Suddenly, McIlroy was standing looking down at him on the other side of the fence.

'You gave her up when you let her down, Stevens! Getting yourself caught like a rat in a trap! So fuck off! Unless youse'd like me to come round there and kick the living daylights out on yer!'

Stevens, powerless against the greater strength of his younger adversary and the physical restrictions placed on him by the captain and Dr Ballow, could only stare and convey his hatred with his eyes. He turned away, spat hard, and stumbled off towards his shack behind Mr Jones's workshop.

An hour later, he was back again, pressed hard up against the fence, whining his loss on an altered theme. But this time there was no one there to hear him.

With the horse securely tied to a bush, the three of them began their ascent, with the swiftly moving Tompani in the lead.

When Will reached the top of the steep, rocky slope, the Aborigine and the boy had already moved some distance away, to the right, and were now crossing a downward-sloping plain. Still panting hard, he set off in pursuit, a little anxious, suddenly aware that he could well be placing far too much trust in the native. When he finally reached them, they were standing above a deep gorge, a long, narrowing inlet where the sea boiled and surged fiercely. Pausing to take in the majesty of his surroundings, he became aware of a deep booming sound coming intermittently from somewhere close by. Then suddenly, a huge jet of water hurtled skyward and although it was more than twenty feet away, down the rocky slope, instinctively, Will and Billy leapt back away from it, Will reaching out frantically for the boy... to the great amusement of Tompani, who had not moved from the spot.

'Ooooh! Mr Twopani...!' Billy cried out, in amazement. 'Again! Show me it again!' And he clutched excitely at Will's hand. 'Again... please!'

Tompani raised his hands level with his face, solemnly, then slowly brought them down; then just as they returned to their original position, he jerked them upwards, and the booming spout once again shot high into the air.

Billy leapt forward, clapping his hands in delight. 'Oh you are a clever man, a... magician!' he cried.

But Tompani, turning to him, laid his hand on his shoulder. 'No, Billy, not Tompani magic. Earth magic. Tompani not make.'

'But you did, I saw you!' the child insisted, jumping up and down, his arms steepled above his head in imitation of the water jet.

'No, Tompani not make magic. Tompani make… joke, Billy.'

The boy looked puzzled, though his eyes were still wide with wonder.

'Listen! Watch!' the Aborigine said, gently, though clearly savouring Billy's misunderstanding.

And after a third boom, the seawater again spouted high. 'Always same,' he declared. And so it proved, as they waited. Billy moved in closer, not seeming too disappointed, and nodded sagely. Then, Tompani turned to Will.

'Your people say it blow hole. Like whale. Look!' And he pointed out to sea where, maybe half a mile away their straining eyes eventually encompassed two huge, though indistinct shapes occasionally breaking through the surface waters, riding the waves in parallel, moving away northwards. And then one of them, as if in collusion with the man, spouted a jet of water. And Billy, perhaps appreciating the simultaneity, if no longer the magic he had previously presumed, once more clapped his hands, exhilarated.

'They're like the ones we saw when we were on the ship, Mr Crosby, aren't they! And those ones sometimes jumped high up out of the sea as well!' He beamed at Tompani.

Will began clambering down to the rocks' outer platform, to make his own inspection of the phenomenon, but then he paused to hear Tompani explaining to Billy that for his people it had another, quite different meaning, in addition to being 'Earth magic'.

'Back long long time, old Nunukul woman go mad and shout and cry all time. Shout cry all time. So people make her live this rock, away, but not very far away. One day, go to find her but not find her. Look everywhere but not find. Now my people say big noise and big water her spirit in this place. It called Wail Rock. She in noise she in big water. You understand?'

Will stood watching the sea, and then walked back, to find Billy nodding seriously. 'Yes, 'cos my daddy is…' The boy stopped, clearly puzzled.

'What is it, Billy?'

'Well, my daddy is…' He looked from Will to the Aborigine. 'How do the people know it is the old lady?'

But before Will, recognising once again the typical Billy mind-twister, could start to wonder how he was to give the boy a plausible answer, Tompani straightened, and gave his own measured explanation, mindful of the child's age, perhaps, and of his race's different way of seeing the world.

'My people not live in house, live in land, little boy. Know how land feel, what land do, what land give, because when Great Spirit make land make my people also. Same time. Land and people feel same know same remember same from Dreamtime, only land never die so remember always. One man die so not remember always. Land make way men remember more than one man life. Like blow hole, like Bummiera, like Kalboora, like Myora. These place remember for my people.'

Will looked at Billy, wondering if he had managed to understand anything of this explanation, for there were questions he himself wanted to ask; and so he asked them, hoping also to help the child.

'Tompani, twice now you have mentioned "Dreamtime". Is that just another word for "sleep" – when we dream, I mean? And what is "Nunukul"? And the other… things… you mentioned?'

Tompani shook his head and frowned. 'Bit like sleep but not same. Big sleep out of which Great Spirit make all thing. When Spirit dream… then he… dream my people make my people, make my people land also. Nunukul my people. They… me… Nunukul.'

Will nodded. 'Yes, I see. And the other names? Are they places? Places on… this island?'

'All here, yes,' Tompani answered. 'Bummiera you say… ah, Brown Lake. Kalboora you say… you say Blue Lake. But now we go.' And he pushed past Will and the boy and set off briskly towards the top of the defile by which they had ascended.

He had waited for them at the bottom, however. And, as Will was untying Bluebell, he asked Tompani what he had meant by places remembering for his people.

'These place all tell story, Mr Will. Like Kalboora. Blue Lake. Many life past, some young man my people go Kalboora to bury king, but not do things old custom say do. So spirit angry. Make Kalboora fall and much big water come fast, and all young man die in water. So now lake – but not always lake. Story tell how spirit make lake. It say also remember custom. Story also say Bummiera special. It... it... make clean man spirit.'

Will persisted. 'And have you other stories like this? Do they all say what to do and what not to do?'

'Many, many story. All say big thing to my people.'

Billy was listening intently, barely moving a muscle.

Yet the sun, Will saw, was already low in the sky.

'Tompani, we must go back to our camp now,' he said, reluctantly. 'But – he considered a moment – I should very much like to come back and hear more of your stories, learn about your people. Is that possible?'

Tompani smiled. 'I hope you find. Maybe here. Maybe long sand.' And he pointed back towards the rocky slope by which they had just descended. Then he looked at Billy, thoughtfully, tenderly it seemed.

But before he could speak the child treated him to another of his beaming smiles.

'You won't forget my bloomerlang, Mr Twopenny, will you?'

LXIII

Like a strutting cockerel, along the yellow sands, colouring towards sundown, came Sean McIlroy, almost skipping in delight at the more than three shillings jingling in his pouch. The sun was scarlet as it dipped down towards the mainland, shooting golden bars in great profusion across the darkening sky so that it tinted everything about him. He could not remember ever having had such riches. But more than that, much more, this day had proved that this was only a start, a modest start, and perhaps nothing he wished for or could ever wish for would be beyond him ever again. She'll pay for you, Seany, right handsomely she will. Pity was though, there was no place here where a drink or two could be had and sunk. But there were other consolations. And at this uplifting thought he stopped and turned about, shielding his eyes, looking for Lizzie in the low sun's blinding glare.

To his surprise, she was lagging quite some way behind. And as he turned, she too stopped, clutching at her stomach with both hands.

'Seany. I feel awful bad,' she shouted. And she swayed unsteadily, then sank slowly to her knees, on the sands. 'I've got such a bad pain in my belly. Come and help me, Seany!'

The man sighed audibly at the trouble she put him to, and he sauntered back to where she knelt, clutching herself. 'Come on with ye, Lizzie, stop playing around; it'll soon be dark!' he shouted, aware too of the approaching tide. Then more quietly, drawing closer: 'What's all this about?' And taking hold of her hand he jerked her to her feet.

Lizzie yelped in pain. 'I feel all dizzy like,' she said, whimpering, 'and sick'. And pulling up her dress front, she moved her hand warily, very warily, between her legs. And when she withdrew it, it was covered in blood.

McIlroy blanched in horror and took a step back.

The girl swayed again, like a tree struck by a sudden storm, and would have toppled over had not he stepped featly forward and caught her in his outstretched arms. 'Oh Seany, what is it, what can be the matter with me, with all this blood?' And she lifted her dress front a little higher and held it there so that he too could see. 'Is it a lot?', she asked, fearfully. 'I can feel it on my legs. Is it on my legs?'

The sight of it running down in crimson rivulets was too much for McIlroy. Braggart and bully though he was, he had no stomach for blood. 'Aye, it is, and still coming… and I know not what it… But you can't be going back through the tents in a state like that, Lizzie, and that's for sure. You'd best clean yourself up… with the water in one of them pools there, first.' And he led her to a shallow-looking pool some thirty yards out towards the sea. 'Take off your drawers and rinse 'em then use 'em to clean yourself with; that'll be best. Aye, so it will. But don't be coming through the tents till you've got rid of it all, mind you.' He paused for a moment, uncertain, but then swung away at a fair pace down towards the camp.

'Where are you going, Seany?' she cried after him. 'You can't leave me here like this. I'm scared, Seany! I'm scared! Help me…'

McIlroy froze. But then, shaking himself, he called back: 'Agh, you'll be all right. Don't worry about nothing. And… get a move on now! I'll be fixing us some grub.' And away he strode, almost running, wanting to put as much distance as he could between this girl, who had suddenly become a liability, and himself. Maybe she was going to die; all that blood said she was going to die, didn't it? Six men – no, seven – had taken their pleasure with her that afternoon. Maybe they'd fucked her to death. All that blood…

Sean McIlroy felt at the coins through the leather of the pouch, and realised it had all been too good to be true. 'Good luck doan't stick with such as me,' he muttered gruffly, 'not ever. It'll be more fucking jobbing for the builders or swabbing out byres for some fat shit of a farmer; that'll be my lot, for sure.'

At about the same time, Will rode into the encampment as he had left many hours before – with Billy in the saddle before him; although now the boy was almost asleep, yawning just the occasional question that sometimes never reached its point.

He raised his head a little, perhaps stirred by the glare of the fires and the lanterns the camp presented.

'Are we there yet…? Oh yes, for there is our tent with my bed in it. I'm too tired to eat, Mr Crosby. Can I go straight to my… bed?' And his head flopped back down.

Will had fondly imagined taking supper with Thomas, with Billy telling him all about their day. Instead, dismounting beside the tent, he lifted the child to the ground, steadying him, so that he did not fall. Then, bethinking himself, he hoisted him over his shoulder, and tied the horse's reins to the sapling that stood between their tent and that of the O'Rourke's, noting as he did so that both tents were in darkness. Inside, he removed the boy's clothes and, leaving him still in his shirt, laid him down. 'There now, Billy,' he whispered, 'you have your wish. So I'll bid you a good night, sweet dreams, and God bless!'

All the while, the child barely stirred. But as Will turned to leave, a sleepy little voice murmured:

'Do you think Mr Twopenny really will make a bloomerang for me?'

'I'm sure he will,' Will assured, reminding the boy how friendly and kind Tompani had been, and what a good day they'd had; and telling him he'd bring back some bread, 'just in case'. But whether Billy heard any of this he very much doubted.

Unhitching Bluebell, he walked her down through the tents and handed her over to Ridley, patting her flanks. 'I'll give her a rub down, Mr Ridley, if you…'

'No, that won't be necessary, Will, I'll see to her myself, right away.'

'She is a fine horse, Joe, that she is...'

'Managed to stay in the saddle, did you... this trip?'

Will looked him squarely in the eyes. 'Not only that, Joe, but I think you'll find the rifle's still where it should be... and that despite the time I spent with a group of the Aborigines...' He smiled, gave a curt nod, then turned on his heel and left, not waiting to hear Ridley's response.

Alas, maintaining civilities was almost invariably difficult, with Ridley.

A short walk took Will to the hospital tent, whose beds – a glance told him – were empty of patients for the first time since they had come to this island. The truth and significance of this passing observation did not immediately register with him, however, so full of his encounter with the Aborigines were his thoughts. And his eyes lighted on Thomas, with Ballow and Mallon, seated about a trestle table, an inviting jug between them.

'Ah, so there you are, Will, lured no doubt by the scent of rum from whatever unwholesome bog or poxy fen you slithered out of, but... in all truth, my friend we were beginning to be anxious for you... But you're back safely, thanks be to whatever. So here's a cup to fill with some cheer on what has been – for us at least – a cheerless day.' And he passed Will one of the spare mugs from the centre of the table.

'Are we expecting visitors?' Will asked, 'Are we...? But he pulled himself up short, suddenly realising the obvious meaning behind this gathering, in this place. 'Dr Mitchell...?' he stammered. 'What has...?

'Our good friend and colleague passed away just before midday,' Ballow answered, 'and we buried him not three hours ago. It was inevitable, given the situation we find ourselves in here, on Stradbroke; though in all honesty, Will, I doubt whether even in Sydney they could have saved him.'

'We hope he has gone to a better place,' Mallon added, 'God rest his soul.'

The priest jerked back his head and pointedly looked away.

Will sat down, uneasily, among his companions. Despite Thomas's initial jocularity, there was tension, all hearts clearly heavy at the loss, at their own helplessness, for which the rum was but poor consolation. What a sadness to come back to, he mused, after such a bright day.

The silence gathered slowly about the little group as each man, lost in his own thoughts, gradually withdrew into himself.

It was the arrival of Captain Kemp and the ship's purser that pulled them round, for they had come with the question that must have been preying on all minds inside the camp.

'We have been wondering… though this day of all days may seem inappropriate, but in your professional opinions, gentlemen, is there *any* sign that the pestilence is abating?' And Kemp stood there, arms akimbo, his stance suggesting, it crossed Will's mind, that it was, after all, quite within the doctors' gift to banish it on demand.

Dr Ballow looked at Dr Mallon. 'In spite of our loss today,' Ballow said quietly, 'inevitable, and long expected as it was, I do have the sense that the tide is beginning to turn. Would you agree with that… feeling, Patrick? For 'tis no more than that: a feeling…'

Mallon nodded. 'It is my… feeling, too. Because, Captain, we've had no new cases these past three or four days. And it's the first time, I believe, that this tent has not housed patients since your arrival here. Only one woman remains over in the hut, though – he grimaced – she may yet result in another death: matron is with her now… Which reminds me, maybe I should walk over there and check… But Captain, we can't be too optimistic… Not yet.' And he glanced at Dr Ballow. 'This… malady does not always obey even its own rules…'

Thomas put his hand on the young doctor's shoulder. 'I could go…' he said, half-rising, 'I don't mind… if you would prefer to stay.'

'Thank you, Father Sheehan, but I think not,' said Mallon, draining his cup and rising to his feet. 'The sight of you would put the fear of God into her, and… begging your pardon… it might finish her off!'

Thomas raised an eyebrow, but then chuckled, realising the implications of the doctor's words and, affecting to adjust his priest's garb, he subsided once more into his seat. 'I see what you mean… if she's that bad…'

'I shan't be long away – Mallon turned, at the doorway – I shouldn't think…'

'Thank you, Patrick, for your assessment,' Ballow shouted after him. 'Now Captain… though do please sit, and take the weight off your legs awhile, gentlemen,' he added, sensing their awkwardness, and then proffering the rum… 'there are, still, several cases in the tents, and not *all* of them will pull through, I fear. Yet, we are cautiously, yes, that's the word, cautiously optimistic that we may soon be able to think of leaving… if not quite yet: it is still a little premature. And thus, I should be grateful to you both if you breathed no word of this conversation outside this tent… Nevertheless – Ballow raised his mug, jovially enough – let us drink to the speedy realisation of our cautious estimate of… the situation.'

Will raised his mug along with the rest, though pensively.

After a few brief and rather formal exchanges, the captain and the purser rose, thanking all present for their hospitality, and Dr Ballow also got to his feet.

'I'll step out with you gentlemen, for I must be looking in on some of the patients I mentioned, afore they and their families start settling for the night. Oh, and Thomas… Thank you for your assistance… earlier.' He nodded to Will and made his exit.

LXIV

Left to themselves, Will and Thomas fell into a more relaxed mood. 'So where have I been?' Will was eager to try and convey an impression of what he'd experienced, despite the cloud of Dr Mitchell's passing hanging over them, but how to set it in the right words, to explain the feelings he had been left with?

'Well, I can tell you straight about the places and the things we saw; Billy was enchanted, as you too would be. But the northern shore of the island, Thomas, with its silence and emptiness – though it's not empty, not at all – believe me, it's the nearest I've ever come to any earthly paradise... not that I've ever been anywhere that even hinted at it. The whole area, it's just so... oh what's the word for it? Clean is the nearest I can come to it.'

'Pristine?' Thomas suggested, enjoying Will's enthusiasm.

'Aye, that's it, I think. The emptiness, the silence and the... pristine beauty – if by that word is meant a beauty that is as the Lord created it, that has never been sullied by feet shod in neat's leather, and all that would imply...' Will smiled awkwardly, a touch embarrassed by his own words. 'I don't know if I'm making sense to you, but I felt at times as though I was looking back over however many thousands of years it is since the Creation, and seeing it as it must have been, and, for a little while yet, will remain, I hope. And then...'

'Remind me to tell you something,' Thomas interrupted. 'Later, I mean... about the date of the Creation. But... go on.' He drained his mug, put it down on the table, and pushed it away from him.

Will smiled at the gesture. 'Out of harm's way now, is it? Well,

I wasn't sure what we would find up there, but it was more, in the reality of it, than I could ever have imagined... or hoped for.'

Thomas frowned. 'In what ways?'

'I'll try and explain... to myself as much as to you,' and he nodded, reflectively. 'It was something at Amity I'd noticed the first time I went there, when I was alone; the birds there, and there is such a profusion of them, they don't take fright at a man's approach – unless it happens to be Billy, I hasten to add.'

'I can well imagine!' Thomas chuckled.

'Oh yes. He went hollering and galumphing towards a colony of kingfishers, so that they scattered in all directions, no doubt fearing Doomsday was upon them!' Will grinned at the memory. 'But my point is this: I've never before encountered such a lack of fear, or call it trust, if you like, among wild creatures. It may just be my fancy, of course, but I felt, somehow, that their world is a good deal more different from ours than even this foreign... terrain... and the climate, of course, would allow for...' Uncertain, feeling his way, he looked to Thomas for some reaction.

'Well, now.' Thomas's face spoke his concentration. 'According to common interpretations of the Genesis story of Eden – and, for that matter, its Renaissance revival in the notion of the Golden Age – man and beast had dwelt in perfect amit...' He glanced at Will, suddenly, clearly amused at something. 'What I mean,' he went on, since Will only peered at him, perplexed, 'is that they lived in *harmony*, one with the other...'

Will shrugged. 'So, what are you saying...?'

'I'm saying that unless this knowledge was at the back of your mind somewhere, it would seem to support your contention about it being a place fit to rival the Earthly Paradise.'

'Maybe it was so... though I can't say I've ever heard mention of those things,' Will said, cautiously, still wondering at Thomas's private mirth. 'Anyhow, this difference at Amity, whatever it was, seemed the right sort of... introduction... to what soon followed.' And he quickly outlined his encounter with the Aborigines, the wonder of the boomerang and the experience and story of the 'Whale Rock', as he'd heard Tompani call it. 'But there was something else, Thomas,' he went on, before his friend could comment. 'These people were almost completely naked. And the little girls there… I fancy to Billy's consternation, though I cannot be sure… soon had *his* clothes off too, showing *great* fascination with his… you know. I suppose because of… its whiteness… Feeling it and then making him feel their own… Yet it seemed to be nothing more than curiosity, with no… obsession, or shame about it; they were just being… children. And this, you understand, was all in full view of the adults, who didn't bat an eyelid… Which was not my first reaction, I can tell you, although later, thinking about it…well, maybe… But to *our* way of thinking it wouldn't be… but it just came out of the children's play, and at that point, I was still unsure how we were going to be received… Their playing together, however, actually opened up our first real contact… and in any case, they all went back to just splashing about in the sea together, and the awkwardness, if there was any, soon passed. So – he shrugged – I just felt inclined to… let it be.'

'Then let's leave it at that,' Thomas agreed. 'Was there anything else struck you about them? About their ways?'

'Oh yes. For one thing, they seemed to lack any sort of… pressure; any notion of time, I mean, or urgency, or for that matter, of where they were. They seemed entirely bound up in the moment… in the place, and whatever they happened to be doing there. I remember Ridley passing some scathing comment about their failure to grow crops, use the land. But looking at them, none appeared undernourished, Thomas – just the opposite, in fact. From the youngest to the oldest, they looked robust and solid, healthy. So, maybe they have other sources of food, and no *need* of crops, and such like.'

Thomas nodded. 'Yes, well, crops, of course, would need tending, forcing them to stay in one place… But, with all this vast continent around them, teeming with wildlife… and whatever else… the seas with fish… I suppose they've never needed to… till the soil.'

'Also, I can't say why,' Will went on, trying in vain to remember something else he had noticed, 'but you just felt there was no planning of any sort, no need to be anywhere in particular…'

"Here now, tomorrow different place…" And he smiled, remembering Tompani's words.

'…And from what I sensed, watching them, they were all very relaxed with one another… The women were gathering shellfish, the men coming out of the forest with an assortment of small, dead animals, leaves of various kinds and what looked like roots… Oh, and as I said, one man took the trouble to show me his boomerang and how it worked, then did the same with Billy, to the boy's great delight. And then another man arrived, and he spoke to me in English – I couldn't believe it! He was called Tompani, and he took Billy and me to see this rather spectacular blowhole and then told us a story about it. He said there were other stories too, all of them linked to different places on the island… And on our way back I kept thinking about these things, but especially the stories and… their… precise geographical locations.'

Thomas leaned forward, and his face was alight. 'It sounds wonderful, Will. Truly. And presumably, you were looking for explanations – am I right? And yet, while their stories might be unusual, and very particular in their detail… there's really nothing unusual about primitive people telling stories, is there, creating myths, or whatever you care to call them? Did you not encounter such things in India?'

'I did, yes. And I may have got this hopelessly wrong, Thomas. But I had the impression that this was different, that here they live… in two different worlds at the same time – no, don't laugh, I'm not joking. I mean this physical world, but also some sort of, well, spirit world, for want of a better expression. The blowhole was a blowhole right enough, and its causes were certainly physical. But it was also the voice of the old woman who had once lived and died there: it was a reminder, a constant reminder of this event in their history. And so, because of this, it was a sort of shrine, I suppose.'

'Sanctified, are you saying?' A holy place, maybe?'

'Maybe. Although the point is, the *place* keeps alive the whole event and whatever significance it has for them. The place communicates something more than just itself, to them. I know from what Tompani said it isn't their only such place, and frankly, I'd like to know more about it… about their world.'

Thomas made a wry face. 'So, in the end, what impression did this whole experience leave you with?'

Will thought for a moment. 'I've seldom felt as much in touch with what was around me, as I did there. But I learnt something else, something more to do with me, too… my life, I mean. And the world, how I… belong in it. Am I making any sense?'

Thomas grinned. 'Just about…! But do go on.'

'It's so different there, from the world we know. And as you know, I went looking for new things, *physical* things. But I stumbled upon something I fancy goes a good deal deeper…'

'Serendipity,' Thomas murmured.

'What do you mean?' Will pondered the word, hunched over the table.

'Well, you'll remember I interrupted you, before?'

Will nodded. 'You said it was something to do with… the Creation.'

'Yes, and what I had it in mind to tell you was, that until now, it's been generally assumed that the date of the Creation could not be much more than six or seven thousand years ago – which has always struck me as absurd, though I could not really say why. Anyway, not long before we quit Ireland, I happened to be up in Dublin for a couple of days – Church business thankfully got me back to civilisation every now and again – and I was in this bookshop, where I came across a collection of essays that had been but lately published. Essays about… about the origins of the creatures and plants that live upon the Earth… I don't know just how long I stood there, reading… And you know, from the moment I started what amazed me was its obvious assumption of a much longer time span than a mere six or seven-thousand years.

'Anyhow, several of these essays mentioned a man – his name escapes me now – who had apparently quite recently sailed round the world in a Navy vessel whose voyage had been purely scientific. Just a few years before that, it was. And they'd been away several years and made a huge collection of things to take back to the British Museum. It seems they were even in these parts, Will, though from what I could tell, it had been mainly in South America. But this man had found fossilised creatures – some of them huge, apparently – whose lives stretched way back beyond even double the usual date of the Creation. Just think of that! Do you ever think about these things, Will…?'

'Not up to now I haven't, not really. But what did you find out that was so… important?'

'Well, I gathered – from the repeated references to the man – that when his findings are published – and for all I know, maybe by now they have been – they'll cause such a stir – and not just among fellow scientists, but in the Church as well. So, of course, I couldn't resist buying it. Expensive though it was, I had to read it… Unfortunately, on my coach journey back to Tipperary a garrulous, sanctimonious, and very ignorant banker and his equally odious wife latched themselves onto me, so that I had no opportunity even to start it.'

Will grinned. 'I find it hard to believe *you* could allow yourself to be so thwarted for that long…'

'Ugh! With their endless babble… well, it was not conducive at all, not at all, to the concentration the matter required. God knows why, but I was politeness itself, Will. Oh, they were too full of themselves to notice… all the smoke from my smouldering…'

Will laughed. 'Aye, I've met such people – all talk… and quite deaf! My first month in Carlisle gaol was forcibly spent with just such a one – a self-righteous, quite immodest, self-promoting embezzler… of Church funds! But… I assume you did eventually read it…'

Thomas shook his head. 'Not much of it. Shortly after I got back home from Dublin, we conceived our plan of escape, Joanna and I, and sadly, that precious book was one of many possessions I had to sacrifice.'

The regret was written in his face, mingling, no doubt, with all the others that had accrued to him since then.

'Nevertheless, what I'd understood of it, Will – as I was saying – suggested that, on yet another vital issue, the religious consensus had been as badly wrong as it had been about the configuration of the Universe prior to Copernicus and Galileo. Perhaps it was the likelihood of that apparently imminent revelation about another piece of elaborate fakery – which kept men in ignorance and ignorant men in power – that loosened still further my ties with the Church. And now I think of it, it may even have played a part in our decision to cut and run towards real life.'

Thomas swung round and placed his booted feet on the empty chair beside him. Swivelling sideways, he raised his right arm onto his chair back, then leaned his head against it.

'So...' Will asked, smiling at his friend's contortions, 'what else did the good book have to say on the matter?'

'Hm... Assuming I'm remembering rightly, some of what I read seemed to be suggesting there was no great, divine historical plan, just blind chance. Chance... Imagine that! Determining which species survived and which did not. Do you see what I'm driving at, Will? Chance! What sort of a god is that which doesn't even know its own mind? When this truth is out, well... the world will never be the same again! How can it be?'

'Sounds like the trump of doom... for the Church, I mean...'

Thomas smiled, regretfully. 'Oh, not just for the Church, but for us too – the human race, I mean – Oh, it'll take quite a while, I think, before that point is reached... but sooner or later, it will be. We mistake our infinite complexity for infinite entitlement, Will. We think it sets us apart from, and above, all other living beings, but the plain facts should tell us that is not so. There is no difference between a dead man and a dead dog, Will. It is the same end of the same road for both... Anyhow, if I've understood these new arguments aright... and I'll follow them all up when I can... they give off the scent of freedom, for the individual, at least – though at a price: the great loss of that sense of security the Church's teaching and prescriptions have afforded up to now. Hm. And who can say whether the freedom or the loss will be accounted the greater? Eh, Will...? Will!'

In truth, Will's mind had wandered... as Thomas now realised.

'Damn it all, Will Crosby!' he all but exploded, 'You've not been listening to a word I've been saying!'

'I have, only...'

'... And you... you had all my attention when you were rhapsodising about your crabs and... and eagles, was it? And those... booming rams and whales, or whatever it was you went on about...!'

Will laughed out loud, at what he sensed was only half-feigned exasperation. 'Of course I've been listening... most of the time, anyway! No, it's just that, when you mentioned this longer time span since the Creation of things, I was half-remembering something Tompani said, something implying much the same... Unfortunately, I still can't quite call it to mind.' He stood up and laying his hand on the jug he poured the remaining rum into their mugs.

LXV

'Lizzie! Lizzie!' McIlroy shouted, strangulating the sound so much that it came out as little more than a whispered hiss, trying to make himself heard over the persistent lapping of the waves yet trying also not to be heard by anyone in the vicinity, unlikely though that was, now that darkness had fallen. 'Lizzie! Lizzie! Where are you?' he tried again, then listened intently. But there was only the slap-slap of the water against the rocks and further off the muted roar of the still incoming tide. After several minutes he called more sternly. 'Lizzie! If you're hiding from me, up to your pranks, now, come out at once, show me you're safe.'

McIlroy had walked away, earlier, and now only the sea's pounding, mocking his frustration, came back at him. After several more minutes of futile waiting he gave up and slunk back to his tent, hugging the shadows to avoid being seen, much less identified, by any who happened to be still abroad. And he cursed himself for his too-hasty abandonment of the girl when plainly she most needed him. But the blood had scared him, really scared him, and he hadn't known what to do, with her still bleeding and all.

For God's sake man, there were doctors who could have helped her, so why didn't you think of that, Seany? But you was scared, wasn't you, shit scared that it would all come out what you'd been up to... selling her to any man who'd pay and there were plenty mind you, oh yes there were plenty... and not all of 'em just plain folk like yourself...

In fact, it was all their fault really... if they hadn't wanted her there'd have been nobody to sell her to, and that would've been an end of it...

And so it went round in his mind, round and round.

Will was tying up the tent-flaps when Thomas came hurrying up, full of apologies.

'Ah, Will, with all that happened here yesterday... hardly surprising it got mislaid...'

'What did?'

'...and God knows how it ended up in the food store...! Anyhow, I went and fetched it, and the matron and I... what a fine young woman she is, Will... we've just sorted through it. 'Yes,' he finished, triumphantly. 'There was a mail sack – dumped on the quayside with the other stuff, from the *Aurora*... So, here you are.' And, still panting a little, he thrust an envelope at Will, and ran off, in the direction of the hospital tent.

Grasping the letter, Will recognised his sister's round handwriting, and felt a sharp stab of disappointment. And then guilt. And for several moments he stood there, holding it at arm's length, both fearing and craving it, as both sore and plaster. It would doubtless bring news of his mother's end, for which he supposed he was prepared, but also news of the still living, and for this his whole being pitched and surged.

His heart beating fast, Will stalked off down a rough track, just off the main roadway leading out of the camp, in search of some quiet spot, soon slowing his pace, however, as if to allow the time and the distance the letter had traversed to settle into his mind and humour, newly shaped by the island. He walked for several minutes. And then, with the camp still visible, away to his right, he sat down athwart a giant tree trunk, lying just off the track. There was no one about. And still he waited, his mouth dry, his hands trembling.

Will closed his eyes, and a moment later, felt his fumbling fingers tear the letter open.

Back in his tent now, McIlroy was paralysed by his fear. But... yes, that was it… he'd shared her, so he had. He'd shared her around, not kept her to himself… like a good neighbour. And it was plain as a pikestaff now, that somebody had done the dirty on her, really hurt her, and left her bleeding to death… 'But Lizzie, Lizzie,' he moaned, under his breath, 'I'm sorry for what I… done. I want you Lizzie, I really do. And I won't ever leave you again like that if only you'll come back to me… I need you Lizzie, honest I do… Them bastards, whichever one of 'em done it to you, if I ever find out I'll swing for him… I swear I will…'

His face was wet, be-slubbered with tears and snot, and the sobs kept breaking through, though he tried to stifle them as they struggled out into ugly, unearthly sound.

And now he was doubly afraid, lest someone had heard him. Or might hear him. And then, if it all came to light, if the girl had… had not survived, they would know his noise had been for her, and they would come for him.

And as this rambling incoherence ricocheted about in his head, he became aware of another sound, one for which he was not responsible, a snickering sound from close by. And by and by he was assailed by a mocking, gloating, disembodied voice that might still be coming from inside his head.

'So you done for her, Seany. She ain't no more, Seany, not for you nor for me. And I knows it, Seany, I knows it; so you ain't safe, no ways! What you done to her, anyway, eh? Where you left her? She's sea-swallowed, ain't she, Seany? Though I wager she'll be cast up again, and that's when they'll pull you in, Seany, you see if they don't! It'll be a dark morning for you Seany, so best get your rest while you can…'

'You little shit, Stevens!' McIlroy ground out through gritted teeth. 'I'll get ye, if you split on me, make no mistake!'

But his conviction was much less than his fear. And besides, there was no longer anyone there to hear his threats, for the gloating, cackling voice had already slipped away into the blackness, still muttering, still threatening:

'Nobody gets the better of old Stevens, nobody! That's for sure.

Poor old Seany! He's got it coming too, and no mistake... And that bloody priest better watch out and all.'

It was much as Will had surmised.

> *My dear William (he read),*
>
> *Unable and unwilling to accept that you have perished upon your long voyage I send you our greetings and good hopes. Indeed, we were much heartened by the arrival, yesterday, of your letter posted from Cape Verde Islands, when you appeared to have been in good health and spirits. It took such a long time to reach us that it had set us to fearing the worst – as you will have understood if you have received the letter, which I sent you, some two months ago now. In that letter too you would have learned that our dear mother was near her end, and the Good Lord took her soon after I posted it. Did you get that letter? I do hope so, otherwise this news will come as a terrible shock to you, dear Will. She had suffered much and was exhausted by her struggle.*
>
> *We are all heartbroken at our loss, as I know you will be too, but otherwise in good health, as we hope you are still. Charlie continues in poor spirits though and whenever...*
>
> *Will hurried on, skim-reading.*
>
> *... still on the colliers... has lately taken to drinking long hours at the Crown and Anchor... often the worse... I try to be patient with him, for it is not like him...*
>
> *Sadly, our Joseph did not manage after all to see mother before the Good Lord called her, but he and Arabella got up for the funeral... pleased to see them and have their news. It seems he is to be promoted to a higher grade at the year end, and then... better accommodation in a more comfortable part of London than Greenwich. He really is doing well.*
>
> *You will be relieved, I am sure, that they had no news of Nancy who seems to have disappeared into thin air. Sarah, John's wife, is now a great deal better and little John... brave start in*

life despite the setbacks at his birth… All of them send you their
love and best wishes.

A week or so after the funeral I received a short note from
Alice…

Will lowers the letter, his heart suddenly pounding. And when he
takes it up again, he consciously slows his pace, trying to read more
calmly, more attentively… if his careering emotions will permit it…

expressing her commiserations on hearing of our sad loss, which
she had read of by chance in the Whitehaven newspaper. It was
sent from Redhills, where she is back at present having left her
place in Kirkby Stephen. Her employer there had brought her
some displeasure, it seems, and she quit the place from one
day to the next. She has been looking for a similar position
elsewhere and tells me she is to journey to Maryport next week
to speak with a well-to-do lady in Netherton, who is seeking
a companion/housekeeper, so I expect we shall find out, all in
good time, whether or not she was offered the position.

Lilian, it seems, has been much out of sorts. As I understand
it, in their haste to get away from Kirkby Stephen, they left Agnes
behind, that doll she was always much attached to, and she has
never stopped grieving for her. It appears that Alice wrote to her
former employer begging him to send it on to them, but she had
received no reply at the time of her writing to me. Charlie and I
have seized the chance to try and heal matters between her and
us by sending the child a bonny little doll, with blue eyes and
long golden hair and the sweetest of smiles. We chanced upon it
in our local market.

The summer has begun well, it being generally warm and
sunny, and that at least affords us some little cheer. We remember
you often, Will, and always with great affection.

Well, I think there is little other news from home, except
to tell you that your old school friend, Teddy Oliphant, lost his
wife, Bella, to the consumption about a month ago. She had

*been ailing for a couple of years or so and had wasted away to
skin and bone by all accounts. They live in Distington. She has
left him with five young bairns to rear. It will be hard for him,
but his mother has moved in with him and is helping as best she
can, though she is not in the best of health herself, being crippled
with the rheumatism.*

So God Bless you, William, and write when you can.
Your ever-loving sister,
Mary.

Despite an enforced cheerfulness, his sister's letter reminds Will, yet
again, of what a short and brutal affair life is for the great majority
of those pitched into it. Dear Bella. She had been a beauty when at
school – or so Will had thought, for he himself at the age of twelve
or thirteen had tried to win her favours, a folly that had caused a rift
between him and Teddy… though not for long, for Bella, even then,
had her heart firmly set on his friend. Teddy had written to him,
at the time of his trial and imprisonment, expressing his concern
and assuring him of his continuing friendship, even though they'd
not seen each other in years. And Will regretted, now, never having
acknowledged the kindness of that sentiment. Alas! It was too late to
do so, even more years later, from this other side of the world.

And Alice. It was obvious she was still seeking some kind of
redress from the cruel hand fate had played her. He hoped the
position in Netherton – if secured – would afford her both peace
and security, and a comfortable place for them both to be in, until he
himself… Yes, that would be best. And he, by stiffening resolve and
sharpening initiative must in the meantime seek to emulate his older
brother – and 'do well' in this new life, with whatever opportunities it
placed before him, so he could go back and lay the world at her feet.

One day, maybe.

Caught as he was, between a fleeting hope and helpless despair, it was
some little time before Will could bring himself to fold up the letter
and return to the camp.

McIlroy went early to the shore next morning, while the mists still curled about beneath the casuarinas, among the rocks, but he saw nothing. Later, when the mist had lifted, he went again, frantic with worry, but still there was no trace of the girl. The sea was tranquil, its withdrawal hushed, but he dared not linger there. And so once again he retreated to his tent and tried to sleep. But sleep would not come, and his heaviness fed the depression into which he had fallen headlong.

If only he could set back the clock, he would know what to do, think more clearly, not panic.

And he tossed and turned, and he dreaded the girl being found dead... for as yet no one knew she was missing... and he dreaded being the one who found her...

Suddenly, he sat bolt upright, his eyes gleaming. But if he found her and could hide her, then no one could pin anything on Seany. No one would ever know. Apart from Stevens, blab-mouth Stevens...

McIlroy snorted crossly. So maybe Stevens should meet with an accident too, afore he made his mischief. Aye, that was it. Snuff out Stevens.

LXVI

Mr Jones was sitting on a pile of planking outside his workshop, smoking a clay pipe, a luxury time had seldom afforded him, since coming to this island. Now – it had become noticeable – things were starting to ease off. And not before time, for he had manufactured nigh on thirty coffins since landfall. Always trying to keep ahead of the daily demand. Damn it! If there was any justice in this world at all, he'd more than earned his pipe.

A natural talker, generally at ease with his fellow men, he had accepted the solitude the dawn-to-dusk anchorage at his bench had imposed, a condition aggravated by the need to stay well clear of the ship's passengers penned behind the fence. Class – and his Welshness, maybe – had also served to keep him more or less aloof from the ship's officers and crewmen, this side of the pale. And maybe their superstitious natures had contributed something too, avoiding the man who made the wooden suits in which they passed through the feared gate into the next world – whichever gate that happened to be.

Mr Jones looked up to see Father Thomas coming towards him, and he cursed his luck. The priest's black garb, which set him thinking of crows, could mean only one thing, and he stood to, reckoning he could draw on his pipe possibly three times more before courtesy and the required solemnity demanded it be extinguished. While still at a distance, however, the priest waved his hand from side to side, as if prohibiting something or other, and so he waited patiently and sucked on his pipe still with a dawning hope that it might yet be able to run its full course.

'Ah, Mr Jones, I have no wish to interrupt your respite, for it is nothing more than a whim that brings me down here, to thank you for your steadfastness, your sense of responsibility in these bitter times. I've never yet had to delay an interment for want of a casket, and that has eased my task, as well as the burden on the poor relatives. The signs are, though, we're heading into calmer waters and I just wanted to say it before a budding optimism of new lives ahead makes us forget any such debt of gratitude from our recent past.'

Davy Jones pondered these words until they settled into sense, and then his face beamed his pleasure, with not a small admixture of pride that his dedication had not gone unnoticed. 'A man can do no more than his best, Father, particularly when we're all up against it.'

'And what'll you be doing, Mr Jones, if our release is indeed imminent?'

The carpenter shook his head. 'I hardly know yet, sir, for the world was all topsy-turvy for me long afore it battened the hatches o'er my head on this ill-starred voyage...' And as Thomas's head tilted, enquiringly, Mr Jones smiled: his ability to ensnare a man's curiosity had in no way been impaired by a lack of practice, then!

''Tis a vexing life, that's for sure,' he began. 'And maybe now'll be the time to quit and get me back to Pandy... Twenty years ago now, when it all started; and with no warning whatsoever...' And he shook his head, wistfully, and attended to his pipe.

'Ah now...' Thomas protested, settling himself down on Mr Jones's planks, 'you're surely not going to abandon me, and let all that... that promise go up in smoke, are you?'

Mr Jones's eyes laughed, contentedly. 'Well, a vexing life, like I said... and story. There I was, see, down in Barry to pick up a load of timber at the docks... I'd been once afore, with my father, see, and he reckoned I was now old enough, and sensible enough, to manage the thing on my own. And I'm sure I must've shared that impression. But events proved us both wrong, as it turned out...'

'Timber, you say, at the docks...?'

With the warmth of the sun on his back, and gently inhaling the scent of Jones's passing clouds, Thomas's mind was only minimally engaged, despite his earnest plea a moment before.

'Yes. I put up at the same inn we went the first time, and where my father had stayed whenever he made the trip down there. If I'd kept to my room that night, Father, bespoken a supper and got me to bed early, my life would've followed a very different course… it would've stayed on course, rather! But what was I? Seventeen? No more than that, I suppose…'

'Seventeen…' Thomas leaned back, a brief sadness in his eyes, as he recalled all he'd been subjected to, at that age: all the harshness, the impositions…

'…A lad away from home alone for the first time: roaming the port area, first into one tavern then into another, eyeing up the women… though not daring any more than that, mind you…' Mr Jones winked, then sucked on his stuttering pipe, finally managing to bring it back from the dead.

'Sorry, Father… Well, anyhow…there I was, suddenly talking with this sailor, see, a man a good few years older… An' he says: "I saw you giving Kate there the glad eye, lad, but take it from me, Kate'd eat ye alive and no mistake, and very likely leave ye with a present you'd find very hard to explain when you got back up the valley. So take a friendly warning, and steer clear of all the Kates in these parts!"'

'Indeed!' At that age, Thomas mused, his own experience of the world had been considerably less than that…

'That sailor's manner and his words completely took the wind out of my sails. "Oh, well," I says, "I was just looking. No harm in looking. And you must admit, she's a beauty…" But the man laughed in my face. "I must admit nothing of the sort," says he. "For a start she's not a *she* she's a *he*… though a novice like yourself would make that discovery only when it was too late. So if I was you, sonny," he says, "I'd get back to shallower waters as you're plainly out of your depth here." Well, my first instinct… What young man could hear that advice, Father, much less heed it? It was like a slap in the face, and I itched to throw myself at him, and beat an apology out of him.

But fortunately – or maybe not, the way it turned out – I put that idea out of my head almost the moment it entered.

"'You'd be surprised at the waters *I've* swum in," I says... or something of that, full of bravado, but the man he just smiled, you know, humouring me, like. "If you say so, sonny," he says. Then after a moment or two he asks: "So what can I get you? Rum? Brandy?" Well, I'd been drinking nothing stronger than pale ale, but I was desperate to impress him. "Make it a rum then... the bigger the better", I says, and the sailor, getting to his feet, says, "Whatever's your pleasure," and away he goes, over to the bar.'

Thomas was enjoying Jones's gentle self-deprecation. His pipe was spent but he hardly noticed, much less cared now. Mr Jones was enjoying himself!

And the priest arranged himself more comfortably, on the planking, to hear the rest of his tale.

Shortly after coming back to his seat in the tavern the sailor had hailed a couple of his shipmates, who'd just then come in, and waved them over. They had all drunk steadily the whole evening, with young Davy foolishly striving to keep pace, and as a consequence he had become more and more drunk. Conversation had become a blur, a distant buzz; faces had come and gone as he struggled to hold onto his senses...

The carpenter clicked his tongue and tossed his head back. 'Inevitably there came a moment when I feared I would not be able to find my way back to the inn – he smiled, bitterly – and so I confessed as much. The three sailors looked at me and laughed.

"'Have no fears on that score, sonny Jim," says one of them. "We shall see you to your bed safely, all right."

"'But you don't know where it is," I persisted, as only a drunk would! But the first man cut me short, and said something like: "Of course we know where it is, for it is the self-same lodging as our own..." And in my befuddled state I could not work out how that could be... "So calm yourself... and drink up."'

Mr Jones shook his head, ruefully. 'Well, Father...' He raised his eyes, comically, towards the heavens, and threw his arms wide, his palms upturned. 'When I woke late the following morning, I had my answer right enough. With a splitting head and a gagging thirst, I put the gentle rocking sensation I felt down to my... degenerate state. But the rocking, I gradually realised, was – he smiled, in remembered disbelief – the movement of the ship I was on...'

Thomas whistled. And the smile on his face vanished. 'Oh, the vileness of it! You poor man! You had... you'd been pressed into service, is that not so?'

Jones smiled fleetingly, still shaking his head at the memory of it. 'Aye, that was it, right enough. But there was nothing I could do.' He paused and knocked out the ash from his pipe, against the planking.

Three days later – three endless, empty days kept in the same small, locked cabin – the ship had finally sailed. And only when they were well enough away from harbour had he finally been let out.

'That I could have been duped so... the shame of it! But I was powerless. My destiny, for the moment – and for a young man there is, of course, only the moment – was sealed, was in the hands of others, and I could only accept and try to survive it on their terms.'

'And what about your poor family...?'

'I'll come to that, Father... But those first days, weeks, I'll never forget them. I soon learnt to buckle to when orders were given, for discipline was harsh in the navy and they'd flog you as soon as look at you. Oh yes, I discovered that early on...

On the second day out, encountering the man who'd betrayed him, he had at once hurled himself upon him – only to be flung off, as though he were a child. Two crewmen had run up, and the man had had him bound to the mast and given ten lashes of the cat for his folly.

'The brute was one of the ship's lieutenants...! "You arrogant young whelp," he whispered in my ear when I was being untied. "I did try to warn you, but you insisted you knew better! Well, now you're off to see the world. And maybe you will learn a thing or two along the way."'

Thomas closed his eyes briefly, in fellow feeling. 'Oh, but what a nightmare… So how long did Her Majesty's Navy manage to hold on to its new recruit?'

'Long enough for him to "learn a thing or two." Two whole years…'

And, fingering his pipe, Mr Jones told the priest how he had jumped ship at Portsmouth and had made for London as soon as he dared. 'I *couldn't* go home, or let my family know where I was, for that was the first place they would have looked for me.'

'What did you do in London?'

'For a couple of years I worked as an apprentice cabinet maker. But I was never happy there. The salt had got into my blood, see; though – a young man – I was loath to admit it. So, one day, I went to my employer and asked him for a written reference saying I'd decided to move on.

'Oh, he tried to persuade me against it, but the more he tried the more I realised I'd made the right decision.' And once the reference was forthcoming, he'd decided to try and find a berth on some merchantman, as ship's carpenter.

'I travelled right across to Bristol, not daring to show my face around the London port area, see, lest I was recognised.'

'And your family? Did you ever…write?'

'Yes – the day I sailed from Bristol, I wrote a letter to my father, telling him what had befallen me and trying to explain my silence for those past… almost four years, it would be.' He paused, shaking his head. 'I did not know it then, but my poor father had already been dead and buried for three years, having missed his footing, apparently, when repairing the chapel roof… a task that would undoubtedly have been mine, had I…'

'God and his mysterious ways, again…' Thomas muttered to himself through clenched teeth. 'So how did this new venture turn out?'

'It paid well, at times. But I never stayed with a ship more than two voyages, as I figured they might still be looking for me, and the crew lists of merchantmen would be an obvious place to start… I was over *this* side of the world, for several years, in fact, working on traders in the South Sea Islands, or pearl fishing. I even did a stint or two on whalers – and that was hard. And yet, Father, while I wouldn't dream of doing it ever again, I was glad, afterwards, that I had.'

'Were the seas dangerous?'

'Sometimes, yes... mountainous. But it wasn't just that. "Exciting" would be too mean a word, but... watching a sixty-foot whale struggling against the puny harpooners, whose skill, nevertheless, more often than not won the day... the thrashing, mighty tail of the giant beast, the sea crimson, the winds and the waves and the huge floating islands of ice... Savage, it was... bloody savage. But also majestic and...' His voice tailed off, lost in the harsh wonder of it.

Thomas was watching the man closely, and for a moment their eyes met.

Jones smiled, wistfully. 'It was there, I suppose... begging your Reverence's pardon... that I knew for certain there was no God, no Hereafter, only the struggle to survive till death severs us, and that's the eternal end of it. I live for each day and would never be surprised to find it was my last. Not that this means...'

'Ah, but you are not alone in your thinking.' Taken aback by the turn the carpenter's narrative had taken, Thomas nevertheless spoke quickly, to reassure him. 'For no "loving God" could countenance the things I saw during the Great Hunger in Ireland... and if that leaves any other sort of sadistic being toying with our lives, then I despise it utterly.'

Jones sagged, utterly flabbergasted. 'But... I don't understand. You, a priest...? But if you see things this way, then, how... that is, why...?'

'Why do I continue?'

Jones nodded.

Thomas got to his feet. 'If you had spent the final minutes of some poor soul's lifetime with as many poor souls as I have...' He took a couple of steps, and turned to face his companion, his arms clasped round his body. 'It's just that, if you had you'd understand, maybe even approve...'

'Yes...?' Jones looked even more puzzled.

'The terror of the believer, great though that can be, Mr Jones, is as nothing beside the terror of the man who has ceased to believe, or who has never believed at all. And when I see someone facing that fear, in his moments of realisation that oblivion is but a breath away, then I have no doubt whatsoever what my duty is, as a fellow human being. I have to try and get him to stand back from this precipice that might otherwise nullify not only his future but the whole of a lifetime lived on the spur of expectation, whether religious or no. Do you see?' He looked hard into Jones's face, seeking signs of comprehension – and was partially rewarded.

'If, in those moments, I can… weave some magic… something, in place of that awful nothing in that person's mind, so that he breathes his last at very least doubting his own doubts, then, rightly or wrongly, I think I have… saved a life.' Again he scrutinised the other's face, and smiled, inwardly. 'Truth is the bright flaming banner throughout our lives, Mr Jones. Of that I have no doubt, and I seek always to live within its glow. But – and of this I am also entirely convinced – it is of no use at all to the man who is about to breathe his last. So there you have it.' And he spread his arms wide, as though appealing to common sense beyond all other possible considerations.

Jones scratched his head: 'Well, that beats everything I ever heard, I'll tell you! I just would never have thought… I mean, I see your point, well enough, Father, that I do, but…'

'And I'll tell you this. Although you and I are, in our different ways, convinced of the non-existence of God, I have latterly come to understand that that fact is of little real importance.' He paused, and when he spoke again his tone was graver. 'What I mean by that is that God *does* exist even in his non-existence. For whilst ever there are churches and believers and laws and customs predicated on such belief, then it is as if God really did exist. And all our lives are touched, indeed, driven to a greater or lesser extent, by this being in non-being. Do you see this too?'

The carpenter stood up, stiffly, rubbing his back. 'I thought I had, until… Are you saying…?'

'…I'm saying that God's non-existence is immaterial in this life because there are so many people and institutions that do believe in his existence and act on their belief. I'm saying that no one, in his daily life, can escape the consequences – which are exactly the same as if God really did exist!'

And that being the case, maybe he would not slough his skin after all, not entirely, anyhow, when… if… this God in his Nothingness released them. For in truth there were too many crossings over in people's lives that would ever need his "magic."

'God exists, Mr Jones! Even if he has no Existence.' And, as if to make his point clearer, Thomas traced a small, then a capital 'E' against the sky.

Mr Jones scratched his head again.

There the priest stopped, shaking his head at where his thoughts had led him. What on earth was he thinking, though…? Most certainly not! He could not commit himself to all that mumbo-jumbo, all over again…

And, in amused disbelief, he raised his hand by way of valediction and turned to walk back towards the fence.

And Davy Jones, in a not dissimilar frame of mind, watched the retreating figure, then sat down, tapped the ash from his pipe and began packing the still tepid bowl with fresh tobacco.

LXVII

He heard them coming, at last, and breathed a heavy sigh. Pulling himself up into a sitting position, he waited with his head in his hands, aware only then that he had not shaved in days... Had he used a razor, perhaps, the temptation would have been too great... But at least he would not have had to face what was coming to him now.

'Mr McIlroy, would you mind stepping outside for we have some important questions to put to you?'

It was a voice full of the kind of authority he had always loathed, and he had a mind to shout and tell them all to bugger off. But it would prove a futile gesture, given the reason for their visit. So he clambered to his feet and pushed his way out into the blinding morning sunlight. In any case, his part was well rehearsed. He was ready for them.

'Ah, gentlemen, what brings you here? "Important questions", you say? On what matter?' He attempted a smile that didn't quite come off, for in that moment he saw that two of his visitors were armed, the third was Captain Kemp, and the fourth – his face darkened – was that man everybody called Sergeant Crosby.

'Mr McIlroy,' the captain said, haughtily, 'a moment's reflection should answer each of those questions for you – as you well know.'

McIlroy did his best to look perplexed, but he was no actor, and one of the two armed men sniggered in contempt.

'Sergeant Crosby, your man,' the captain snapped.

'Where is the child, Lizzie, Mr McIlroy?' And Crosby took a step forward so that only a yard or so separated them.

McIlroy gulped, unnerved by the directness. This was all wrong; it wasn't how they should have begun. That bloody Sergeant Crosby…

'Lizzie?' he stammered, as though hearing the name only now for the first time. 'Lizzie?' he repeated, stalling for time to try and get his mind working along different lines from those he had rehearsed. 'Why, I cannot rightly say in this moment… Why do you ask?' And he tried to shift the script back to where it should be.

But Crosby, it seemed, had not learned his lines at all, for the script was once again ignored. '"In this moment", you say? So tell us, when was she last with you?'

It was on the tip of his tongue to say it had been but an hour ago, but he stopped himself. For if they had already found her, with that bold statement he would be done for. So he hedged. 'Last with me? Oh, I'm not sure.' And he affected a deep concentration. 'Yes – I'm pretty sure, it was… three days ago. Yes. That's right.'

Crosby looked at the captain. 'But she was *living* with you, McIlroy, in this tent. Or so you told Father Sheehan.'

Damn that meddlesome priest! He'd be the death of him yet! 'What…? Well yes, she was. But…' His interrogators seemed to be hanging on his next words, the ones that might even go and hang him. Damn them all!

'But?' prompted the sergeant.

McIlroy's mind reeled this way and that in the small and still-diminishing space his predicament and feeble imagination allowed him. He was no Stevens. Yet he was fighting to survive, and suddenly he had it: 'But I sent her back,' he said. Then all in a rush: 'That day, after the… unpleasantness here, with that priest, she confessed to me that what the priest had said was true. She wasn't eighteen, nor nothing like it; she were a child still. So I told her she were a wicked, wilful child what had already got me into a whole lot of trouble and could well have had me in much worse… And I sent her back.'

Crosby looked him straight in the eye. 'Back? Back where?'

McIlroy flinched at the sergeant's gaze. 'Why, where she come from, with those old people she was with all along. I were horrified at the sin I almost fell into over that child and I thanked God right heartily that he had saved me from it at the last minute. It were a close-run thing…'

Had that convinced them? Was their grip slipping? It had to be.

But still Crosby's eyes remained on him. 'Mr and Mrs Parry, you mean?'

Sweating profusely, McIlroy nodded.

'Well, McIlroy, they have not seen her, not since she came away here with you. So how do you explain that?'

The sergeant's voice was controlled, but the effort it was costing him did not escape the Ulsterman, and he shrugged, casually. ''Tis mighty strange! That were the last time I seen head or tail of her, honest to God.' And he crossed himself, lingeringly, piously, he hoped.

But they were chuckling, now, all laughing at him. McIlroy gave them what he hoped was a pained look, but the chuckles seemed only to increase.

'On the other hand,' Crosby began again, coolly, 'we have it on more than one person's authority that you were with her for most of the day, *three* days ago, and you were seen returning to this tent alone, late in the afternoon, just as dusk was falling.'

'Then they are liars, whoever they are, just trying to make trouble for me,' he blurted, his mouth, as usual, leaving his head far behind. 'I have my enemies here, you know. That Stevens for one – maybe you should be asking *him* where she is, not me!'

'Oh, we know where she is, McIlroy,' Crosby announced, wrong-footing him completely. 'But what we want to know from you is how she came to be there. We are sure you can tell us.'

'Well, if you know already, why are youse asking me?' he blustered, affecting outrage.

'Because, McIlroy, we think… indeed, strongly suspect,' Kemp snarled, impatiently, 'that you were the last person to see her alive and may have been responsible for her… fate! Well, how do you answer us now?'

McIlroy considered this last pronouncement. So, she was dead, then? Poor Lizzie. His mind thrashed about, trying to decide whether to stick to his original story about 'sending her back' or whether to tell them the truth and hope they would believe him when he said he had left her alone on the strand…

'Well, McIlroy? We are waiting.' Crosby's voice was level, still, but his tone had turned icy.

'All right,' he said, suddenly deciding. It would mean having to relive all the anguish of the past three days, but what else could he do? The truth was the less risky of the two courses open to him. 'All right, I'll tell you exactly what happened.' Already though, he was casting about for ways in which, in the telling, his own responsibility might dwindle to nought.

'Ah, some sense at last…' Sergeant Crosby stepped back. 'Before you do that, McIlroy, we insist you look on the child – what is left of her – and reflect on how she came to be found in the state she was.' And Crosby seized him roughly by the arm, as if he were a prisoner.

The little group then escorted him, as he knew they must, to the shore at the northern end of the camp, to the point where he had last seen her. Not a word was spoken. They marched him onto the sand towards a large rock, where one of the ship's officers was already standing. And as they rounded it the man pulled away a piece of sheeting.

McIlroy gasped, his eyes almost starting out of his head.

She was lying on her back. Her mouth was open, but her lower lip had been partly torn away. And the more he stared at her naked body the more he became aware of other rips and tears in her flesh. How small she is, he thought, fingering his chin, nervously, her breasts that had so excited him, how small. He saw too that she was without her drawers; she had followed his instructions, then! And momentarily, unaccountably, he felt some satisfaction in that.

Yet he realised, too, that this fact would be interpreted in such a way as to incriminate him further.

Sean McIlroy was suddenly moved by the sheer tragedy of it, the loss, for him, for her, and his eyes filled with tears.

'Poor Lizzie!' he murmured. 'Oh my poor Lizzie!' he wailed, 'I never knew...'

Will slackened his hold, and McIlroy fell to his knees, reaching out to touch the damaged body, brought home by the tide.

'Why is it the child is all torn like this?' His face twisted up at them, contorted with genuine grief.

'Most likely they are teeth marks... made by the fish,' said the captain. 'Not sharks; smaller fish than that, the crabs and... such like,' he ended, lamely.

McIlroy could hold back no longer. He fell forward, across the child's inert, mangled body and sobbed, his guilt sharpened a thousand-fold by the hideous manner in which she had been given up by the sea.

LXVIII

'So what did you conclude from McIlroy's version of events, Will?' Thomas asked, later that same day.

'I have to say I'm inclined to believe it for the most part. I don't think he has the wit to devise such a story. Do you? Whenever he does try his hand at... embroidery... or evasion, it comes over so heavy there's no doubt about what he's up to.' Will accepted the glass Thomas had pushed towards him.

'Thoughtful of the captain – Thomas murmured, setting his own cognac down – though quite what put it in his mind I have no idea!'

'His way of saying "thank you", I should think.' Will smiled. 'You know, Thomas, earlier, when they came to tell me about the body they'd found, I immediately got it into my head it would be that girl who disappeared a few weeks back – you remember, whom we never found in spite of our extensive searches: Elizabeth Wade. And even then, when I was standing there, looking down at the body on the sands, it took me a while to realise just who it was... Not her, but poor Lizzie.' He shook his head, sadly.

'Well, of course, none of us had any inkling that Lizzie was missing, that she wasn't still with McIlroy.'

'No... But, going back to McIlroy,' Will continued, 'his grief and remorse seemed real, in the end. That doesn't exonerate him, of course, in his dealings with the child, while she was in his... "care" hardly seems the right word, does it? But knowing she was still only a child, as I guess he must have, then he was responsible for her.'

'Yes, you're right, of course, though I suspect the man's ignorance, including about women, also contributed to the tragedy. The girl's too, I shouldn't wonder, for in her cocksure way she was always floundering. How we fail people, Will...!' Thomas tipped the bottle and allowed himself another generous measure of cognac, then looked enquiringly in his friend's direction.

Will shook his head. 'Lizzie, well maybe... though not Billy; we're doing better there, don't you think? And you certainly tried your best with Lizzie – a case of the horse and the water, I would say. The knowledge is there, available, and sometimes, even the man who's willing to impart it; but ignorance and arrogance are often close companions and will not be gainsaid.'

'Holy Mother Church's response to that particular teaser used to be quite uncompromising,' Thomas retorted, though he was unable to restrain a sceptical smile. 'Conform or roast! Mind you, the knowledge she sought to diffuse... and protect with drawn sword, as well as fire and brimstone... was itself not a little compromised!' His ironic smile transformed itself suddenly into a burst of scornful laughter, which carried Will with it. 'Still, the "methodology" evidently had some merit – and there was now no mistaking his disgust – since The Church persisted in it for so long...' He shrugged then picked up his glass and drained it once again. 'So what is the answer, Will?'

'I doubt it's coercion of any kind,' Will began, lightly. 'Yet having said that, I also doubt you can often do little without it in some shape or form, whatever system you devise for instructing the ignorant. Maybe you're right about McIlroy and Lizzie... If only they'd had that very little, necessary knowledge in that one situation...'

'...whose consequences were so terrible...'

'Yes... terrible.'

The two men fell into a long, contemplative silence.

Thomas was the first to break it. 'Will, I have to say... something. I must, to get it off my chest.'

Will set his glass down, somewhat taken aback by his friend's sudden change in tone, the slight slur in his speech. 'What is it?'

'I did try and help the child, Will, to be sure I did… to see the folly of her conduct. But only to a point. You see, in the end, I… stopped trying. You remember the day I brought her to the tent?'

Will nodded.

'Well, after a while, she simply walked out on me, and I had no answer to that. I had no right even to try and restrain her, so… I did nothing.'

'Well, then. But what…?'

'No… let me finish, because if I don't say it now, I maybe never will, and I feel I must. You see, even after that rebuff I would likely have returned to the task, only… only…'

'Come on,' Will coaxed, 'you've got this far, so out with it… whatever it is.' He sat back in his chair, acutely aware of the irony of the situation, bracing for what seemed to be… a priest's confession.

Thomas cleared his throat. 'The truth of the matter is, Will, that I had a dream; a very disturbing dream, involving Lizzie and… myself. And – he held up his hand – before you tell me, like Pertelote, down from the rafters, to take no heed of dreams, I have to say its effect on me was not accountable to any sort of superstition but rather to what it told me, and that very starkly, about… myself.' He looked hard at Will, and then rushed into his confession.

'Will, I was on the point of… taking her myself.'

'But…' Recovering quickly from the shock of it, Will sought to reassure. 'Thomas, it was a dream, just a dream. In waking life you would never even have considered…'

'True enough.' Thomas nodded impatiently. 'But there *is* a conflict here, Will, between my rational, waking self and whatever it is of us that feeds our dreams; for they can only come from inside us.'

'Well, evidently.' Will conceded, reluctantly. 'Nevertheless…'

'…And therefore they must say something about us… They are in no way detached from us. Of this I am convinced.'

Will nodded slowly. So that was why Thomas had vowed to pursue the matter no further, was it, he was afraid – of himself?

'I failed the child, Will, because I was forced to question my own motives, and thus I left her where she plainly wanted to be, but should never have been – with Sean McIlroy. And what's more, in my flight, it took little to persuade me that that was all for the best. *Even though I knew full well it was not!* And now the child is dead, Will, and there is nothing can persuade me that my cowardice, born of that revelation about myself, was not a primary, contributory factor in that so unnecessary tragedy. Nothing. Nothing at all!'

The priest leaned forward, his face in his hands, his elbows propping him up on the table, in silence.

Will rose to his feet, at last understanding the full implications of this confession. But what could he say to alleviate his friend's misplaced, as he saw it, sense of guilt?

At length, Thomas raised his head. 'Tell me, Will, who is the more guilty, McIlroy or I, in the matter of the child's needless death?'

But suddenly, Will was feeling uneasy himself, recalling his own not dissimilar, unwelcome self-discovery... on the occasion when Stevens had offered Lizzie to him.

Thomas, at least, had found the courage to admit it openly.

LXIX

Musing, later, alone in their tent, Will realised it was essentially all about finding ways of stemming the flood. Mr Machiavelli's dykes and fortifications constructed not against Fortune, this time, but against the contagion we all seemingly harbour within. Yet how can a man fortify against himself, protect self from self? In those particular circumstances, Thomas had undoubtedly taken the right course of action, stepping back when he came to suspect his own motivation.

But then, by abandoning the girl to her own devices... hadn't he left the way open to Machiavelli's 'river in spate'? He had, and it had overwhelmed her.

Restless, Will quit the tent and wandered over in the direction of the sea. But his train of thought went with him.

In all fairness, though, Thomas could not have known that things would go the precise way they had for Lizzie. That would have been impossible, more than any human being could foresee. So... *Could* he have done things differently?

And then again, to set against that, there was Billy's case. But what a contrast: Billy was much younger than Lizzie had been and had offered no resistance. He had been garnered, as chance would have it, in the very moment of his greatest need, at his most vulnerable, and unlike Lizzie, neither time nor any previous experience had inured him against the cruelties of the world upon which she, evidently, had been weaned. Will recalled Thomas telling him about 'Fat pig Beales', and a wan smile flickered momentarily, but then he smiled warmly, remembering something Billy had said, just the day before.

'I think I'll just go on knowing new things forever and ever, Mr Crosby. That's what I think.'

Billy had been fortunate, in that the community – even if at present represented, in practical terms, primarily by Thomas and himself – had reacted spontaneously, generously, and with the utmost rationality, to the little boy's plight. And he appeared to be thriving, even if on occasions he did lapse back into insecurity and grief.

Lizzie was older, harder, already badly scarred. The poor child had absorbed too much poison in her tenderer years, and out it gushed whenever she felt anew the pressures of adversity.

Will stood for a while, contemplating the seashore, its rifts and folds, its rock pools, and the incoming tide.

Was it inevitable that the Callaghans, Stevens, and McIlroys were always, sooner or later, going to descend upon the girl's misshapen world? Surely it was. And however much Thomas had persevered he might never have been able to save her from the self the world had made her... a victim. And she, poor thing, had never been able to rise above that affliction in her short life. Thomas, Will reasoned, his thoughts settling, was no more responsible for that, than *he* was.

He turned away from the sea and ambled slowly back into the tented area, and once there, encountered Dr Ballow and Dr Mallon, coming from the hospital hut.

'Ah, Mr Crosby,' Ballow greeted him, hardly able to control an apparent elation. 'Despite the death of that poor girl, news is not all bad on Stradbroke Island.'

Will cocked his head to one side. 'Really? Tell me...'

'Yes, indeed. Well, we have but one patient left in the hospital hut now, she is young and strong and seems set for recovery, and none at all – as you well know – in the tent. It is over a week now since we found any new cases, and we are almost inclined to declare that our emergency is over... It's certainly beginning to seem that way, eh, Patrick?'

There was all of Edinburgh in his voice, Will noticed, smiling, and that in spite of his almost two decades away from his native land.

Mallon nodded, also smiling. 'From what I have read, a gap of a week suggests it is very unlikely we shall have any new cases. Until now, confirmation of one has always led us to another, after two or three days, at most. However, the chain of contagion does seem to have been broken. But David, let us wait a little longer before we convey these tidings to the world at large.'

Greatly relieved to hear this news, Will signalled his agreement, too. And though he could not help but notice Dr Ballow's frown, on hearing Mallon's counsel, he found himself asking, since the undertow of his previous line of thought was still with him… 'Do you think… That is, gentlemen – and he looked from one to the other – what is to be done about the girl? Is some form of post-mortem examination possible? Is it necessary?'

Mallon looked at Ballow, who explained: 'We are certainly not equipped for any major post-mortem operation here. But… in the present circumstances of the ongoing absolute imposition of quarantine regulations, clearly her body cannot be shipped back to Brisbane.'

'No…' Will frowned, though in truth it was no more than he already knew. 'So, what can you suggest, if anything?'

'There are certain basic things we could do, if you think there is the need – if, in fact, you have reason to believe that the child's death was not from natural causes…'

Will considered a moment. 'Captain Kemp, the First Officer and I examined the man, thoroughly, and we are all much inclined to believe McIlroy's story – which means it was more likely a case of criminal folly than of criminal intent or acts which led to her death. But it's the other things… her age, the likely… sexual things… And it might help in any eventual prosecution…'

'I see your point,' Ballow said. 'And McIlroy will surely have to face yet more questioning…'

'Once we can get him to Brisbane, yes, undoubtedly. And that, incidentally, goes for Stevens too, because our questioning of him here can have no legal status, of course. But in McIlroy's case, one of Kemp's officers did keep a detailed record of our interrogation… and

McIlroy's answers. And that will be passed to the proper authorities when the time comes.'

'But… I'm intrigued, Mr Crosby,' Mallon broke in. 'What is it… specifically… that leads you to see it as "folly" rather than anything criminal?'

'Because, although it is clear the girl died from drowning, there is still the question of the bleeding McIlroy spoke about… which caused him to take fright and run rather than stay and help her. And if that is the truth, then who or what caused it? And even if this points to criminal acts against the girl, specifically sexual acts, it does not necessarily suggest murder… or anything approaching it. So if you could find an explanation for the bleeding, it might help…'

'I see,' Ballow said, his tone suggesting this explanation put a degree of pressure upon himself and Mallon. 'Then we'll take a look at her, right away, if that suits you, Patrick? For I suppose we should get her underground as soon as possible. We can make the examination in the hospital tent – I take it she's still…?'

Ballow broke off, suddenly aware of a man and a woman standing near, hesitating. 'Excuse me, but was there something…?' he asked, officiously.

The man stepped forward, although it was the woman who spoke. 'Well, sir, it is really the sergeant we were a-seeking…'

'It's about them missing women,' the man piped up, shooting a glance at the woman.

'Tell me, then,' Will said, although he had more or less dismissed that mystery as a case that never would be resolved… 'what news have you?' And he signalled to the two doctors that they need not tarry.

Ballow exchanged a few hushed words with Mallon as they departed, calling something back to Will, about the matron, though his words were mostly lost to breeze and distance.

'There's a tent close by ours,' the woman resumed, in her sing-song accent, 'down at the bottom end of the camp there, see.' She pointed vaguely in that direction. 'And we noticed over a week ago that the two young women what shared it… well, suddenly they seems never to be there, see, whereas afore that we'd hardly been rid of 'em. They was a real pest, and all, what with their noise and shouting... and goings on.'

'And using language, and all,' the man chipped in, sounding even more Welsh than his wife. 'Downright vulgar, they was with it, too…!'

But the woman was speaking again, and Will forced himself to concentrate, even though something about the pair had begun to irritate him.

'...Anyhow, though we never had nothin' to do with 'em, we got a bit concerned... So... to cut a long story short, we took a peek inside their tent…'

'Yes, that's what he done. He 'ad a look inside,' the woman confirmed.

'And what did you find?' Will asked, tersely.

'It were very untidy,' the woman said, ratcheting up a righteous edge to her voice. 'Filthy it were! Which come as no surprise, mind. But there weren't nothin' to suggest they wasn't about. The opposite, in fact. Anyhow, Daffyd here had this idea, see...'

'I did and all. I thought that if we tied up the tent again in a particular way – I'm a dab hand with knots, see – we could keep lookin'... you know, to check, like, whether or not they'd been back. And that's what I done.' The man winked, conspiratorially.

'...Aye, that's what we done, right enough…'

Would these little people ever get to the point, pressing hard on what they perceived as their moment of glory?

'And so...?' he inquired, icily.

'And... well, for a few days it were clear they'd never been near the place. Then suddenly, yesterday…'

'…there they was again,' the woman interjected, with an indignant sniff, 'with their noise and their foul language and their dirty ways...'

Her husband looked at her, with something akin to loathing in his eyes. Then he turned to Will. 'One of 'em's called Sarah, I think. And t'other's... eh, I can't just bring it to mind... '

'It wouldn't be... Bunny, by any chance, would it?' Will suggested, remembering the note.

'Aye, that's it,' the woman yelped, 'that's it, right enough!' And the man jerked his head up in silent confirmation.

'Well, I'm grateful to you for your public spirit... for bringing me this information, Mr and Mrs...?'

'Lewis,' the man answered quickly. 'But...'

Will cut him short. 'When did you become aware that I was looking for them?' he asked, testing that 'public spirit' which, to his mind, seemed tainted.

'Only yesterday, actually, and quite by chance,' the woman answered. 'I just happened to be waiting at the water trough see, when I overhears a bit of tittle-tattle, like. One woman says, "I see they're back," and t'other says, "Aye, seems they've made quite a bit in the town and got fixed up with jobs for when they gets back there official, like." Then the first one says, "I reckon we should get summat for our pains, leading that bloody policeman a merry dance like we done."' And Mrs Lewis blushed – 'a-begging your pardon, sir, but them was her very words, sir.'

Will waved away her apology, shaking his head.

'So when I told Daffyd what I'd heard he thought... That is, he said we best come and tell you 'bout it, see... There isn't by any chance a... a reward going is there... by any chance...?'

LXX

'It just never occurred to me,' Will said, something like scorn colouring his voice, 'that the missing women could have been from a *different* sector of the camp and were using that bathing expedition as a cover. That's how good a policeman I am!' And he slammed his right fist into the palm of his left hand. 'And... What's more, Dr Ballow, I'm not sure what we can do about it now, if they are back here. Certainly, they'd deny ever having been away...' And if the general response to his inquiries was anything like it was the last time then he'd get nowhere...

Ballow nodded, but then asked Dr Mallon to check whether there was any quinine among their medical supplies.

'Maybe it's your decision, Dr Ballow, not mine,' Will said, as Mallon went to the medicine cupboard. 'For they have almost certainly broken quarantine restrictions, and that is very much your concern.'

'Well, what damage they could do they have presumably already done, Sergeant Crosby. The quarantine regulations were always intended more as a deterrent than as a cause for punishment. Nevertheless, however long these women were away, plying their particular trade – and we don't have any clear picture of how long that was – they were continually risking other people's lives for their own selfish ends. And if what we hear now is true, then they will be returning to that trade as soon as they get back to Brisbane. Actually, for me – his tone changed – the question is also a moral one... Do we want that sort of person in the town?'

'But Dr Ballow, we can't detain, much less convict them, on the basis of a moral principle.' Will looked pained. 'The fact is, we have nothing but hearsay and no concrete facts on which to proceed. Maybe the best we can do is to keep a watch over them and let the Brisbane authorities have a report of our knowledge of them and their activities. Then leave it up to the magistrates there to take action when the women are actually involved in breaking the law – always presuming brothels and prostitution are illegal in New South Wales… Are they?' he inquired, only half in earnest.

Ballow laughed. 'Well, the law as written is clear enough… but all too often the authorities turn a blind eye, don't they, Patrick, in these wilder parts of the country? The brothel is a sort of social safety net, I suppose.'

'Aye, but it certainly causes the medical profession a lot of headaches,' a disgruntled Mallon observed, as he was locking the cupboard. 'And wastes a lot of our time… No quinine, David, I'm afraid.'

Ballow groaned. 'I wonder – is it worth ordering any, now?'

'Hardly, I suppose,' and Mallon shrugged.

Will hesitated to be sure neither wished to say more, and then brought them back to the question of the women. 'As you both know, *here* we have no authority even to question these women, let alone place any restrictions on them. So, I was wondering… Might it not be best to let them think they've got away with it, and then have them met by it as they arrive in Brisbane? Always presuming we could get a message to whoever was responsible for such an action, in the township…'

Ballow looked pensive. 'Let me sleep on it, Will. I'll give you my decision as soon as I reach it… if I reach it, that is! Clearly, there's no immediate hurry. The *Aurora*'s not due back here for – he calculated rapidly – another five days. As far as… this poor child is concerned, Patrick, shall we see to it now?'

And the three men left the store hut, Ballow shutting the door firmly behind them.

After spending an hour or so in the company of Burke's *Reflections*, and encountering frustration after frustration, Will decided a lesson with Thomas was what was needed.

On entering the hospital tent, however, which in these past few days had become more a place of ease and recreation, he was instantly reminded that, for want of a better place, it was where they had left the body of the drowned girl. And he remembered the post-mortem. Yet although the covered corpse lay there on a wooden board, towards the back of the tent, neither of the doctors was to be seen, despite their declared intention of examining the girl's body "at once". Surely, they had not completed their work, already?

Will's bewilderment was interrupted by the young matron, just then pushing into the tent. 'Oh, Mr Crosby,' she gasped, 'you gave me such a fright. I thought you would have been away with the others.'

'Away?' Will questioned. 'Away where?'

'Oh dear, have you not heard about… the accident?'

'Accident? No… What accident?'

The woman was clearly in some distress. 'The doctors were called away… more than an hour ago, before they had time even to begin…' She glanced across at the inert figure. 'Oh, Mr Crosby…'

'Tell me, matron…'

Miss Labone sat down, heavily, on one of the benches. 'It seems a little boy fell into a cooking fire and he's been badly burned. The man who came with the news said it was young Billy…'

'What! What are you saying…?' Will interrupted, his face turned ashen, he leapt past her, not waiting to hear more, realising he had not set eyes on Billy since…

Brushing the blinding tears from his eyes, Will raced towards the hospital hut, his heart pounding.

'Sergeant Crosby! Sergeant Crosby…!'

The matron ran out after him, calling his name in vain.

Miss Labone went back inside, and flopped down on the bench once more, her chin in her cupped hands, elbows on the table, sunk in her own private turmoil.

Poor George, whom she had loved, still loved, though he had

gone to his Maker… Nothing could ever undo that love, though he never knew, so… what had been… what was the good of it… now? But this new thing… Goodness! There she'd been, grieving over dear, dear George… when… it had felt like a tremor surging through her, as though his gentle, genuine concern for her had become something quite… physical, coursing through her. And instantly she had felt… had known… she was no longer alone…

It was just the same as when dear mamma had closed her eyes, finally, and Dr Mitchell – George – had put *his* arms around her…

It was the same… These good, kind men…

Yet, with George but newly buried, how unseemly, how fickle, and faithless she was… And yet, George, she was almost certain, had been entirely unaware… Unless, of course, he had affected… But no, no… it didn't bear thinking about…

She sighed, fighting back her tears. But the feelings were real enough. With no warning, *this* man, towards whom she had been disposed to feel, nay, had felt, an open antagonism… *this* man, who was surely old enough to have been her father… Now, every time she set eyes on him, or heard him speak, her heart beat faster. It was ridiculous…

Except that *he* was now… he is *now*, and the *next* moment and the *next*. And what if, despite all we are told to believe, there *is* only now…

Miss Labone ceased to struggle and gave way to tears. It was all a great deal more than her twenty-one, quite sheltered years, could cope with.

If Will had shied away from acknowledging just how central to his own life the little boy had become, it was certainty borne in upon him now. The very thought of losing the child drained him of all hope for the future; without Billy, the future here would lose all sense of the purpose it had been gaining latterly, by stealth almost.

He burst into the hut where, immediately, his questing eyes found the doctors bending over the only bed that was occupied.

'Billy!' he all but shouted.

'Sorry, Mr Crosby, but you must not interrupt us…' Dr Mallon pushed him away.

Will caught sight of the singed and tousled fair hair of their small patient, then saw the extent of the damage to the boy's face, which was no longer recognisable as a face.

Oh Billy…

Feeling light-headed, sick at the horror he beheld, he sank down on the adjacent bed, pushing his head between his knees, gasping, his gasps turning into sobs.

'Shush, Mr Crosby.' Without breaking off from his ministrations or raising his head, Dr Ballow reproached him, quietly. 'Be calm, now or… preferably… leave us. Can you not see we need to give the boy our full attention?'

Still reeling from shock, Will attempted to stand. He shuffled miserably towards the door, then looked back at the bed.

Mallon caught his eye momentarily. 'Mr Crosby,' he said quietly. 'This is not… this is young Billy Griffith.' And he bent forward to apply more salve to the seared mass.

Will stood rooted to the spot, his eyes widening at this second shock, streaming with tears, still. He flopped down on the steps outside, rocking back and forth in his anguish, back and forth until his tear-tempest finally abated.

Billy, oh yes, with all his day-to-day needs, his schooling, his whole upbringing…

The pleasure in those necessities, in themselves, would also, surely, make the distant date of his return to England seem less far off… With Billy at his side…

The immediacy of the love and deepening sense of responsibility he felt for the child would help alleviate the fears his other, projected future continually stoked within him. Alice and Lilian…

Without Billy, the years that stretched ahead, until then, would be bleak indeed.

When Will eventually rose from the step, he felt dazed, as though he had suffered some harsh physical pain, with all semblance of normality now hopelessly destroyed. He stumbled forward, blindly, his temples throbbing, his mind reeling, and came to a sudden halt, his eyes closed against the sun's glare, which seemed to intensify his feelings of dizziness.

But finally, with a strenuous effort of will, he gathered himself together and made for his tent, and upon reaching it fell face down upon Billy's bed and sank immediately into sleep.

'Wake up, Mr Crosby! Wake up! You have to wake up!'

'Billy?' Will was pitched once again from one extreme state to another.

'Mr Crosby, why are you asleep? It's still daytime! And you're on *my* bed, and... but I don't mind,' the boy added quickly. 'I hope you are all right because I have to tell you... I just *have* to tell you what I've seen! Mr Crosby...!'

When he was sufficiently aware of where he was and what was happening, Will found himself wondering whether the desperate scene he had witnessed in the hospital hut had been a nightmare after all. For here was Billy, as usual larger than life, with his innocence, earnestness, and boundless enthusiasm. He looked at the child, half sat up, and drew him down onto the bed beside him.

The boy came willingly enough, yet the urgency persisted, uncontainable.

'Oh, Mr Crosby, do you know what I've seen? You'll never guess, so I'll just have to tell you. I've seen a real, live kanguloo, and it had a baby one in its... its... bread-basket.' And he chuckled mischievously. He wriggled free of Will's grasp and hopped around at the foot of the bed. 'Watch me Mr Crosby! I'm a kanguloo.' Then he came back panting and stood beside Will. 'You've not seen one yet, I know, but I'm sure you will one of these days. I could take you to where I saw mine, if you like, but I don't think it'll still be there. And do you know what? It was ever so funny. It sort of hopped and... and... lolloped. Like this!' And away he went again. 'It was at the lake, where Father Thomas and me went exploring, and I saw it first, and... Mr Crosby!'

Laughing aloud at the boy's headlong rush, Will felt the anguish of two hours before slipping away from him. And still laughing, he held up his hand.

'Billy. Billy. Don't you ever pause for breath? But... how exciting it must have been for you!' And he sat up fully, swinging his legs over the side of the bed. Reaching out, he put an arm round the boy's shoulders and hugged him tightly, until the hopping urge seized the child yet again.

'Oh, Billy, you have no idea how glad I am to see you. And, well, I must say how envious I am of what you have seen, and I haven't.' Then, making some sort of connection between the kangaroo and all the other presumed, yet-to-be-revealed wonders of the island, he added: 'I think maybe it's time you and I went off to find Mr Tompani again. What do you say to that?'

Billy ceased hopping and seemed to consider the proposition for a moment or two. Then he nodded, gravely, and came and stood before Will. 'Well, yes, you could be right, Mr Crosby... because... he's probably had enough time by now to finish my bluemerlang and, I 'spect he's very likely wondering why I haven't been to collect it. Yes. Yes! Can we go tomorrow?'

And without waiting for a reply, off he went, skippety-hopping, kangulooing out of the tent.

LXXI

Billy was gone as swiftly as he had come, presumably to tell the rest of the world about his 'kanguloo.'

If the child only knew how he had so... disarmed the man. And it was a moot point, now, which of the two depended more on the other... How on earth had he allowed himself to fall into this trap, set by this... Will-o-the-Wisp?

But, for all that, Will was smiling with amusement, as well as, still, an immense relief. And in this frame of mind he once again picked up the dead judge's copy of the Reflections and read through the passage that had defeated him earlier.

On nearing its end, however, he realised his thoughts had been mostly elsewhere, and thus he had come no nearer understanding it than he had on the other occasions. Frustrated, he thrust the book aside. And yet, it was hardly surprising. The shock of what had happened – the extent of Billy Griffith's terrible injuries, and the relief that they were not his Billy's injuries – had locked onto his mind infecting all thought.

By this time, the poor child had probably died. And though he had not known the boy or his parents, Will grieved for them, and with them... for the whole of humanity, himself included, endlessly exposed to the vagaries of chance.

As a young man he had believed his physical strength and agility sufficient bulwarks against any assault from without, invincible even in the face of death itself. Yet India, with its endless violence and bottomless poverty had gradually unseated that certainty. And then

– though not a death, yet very like one – his sudden separation from Alice and Lilian, his trial and judgement, his imprisonment and loss of respect and self-respect... Each of these events had driven nail after nail into the coffin of Will's presumed invincibility and made him understand how vulnerable each person was, at all times. Chance, and little else, stood between a man and his end in any moment. The long sea-journey followed by Stradbroke Island had confirmed him in that opinion and, he was sure, nothing would ever shake him from it now.

We live, he realised wryly, as precariously as the tiny blue crabs at Amity, our margins of safety every bit as slender; and we should give thanks for every new day which dawned upon us...

And if he could share these thoughts with Alice... surely, she might come to realise how little importance should be given to a moment's human weakness? Particularly when his whole thought had been for something much greater, their being together, at all costs. Surely, she might see that... now?

...And yet, although his every action was rooted in that knowledge – of the frailty of human existence – his every action seemed to deny it: spurning it and striving instead in the service of a continual reaffirmation of life... which was why he had been trying to understand the thoughts of this man, Burke...!

Will frowned, still in the shadow of this pessimism, which lodged like a cancer at the bottom of his soul. For it was wholly irrational to expect that Burke, or indeed any other man, could have anything to say that might ameliorate this baleful human condition.

Groaning inwardly, he picked up the book and read one of the difficult passages again, straining hard to concentrate as his eye, and his forefinger, moved slowly along the lines.

You see, my dear Lord, that I do not go upon any difference concerning the best method of preventing the growth of a system which I believe we dislike in common. I cannot differ from you

*because I do not think any method can prevent it. The evil has
happened; the thing is done in principle and example; and we
must wait the good pleasure of an Higher Hand than ours for
the time of its perfect accomplishment in practice in this country
and elsewhere. All I have done for some time past, and all I shall
do hereafter, will only be to clear myself from having any hand,
actively or passively, in this great change.*

The evil – which evil? And whose Higher Hand? Will's present mood
was against further understanding, so he rose and went out, with a
sudden need for food, drink, and company.

After quickly consuming the piece of bread and lukewarm fish
soup he was given at the mess tent, he made his way over to the
hospital tent where the matron was pouring tea for Thomas out of a
large kettle.

'Mr Crosby, you must have smelt the tea,' she said, smiling.

'…And *you* must have sensed my need of it!' Will laughed, settling
himself at the table, opposite Thomas. 'Is there any news of the poor
little lad who fell into the fire?'

'The doctors are still at his side,' the matron said quietly. 'His
poor parents… they had been over to the lake to wash some bedding,
and knew nothing about it until a little while ago… I'll call in again
now. He's not expected to survive, poor boy.'

'It must have been a terrible shock for them,' Thomas said, his
voice heavy with the pity of it, 'though I didn't see them at the lake.'

And a deep silence descended upon the two men.

At length, Thomas looked up at Will, his face breaking into a wistful
smile.

'Did Billy tell you about the kangaroos? Ah, that boy, he had me
running round the lake all afternoon, you know, chasing them! And
I'm supposed to know all about them even though I had never set
eyes on one until he did… Do they do this? Do they do that? Why…?
What…? When…? Oh, God save us!'

Will laughed. 'He has exactly that effect on me! He never stops

443

with his questions, does he…? Oh yes, I heard *all* about the kangaroos! Still – he added, unwilling to break the mood, yet seeing if he might gently steer the conversation – with the admitted exception of these wondrous creatures, you *can* provide him with many more answers than I can!'

'Me, with my cloistered life? I'd say that's questionable,' Thomas laughed, pouring himself a second mug of tea. 'Whereas you, with your extensive travel and exotic experience… you're a practical man, and in the main it's these things that interest young Billy. My cloistered life gave me nothing of the sort, unless it came from a book…'

'Books, ah yes. And speaking of books – Will chuckled inwardly – I have a question for you too. I've been trying to read Burke. And I freely confess he has me befogged. I've read one paragraph a half-dozen times and I'm still no wiser!'

'Edmund Burke?'

'You know of him, then?'

'I do indeed, though he's hardly my favourite reading!' Thomas snorted. '"Befogged", you say? That's Burke right enough! But whatever did you choose him for…? I thought…'

'…because the title sounded promising: something I ought to know about. This man was, if I've understood aright, much opposed to the revolution in France… so why don't *you* approve of him?'

Thomas clicked his tongue. 'No. I have sympathy with things like his condemnation of the French Revolution – the manner of it, that is – but I can't stomach much else: his pious adherence to the old paternalisms – you know, the Church, the Nobility, the landowners…' Thomas almost spat the words out. 'No, as far as I'm concerned Burke is the worst kind of reactionary: a man in the thick of governmental politics, who clings to the old ways, and does so in spite of his recognition of their many flaws and their eventually doomed nature. That book, Will, is a very long-winded declaration of cowardice, actually! That's my view anyway!'

Will nodded, reflectively. 'Fair enough. But still, it galls me that I cannot even follow the sense of it on the page.'

Thomas laughed. 'All I can say, Will, is that in this case your failure is a positive gain – at least your mind runs no risk of pollution… Agh, these traitors to mankind! But is it my view on what you've read you're seeking…? It is? Well, if we must, we must! I'll cast an eye over it, to be sure.' Rising, Thomas drained his mug.

'So…?' he queried then, since Will had not moved, 'do you want to know what the bloody man says, or don't you?'

Grinning, Will leapt to his feet, and followed the priest out of the tent into the damp air outside.

Beyond all horizons, a woman turned another page. She could not give it up yet, this book she was reading for the third time in as many months. Catherine and Heathcliffe. Reaching out across the vast nothingness left to them. She, cold in the earth, and he prostrate above. There was no sense in it, the all-severing wave. The eternal rocks beneath. The endless emptiness above. Ridiculous, the wasted years.

'What are you reading, mummy?'

Alice turned another page, then closed the book. 'Oh, nothing much. Just the same silly old story. It's just a story…' And she placed the book on the low table before her. 'Would you like me to read you one of your stories… before bedtime, my pet?'

Lilian's eyes lit up. 'Oh, yes please! The one about Hansel and Gretel we started last time.'

'Then go and fetch it, and we'll see whether it has a happy ending. Let's hope it does…'

When he had the volume in his hands, Thomas ran his eye swiftly over the passage. 'Well, is this not just typical of the bloody hypocrite? He's saying here that what the French Revolution has unleashed, that is, the democratic ideal… though evil in itself, it will sooner or later engulf the whole of… I suppose he means, of British society. But he's saying he wants no part in it. Doesn't want to soil his hands with it!'

'Ah, and that means…'

'Yes. Even though, it would seem, he sees it all as part of the Almighty's Great Plan for mankind…!'

'So why doesn't he…?'

'Because this so upright man much prefers to live on borrowed time, Will, and maintain class privilege for as long as is possible. And my god! That was certainly long enough to murder a million or more of his fellow Irishmen fifty years later!'

Thomas threw the book down on his bed, wiping his hands on the counterpane, as if to cleanse them.

'Will, you'd do well to read the counter-blast to this outrageous dishonesty, which came from a certain Tom Paine: *The Rights of Man*… Not that you are likely to find that sort of smouldering subversion in the dead man's chest…!'

Will smiled in admiration of his friend's volcanic passion. 'But do you not find that ideals are, well, one thing, and realities… quite another? Until whatever it is that drives human nature undergoes a deep change, surely any system will always find itself… adjusted, sooner or later, to operate in the interests of the already better-off, wouldn't you agree? And that must include this "democracy" – whatever promise it may seem to offer for the future! And truly, I see little evidence of such a change happening any time soon. Oh, Thomas, the bulk of humanity is but a poor recommendation for the skills of its Maker!'

'Well, well!' Thomas laughed, 'You do seem to have taken your Machiavelli to heart!'

'Maybe so! But remember – Will's brow puckered – I too have seen far too much that is unlovely in this world.'

'Yes, Will, and you didn't really need a Machiavelli to point that out, did you? And if there was one thing the early Church Fathers almost had right, it was that. Mankind is in a fallen state, sure enough, though *not* through falling… Our state is not "fallen" but "un-risen" in the first place. And so it will ever remain, I fear – though I am mindful, even as I speak, that I, like the foolish Burke, may yet be declaring much too soon…' He shrugged, then grimaced. 'In truth, I don't actually know. I have all the questions but none of the answers…'

'Oh, I don't think you do too badly in that department, my friend.'

Will smiled. 'I only wish I had even a smattering of your knowledge, your... good sense...'

Thomas waved his hand dismissively. 'But one thing I do think is that if the reports that have filtered through to us are true – about the state of Brisbane right now – then it's a mightily sad thing.' He pursed his lips. 'No doubt it will suffice for many of our fellows who have survived this far, since what they desire, in the main, is more of what they know, but coming to *them* more abundantly this time, and not to others... Just a re-shuffling of the cards, really.'

'So then... when we get there, what will you do?' Beset as he was with his own uncertainties, Will felt troubled, having hoped for a more optimistic slant on things, from his friend.

'In truth, I cannot tell, but I suspect I shall not be too long before I shake its dust from off my feet and try to start all over again in some new, unsullied place. But honest to god, Will, I don't really know. I need to find, well, a new "calling", I think.'

Will fell silent, digesting this. 'Yes... And there's young Billy to think of.' And he paused, acutely aware that whatever Thomas responded would be as a watershed for his own future life. 'He'll need an education, won't he? And not just schooling, but in the broader sense, if he is ever to make his way in the world after the indifferent start fate has dealt him...' Will's tone was light, but inside him, once again, that suffocating feeling was edging its way forward: that his responsibility for another human being, a vulnerable human being at that, would close off so many roads and pathways, until he was prodded down the very one he most wished to avoid.

Thomas scratched his chin. 'About Billy, yes, you're right, though that is not to say we have to submit to the conventional ways that our society prescribes, now, is it? Come on, Will, think! After all, it's what you're becoming practised at! This land is thought to be vast and empty, and for me, that, right now, is its beauty...'

'Yes, that attracts me, also... but...'

'The newness and the differences it offers should be our compass, Will, not the things we know, replicated – maybe shoddily replicated

– in Brisbane. Anyway, we should not be afraid to take Billy along with us. Do you not agree?'

That casually spoken 'we' told Will all he needed to know.

At last.

A great sense of relief washed over him, and he leaned forward, his mind racing.

'Thomas… and I'm not changing the subject, but tomorrow I shall go exploring again, on the other side of the island. Will you not come along too?'

'It's tempting, Will, but I may still be needed here, and besides, I've never been astride a horse in my life!' Thomas laughed, 'although doubtless that particular innocence must shortly end if we are to become pioneers…' He shook his head. 'We make plans for our future, Will, but that future depends on the reality we are still living here, one that – as it has demonstrated – is capable of throwing up all manner of shocks and surprises…' The priest placed his hand on his friend's shoulder. 'I thank you for the thought, but I feel my duty lies here, still… Do you understand?'

And Will nodded, having known this all along, yet battling, nevertheless, against his disappointment.

LXXII

'I can't, Mr Crosby. You see, all the flowers in my mammy's garden have died, and it looks an awful mess. I think I should stay and plant some more for her or she might be sad.'

The still bleary-eyed child sank back on his pillow, and it was in Will's mind to reject his request. But then, as on so many previous occasions, he relented, won over by the innocence and simplicity of Billy's declaration.

'I know that's what my mammy wants, because she said so, in my dream.'

'Did she now, Billy?' Will said, swallowing his disappointment. 'Well, then, of course you must stay.'

'Mr Crosby?'

'Yes?'

'Are you sad, Mr Crosby?'

'Yes, Billy, I'm sad. But that's all right. I'm sad I shan't have you along with me, for we so much enjoyed ourselves last time, didn't we? And I'm sure Mr Tompani will be sad too, not to see you, especially if, as I suspect, he has the boomerang ready...' And he paused, in a half-guilty, half-hearted attempt to stir the little boy's... awareness of what he might be missing.

But Billy's mind was quite made up.

'Mr Crosby, I'm a bit sad too. But my mammy was also quite sad about the garden, so you see I just can't go...' And his lips clenched together, in fierce determination.

Will ruffled his hair, admiring the child's forthrightness, his clear sense of responsibility, and the priorities it seemingly demanded – whatever the adult might think of the reasons for their justification.

'… and I do hope you won't miss me too much… Will you be all right on your own?' Billy sighed, then grimaced comically. 'I suppose I could…'

'No, no Billy,' Will laughed. 'I'll be all right, and you are quite right to stay. But you take care, now. Always let Father Thomas know what you are doing, and where you will be. Promise me? I'll tell him you are not going with me. Oh… and stay well away from any fires, long grass, and… rainbow-coloured snakes! Do you hear me now?'

And so it was that Will set out alone.

Familiar now with the track to the north coast and the time needed to reach Whale Rock, he was determined to make no diversions on this trip, for what he did not yet know was quite how he would coax Bluebell up the steep rocky headland at the far end of the north beach, or indeed, how far he would have to travel once that task had been accomplished, if accomplished it were.

He had warned Thomas not to worry if he did not return that day, while suggesting, half-jokingly, that a search be organized if he did not show up by sundown on the third day! But then, with these words in mind, he had sought out the quartermaster, and packed additional provisions, sufficient for three days. And then, back to Thomas, to explain his intended route…

At first, Will allowed the horse to walk so as to get used to carrying a load on her back once again, but after twenty minutes or so he spurred her into a trot and then, minutes later, to a canter. He went past the spring at Myora and the clearing in which the coloured poles were set, and although he had the fleeting impression something was different about it, he rode on, intent on covering as much ground as quickly as he could, as far as the anticipated difficulties at the high, rocky headland. He was anxious to find Tompani, though with no clear understanding as to why, and was hoping he might encounter some of his people along the north shore. But even using the telescope he could see no one, no figures gathering shells as they had been that first time.

The golden sun flamed, transfiguring all about him; even the white sands had yellowed. Halfway along the beach, Will slowed once again to a walking pace though he did not dismount. The breeze coming off the sea was cool and to some extent countered the increasing heat of the day. He rummaged about in one of the saddlebags for the old felt hat Barney had mentioned, and put it on his head, fastening his neckerchief higher, especially at the back.

In not much more than an hour and a half, he judged, he had arrived at the foot of the rather forbidding rock-face.

'Well, Bluebell, what do you think? Can you make it?'

Will dismounted and surveyed the headland from different positions all along its length. It was much higher and more rugged than he had remembered, and certainly more so than the small outcrop they had crossed with relative ease, a mile or so back.

The best place to attempt the climb, he decided, was through the rocky defile by which they had ascended and descended on his first visit, with Tompani.

Tying the horse's reins to the lowest branch of a shading tree, close in by the forest belt, he clambered some way up to try and work out the best ways of manoeuvring her at points that appeared to be particularly tricky. The higher he went however the steeper became the incline. And he then he saw, to his dismay, what he had clearly forgotten: near the top, the track – in the direction from which they had come in their previous descent – began in a series of steep, narrow, natural steps that would have presented an impossible obstacle even for a goat, let alone a horse. Accepting defeat, for the moment, he completed the climb on foot to explore other possibilities – if such existed.

Reaching the top of the 'steps', Will stood gasping for breath, much as he remembered having done on that first occasion: how all these months of relative inactivity had taken their toll on his physical fitness! As his heart continued its pounding, he let his eyes wander about him: first, out to sea, where yet again three or four leviathans of the deep, like the new-fangled railway engines back home, were blowing out their jets of steam as they pursued their route northwards; and then, involuntarily, distracted by its periodic booming, in the direction of the deep gorge, some way over to his right. And once his breathing had slowed, he turned his steps towards the gorge.

Swinging round, he looked back along the strand in the direction of Amity Point, across the splendid golden emptiness he had lately traversed, by the land's edge. And he marvelled at its blue, tranquil magnificence. Far below him, Bluebell stood where he had left her… patiently awaiting his return, he liked to think. And in that silent moment he felt that the Earth was his alone, as though everything representing the human race, including his own experience of life lived, had all yet to happen. It was perfectly possible, he mused, one might even think natural, to encounter a living god beyond the next rise, or through that nearest stand of trees. In that moment, everything seemed possible, *everything* – even the fulfilment of his wildest dreams.

It was the moment before everything; and he stood transfixed, unwilling to move and destroy that complete sense of imminence, and perfection.

Some minutes later, Bluebell's neighing broke the spell and reminded him of his immediate task. He closed his eyes for a moment, breathed in deeply, then set off walking along the rocky ridge that led over to the gorge. It crossed his mind that he had perhaps been foolish to leave the rifle behind, not so much for fear that he might need it to defend himself, but that, like the other one, weeks ago, it too might disappear, and yet again – though justifiably so, this time – provoke the wrath of Mr Ridley. But it was too late now. And in any case, he was unlikely to be out of sight of the horse for long.

Ahead was a mixture of trees and high grasses with some relatively open clearings, and the sloping plain he already knew. And he was struck by the silence of it all. Here, even the sea's roar was stilled to a vague and intermittent purr, the borehole's still distant thunder muted.

He took one last glance at Bluebell then set off at a much-quickened pace, very soon covering the ground that brought him to the point where the peninsula merged, southwards, with the main body of the island. He moved then, almost at once, into the large, downward-sloping clearing and veered away westwards, to the right, hoping to find an area where the incline down through the trees to where Bluebell was, would be much gentler than the rock face by which he had just ascended. However, the trees seemed quite impenetrable. He persisted a little further and was relieved, at last, to find a deep gully snaking downwards. Yet it too was thickly overgrown, and he hesitated to enter it, afraid lest, as seemed likely, it was home to some of the deadly reptiles he had heard tell of, but of which he had no real knowledge.

He looked about him for a suitable stick or branch, but those lying about on the ground were bone dry, and either snapped or crumbled in his hand. He tried to break off a low-growing branch by swinging on it, but immediately let go as he felt the first stabbing bites from a division of red ants marching along it, enraged by his sudden intrusion into their ordered universe. Ruefully, he remembered too late the advice he had been given even before setting foot on the continent – by whom had also slipped his memory – that one should never reach out to touch anything, however innocent it looked... And as Will wiped away the still avenging ants from his hands, he realised it could just as easily have been a tree snake, or one of the many fatal spiders, and he shuddered.

Certainly, Bluebell could not possibly make the ascent of the rock, and if he was to make any further progress, he had to find another way, stick or no stick. Gingerly, and deliberately dislodging any loose stones in his path as he went, Will picked his way down the gully, avoiding patches of long grass, or clinging onto any bushes.

After a while, the gully narrowed and became deeper, swinging away suddenly to his left. And at this point of deviation he turned and looked back to try and assess whether or not that section already traversed would be feasible for the horse ascending and descending.

Will stood, blinking at the sunlight shafting down through the trees, not immediately focusing properly. And suddenly there was a face staring down at him from the topmost rim of the defile, a figure almost entirely hidden by scrub and leaves. With an involuntary gasp and shivers prickling down his spine, he brought up a hand to shield his eyes, the better to see what manner of man confronted him. And when his eyes finally adjusted, he was struck by the devilish impassivity of the motionless face, which was long, thin and grey… And all at once, because of the sharply pointed ears surmounting the face, it became clear. Neither man nor devil, but simply an animal, and even as he watched, it moved and loped away out of sight. Banishing fear, and collecting his thoughts, Will presumed he had probably just seen his own, first 'kanguloo'.

Just wait until he told the story to Billy! And Will laughed to, and at himself, for he had been utterly unnerved by the experience, coming so soon after the sharp warning delivered by the ants.

Again he stood and deliberated. But this time he was wondering about his fear: he had been unnerved because he was predisposed to be so. And what was it that so undermined one's whole being as to negate completely any semblance of rationality in these present circumstances? Fear of the unknown, yes, but it was far from the whole story. Was it not also a lifetime's preparation for that fear, starting from the adventure stories read at school, in which 'the jungle' was as baleful a character as the fearsome beasts (or black savages) that lurked behind, and in, every tree, bush, patch of long grass, or indeed, in every river? A fear nourished, of course, by the flat, totally uncompromising warnings about the treacherous, unforgiving nature of this land itself.

India, Will mused, had been different. Only rarely had he found himself in thick forest, and never, so far as he remembered, alone. The tigers, crocodiles and rogue elephants were always far away in other parts of that vast, teeming country, and thus this primeval fear had never really been engaged.

There, he now recalled, his fears had always had a human cause. Stradbroke, he faced alone.

The forest, of course, was neither malevolent nor benign. It was – like any other sort of terrain – whatever you made of it. True, experience of it privileged you, so that its animals, whether hunters or hunted, knew how to use it to their advantage, and they had the advantage of you whilst ever you remained a novice, and were panicked by silence or superstition or sheer ignorance.

These factors notwithstanding, one's mind was hardly devoid of answers or understanding, surely? And Will acknowledged to himself that the vast majority of animals he had encountered in other places had been anything but confrontational. And the reason you saw so few of them was because, in general, they were aware of you first and made sure that you did not see them... A lesson an old sepoy had once imparted, up in Kashmir.

Not waiting to pounce, then, but to avoid being pounced upon. Indeed, it was said too that predators – though that surely meant the whole of animal life – did not kill wantonly, but only to satisfy hunger, or in self-defence. Common sense (or was it really superstition?) told him to be wary of such a generalisation. But, in any case, since big predators were absent from Stradbroke, it hardly applied. Only accidental contact – as with the ants or stepping on a snake – was to be feared, with caution and vigilance the main weapons in one's armoury, and powerful ones at that. Mr Machiavelli would have approved of this reasoning, he felt sure! And yet – he fancied that same sage whispering – a stout stick would not come amiss...

Will resumed his search a little further down the gully. His patience was rewarded, and he soon had his ideal companion, a fairly straight, quite sturdy stick. Soon too, and to his great surprise, and relief, he was standing on the wide beach looking back to where Bluebell was tethered, less than two hundred yards away, still in shade, in the lea of the forested hillside, though the sun was now well-nigh overhead.

Bluebell whinnied as he approached her, and yet Will's relief was tempered by his disappointment at having found no trace at all of the Aborigines – Tompani's final words notwithstanding, before their parting not many days before.

Here now, tomorrow different place...

Of course, the island seemed large enough to conceal a good

number of such groups, so he might well track them down eventually. But he was impatient now: that was the honest truth of it.

Reaching Bluebell, he sat down on a flat rock, feeling the warmth of the sun on his back, and drank a little water from his flask, and after pouring the horse some water onto a dished rock, led her up through the gully by which he had just descended. It proved less difficult than he had surmised, mainly because she selected her own route. And quickly realising her good sense, Will reached up, fastened the reins around the pommel, and left her to her own best devices. She gained the top well ahead of him, and he found her lazily cropping the lush grass there, when he at last caught up.

After a short wait, Will remounted and set off in what he calculated must be roughly a southerly direction.

Before long, he was conscious of having drawn near to the sea again, hearing its pounding on unseen rocks, with a strong, salt-laden breeze whispering through leaves and branches. And all of a sudden, without warning, he was transported back in time, to the Cumbrian coast, when they had lived at Tithe Barn.

There was that particular path where the sounds and the smell of the sea were with you well before the sight of it, and once she became aware of their presence Lilian had invariably tried to break free of his hold and run towards the water. But he and Alice had always been vigilant and never allowed her to do so: although not of any considerable height, the cliffs there could well have been a danger to a little girl. And at more or less the same point she had ever needed some distraction – usually in the guise of a piece of Alice's toffee or an apple, brought along for that very eventuality. He remembered too that on those occasions, once the child had been pacified, a certain look or even a brief kiss had passed between Alice and him. His world... their world, he quickly corrected himself, had been all certainties, then, and had seemed likely to remain so for the rest of their lives. And where were they now, his Alice and Lilian, those certainties?

Will brushed the back of his hand across his eyes.

Yet, dismissing these sorrows, he pushed on. And soon, to his amazement, he came across a poker-burned plaque nailed to a tree, announcing that the spur to his left was Point Lookout, so named by Cook on his first voyage in those parts; it was reputedly the discoverer's first sighting of Australia, prior to his eventual landing at Botany Bay. Will looked at it in some doubt, but then realised that here was proof positive of what he had told Mary in his letter home, the day they had made landfall here.

And who, he wondered, could have thought to set up such a memorial? Disappointed, he recognised that its presence put paid to any notion he might have entertained of being the first European to set foot on that side of the island. Someone maybe connected with the former penal colony, years back, had beaten him to it. Of course they had. It had been foolish to presume... and, for that matter, for it to have become so childishly important to him.

The sudden incursion of a flock of multi-coloured parakeets distracted him. They landed high in the trees, squawking and squabbling as they did endlessly, it seemed, from earlier encounters with them. Their sound was ferocious, but he presumed they were unlikely to vent their anger, whatever caused it, on a human being.

Will retied his neckerchief and pushed on again, moving slowly behind Bluebell, until they reached another huge outcrop of rock that sloped away down towards the sea. And looking down from his vantage point, once back in the saddle, he was delighted to see dolphins leaping and diving and riding the waves, and utterly carefree – or so he interpreted their frolicking. He watched for only a few moments then spurred the horse on, round a small hillock along what appeared to be – for a good few yards, at least – a well-worn, sandy path. A little further and he was looking down from some considerable height upon a white, sandy beach that stretched away southwards, as far as the eye could see. To the inland side of the beach, though a little way behind it, were low stunted trees and bushes, beyond which – his adjusted telescope, reached from the saddlebag, told him – were what appeared to be long, yet separate stretches of black water thickly bordered by reeds and rushes, surely an area of swampland? He surveyed the whole scene before him and once again quietly revelled in its glorious peace, its emptiness and the absence of all the usual sounds that came with humankind; only the ocean breaking onto the beach, the intermittent breeze setting the trees a-whispering, an occasional bird call… as it had been since time immemorial, he surmised.

Will dismounted and led the horse down the long slope towards the dazzling white sands.

LXXIII

Most days began like this for the lapsed priest. He had grown accustomed to the shifting, early morning mists, fond of them, even, and of the shapes they revealed and concealed by turns, as he plodded over to the top corner of the burial ground.

Thomas stood by Joanna's grave: remembering, inevitably, and regretting; yet more and more of late, he had noticed, absorbing a sense of strength, of power, which the place seemed to stir within him. Of course, it defied all reason. Joanna was dead and that was an end of it. But the sensation was real enough. And he recalled how, on the second or third day after he had buried her, he had stood here as he stood now, and been first startled, and then, inexplicably, elated by the sight and sound of a small furry animal moving about in the branches of a misty tree not a dozen yards away. It had seemed such an affirmation of life and living, and somehow it had seemed to include Joanna too. He could not understand, let alone express, the powerful feelings that had gripped him, then; but they had remained with him constantly, and were with him, even now, as he talked quietly, quietly, to his departed soulmate.

And he realised, as he had done the day before, and the day before that, that when the time came to leave this island, tearing himself away from this place would prove one of the hardest tasks he had ever had to face. And it was no use appealing to reason – he knew that, too; for the heart's reasons were of an entirely different order.

Thomas knelt down, as he usually did, before bidding her... au revoir. And he laid his open palms upon the roundedness of the mound, as he had done so many times, on her naked body.

When he rose again, through the mist, he caught sight of Will passing their tent, leading his horse by the reins, starting out on his journey north. He had disappointed his friend, of course he had; and he had been a little less than honest in the reasons he had given him – for which he was deeply sorry. But this need of his, this... he could find no other word for it... this spiritual duty become a daily ritual with him... it was entirely private, a communing, which to others would seem foolish. And yet it was the spark that fired him each day, that gave him the will to go on. Today, tomorrow, and...

The early mist was still hanging under the trees and, reluctant to give it up just yet, Thomas stepped down onto the sands and walked over to the rock where he and Will had found Callaghan that day. Poor Callaghan whose story and song had miraculously translated him from monster into man, into suffering mankind in its myriad manifestations; just one more example, if an especially poignant one, of the peculiar oppression the English and their Irish landowning friends visited on his fellow countrymen.

Thomas shook his head in disgust. And in the next moment – appropriately, he felt – he remembered Burke.

What was it about Burke's language that stuck in his gullet? It was years since he had read the book, but from what he remembered it had been, above all else, his epithets, his terms of comparison: he might check back, perhaps, in Will's copy. But yes, all was reduced to... pounds, shillings and pence, to 'banks' and 'capital', to 'contracts' and 'partnerships'... whatever the subject! To Burke, the State was nothing but a huge marketplace, and it mattered not that it was the lives of countless millions that were sold in it – the Callaghans of this world!

But Edmund Burke had picked up his pen too soon, hadn't he? Exposing the poverty of all the theorists, revolutionaries, and reactionaries alike! And in a way Will was right. Theories expressed hopes – often in the form of certainties – and bred expectations far beyond the capabilities of mankind to deliver. Wasn't the French

Revolution demonstration enough of that? Within a couple of years of the business at the Bastille, revolutionary faction was murdering revolutionary faction in very un-idealistic ways! And a mere ten years after that, having butchered the royal family and eradicated much of the old nobility, they went and set up a super-king, the Emperor Napoleon! Then ten years after him, both 'revolution' and 'Empire' were gone, and the Old Regime was back in harness... So what had it all been for?

And the whole plot was still bubbling away, wasn't it! For what were the great upheavals of not two years back... in France, in the Italian Peninsula, in Hungary, in Germany, and elsewhere... if not aspirations fired by the meagre success of those original revolutionary ideals?

And now, here in Queensland...? Could this new, southern continent fare any better?

The sea crashed and roared, the sunlight refracted into myriad flashes and bars of gold in the consequent spray, and the glare continually transmuted whatever one's eyes lighted on into forms and colours that made their mundane realities often impossible to guess at. The sand was brilliant white and seemingly endless, and the swampland, beyond the dunes, maintained a constant presence, announced occasionally by birds not seen in the drier parts of the island – the kites he had known in India, swooping out of the swampland and over the shore, and even larger, wedge-tailed birds of prey, which must be some sort of eagle.

Initially in profusion, then sporadically as he progressed, Will came across what seemed to be meticulously formed heaps of seashells, such as he remembered having seen – then too, to his surprise – during his last visit to Amity Point. And perhaps they did testify to the nearness of the Aborigines, as Ridley had suggested; though some of them were so overgrown they had to be years old, and he made a mental note to ask Tompani about them... should he have the good fortune to meet him again.

During his ride down the length of the island beach, Alice was never far from Will's mind. Alice nursing Lilian. Alice combing her long brown hair by candlelight before jumping, shivering, into bed beside him. Alice in that pale blue Sunday dress he had always loved... Did she still have it? Wear it? And maybe also remember their intimate times together, whenever she did?

The child, Billy, occupied his thoughts too. And once again he became deeply aware of the conflict that must necessarily exist between his commitment to the boy, in its immediacy, and that to Alice and his daughter, in its remoteness. Reluctantly, and with a heavy sigh, he acknowledged that 'immediacy' and 'remoteness' were simply an ordering of priorities, whatever his conviction or desire in the matter.

He had set himself a limit of seven years' stay in this continent, hadn't he? – the time the law prescribed for the annulment of a marriage in the event of there being no contact between the two parties involved....

Although by no means the only reason for Will's migration so far across the world, it had been the most significant. Nancy had vanished from his life; yet had he stayed, she could always choose to reappear before him, thereby cancelling out whatever time had accrued towards his eventual 'release.'

Seven years. In seven years, Billy would be... thirteen. He could not suddenly be abandoned and left to fend for himself. Nor could he be left solely in Thomas's care... always assuming that Thomas himself stayed.

Will stopped and looked about him. The fold of dunes seemed suddenly to be extending, their height increasing the further south his eye traversed. The swamps were fully hidden now, or maybe they had even petered out; he would check by and by.

But no, for a thirteen-year-old boy, the disruption would be far too severe, its effects impossible to predict... Seven years! Such time seemed endless; how on earth would...

Will swivelled his eyes seaward, fixing a spot far out, trying to determine whether it was anything more than the movement of waves on water. The glare dazzled and danced, misting his vision, and he closed his eyes against the ensuing dizziness, before urging Bluebell on.

And the alternative solution? Uprooting the child from this land, and whatever life they might then be living, might be equally destructive – the more so since it would drag the boy towards an uncertain future in an alien land, however it turned out for himself. And Alice…? Even if she were disposed to reconciliation, he couldn't expect her to welcome into her home a boy of thirteen she knew nothing about, in whose upbringing she had played no part, and whose whole life had been as remote from her as Australia itself… How could she relate to him? There was also, of course, the not unnatural fear she might entertain (given his original sin) of just whose child she was accepting, regardless of whatever assurances he might give her…

But he was being over-dramatic: the boy's age meant the question should never arise. Yet that it had, was symptomatic of the chaotic state of his mind whenever these matters drifted into it, and he sought to settle them.

Will dismounted to stretch his legs for a while and give Bluebell a rest. Ahead, at the ever-changing extremity of the tide line, were a small number of birds pecking furiously at the sand, looking, and behaving very much like the oyster catchers they had seen on Cumbrian beaches… As he approached, they flew off to a safer distance and began their foraging all over again.

Watching them, his spirits lifted a little. Unless Alice had changed in her character so much as to be unrecognisable to him, her natural disposition would be towards understanding and an active charity. And surely – please God, he willed – she would make the effort to overcome any difficulties that stood between them… if indeed they ever came as far as that moment of discussing future possibilities… And Billy were amenable…

And what of Lilian? In seven years' time she would be approaching thirteen herself. By that time, a little lady. Will smiled at the thought, striving for an image of her then – her brown curls, that resolute chin, still wilful, no doubt. Could she cope with the return of a by then, long-forgotten father with a… with something like a brother in tow, a boy who might well be resenting the fact of his own uprooting, and feeling all the apprehension that a new life must hold for him? Would she be prepared to welcome these… strangers, especially in view of her mother's likely tension? There might be scenes, and tears, and… The more Will considered, the more it all seemed like a recipe for disaster – for all of them… Or was he being just too pessimistic? Instead, they might just be shy, and willing to try, to forge something together…It might be what they both most wanted: a proper family…

And yet still, there was Billy…

Will led Bluebell to the water's edge, where he stood and marvelled at the hushed rustle and murmur of the rippling waters, the westering sun's slanting rays glistening silver almost to the horizon. Yet the calm, he knew, belied the monstrous power of this endless ocean and even in his delight he found himself backing away, pulling the horse after him, to resume his journey, and this persistent, tormenting train of thought.

No, labouring seven years for his 'Rachel' might well have been possible, without Billy. And Thomas was right – damn the man! Seven years was too long a time, and if he were looking to start again with Alice, it would have to begin sooner rather than later… and without the child. Yet Will was bound to the boy, he knew it now, and would do anything rather than abandon him. Could Mary help, he wondered? Perhaps he could write again to her, and explain this new complication and ask her to make tentative, tactful enquiries of Alice…

It was a solution of sorts. But Will dismissed the idea almost as soon as it came into his head: it would further burden his poor sister; and it would only look like cowardice to Alice; but most of all, as he dreaded the possible finality of Alice's reply.

These seas, these shores, these lapping waters, the white sands, the silence, the sun-haze, wave-mist, imaging aeons of time here – past, present and, yes, the uncertain future too.

Will had experienced with Alice, he suspected, the nearest one could come to perfection on this Earth, and now, at a distance of twelve thousand miles or more, he found himself in this new Earthly Paradise without her. Without her. The irony of it was unbearable. But why not a future here? What was there to hold it back, what that really mattered?

Will paused to scan the furthest horizon, as if he might find an answer there to these questions that plagued him endlessly. What was it, if not hurt and hurt pride, a sense of deep wrong – his folly, that first disobedience to truth and trust – that had cast them out into a wasteland? Yet these were, in the main, themselves simply effects become causes. For behind them, a towering iron barrier loomed always: the law, both moral and civil, and customs that had evolved over many centuries, the very soil out of which both he and Alice had grown and then, unquestioningly, grown into. But what he now knew – because of where he was and of what he had newly experienced, and that Alice could have no inkling of – was that even those cyclopean walls could be thrown down, or by-passed, to reveal the possibility of a new beginning… not just for them but for any who cared to make the hazardous journey. It was something akin to what the churches called grace, the freely given opportunity resolved here, now, into this place, to live wholly in a world of time that stretched away, like this white beach, like this ocean, beyond the moment; a life to resign the old life for.

Yet all of it, balanced on a knife-edge. For it was nothing if Alice and Lilian did not enter into it.

A half hour or so after Will had resumed his trek down the long beach towards Jumpinpin, the reputedly sandy isthmus that led to the southern part of the island, he guided Bluebell off to the right through a gap in the dunes, in search of water for her, while also looking for signs of Tompani and his family. The former they found almost at once in a spring that bubbled up out of a low dune and emptied, after only a few paces, into the swamp itself. Curious, Will dipped his finger into the water where the spring spilled out, and tasted it, cautiously. Brackish, a bit… sulphurous, but not too much.

'That should suit you Bluebell, old girl.' Set free, the horse bent her head and seemed to relish the water right enough. But as for the Aborigines, nothing. Not a trace. Maybe they had indeed gone off to one of the neighbouring islands.

The going was easy now, and he rode at a leisurely pace, noticing the sun moving steadily down the sky towards the west, and realising that somewhere along the way he had quite unconsciously taken the decision not to return to Dunwich. Not until the following day at least. It would give him time... time, though a different sort of time, for sure, from that of the time of separation.

If what the two doctors were all but predicting was true, Will's time on Stradbroke, was growing short. And when that hour was called, he would depart with the rest, having, like them, no say in the matter. He would leave, and not return: the island's dedicated function as a quarantine station precluded that possibility, clearly.

Yet Will was in no hurry to leave this island, this seemingly timeless place.

And the Aborigines, he wondered? Even though the quarantine colony was unlikely to extend this far, to this remoter side of the island, they too might be forbidden access, at some point. And he wondered, vaguely, whether Tompani and his people were aware of this.

He also wondered whether anyone else felt as he did. Was anyone else in this state, not really wishing to move on, despite all the suffering and the sorrow the pestilence had brought? Thomas, he knew, was eager to 'start afresh', while for him, the thought of quitting Stradbroke felt like... like erecting yet another invisible barrier between himself and Alice and his child. Silly, really, finding the thought of another 'moving on' depressing, for wasn't it also a 'moving nearer'?

Quite suddenly, the character of the terrain seemed to alter. The swamp was replaced by low scrubland which, in turn, gave way to more sand over to his right. A little further forward and Will realised he had achieved his goal or, at least, the first part of it: the narrow, sandy isthmus.

Calmly, he surveyed the scene around him. It reminded him, at first, of the long sand-spit at Amity, but only for a moment. For this place, being more exposed to the open ocean, was much wilder, and in one or two places, not too far ahead, shallow streams ran through it, from the seaward to the western side. In high seas and violent storms, did the isthmus become impassable, he wondered, effectively cutting the island in two? As it was, even on this balmiest of days, a salt-spray mist hung over the eastern side of it. Turning his gaze southward, beyond the isthmus, his attention was arrested by a distant view of… he couldn't really be sure what, for the sunlight was refracted through the spray, but was momentarily much brighter over that far off vista, like looking into a brightly lit room from darkness outside… way beyond the island, he surmised. Then a cloud seemed to blot out the sun, but it had been a… vision, a view of…? They seemed like giant towers; strange, elongated shapes touching the sky… A trick of the light, he decided, yet strange beyond comprehension.

Ahead of him, at the other end of the sand bar, he could see the beginnings of vegetation once more, though noticeably sparser than on this side. There were the inevitable mangroves to the west but nothing like the profusion of trees, especially tall trees, he had been expecting. The backdrop was hazy mountains, far away, on the mainland. The seaward side was largely composed of dunes and grasses as far as he could see, so he opted to go no further but to make his camp for the night where he was, on this northern side of the isthmus.

Will set about unloading the horse, freeing her of saddle and harness. But by the time he had pitched his tent and collected enough brushwood to maintain a fire for an hour or two, darkness had all but fallen, and he decided against tethering her for the night, thinking it unlikely she would wander far. Settling into the circle of flickering light his fire cast absorbed him a while; and each time it flared, he would catch its gleaming reflection on the horse's hide and be reassured by her good sense. And eventually Bluebell lay down on the sand not a dozen yards outside the circle.

As he ate the bacon and beans, he had slowly reheated, Will

stared out into the impenetrable blackness all about him, its intensity alleviated only by the star-spangled heavens above him and – surprisingly, he thought – the caress of the unseen waves less than a hundred yards away, gentled to a peaceful murmur; and it was somehow fitting that it should be so.

He crawled into his tent. And as he recalled the different sights and sounds of his day, he wondered again about Tompani, about his people and how they lived… and slept; and he realised that this total peace, which in these moments seemed so entirely to possess him, was what surely awaited them at the end and the beginning of their every day.

And, agreeably lost in these speculative thoughts, Will drifted into sleep.

LXXIV

Something had touched his foot.

Will jerked bolt upright out of sleep, victim of that primeval fear he thought he had understood, and even exorcised only the day before, when exploring the gully. His fear, however, soon turned to laughter: the towering Bluebell had thrust her huge head through the tent flap and was nudging him into wakefulness. 'So you've decided we should be moving, have you?' He leaned forward to stroke her muzzle, affectionately. 'But… what's the hurry? There's no time here.' And yet, for all that, he bent sideways, took hold of his boots, and pulled them on.

Shuffling out of the tent and climbing to his feet, sleep clinging to him still and weighing on his every action, Will began to look about him, to get the feel of the day.

A strong breeze was coming in off the sea again, and the breakers rolled off their white-crested peaks to sweep high up onto the beach. Slowly, he turned his head to survey the whole scene about him, and a clump of yellow flowers caught his eye, tossing their heads, waltzing, it seemed, in time to the music of the breeze, not a dozen paces from him, over to his left; flowers – he was sure – that had not been there the night before. He marvelled at their delicacy and their resilience, riding the breeze. Then he looked towards the sea once more, at its peerless turquoise becoming pearl then frothy white close in, its indigo depths not far out. A sea he never tired of watching. It drew him, dazzled him, amazed him. Its awful rhythms, its murmurs and its furies held him spellbound, its all-transcending presence.

It was still quite early, just after eight when he checked his chronometer, but the sun was already pushing up into a pale blue-and-white-streaked sky that had seemingly not yet decided how to dispose of the day.

Bluebell whinnied, and Will turned to see her ambling off along the beach, her head lolling from side to side, as if, he thought, amused, quite out of patience with him. 'Hey, Bluebell!' he shouted. 'Haven't you forgotten something?' And, dashing after her, he turned her back, to straps and harness and panniers. 'Oh surely, you didn't expect me to carry all this, did you?' he tutted, tethering her loosely to the nearest bush. 'But a man has to eat! 'I shan't be long...'

He folded his blankets and dismantled the tent before setting about relighting the fire to boil his tea and fry a little more of the salt bacon. Busying himself, he noticed that the breeze had strengthened to a wind; it picked up some of the dry sand and whirled it about, before depositing it along the mounds that fringed the southern and eastern edges of the swampland and the more distant forest.

'Let's hope we're not in for a storm, old girl,' he said earnestly. 'That would be an inconvenience, to say the least. It would put paid to any ideas we might have of going further south.' But Bluebell, he now saw, had broken free and wandered a little further off, most likely searching for something edible; an awareness that caused him a pang of guilt as he slowly sliced the bacon and put it into his mouth.

It was while thus occupied that he first heard it. A low, intermittent droning that might well have been a trick of the strengthening wind in the trees. And for a while, after his initial awareness of it, he let it drift out of his consciousness, for his thoughts had returned to yesterday's preoccupations about the future and who would share it with him, and where. Every now and again, however, he sensed the sound's continuing presence: sensed rather than heard it; it was at the edge of consciousness, coming in and drifting away, according to the wind's whim or mood.

There came a moment, however, when it forced all else aside. The sea-wind had dropped below a whisper, in odd moments missing a breath altogether, but the droning sound was still there, its tempo subtly changing even as he listened for it. And he realised it was unlikely to be a sound devised by nature alone. Yet, even as he came to this conclusion, he remembered the blowhole, and for a little longer still, held back his judgement. But the sound persisted, and after turning first this way, then that, he surmised it was coming from the north rather than from the south. If it were not some trick of nature then, he reasoned, it must signify the presence, not too far off, of some of the native peoples. Storm or no storm – though the sky now seemed to suggest that that possibility had receded, at least for the time being – he would go and seek them out... if they would be found.

With his fire smothered in sand and his cooking utensils washed at the water's edge and put away in the saddle bag, the bag and harness once again in place, Will took hold of the horse's reins. But then, deciding to walk, he let go of them. And the two of them strolled at an unhurried pace northward along the blinding-white strand.

The wind had once more hushed to a listless breeze, and a calm settled over the water, much as he had witnessed it on the previous day.

As they progressed, the droning sound increased in volume until, he judged, its source lay not too far to his left. Will searched for a break in the dunes. But when he found one, he discovered, to his consternation, that it led him straight into the southern-most extremity of the swamp, and he had to retreat at once, not trusting its inky blackness. They proceeded another mile or so along the shore before another such opportunity presented itself.

Here, the ground was firmer, the water being now some twenty or so yards beyond the dunes and the perimeter hedge of bush and thorn; indeed, though he judged it to be the same sheet of water he had earlier almost plunged into, he realised that they were now not too far from its northern end and that the more or less dry ground around it should serve as a path to its landward side. Before mounting the horse, he listened again to check on the direction the sound was coming from.

It had stopped.

He waited five long minutes, before it resumed. Then taking a bearing on it, he stepped up into the saddle and set off around the swamp-water lake. A moment later, a huge lizard dashed away into the undergrowth from the rock where it had been basking in the sun. Startled by its movement, then its speed and its size, he reached for the rifle, and checked that it was loaded.

Passing round the end of this stretch of swamp he attempted to survey the possibilities on its further side. Once again, however, the vegetation was thick right down to the black water's edge and seemed to afford no passage. He rode on then into the trees, with the swamp to his left, and saw at once that movement was possible among them, the scrub being sparse over much of the area, owing, he surmised, to the almost impenetrable, overarching canopy of the treetops.

Will dismounted but held on to Bluebell's reins: the trees were too close together to allow her much room in which to manoeuvre, but he was afraid that if she were startled and panicked, she might injure herself badly seeking a way to escape.

Once more, he stopped and listened, but the sound now seemed to have ceased altogether. And so he set off towards what he judged to be its most likely location.

After passing under an arch of trees to enter a wide clearing, he remounted. But as he was making his way into the space, he sensed a sudden movement at the far side. Looking into the shadows cast by the gigantic trees at the farther edge of the sward, as if casually, his heart skipped a beat. There was a figure, standing there, seemingly watching him.

He tensed in the saddle, but then consciously steadied his breathing, before riding slowly forward. And as his eyes adjusted to the rush of sunlight in the clearing, he realised that the man's body was all but naked and was painted with curious designs in which the predominant colour was a dull yellow.

Feeling he had come far enough, Will jerked on the horse's bridle, stopping her abruptly. And he sat waiting to see what the other would do. After what seemed like forever, and with mounting unease, bordering on fear – if swiftly controlled – he saw that the watching figure had been joined by another. Then a third man appeared between them. And all the while, hearing no sounds of movement, he wondered if all three had been there all the time, only now becoming visible as his eyes finally adjusted to the light. And while telling himself there was nothing to fear, that these might even be Tompani's people, he found himself pulling Ridley's rifle from its holster to then lay it across the saddle, his finger on the trigger.

Yet more painted savages began to emerge everywhere within his field of vision, and Will started to back the horse away in readiness for turning and a dignified but rapid retreat. But as he did so he discovered that the menacing figures were also behind him and that he was, effectively, surrounded.

Slowly the men advanced towards him. But surely… surely, they wouldn't…?

And now he panicked. Gripping the horse's flanks with his knees, he brought the rifle up to his shoulder and levelled it, focusing on the nearest savage.

All movement towards him ceased instantly: evidently, they knew what his action signified. And his mind raced to find a solution that might yet injure no one. He could shoot up into the air. Or spur his horse round suddenly, and break through the tightening cordon, back to the seashore…

He blinked and looked again at the man on whom the rifle was trained, noting now that his arms hung at his sides, inert; and this small shift in Will's perception prompted him to move his eyes from that one to another, then to scan the whole group. Not a single one of them was carrying a weapon of any sort. Yet the sense of menace persisted; they had stopped, but none had retreated.

Hardly daring to move, though aware he must, Will held the man in his sights and slowly, laboriously, began manoeuvring Bluebell round, ready to bound away at the slightest movement.

Suddenly, a cry from behind him made him twist round in the saddle… to see one of the yellow-painted savages moving rapidly towards him. His heart pounding, he swung the rifle round and pointed it at the man's chest, his finger on the trigger.

'Not shoot! Not shoot…!'

Will's mind had been in utter turmoil, but now a torrent of relief, then shame, washed over him, like a deluged river in full spate.

'Not shoot, Mr Will…!'

Tears pricked his eyes, and, thrusting the rifle decisively back into its holster, he leapt from the saddle, and troubling to maintain neither self-composure nor dignity, he hurried towards his deliverer with arms outstretched… and a flurry of words spilling from his mouth.

'Tompani! I am so happy to find you! For it was to see you again that I made this journey, and I was hoping… and I hadn't seen you… And…But I had no idea how… how… crucial it would be, finding you, when I finally did…! What was that sound, that… buzzing sound I heard, like… like bees?'

And he laughed, almost crying, at the strangeness of it all – the laughter of release.

It was difficult to gauge just how much Tompani comprehended, for the markings on his face rendered him not only unrecognisable but veiled all muscular inflections, and even the language of his eyes. Will's gushing confession was met initially by silence, perhaps a bewildered silence, before the painted face finally opened up into a wide grin. But then, immediately, the Aborigine's brow puckered.

'But where is Billy? Why he not here?' he asked, his voice registering disappointment, and perhaps displeasure.

Will explained Billy's absence as best he could, again not sure how much Tompani would understand even if he had the words. But Tompani answered him almost immediately.

'It good he plant flower when mother ask it. Long time, yet, before she go back to Dreaming.'

'Dreaming?' Will queried since Tompani's use of the word did not seem to reflect what he remembered from their first encounter.

'Where all spirit in end gather. But she not there for long time still if die after you come in this island.'

Will simply nodded, as if in agreement, for he had so many other questions to ask. 'So, if, as you…' But Tompani cut him short.

'You come today when our people here to send old dead man to Dreaming. Some my people much angry, you come. All right now because I say you friend.'

Will smiled and nodded again. And, intending to make some acknowledgement of the others' presence, he looked around him. But they had all vanished as quickly and as silently as they had materialised out of the bush.

Tompani smiled his broad smile, then explained. 'They go back… to *corroboree*, Will; put dead man in tree, so he begin first part journey. Then dance again and sing again so *mokuy* spirit go 'way and *birrimbirr* spirit can start long journey back.'

At this explanation, which was for Will no explanation at all, he could only shrug his shoulders in ignorance.

Tompani grinned. 'Come,' he said. 'Better you see.'

As they moved across the clearing, the droning sound that had led Will there started up again, accompanied by a rhythmic tapping. But before he could ask about it, Tompani said: '*Didgeridoo* and *bilma* stick. Yes. Nunukul always play at important time.'

But despite Tompani's attempts at clarification, the questions, Will realised, were only piling higher. And perhaps they could never be answered adequately. Words perhaps might never suffice to bridge the chasms that plunged between their two ways of life.

Soon they came into another, smaller clearing, and Will saw at once that something was being hauled to a platform that had been constructed high up in a grey-barked eucalyptus, and that two of the painted tribesmen were there awaiting its arrival. Again, Tompani began to explain what was happening and why, something of which Will understood, though not all. Then these staccato words and occasional gestures were interrupted by the commencement of a slow, gyrating dance about the bole of the huge tree, and intermittent chanting of what appeared to be the same sounds made over and over again.

'Old man body stay in tree many moon, many many moon, then take down, clean bone and paint and put in *dupun* pole at Myora. Not forget dead man. We think him, always, on journey back to him other spirit in land of Dreaming.'

And still the chanting continued, though changing tempo, becoming somehow more aggressive in character. And the dancers began to jerk and grimace and to plunge painted, pointed sticks into the earth about the tree as they circled it. Some cried out from time to time, their voices echoing eerily, as the pace quickened.

'Here we... drive out evil *mokuy*. When he go, *birrimbirr* go free through tree and water and stone, all thing, in our land. Him touch all last time. But come, we must get boomerang for Billy.' And Tompani led Will, yet again, out of the clearing and further into the bush beyond.

At length they came to a place where there were several women sitting in a group, on the ground. And Will realised, only then, that he had seen none participating in the funeral rite back in the clearing. Tompani behaved as though the women were invisible, speaking to none of them, looking at none of them. He strode across to a bush, and from a bag that was hanging there drew out a smallish boomerang which was decorated with bright colours and strange shapes and stylised animals.

It was an object of great beauty. Will ran his palm over its curving length and felt its smoothness. And he held it high, at arm's length, admiring above all its... balance, its... rightness in his hand.

Just then, a seated figure, propped up stiffly against a tree some distance away from the women, diverted his attention. He too was painted all over, though in bright colours, and with designs that, even at that distance, he could see were quite different from those worn by Tompani and the dancers. The figure did not move, did not even appear to be breathing, and Will wondered whether he too was dead and awaiting burial. He pointed to the man but did not know what to ask, becoming suddenly aware that his curiosity might well be seen as impertinence.

Tompani nodded, and whispered in a hoarse, almost cracked voice: 'Him karadji. Clever man. He go now in spirit world long way past star...'

'You mean he can travel great distances, and still be...?' But Will checked himself, realising an involuntary note of amused scepticism had crept into his question.

But Tompani simply nodded. 'Him go to long time past or long time come. Always like lightning.' And he made a swift, sharp movement, with his hands crossing in opposite directions.

Will waited for a moment or two, then began to ask some of the questions that had accumulated in his mind following their first meeting, a few of them linking, though, with things Tompani was telling him now.

'What is this other world the old man goes to? Does your "clever man" go there too, even before he dies? What is that world's connection with this earth here that seems so important to you…? And the 'Dreaming'…? I know you explained before, but…'

Patiently, within the limits of his means, Tompani made his explanations. And as Will's knowledge grew – not so much in the detail as in the deeper significances the detail encompassed – he gradually became aware that his first impressions of this radically different kind of vision of the world and its meanings had not been so wide of the mark. The few words they shared were proving splendidly sufficient, after all.

Keeping his eyes fixed on his host's face, Will slowly lowered himself to the ground and with a movement of his hand suggested Tompani might do the same. And as he did so, Will allowed his gaze to travel swiftly round, taking in the karadji, the silent women, the boomerang in his hands, the intricately painted, naked figure before him. And he marvelled, feeling himself to be on the threshold of a new, different world. And yet, there was Bluebell, at the edge of the clearing, cropping the grass, as though she had always been here.

LXXV

On the other side of the island, at about the same time as Will and Tompani were engaged in that conversation, Father Thomas had walked in at the hospital tent, ostensibly to see whether a mug of tea might be had, if the young matron was not too busy to make it. And she had obliged, so that now the two of them sat facing each other across the long trestle table.

'Well, Miss Labone,' Thomas said, treading warily, 'your tireless efforts… remarkable! You may be lacking in years, yet you are clearly not wanting in good sense or practical knowledge.'

The young woman lowered her head, modestly, and the priest saw that his earnest compliment had caused her to blush, though he affected not to notice.

'It is kind of you… Father Thomas… to say such things, though I confess I do not feel they are warranted, myself. I have made many mistakes, even if none but I have been aware of them…'

'Ah, my dear, error is a common enough failing among us mortals: none knows that more than I, I do assure you. But recognition of that fact is a first step towards redress, is it not…? Though in your case… I am sure you worry unnecessarily. And additional to all that… your tea-making is especially to be appreciated…' And he smiled, for his compliment was genuine enough.

Laughing now, the matron looked up at him. 'You are very… kind… with your blarney,' she said, but she was suddenly looking serious again. 'And just how kind, I did not realise… for quite some time after we came to this island…' And she reached out, and laid her hand gently upon Thomas's own, which had just then strayed away from his empty mug.

Somewhat startled, Thomas looked down at the long, delicate fingers that lay so lightly, barely registering their presence upon the back of his hand, and he struggled to find words. It was... it was as if... some invisible line, whose existence he had not even been aware of, had suddenly been crossed. In that moment, however, the tent flap was suddenly thrown back and in rushed Billy, who threw himself down on the same bench as the matron, sighing noisily.

Since the sigh was not followed by any explanation, Thomas leant forward, and raising his eyebrows, looked intently into Billy's eyes. 'So what is it that can squeeze such a huge sigh out of a not very big body, Billy?'

'I'm bored, Father Thomas! I've finished off doing my mammy's garden... again, and I've read that same old book... again! And I can't find anyone to play with. When will Mr Crosby be back, do you think?' And the child looked from one to the other of them, hoping for an answer.

Only now did Miss Labone slowly withdraw her hand.

'Well, Billy, we can't be certain...' she answered. 'But...'

'Will you play with me, then, Miss Labone?' And as if the request had already been granted, Billy jumped up and performed a little jig for her. 'But... when will he? When will he be back?'

'Possibly later today, Billy... though it might not be till tomorrow... So why don't we...?'

'Not *another* day...! Oh, I just hope he hasn't got himself lost... I really should have gone with him...' Billy confided, a look of genuine guilt settling into his small face. He sighed heavily, again, then leapt to his feet and ran out of the tent as suddenly as he had come.

The Matron and the priest exchanged amused smiles. 'Ah, that boy, he is nivver still a moment!' said Thomas, and his smile seemed to turn inwards. The young woman rose to her feet. 'I'll just fetch some more hot water and see if we can revive what's still left in the pot.'

As the morning slowly wore on, Tompani's world flooded out all around him, and Will gradually became aware that a gap was beginning to open up between himself and beliefs or values he had till now never thought to question.

'Whitefella only take from earth, not give, not know earth…

Whitefella live too many one place; fight earth, forget earth…

Blackfella all life together with earth till through earth go back in sky.'

With these closing statements, Tompani had summarised the ways in which his people most diverged from the untenable ways of the Europeans.

'My people talk with earth, sing to earth, listen to earth and earth tell them many important thing you Whitefella not know…'

'Come, I tell you.' And Tompani led Will along a twisting track, away from the clearing.

The white people Tompani had known for a time at Amity, and on Moreton Island (further confirmed by his one visit to Brisbane), were sick at heart because they had come adrift from all the subtleties and modulations that life in harmony with the land afforded – or so Will interpreted his words. They worried about the future, about the past, about themselves, and found refuge from uncertainty in the most ridiculous ways, automatically – or was it instinctively? – opposing anyone or anything manifestly different, failing to understand because unwilling to understand; laying claim to things they had no affinity with, to exploit until utterly exhausted, to then be discarded. For Tompani, the ever-increasing mountain of stinking 'waste', just outside Brisbane, was proof enough of the sad plight of the Whitefella; and as the mountain grew so the Whitefella's problems would grow.

Conflict with the earth, it seemed, ensured that all else turned, sooner or later, to conflict with all else.

From an upstairs window, that same morning – ten or so hours later than in Will's world – Alice Fallowfield stood watching her little daughter and Winnie, a new-found friend, playing together down in the wide back yard at Ghyll Mont.

What a rapid transformation had come over the little girl in the few days since they had moved to their new situation. But it didn't surprise her really, for she too had almost immediately felt a new sense of purpose, largely as a result of Granny Abbot's many kindnesses and genuine gratitude for even the smallest endeavour, and of her own returning self-esteem. Cautiously, she found herself thinking that this could well be the start of a new life for her and her little daughter.

Yet even as she thought it, her eyes would fill with tears. It was not a new life she wanted was it? It was her old life back again, her re-entry into the... rose garden. 'Stop it!' she commanded now and turned back to stripping the beds in readiness for the wash.

It turned out to be a circular route, and before long they were back at the clearing, with Will still undecided about whether or not, before another night fell, he should set off back to the station at Dunwich. The *karadji*, now seemingly returned from his travels among the stars, came forward to address Tompani.

Will had known of other shamans who made equally preposterous claims during his time in India, and had always thought of them as charlatans, and the people whose minds they apparently controlled as gullible children. While appreciating more and more the good sense of what Tompani told him about his people's way of life, he none the less remained sceptical about its spiritual aspects – how could he not? – although he did not say so in so many words. It had not escaped his notice that Tompani, a man so hugely imbued with common sense, spoke of those spiritual matters in the same, matter-of-fact tones as he did about the more tangible, everyday features of their lives, treating them as merely different facets of the same united whole, and this, frankly, surprised him. Was he simply paying lip service to the beliefs of the ignorant? Or, like a good teacher, laying out the whole case as dispassionately as he was able, leaving himself quite outside his words? Will really could not make up his mind at all on this point, waiting for the conversation between his friend and the *karadji* to end.

After Tompani had explained to the *karadji* who Will was – or, at least, that is what Will presumed he was doing – the man nodded, then turned to Will and spoke two or three words to him, perhaps in greeting. And then he held him fixed with his deep, penetrating gaze, and Will felt he could not avert his own eyes without seeming discourteous. As the moment lengthened so too did his bewilderment, but then thankfully, Tompani intervened.

'*Karadji* want to know what this deep trouble you fight with inside you. If you wish, you say him.'

With the sudden shock of it, followed at once by a rush of northern English pride, his first thought was to deny any problem, or state that these were personal matters and not for public discussion. But he was drawn back to the *karadji*'s eyes, and this upsurge of truculence melted away as quickly as it had come upon him. He turned towards Tompani.

'Ask him how he knows I have a... deep trouble.'

Tompani spoke, then listened to the *karadji*'s reply. The answer was short and Tompani translated at once: 'He say your body all speak it, it feel fear, smell fear.'

Taken off-guard, but also unaccountably submissive to this painted, grotesque-looking priest – for that was surely what he was – of a primitive race far behind his own in its mastery of... of... but even as the thought was forming in his mind, he rejected it. How could he not? Hadn't he been courting doubt about 'modernity' in seeking out new certainties? It seemed also that this man, in his tribal functions, was regarded by his people as a key figure in the substance of those certainties, repository of an ancient wisdom that for them, at least, had never lost its relevance. Why should 'primitive' always be negative, especially when it came to questions of truth...?

As simply as he could Will explained the dilemma upon which his life had foundered. Nancy. Alice. Lilian. And now, Billy.

How well Tompani conveyed it he had no way of knowing.

With a casual gesture, the *karadji* summoned them over towards one of the fires that had been lit even as they were speaking and invited Will to sit. He too sat down facing Will and took something from the bag he carried over his shoulder. He turned to Tompani, who had first crouched, then sat a little to one side, and spoke again. Will was instructed to focus on the object the man would hold before his eyes and not to allow himself to be distracted from it.

Will signalled his agreement, but even as he did so, could not believe how easily he had acquiesced – the irony of it; was this not some sort of séance, such as he would have rejected out of hand back home? – yet he was too curious to pull back. He fixed his eyes on what appeared to be a white stone, which glinted fiercely in the glow and growing heat and dance of the flames, and from one moment to the next felt himself whirling away into a radiance that was so intense it seemed to absorb him entirely…

This was no faint, but it was a condition Will had never known before, in which his senses were so sharp, so engaged, that his perception seemed to penetrate to the very centre of things that came into his mind, whatever they were.

And strangely, when it was all over, he would remember every little detail of the 'journey' in all its varying facets.

Whatever it is the *karadji* is dangling before his eyes fractures into innumerable slivers of light that dart away from each other at a prodigious rate. But then, just as suddenly and as swiftly, they slide back towards some invisible centre, aligning themselves in circles of light around it, rank upon rank, stretching away towards a shimmering horizon of blinding light.

And all the while, he is conscious… entirely conscious of slipping away into an alien dimension.

Fragmented images begin to flash by, too quickly to gather them in, though fleetingly recognised, they slow gradually, everything slows until he is standing on a darkened street, before a window, gazing in. And there she is. Alice.

A door opens. And Lilian comes in, serious-looking, and taller, yes.

And there is an old lady dressed in black, seated regally in a chintz-covered, high-backed chair... a lorgnette held regally, almost, between finger and thumb. And smiling, Alice and Lilian approach her. The old lady reaches out a hand and Lilian takes it.

And now... he is on a country road looking into a sunlit garden with a gushing beck speeding through it down towards... yes, a lake, which shimmers and sparkles, and between the garden and the lake a steam train, billowing smoke, panting slowly past. And...

And he is spinning away, again.

The same place but it is autumn, now. He has passed through the same garden gate, his eyes fixed on a young man bearing a huge wicker basket full of bread. There are two adjacent cottages and the door of the nearer one stands open, and suddenly, there is Alice, beckoning the bread-man in. He sets the heavy basket down upon a table just visible through the open door and Alice is smiling, speaking to him, and now slowly closing the door behind her, pushing it with her back until the latch snaps shut. Alice, closing her eyes, sensing the air, and waiting. The man approaches her, takes her breasts in his hands, and kneads them, gently at first, then unable to contain his lust so plainly fed by hers, he lifts her skirts. And Alice...

He feels dizzy... And yet again, a momentary shifting of the light crystals, and there is a new Alice, lying naked in a large bed, watching a tall, thinnish man, slowly removing his clothes before climbing in beside her.

LXXVI

A humming sound – intense, insistent – wakes him. A glaring brightness. Blinding. To escape it he sits bolt upright, his hands instinctively covering his still closed eyes. And when, at last, he ventures to open them a fraction, he realises it is the light of the sun cascading down through a gap in the tree canopy. Some way off, to his left, he sees women and children; to his right, sitting on the ground not many yards away, Tompani and the *karadji*, watching him intently.

And then he remembers the scenes he has witnessed and is plunged into abject despair.

Tompani rose and came towards him, offering a gourd full of water. '*Karadji* say what you see not happen yet.'

Will looked at him, confused.

'Happen sometime... *karadji* say... Can change. All... still...'

The *karadji*, still seated on the ground, explained through Tompani that if left, then before long each crystal light would reattach itself to the whole and possibility would become reality.

Could this be true? Could he really be the sole agent of his own destiny? And what of Alice's and Lilian's? And Billy's... his too? Where all had been in turmoil, Will now had a sense of... not exactly peace, for the powerful images had been all too real, but of anxiety lessened... lessening. Just a dream, superstition, everyone would say.

But dream it was not. Its sequences were too real, its locations so believable in their ordinary detail.

Will made the return journey to Dunwich later that same afternoon, a sense of optimism beginning to form within him.

For much of the time, he was unaware of the terrain he passed through, that same terrain he had lately imagined as the Earthly Paradise. The *karadji*'s visions had brought him no comfort, and he could not say what hope they could offer to his foundered life. Yet a feeling of inner strength, a gathering sense of resolution persisted.

The substance of those visions, however, troubled him deeply, for they revealed an Alice he didn't know.

Of course, he had no way of telling how much time must elapse before these visions were actualised... if there was any credibility in the *karadji*'s words. And Will was torn between the wish to doubt and the fear of believing. But if he must believe, then how to adjust to the shock of those revelations about Alice's life?

His first instinct was to back away from reason. And yet the guilt inherent in such a reaction was surely as much his as hers, since in his fancy, his... adoration, he had elevated her to the status of demi-goddess; not just as an object of veneration but of expectation, as one incapable of wrong judgements, or wrongdoing. In that, at least, the silent visions had served a purpose, bringing him – and her – back to earth, and a reality he had never really accorded her.

These were sobering thoughts, indeed. And now his accustomed sense of guilt and awe in her imagined presence must give way to a compassion she was as much in need of, and entitled to, as he: something she had flatly denied *him*. And yet, in the future, if Alice ever relented, it would surely be *her* need for such compassion that prompted her, this time. And if she decided to sunder the threadbare ties that had bound her to him, and embark on a new relationship, she would still be seeking compassion, from whoever it was. Perhaps love was also recognition of a profound, mutual need of pity.

Will slowed Bluebell to a walk, as these thoughts and conjectures filtered through his consciousness. And soon, something else was teasing out of those same visions, something of a different order: a vague sense of time's apportioning that he could not pin down in words. Maybe it had to do with the running of the hour and keeping pace, while knowing that Time allows us but little time to accomplish what our hearts are set on. And didn't it mean that a failure to act in a given small space, to grasp, to nullify time itself, could make an endless nonsense of all that followed?

Will thought back to the skittering blue crabs at Amity Point. In the running of the tide, one moment's hesitation brought their tiny lives to an absurd nemesis in the beak or jaws of a banal obliteration... He rode on, his mind picking its way through these thoughts as if through a swamp. This new, approaching tide could also, he realised, drown a man's dreams, and his reason for being. And so here, confusingly, was a new, acute anxiety. Ah, Machiavelli...!

When Will raised his head and looked about him there were tents, the drifting smoke of fires, and people, some he recognised, others not, going about their little lives in this still strange-seeming location. He smiled, realising that Bluebell, gentle mare that she was, had brought him safely home.

Yet even as he was leaning forward to pat and stroke her neck in gratitude, his attention was drawn by a crowd of people, splintering like a starburst, moving away – he realised – from the burial ground over to his right. Will's heart froze. He had been away for two whole days, time enough for any number of new calamities to have befallen the imprisoned community.

Concern for his fellows rushed in upon him: they too had already embraced so much grief and sorrow. And as he brought the horse to a halt, he peered anxiously, this way and that, at individual faces, as if to identify and reclaim for himself those who had become... part of him, over these past few weeks.

Only someone known to all could have drawn such numbers to a funeral. And Will's unconscious journey and its revelations were thrust further back in his mind as he recalled Thomas's account of Dr Mitchell's interment. Someone respected, revered...

He had already decided to stop the next person coming his way, to learn the worst, when he caught sight of the O'Rourke brothers, detaching themselves from the rapidly diminishing throng, and coming towards him. And, inexplicably, in this brittle moment, he found himself wondering yet again just why it was that John never addressed a word to him, his brother always accounting for the doings of both... Did he speak to others, perhaps? As they drew near him Will slid out of the saddle and took a step towards them, suddenly aware of his painful, stiffened limbs.

'A sad business, Mr Crosby, and no mistake. But – James O'Rourke frowned, in bewilderment – you were not at the funeral, I see. How is it that...?'

In desperate need of an answer to the one, overwhelming question, whose answer he was dreading, Will cut him short.

'No, James, I was not. But tell me... whose funeral have I missed? I arrived back not five minutes ago, from the far side of the island...' Anxiously, he scanned the middle distance. 'Please... Whose passing?'

And in that terrible, silent abyss between his own last words and his neighbour's next, Will found himself remembering the fire, and Billy, and hurriedly shuffling names and faces into a makeshift order of priority in his own love and esteem, as though by such mental conjuring, he could even now influence the terrible answer when it came.

'The other side of the island? Well, I never...' said the blacksmith, slowly. 'But why ever would you want...?' And he shook his head in plain disbelief. 'Irreparable is his loss. A thoroughly honourable man... 'Tis the good doctor. Dr Ballow that has been taken from us.'

'Dr Ballow? Dr Ballow! Dr B...' Stabbed to the quick, all Will could do was repeat the name over and over again.

'Aye, Mr Crosby. The very same as laboured tirelessly night and day for us all. May God rest his soul!' He turned then towards his brother who had stood all the while two or three paces behind him, to his right, as if to make sure he was still with him. Then he faced Will again. 'To us... Well, more rightly to John here, he was especially kind, for even with everything else he had to attend to for so many of our neighbours, he still found time to try and pry out the mystery of John's... lack of recall for things but lately happened...'

Will nodded, though his stunned mind was still taking in the sudden death of David Ballow.

'...an affliction he surely does not... And the deafness blighted him since... Oh, yes it has, right enough, ever since birth!' James tipped his hat, signalled to his brother, and moved past Will. But then he turned: 'The other side of the island, you say?'

Will smiled briefly but refused to be drawn further, his mind having become a battlefield, its assaults too pressing. Ballow and the mystery of his sudden death crowded out all else, yet the passing thought of his neighbour's enduring responsibility for his brother's well-being did not fail to register with him, nor the lightness of his own for young Billy, when set beside it.

Mechanically, almost, and certainly without concentration, Will began to remove the panniers and his bed roll from the horse, who stood un-tethered, quietly neighing, as he did so. Every few seconds he looked around him, hoping to find Thomas or...

And then, in the distance he caught sight of a small figure running and then bounding towards him, a happy, smiling face in a sea of misery.

'Oh, Mr Crosby, we have missed you so. Father Thomas and me. We have! We have!' said the child, breathlessly.

Will seized hold of the boy, crushed him momentarily against his own body, then just as suddenly released him. 'Billy, Billy! I'm sure you've grown at least another inch!'

'Have I really, Mr Crosby? Did you know that Mr Ballow has just gone into the ground, like my mammy did, and everybody's very sad? And Father Thomas says that when Mr Callaghan has finished putting all the soil back, I can make him a nice garden, just like my mammy's... You must see my mammy's garden, Mr Crosby, you really must, 'cause I've made it even better than before, with more flowers and a big stick I made. And I got Mr Jones to paint it for me like the ones we saw that day when we met Mr Twopenny, and... Did you find Mr Twopenny again? Did he...? Did he give you... anything for me? I 'spect he was quite upset when I wasn't...'

'Billy, slow down!'

The child took a side-skip round Will. 'Oh, hello Bluebell! I didn't see you there, hiding behind Mr Crosby. Did you have a nice trip too?' He patted the horse on her foreleg, and then straightened. 'Do you know what, Mr Crosby? I'm going to make a garden round Mrs Father Thomas's grave as well, but that's a secret. Do you think Father Thomas will like that?' The skipping stopped momentarily, and the child thrust a grimy hand into Will's. 'Do you think he will, Mr Crosby? *Do you?*'

Will's eyes were alight, as he followed Billy's every move, and endeavoured to keep up with his continually shifting soliloquy. 'Oh yes, Billy, I'm quite sure Father Thomas would be... so grateful to you, if you were to do that. Quite sure...'

The child's bursting energy, his endless reaching-out to embrace everything all at once, as if he feared some part of it could slip away before he claimed it, was working its magic yet again, lifting Will's flagging spirits. And thus prompted, he put his hand into the saddlebag on the horse's nearer flank, then slowly, like a magician, withdrew the object, which had been conveniently wrapped in palm leaves, and without a word, handed it to Billy.

The boy took it gently, reverently, peering inquiringly up into Will's face all the while. Then slowly and carefully, as if wanting to preserve perpetually the possibility of final delight, he peeled away the palm leaves until the boomerang was fully revealed in his hands. He stared at it, his face registering amazement, then the fleeting shadow of disbelief, then something like pride, by turns. 'Is it really for me, Mr Crosby?' he whispered, his eyes wide with wonder. 'Did Mr Twopenny make it... just for me?'

'I'm glad you like it, Billy, and I'm sure that Mr Tompani – who really is a very kind and thoughtful man – would be happy too. And yes, it is yours, Billy.'

Billy brought the precious object up to his lips then slowly, strangely, ran the length of its blade across them. Then he did the same across both his cheeks.

Equally strangely, however, Will felt he understood perfectly, the meaning of the child's action.

'To tell you the truth, though, Mr Tompani was a bit upset that you had not gone to receive it yourself. But when I explained what it was that kept you here, he understood, and he entirely agreed you had made the right decision, so...'

Restraint, Will knew well enough, was one of Billy's lesser talents. And yet he was still taken aback by the child's next words:

'Well, Mr Crosby, we could go tomorrow, and thank him, couldn't we? I think I could be free then, as I'm sure Mr Ballow won't mind waiting an extra day for his garden...' He sucked in his lips. 'You never know, Mr Crosby, he might even – and he grinned mischievously – be glad of the time to properly get to know the others who are in the ground, and to talk to my mammy, who is sure to remember him, and... Shall we be leaving, early, Mr Crosby? I don't mind getting up even early early, just for once. And I could...'

'Billy, Billy! Stop for just one moment, will you?' – Will remonstrated. 'For you have my head all in a whirl!' But then he could not hold back his laughter. 'We can't just go off like that!' he chuckled. 'For one thing, I've only just got back! And for another, Tompani and his people were... well, very much farther away than they were when we first saw them. And besides...'

The boy's face clouded. 'Oh, but Mr Crosby, isn't it bad manners if I don't...?'

'...Besides, Billy, he told me they will be moving on again soon, for they never stay in one place for long, you know... They are not like us; they don't have houses in fixed places and build all they need close about them. They go to the places where the things are that they need, but as there are many such places, they are never still for long... A bit like you, in fact, Billy,' he said, smiling.

But his reasons, of course, were making no impression at all on the child's drooping spirits... and shoulders.

'Anyway,' he hurried on, 'as soon as I've taken Bluebell back to Mr Ridley, I must find Father Thomas and Dr Mallon to see what has been happening here... I mean, what else has been happening, since I went away.' And he must also, he knew, pay his own last respects to Dr Ballow.

Billy stood there, twisting round, dismally, this way, then that, his frail form visibly sagging under this weight of words telling him 'why not.' And Will sought to make amends.

'Now, then, before dusk falls, would you like to ride Bluebell back down to Mr Ridley's place? Would you? Right now?'

Billy nodded, still sulking but raising his head just a little, and Will lifted him up into the saddle, and gave him the reins – not mounting himself.

'Hold on tight!' he said: 'Oh, and you'd better put your boomerang back in the saddlebag, until we get there. It will be safer, there.'

Billy nodded, sagely. 'Yes…you could be right, Mr Crosby.'

LXXVII

The ride down through the camp was rather less triumphal than Will had anticipated, and perhaps Billy had imagined. Only once did he have the opportunity to raise his hand in a studiedly casual, quite regal salute, to one of his friends. Yet, given the hour, all the others must already have been at supper, or in their tents, making ready for bed even, and so were quite oblivious of who was riding by.

Poor Billy. Will tousled the boy's hair as he lifted him down. Billy asked for his boomerang and ran off to show it to Mr Barney, while Will, aware still of his stiffness, handed over Bluebell to an unusually affable Ridley.

The two of them then walked back to their tent, hand in hand.

'Can we play with my boomerlang, now... on the seashore? I want to see it fly! And you have to show me how to do it, to make it come back! Pleeeease!'

The sun had now all but sunk below the horizon, and Will was on the point of explaining that it was too late, and besides, he was quite tired... And then he remembered that the tide would be turned and coming in fast by now. So he smiled, benignly and agreed they could 'for a little while,' not wanting to be the cause of yet further disappointment for the child.

They drew near the shoreline, and sure enough...

'Oh, just look at that sea, Mr Crosby!' Billy said crossly. 'It's coming all over our sand...'

'Oh! What a bother!' said Will, feigning his own disappointment in the same cross tone. 'I suppose we'll just have to be patient and wait until morning.' And he paused, mostly to repress a smile but also to impress upon the boy the decisiveness of the moment. 'Now, I really must find Father Thomas or Dr Mallon... So, you can either come with me, Billy, and show off Mr Tompani's present, or go and play by yourself, or read for a while... if it is still light enough at the tent.'

Billy decided quickly for the second option, saying he 'might just' go and see if he could find John, George, and Margaretta, to show them his special treasure – though Will cautioned they might already be on their way to bed. The boy was almost desperate in his desire to astound someone, Will recognised. 'Mr Barney' had not shown anything like enough enthusiasm when Billy had thrust the boomerang into his hands. And Will knew that Billy had understood well enough that adults in conversation were no fitting audience for something as important as a painted boomerang.

Thomas was standing with Dr Mallon, outside the hospital tent. They were deep in conversation, Thomas, gesticulating energetically, and looking decidedly relieved to see Will approach.

'Ah, safely back among us, at last, Will...! Though, as you will have learned – he put his hand affectionately on his friend's shoulder – it is to a greatly shocked and saddened community that you return.'

'So I realise.' Will smiled sadly. 'Tell me, what happened. Dr Ballow seemed hale and hearty enough, the evening before I set out... Patrick?'

'Oh, I hardly know what to tell you,' Mallon answered. 'I have never heard tell of, much less witnessed so sudden an onset. And then a decline so precipitate that in a matter only of hours it swept our dear friend away...' His voice was toneless, bleak. 'He went to his bed late, last night, complaining he felt out of sorts, but attributing it to nothing more than a long toil of a day.'

'But how then did you know...?'

'By the early hours he was in a raging fever; by dawn, he he'd fallen into a coma, and a little before midday, all was up with him.' Mallon explained, his lips pursed, the mask of grief.

'And you are certain it was the fever,' Will persisted, and not some other...?'

'Well, as he constantly reminded us,' Mallon said, slowly, 'and his passing so tragically demonstrates, we know nothing... nothing, about this terrible adversary we seek to quell... I was helpless,' he sighed, shaking his head. 'With all the medical training I had I was still helpless.'

'Patrick...' Thomas said quietly. 'Do not distress yourself, so. There is nothing you, or any of us, could have done.' He turned to Will. 'The real irony, Will, is that only yesterday morning, our two doctors declared it was now safe to petition the authorities in Brisbane for our release, since there had been no new outbreaks for over a week. And believe it or not, Dr Ballow sat down there and then to pen the letter – to be conveyed by the *Aurora*'s captain when the ketch returns tomorrow.' He looked at Will, disbelief still plainly written in his face. 'So convinced was David that the pestilence had left us for good and all that he suggested we try and lift everyone's spirits by announcing this *publicly*, telling everyone their long ordeal was at last over! Only the good sense and caution of Patrick, here, prevented him from doing so...' He sighed. 'Thank goodness, as it has turned out, that Patrick's view prevailed.'

'What a loss,' Will murmured, feeling he would regret, now, never really having got to know David Ballow. Of course, he had admired him, if at first grudgingly: his good sense, his modest yet firm mastery of situations as they arose. Yes, Ballow had had a quiet sort of conviction about him... a man with a calling. And now? Will shook his head, realising the bitter loss the doctor's passing meant for him personally, and for all. He looked up, beyond the tents, into the forest, and it flitted through his mind that the *karadji* might well have saved him...

'Well', he said, after a lengthening pause, 'I imagine we'll be heading to the mess tent, so I'll go and fetch Billy...'

'Ah,' Mallon sighed, 'but we are dining in the hospital tent, this evening, Mr Cros... Will, at Captain Kemp's request.'

'Indeed we are,' Thomas said grandly, mockingly. 'The captain and

his officers are to honour us lesser folk with their gracious presence...'
And he winked, exaggeratedly, at Will.

'Then I'll away and bring Billy,' Will responded. 'He has something rather special to show you all... by the way.'

It was towards the end of what had proved a sombre meal, and something of a trial for all present, that Thomas, who had been unusually silent, visibly morose, suddenly slammed his fist down hard on the trestle table.

Will almost leapt out of his skin. Billy jumped too, alarm in his eyes, and then he giggled.

'My god!' the priest exclaimed, 'but that good man should never have died here!' And eyes ablaze, he looked round the table at the startled company 'Betrayed by an unquestioning, selfless sense of duty, he was... and Patrick here, too. Then trapped here with the rest of us, by the decrees of faceless men whose only concern is to preserve their own skins and ensure that their comfortable lives are not in the least disturbed by the inconvenience that, through no fault of our own, our ship has brought them! If there were any justice at all, he should never have died here.'

Billy, who was sitting on the other side of Will from Thomas, plucked at Will's sleeve, and whispered, wide-eyed: 'Why is Father Thomas so cross... Mr Crossby?' and he giggled again. 'Shall I show him my boomerlang?'

'Hush, Billy. Not just now,' Will whispered, struck yet again by the child's sharpness. He put his finger to his lips, indicating, with puckered brows, that he should speak no further for the moment. Then smiling, he patted the boy on his knee, and Billy's hunched shoulders slowly relaxed.

No one spoke for several seconds. Some fiddled with their napkins or cutlery. Mr Williams, the young boatswain, dropped a spoon that clattered on the bench. Others concentrated their energies yet more intently on their ale.

Dr Mallon was the first to recover some composure.

'Nay, Father Thomas,' he began, calmly, 'while I... while we all share the anguish that puts these words into your mouth, I nevertheless believe that your judgement of the City Council is... a little harsh.'

The fidgeting stopped and, perhaps scenting a disagreement, even an open quarrel, the shipmen, in particular, fixed their eyes on the speaker.

'Their first duty is the protection of the community that appoints them,' Mallon continued. 'David knew that well enough, poor man, and willingly accepted the responsibility, and the risk it implied. As do we all...'

Thomas's face showed clearly, he would have none of this. 'So he did, to be sure. Of course he did. But with your own very honourable exception – and I mean that from the bottom of my heart, Patrick – how many others in Brisbane have chosen to come out here and put themselves at risk? How many? Tell me that! Ballow came, even neglecting his other duties, if I have understood the situation properly, precisely because others cared too little or had not the courage to do so. Now could you disagree with that, Patrick? Anyone...?' And his eyes once again circled the assembled company, looking for dissenters.

However, since it was murmurs of approval that came from several different points about the long table, Mallon shrugged helplessly, and slumped back in his chair.

'No, I thought not!' Thomas growled. 'They are keen enough to have the human cargo the *Emigrant* has brought them, once it has been dusted off and re-packaged, to labour in their different ways to increase the prosperity of the good burghers in their established trades and commercial enterprises. But apart from the not over-generous provisions the *Aurora* drops here each week – and I mean drops! – what responsibility have those same burghers demonstrated towards their future *employees*? This place itself, its lack of facilities, a disgrace!'

'*Employees*, Father? Pray, explain yourself...' piped up Mr Fothergill, from the far end of the table. And Captain Kemp nodded vigorously.

Thomas turned to answer the officer. 'Mr Fothergill, be assured, my choice of terms is precise.' Some of the earlier heat had gone from his words, but in its wake had come an icy disdain. 'For only in a very secondary, grudging sense are our "cargo" likely to be welcomed as fellow-citizens.'

Mallon, a troubled look on his face, opened his mouth, but Thomas waved aside the protest forming on the doctor's lips:

'What responsibility have they shown? I'll tell you what sort of responsibility!' He leant far back in his chair, placing his hands squarely upon its arms. 'It was well represented by that snivelling fop, Weatherall. You'll all surely remember – and his eyes swept the table, seeking confirmation, even before his judgement had been spoken – how Weatherall, with his prissy handkerchief pressed to his face, had not the courage, or the human decency even, to set foot on the island, where others were shouldering the responsibility that was rightly his! And if it is not quite clear to all present, what I refer to is the vexed question of the law here, and who should be responsible for upholding it. No clear directives! No authority of any sort! The question of Stevens, and now McIlroy, left in our hands...' Thomas shook his head in anger, and dismay. 'In our poor, powerless hands.'

Billy snuggled closer in towards Will, his eyes every so often sneaking an anxious glance in the priest's direction; for this was a side to Thomas which, Will realised, was wholly unknown to the boy.

'The chaos that man left us with,' Thomas continued, 'after his brief... memorable visit, might well have proved disastrous. But his attitude and shirked responsibility, as I say, typified that of those same Brisbane burghers for whose benefit we have all been so cheaply bought. But *that one*, that Weatherall...!' The table shook again as his fist thumped down upon it. 'He should be horse-whipped. And I, for one, would willingly oblige!'

'Thomas, Thomas!' Mallon cried, rising to his feet, 'Stop and think what you are saying! True, the man's manner and execution of his authority were woefully lacking, in tact...'

Thomas snorted in disgust. 'And a good deal else besides...'

'That I grant you, too. But *please*, Father Thomas, let me finish.

In spite of the anguish Mr Weatherall left us with, his decision was the right one. Yes, the right one,' the doctor persisted, as Thomas threw back his head in a gesture of disparagement. 'He *had* to have regard for the good of the greater number, those already dwelling in the township... And as for the citizens themselves, well, I very much doubt that many, if any at all, have even the slightest idea of what is going on here, of what we are living through, so your... your blanket condemnation strikes me as...'

'Patrick! You make my point for me, and I thank you! It is either gross negligence or gross inefficiency that keeps them in ignorance, and we in dire straits. And as to the greatest good of the greatest number, 'tis nothing more than the underhand cloaking of vile actions with common-weal pretences! Forgive me, but Patrick, aren't you being just a little bit naïve, trotting out my "blanket condemnation" in these desperate circumstances – desperate for us, here on Stradbroke, I mean – without pausing a while to question its real causes, meaning and function?'

Thomas turned his head slightly, and smiled, catching Will's approving eye.

'Naïve?' Mallon faltered.

'Patrick...'

'I know not what you can mean by that... It was but an expression...'

'Yes, yes... But I am willing to wager that the ordinary citizens in Brisbane would be quite surprised to hear that *their* 'greatest good' was being upheld by the City Fathers. For if those same City Fathers replicate what we have all known and suffered back in the home country, such solicitousness would be... uncharacteristic, to say the least. Don't you see that?'

Will watched Mallon's brow pucker into a frown, though he himself saw the priest's point well enough. The "common man" was being used to protect and further the interests of those who assumed they had the right to pronounce in his name! And he smiled bitterly, glad his friend had spoken out. But he'd put the cat among the pigeons, right enough!

Thomas stabbed at the last few morsels left on his plate and downed his remaining ale. 'You are a good man, Patrick,' he said quietly, 'and I own I have yet to set foot in Brisbane. But here, as a recipient of its niggardly charity, I have seen and heard enough about its workings to realise that the same old paternalism is still hard at work, whatever impressions its rhetoric and its silences seek to promote. Like the ship-fever, this... dissembling... is a disease of our times.' He glanced at Will, smiled once again, and winked reassuringly at the perplexed, wide-eyed Billy peeping across Will's chest, and then extended the same broadening smile to the doctor.

'I'm sorry, Patrick, truly I am, for all this... clangour!' And he laughed, good-naturedly, and clearly at himself. 'But these things have been a-festering in my mind ever since we came here, and David's death has brought them to a head. I mean no offence, either to you or to anyone else about this table.'

Will smiled, applauding his friend's sincere contrition, as well as his humility. 'Please,' Thomas added, quietly, 'accept my apologies, one and all.' His glance traversed the gathering, seeking acceptance. Then, gratified, he leant back in his chair, and then signalled his desire for the jug of ale.:

The jug came slowly down the table, in complete silence, with one or two arresting its passage to replenish their own mugs. And there perhaps, the matter might have rested...

Captain Kemp took up his mug, then added his own assurance that no offence had been taken. But then – casually, it seemed – hazarded the view that the understandable sadness, and frustration, or tiredness, 'or what you will' – the result of 'being ever at the forefront of the battle that has been lately hard fought on these shores' – might have had a somewhat distorting effect on Father Sheehan's view of things over in Brisbane, of civil society there... quite understandably. And, looking rather pleased with himself, he raised the mug to his lips.

Thomas frowned, and then jerked forward. 'Surely, Captain Kemp, you jest with us', he said, lightly enough – his mild demeanour surprising Will, who had seen his rekindled outrage. 'But "civil", did you say? "Society" did you say?'

The captain blushed scarlet. 'No, I speak in all seriousness,' he said, shaking his head at Thomas. 'Surely, any civil society's fundamental principle is that each citizen should be rewarded in proportion to his labours. And from what I have seen in Brisbane... and *I have been there*, on two previous voyages – he added, provocatively – it appears to be a model of that principle and its desired effects. And what's more, with the added virtue that, as it is a society still in the making, every man has equal opportunity to make the best of himself according to his labours and his talents... would you agree with that, Patrick?' And he looked round at the doctor, sitting beside him.

Smiling, Mallon looked up at Kemp but remained silent.

Thomas once again caught Will's eye, and groaned, and once again let his gaze move round, perhaps trying to gauge the impression Kemp's words had left. But when he returned to Will, his friend was leaning over Billy, whispering something into the child's ear.

Thomas turned back to Kemp. 'With all due respect, captain,' he said slowly, 'the opinions you have just expressed both miss and yet, oddly enough, illustrate the very point I was trying to establish... But no matter. Shall we move into calmer waters and speak of other things... if we have a mind to...'

'Aye, Father Sheehan, fair enough. But just let me say this, then I am done. Just that I am a practical man of the world and pride myself in knowing something of the workings of that world. Nevertheless, I admit, the subtle arguments of a... a bookish man, such as yourself, may have passed over my head! All I know is that commerce is, as it has ever been, the foundation stone, nay, the very lifeblood, of our commonwealth. If it flourishes, then so does the commonwealth. But if it is defective or ailing, then the commonwealth shrinks accordingly from its former self.'

There was some obvious assent at this, though some uneasy shuffling too, and Will's eyes darted between Kemp and Thomas, observing the curious gleam in the priest's eye, even quaking a little, fully aware that Thomas roused was a force to be reckoned with, as formidable as the fabled Indian juggernaut whose fearful, fateful passage he himself had once witnessed.

But Billy, Will was also aware, could hardly hold his head up or keep his eyes open. And he knew that very soon, to be fair to the child, he must carry him off to his bed. All the same, he was reluctant to make the move, not wishing to miss out on the company, the exchanges, or the promised fireworks.

Thomas cleared his throat, but as soon as he opened his mouth to speak, Billy yawned loudly. Everyone laughed, and the palpable tension was diffused in an instant. The boy murmured something inaudible, which Will took to be an apology for his rudeness, then he slumped asleep again across his guardian's lap. Seeing this as a reprieve rather than the moment for action, Will relaxed and sat on.

LXXVIII

Thomas looked soberly at Kemp, considering his riposte. 'Gentlemen,' he said firmly, 'I wish to disabuse you of one or two... common assumptions that the captain's words call to mind, and the more so since I have no reason to doubt but that they were spoken earnestly.'

Kemp's mouth twisted into something that seemed to Thomas uncomfortably like a sneer. But then, with a nonchalant wave of his hand, an indulgent smile playing about his lips... 'Please... do go on,' the captain muttered, as though the floor, or the rostrum, were somehow within his gift.

'I am obliged to you, Captain Kemp,' Thomas began, with a mocking tilt of his head. 'Now, I have long observed that it is possible to have very full, rich, and varied experience of the world, and yet fail to question it. You see,' he said smiling graciously, his voice quiet but precise in its enunciation, 'either we're too busy with the experience itself, or we're too enmeshed in the age-old patterns of values to question, much less appreciate, any significance beyond the momentary and the obvious. You see the truth of that, do you?'

He cleared his throat then saw off the ale in his mug.

Kemp stared at him, seemingly on the point of responding, but then failed to do so, for whatever reason.

'Maybe in the end, captain,' Thomas went on, 'it is only those who have the leisure or the inclination to distance themselves sufficiently from the experience, "bookish" men, such as poets, philosophers... or even priests – and with a twinkle in his eye he winked at the captain, who missed the playful gesture since he was just then wholly engaged in attending to his fob watch – who can see things in a broader context, see them for what they truly represent...'

Will smiled, admiring these parentheses by which his friend systematically shut off, one by one, the cul-de-sacs, the possible false turnings to keep his audience focused on the one direction... if Kemp was keeping up with him... And he glanced at the captain, whose face, half-turned away, showed nothing other than the evident control he was exerting over his emotions.

'Please forgive my bluntness captain – and Thomas raised what he hoped was a calming hand – but it is a nonsense to say that "every man" in Brisbane or, indeed, anywhere in the world, has "equal opportunity to make the best of himself." It simply is not so,' he added, seeing Kemp preparing to remonstrate, 'for the simple reason that attitude, aptitude, and ambition, are never alone sufficient for such self-realisation. How can they be? However hard a man may be prepared to strive, he will all too often encounter a whole hinterland of precluding factors, which so limit ambition and effort as to negate them entirely. For all but the privileged or the fortunate few, of course...!

'Yes, my friends,' Thomas went on, gratified to see at least half their company acknowledging this truth. 'Ours, certainly in Britain and, I have no doubt, here too – given the age-old model – is a society rooted in privilege, above all of birth, which...'

He broke off, as Kemp swatted angrily at an intrusive fly.

'Certainly, in Britain, did you say?' and the captain all but exploded, the blood rushing to his already florid cheeks. 'Certainly, in Britain, Father Sheehan? Oh, but excuse me, I had thought that your experience was wholly Irish. And that being the case...'

'And is Ireland not, then, a part of Britain, Captain Kemp? I had always understood that it was. Certainly, Ireland has no government of its own that I have heard tell of...'

'A part, yes, well of course it is,' Kemp blustered. 'And that is what

I am saying: it is a part, but a significantly different one, and that means…'

'And what makes it different, captain? Those who have the power to shape it… or those who have no power at all?'

'Oh, come now!' The captain threw his head back and laughed loudly, at the same time looking towards his officers, soliciting their disparaging laughter too. One or two obliged, notably Fothergill, followed by Seymour, the Second Officer, though somewhat less than fulsomely. 'Why, Father Sheehan,' Kemp declared, playing to his audience, 'I should have thought it was obvious what makes it different… 'tis the Irish themselves!'

This time, the laughter round the table was less restrained, though there were those whose restraint, even pained restraint, was noticeable.

Thomas, his eyes lowered, crumbled a small crust of bread into atoms on the table in front of him.

Only when silence had finally fallen did he look up. 'Privilege, as I was saying,' he resumed, quietly, 'is the habitual mode in British society. And the privilege of a decent education is universally denied to the common man… which "naturally" includes the common Irish man… And this one factor alone guarantees that the vast majority of citizens remains mired in ignorance; an ignorance to which, throughout their entire lives, they are continually persuaded by one ploy or another to acquiesce, as though it were indeed, sure to god! decreed by the iron laws of nature herself.'

The ensuing pause was occasion for embarrassed coughs, murmurs of assent, and one or two nudges, while a scowling Captain Kemp kept his own counsel.

Leaning forward, his elbows planted firmly on the table, Thomas launched into a further observation, but his discourse was interrupted suddenly by the sound and then presence of the matron entering the tent.

Miss Labone stood in the doorway for a moment, then excused herself and swiftly rounded the table to speak quietly with Dr Mallon, who nodded from time to time as she spoke.

When she had finished, the doctor made as if to rise but she laid a restraining hand on his shoulder:

'Oh no, Dr Mallon, that will not be necessary, I assure you. It is a thing I can attend to easily enough, now…'

The young doctor subsided into his chair, and Miss Labone moved away again, apologising once more for her interruption. But having raised the tent flap, she glanced back, and that action took in the sleepy little boy being propped up, awkwardly, by Will's arm.

'Mr Crosby! Whatever are you thinking of… keeping that poor mite from his bed at so late an hour…? 'Well, Mr Crosby?' the young woman persisted, crossly.

And Thomas felt for Will as he shrank from her fury, the guilt plainly written on his face.

Will's discomfiture was exacerbated by the barely suppressed sniggers at the far end of the table. He muttered a quiet *mea culpa* – as, he hoped, the quickest way of extricating himself from this difficulty, and getting the boy to his bed – and stood, gathering the child up in his arms.

'Aye,' he agreed. 'Utterly thoughtless of me… I admit.'

Visibly appeased in some measure, the matron smiled a rare smile, which transfigured her face, for a brief moment, into real beauty. 'Poor little chap, he's dead on his feet,' she said, wagging an admonishing figure at Will though continuing to smile. 'If you will carry him over, Mr Crosby, I will see to the rest.'

And as they went off together, Will's thoughts centred wholly and not unwillingly, now, on the boy's welfare; and Billy slept on, oblivious of the skirmish that had just been fought over his needs.

At the southern end of the camp, Sean McIlroy woke with a start. His sleep had been troubled, his dreams full of fear. His eyes were wet, and still half asleep, he brushed them with the back of his hand. There was the water, swirling… swirling… and the blackness, that he remembered, of his dream. But then, 'Oh Lizzie! My poor Lizzie!' formed on his silent lips, and immediately his eyes were damp again.

He reached out his hand into the empty dark and choked back the insistent tears...

Not fifty yards away, naked, with his hands thrust deep down between his legs, rocking slowly back and forth on the edge of his bed, Johnny Stevens gibbered incessantly to himself, insisting time after time that the garments hanging from the washing-line were his by right, and he would have them, by God he would...!

Making his way back to the hospital tent, Will passed among the grunts, cries and groans, the snores, and the whimpers of his fellow *Emigrant*s in their fitful sleep. Here and there the last embers of their fires started at the passage of a breeze, which in stirring diminished them, scattering their flimsy substance all ways away.

Mid-way across the sward, Will changed direction, almost without thinking, becoming suddenly aware of the star-spangled heavens and the silver moon riding high up the sky. He went on towards the lip of land, hanging above the water, skirted the line of graves and stepped out into the light, drawn to the sea of molten glass.

He stood and gazed, his mind emptying of all but this mighty magnificence. The crystalline purity of it all! Breath-taking, in its exquisite beauty. But – slowly, the thought came to him – entirely without meaning in itself, for itself. It existed in its own dimensions, and maybe the only meaning we could assign to it was nothing other than its visible existence. Or maybe we were its meaning, every one of us, in the time of our living... but outside its symmetries, its wholeness, perfection... all endlessly longed-for, but far, far beyond human reach...

How long he had stood there, staring up at the endless night sky, Will could not say, clutching unavailingly for some fragment of understanding... While back at the tent they sat on, perhaps, still trying to come to terms with a more tangible sort of understanding...

He started off towards it, leaving the narrow sands and stepping back into the gently swaying shadows of the trees.

Passing the graves, however, he stopped at the last one, and knelt on the damp earth. 'Ah, David, I never thought when I... only two mornings ago... Where is the sense in it? Where the justice of it?' he muttered.

Finding only commonplace words that failed entirely to satisfy his need, Will thrust his hand into the still loose earth, and immediately its peculiar moist smell filled his nostrils, and he raised his hand full of soil and brought it up to his face, inhaling deeply. Then opening the hand gradually, he felt the soil filtering back through his fingers, raining back down onto the mound... And inevitably, he supposed, Tompani's words leapt into his thoughts...

Blackfellow talk with earth, sing to earth, listen to earth... and earth tell him many important thing you Whitefella not know...

Nevertheless, he suspected, the real remoteness of everything... that earth smell, even the things we touch, taste, see... they contain us; but they shut us out, absolutely.

LXXIX

'Oh, but Ireland... Surely, Father Sheehan... *that* is a special case...?'

'*That* I cannot allow, Mr Fothergill...' Thomas leaned forward, bringing both his hands together, arched, touching only at the fingertips. 'And you shall be answered shortly, but what I meant was... well, Captain Kemp, you made a statement a while back to the effect that if commerce goes into recession then the whole commonwealth suffers.' He looked across at Kemp: 'Is that a fair representation of your point?'

Kemp nodded – though barely – in grudging assent.

Thomas directed a nod at Will as he resumed his seat. 'Certainly, we agree on that point, at least, captain. But what you omitted to say and to take into account was that the commonwealth's people do not suffer equally during a recession, just as they do not benefit equally when commerce is flourishing... which in a roundabout way brings me back to Ireland... and to Mr Fothergill...'

Thus alerted, the officer sat up straight, and well forward on his chair.

'Now, Mr Fothergill, I am not privy to the good captain's definition of a 'practical man', but I can assure you, gentlemen, that during my latter years in Ireland, despite being what the captain described – perhaps just a trifle disparagingly – as a "bookish" man, I too was also a very "practical" man. Eh? Very practical indeed!' Thomas let his eyes sweep the table, grandly.

Will noted the look on Kemp's face – somewhere between

embarrassment and shame, was it? An aloof sort of man, and not one he had ever really warmed to.

'Here, on Stradbroke,' Thomas continued, 'you have seen me bury upward of twenty of the poor, expectant souls who braved those endless seas with us, in the hope of finding a new and better life. But in Ireland… oh, I was called upon to perform that sorry duty for ten times that number, at very least! And so, I come to the point I feel bound to make in this company – *especially* in this company – and it is this. Of that huge number, I could count on the fingers of *one hand only* – and he paused again, so that the significance of that minute proportion should not be missed – those of easy circumstances I saw into the earth. And believe me, for I am not given to compromising on truth, not one of those died of hunger. *Not one!*' Thomas leant forward, full of defiance. 'And, what's more, there was nothing extraordinary about my particular experience. It was happening, and I do not doubt still is, in every parish throughout that sorry land.'

'Well, that's all as may be, Father Sheehan,' the First Officer declared, his lower lip curling. 'But you've not put forward one single point to gainsay my argument that Ireland is "a special case" – just the opposite, in fact!' And he nodded vigorously, seeming well pleased with his broadside.

Will frowned in bewilderment, failing still to connect with Fothergill's point.

'And furthermore,' the captain added, capitalising on his officer's observation, 'Ireland did not represent anything like the collapse of commerce that was the nub of my argument.'

Thomas leant back in his chair. 'Did it not, captain?' He smiled a tired, yet clearly ironical smile. 'Are you *quite* certain of that? Ah, to be sure,' he went on before the captain had time to answer him, 'the ships kept coming in and going out, and the counting houses and banks continued in their brisk trade. Yet, with the arrival of the blight, my friends, the economy had collapsed right enough! Make no mistake! The potato was the staple diet of the great majority. It was often the only diet! Everybody grew their own, but when that was no longer possible, their economy – a subsistence economy –

crashed absolutely, with results more dire than occur with... with the bursting of South Sea Bubbles and... all the other forms of ill-judged financial flummery that fat commerce indulges in periodically...'

There were several sharp intakes of breath, unease now open hostility in some quarters. What else had been said in his absence? Will wondered.

'Holy Mother of God!' Thomas almost shouted, half-rising from his chair. 'But death by starvation is a cruel, lingering way to quit this life. And most especially when it is in the midst of plenty, elsewhere! Mark my words, captain, I know, for I have seen it, not once, but a hundred times and more. I was *there*!'

Thomas sank back down, and though nodding, as if in further affirmation, seemed disinclined to make further comment. But a moment later, he stood to fetch the jug of ale, which he set, a clear peace offering, before Captain Kemp.

Kemp nodded in acknowledgement, then quaffed in satisfaction from his replenished mug, perhaps grateful at his seeming release. But then, to Will's bemusement and irritation, the young Second Officer broke the silence, perhaps desperate to have his say – to make his mark.

'From what I have read in the news sheets about the famine in Ireland, sir, well... I mean... was not much of it, in a sense, well... self-inflicted? There was no real shortage of food, not really. It was just that so many of your fellow-countrymen, Father Sheehan, sir, well, they stubbornly refused to... to eat the alternatives to their beloved spuds, generously supplied by the government in London! That's what I've read, anyhow... about the wheat shipped over, and the like. He paused, glanced at his fellow officers, his face red with excitement. Then he enquired casually, almost trembling: 'So how do you answer that, Father?' And he risked a smile, perhaps convinced he had administered the *coup de grace*.

The First Officer looked at him askance, almost bristling. Some private rivalry Will wondered. And then it occurred to him that, for all his faltering, this man had been more eloquent than his superior. Or more importunate! And he smiled to himself, curious to see how this developed. And Dr Mallon too, he noted, was looking on with rekindled interest.

And what of Thomas? Thomas was plainly in no hurry.

'How do I answer that, Mr Seymour?' he said, at length, his tone scornful. 'Well, for a start, I would say you should look with a more... sceptical eye on what you read in the news sheets! But more to the point, it was hardly a case of "wouldn't" eat what was available, but of "couldn't!" And I don't doubt your fine English news sheets skipped over that simple but decisive fact – and with that omission misinformed the entire nation. And clearly, not excluding... yourself, Mr Seymour!'

'"Couldn't", Father Sheehan?' Seymour stammered. 'Forgive me, but I fail to comprehend...'

'Do you indeed! Well, this is precisely – Thomas went on – what I meant about *Ireland*'s economy collapsing totally. They couldn't eat them because they couldn't afford them, man! Those in work, in Ireland, were ever paid pitifully low wages, yet were compelled to pay scandalously high rents for their land. So, for most of the labouring population there was never any surplus for such *luxuries* as flour or bread. Especially since, with the coming of the blight, all who were engaged in the grain commerce, from the wholesaler to the miller to the baker, scenting profit from adversity, raised their prices accordingly! So, Mr Seymour, it was more a case of mass murder, than mass suicide, as you would seem to have it. Just remember, young man, *I* lived through it... alongside my poor, stricken parishioners, and I received *my* information directly – from my dying parishioners, day after terrible day, and not from your... mealy-mouthed English newspapers, which were hell-bent on exonerating the English and Irish landowners, the commercial classes, the profiteers – from all blame... with their selective 'facts' and spurious arguments. Well... are you answered *now*?'

This time, a total silence met the priest's words. And Thomas's eyes, still flashing anger, fixed on each of his principal adversaries in turn, challenging them still.

Kemp muttered something indistinctly.

Mr Fothergill stared into his ale.

Mr Seymour – his face scarlet – sat nonplussed, not moving so much as a muscle.

'Well, then.' Thomas cleared his throat. 'I promised I would answer Mr Fothergill's observation,' he said, his tone noticeably calmer, 'about the Irish… Well now, I have long observed that, in general, among the English – and he winked mischievously – the word "Irish" has a very particular taste in the mouth. Like something that, once you're aware of, you wish to spit it out, at all costs!'

Will reached for the ale, agog, excited even, at the seemingly new direction his friend's crusade was taking.

'Then, there's "special case",' Thomas said, almost casually, 'which, when placed beside "Irish", as you used it, Mr Fothergill, sets it apart as something not worthy of our attention, or consideration. And if we add "surely" to this thickening broth, we further feed prejudice: the "special case" is summarily dismissed, as nothing of the kind, and justice falls on its blind sword.'

Will leant back in his chair, full of respect for Thomas's slow roasting of his adversaries. So fired was he, in truth, that he suddenly found himself voicing his own thoughts. 'Indeed, yes… and how effective these… blustering little words can be with those not overly given to thinking…'

Kemp barely concealed a yawn.

Seymour hung his head, seeming to shrink back down into his seat.

And Will stared at Kemp, thinking the man was either a dolt, or else, felt too much revealed, so that all he could do was boorishly spurn this observation, if he were not to lose face – for all his superior class origins. And suddenly, he realised he now had the measure of these men: their airs and graces merely fronting an intellectual void…

'Sergeant Crosby's is a telling point, gentlemen,' Thomas continued. 'Just… think about it as… as dispassionately as you are able. Such pronouncements, they are often grounded in no first-hand experience of their subject, and thus are expressed in words that are tainted: they are not really our words, but nevertheless are the ones which, miraculously, it would appear, leap to our lips, unbidden. And they attest, these words or phrases, to a deep-seated, intricate pattern of controlling prejudice that infects all our lives in differing proportions...' He paused. Then with perfect timing, added: 'And not just Mr Fothergill's... or Mr Seymour's.'

Despite this last, seeming concession, the shamefaced Fothergill raised neither his head nor any further objection. Kemp – Will was certain – swore under his breath. But that was all.

And still no one answered the priest.

For his own part, Will, easily recognising the truth of Thomas's statements, searched for something to add, even some neutral, non-offending comment. Yet the exertions of the past two days, mental and physical, were weighing on him, and no words came. Not that Thomas had any need of allies...

'And just one more thing,' Thomas said, 'and I swear this is my last word – to be sure it is, for I... like all of you, I observe... have need of my bed, after what has been for us all a harrowing day!'

Grateful, Will relaxed a little.

'So,' Thomas proceeded, smiling round at the tribunal, 'I ask you again: are "Ireland and the Irish" really such a 'special case'? You gentlemen' – and he gestured broadly at the officers – 'you, gentlemen, have brought a ship-full of malcontents on a perilous journey to the farthest side of the world... a journey more perilous, as it has turned out, than most of us could ever have imagined. But my point is that all of us were willing to risk the unknown, to face whatever hazards this journey brought. And why? Oh, and by the way, why "malcontents"? For that is most surely what we are. But take note, a sizeable *majority* of them are English, not Irish. So... Why then?'

Will looked up at this last observation; for plainly it was true, though he had never thought of it in such terms until this moment.

'The answer is quite simple, but also tragic. It is that they... we malcontents... are aware, each in his own way, and out of his own particular experience, that in England, as in Ireland, all were compelled to live life under the tyranny of an unequal, harsh justice which severely restricted choices and hugely undervalued labour, the labour of each, for it was cheaply bought; though… mark my words, not so cheaply… or so dearly… as in Ireland.' Thomas's eyes suddenly flamed again. 'For in Ireland we are talking of slavery.'

Slavery? Will was quite taken aback – like most of his fellows, judging by the sudden flurry of murmurings. One officer opened his mouth wide to say something, to protest anew, perhaps, but either he lost his nerve, or his comment was drowned in the rising volume of these reactions.

'Oh yes, "slavery" is the word, right enough! Slavery. Hundreds of thousands manacled by inescapable obligation to landlords, and enforced, crippling debt. However… and just think of the irony of it! Each of our shipmates chose to come to a land where, until only a couple or so years ago, British Justice regularly dispatched its unwanted citizens, those whom, for often the most trivial of offences, it labelled 'criminal'! And that fact alone is a fair measure of how intolerable they found life back home!'

From the look of his tired face, Thomas was done, and he made as if to heave himself up, out of his seat.

'Ah, no sir!' Kemp boomed, his outstretched hand almost physically restraining the priest. 'Surely, you exaggerate the case…' His tone was more conciliatory, almost jovial. 'And that out of all proportion to the reality!'

'Oh? Tell me, captain.' Thomas sank down again, wearily, on his seat. 'In what way do I exaggerate?'

'Because my "ship-full" is but a drop in the ocean!' And he too, having soon forgotten the late foolishness of Mr Seymour, his Second Officer, looked about him seeking recognition of his wit.

His officers, however, looked merely perplexed, and most noticeably, Fothergill.

Thomas shook his head, a wry smile on his face. 'Captain, I will not be gainsaid by these… idle contradictions… this too literal interpretation of my words! Think about it just a little… bit more.' His voice betrayed his tiredness, but he persisted. 'There are surely very many reasons why a man cannot choose to emigrate to the other side of the world. The prohibitive cost is only the most obvious

of them. Yet that does not mean he would not do so if he were able.'
And his eyes met Kemp's squarely, and held them, until Kemp rose
from his chair, laughing good-naturedly.

'Ah, Father Sheehan, you have a ready answer for everything!'

Thomas was also laughing. 'Do I, now? Well, if one is to survive…
one needs must have a "ready answer…" or rather, a "ready"
question… for everything! Now, shall we…?'

And, taking their cue from the two principals, everyone else
stood, all tensions drooping, as sleep beckoned.

Dr Mallon, looking from Kemp to Thomas, then back to Kemp
thanked them for 'a most entertaining evening.'

Thomas bowed graciously. 'Well then, I bid you *all* a… peaceful
night, gentlemen.'

As this company was dispersing to its different quarters, on a bright,
blustery autumn morning, Alice Fallowfield was hanging out sheets
and pillowcases on a billowing line. As she bent to the basket her eye
was caught by the sight of withering dahlias all down the border to her
right, then her disapproving look carried on into the veritable jungle the
blackened flowers fronted. She turned and saw the same dilapidation
and neglect in the border behind her: climbers too rampant, ramblers
tumbling down from the high wall, invading the earth beneath it, and
bindweed, couch-grass and ground elder throttling all that remained
of a perhaps once pretty cottage garden. The shame of it, for the high-
walled yard must be a suntrap in summer, and well sheltered from
winds and frost, in all but the worst of winters…

Straightening up, she resumed her pegging out, exhilarated by
the swell and flap and crack of white sheets on this high and windy
morning. But her eyes kept straying back to the borders, which
were cleared in an instant, in her imagination, to take on a new
configuration, with new planting, careful tending, and ordered taste
of colour, shape and proportion everywhere… A rose garden.

Alice took up the empty basket and pushed open the kitchen door.
She would put her shaping fancies to Granny Abbot the moment the
old lady made her appearance in the parlour.

LXXX

The following morning, when the *Aurora* tied up a little after eleven, Patrick Mallon was there to meet her, to hand over the letter he and Dr Ballow had composed recommending the early lifting of the quarantine restrictions.

The junior doctor felt anxious, not having expected to be the company's chosen delegate. Still, he agreed with Kemp that even posthumously Dr Ballow's judgement and signature would be respected, whereas any new petition signed by himself alone might just lead to further delay. Lieutenant Seymour had even suggested that no mention need yet be made of Dr Ballow's death; but he'd refused to be party to that and had instead written a short covering letter, explaining the circumstances of Ballow's passing, yet insisting that this sad event in no way negated the recommendations stated in the main communication.

'I'll fetch it, Mr Crosby... *this* time,' shouted Billy, his face contorting in frustration.

'Sorry, Billy!' Will smiled ruefully, sensing that the child's suspended sentence had somewhat more significance in the breach than in the letter.

Billy's small feet skipped him away, lightly, over the still wet sands. 'Watch me!' he cried, concentrating only briefly before sending his boomerang flying into the air, to land at the water's edge, startling a squawk of gulls. 'Your turn next!' he called, scampering off to retrieve it.

How long did it take to learn, by trial and error, how to throw the curved object skilfully enough for it to return full circle to the hand that cast it? Will took the boomerang from Billy's outstretched hand, aimed carefully, and failed once more, to Billy's chuckling amusement.

'You try and get it right, Billy. You're much better at it than I am. Away you go!'

If Billy was enthralled by the object for its own sake and for its latent magic, Will's own state of mind, another kind of captivation, was dominated more by what it represented: that different way of life, whose principles, as he understood them thus far, he might have tried to explain to last night's company, in counterpoint to Kemp's fixation with commerce... if he'd had Thomas's confidence, his eloquence, and there'd been an opening.

The difference, he knew, was at the very root; it concerned the true nature of things whose single natures were comprehended and evaluated in ways that the life he and his fellow Britons came from had long lost sight of, or indeed, had perhaps never known. And, if Thomas was right, their own traditional ways... or words... were a powerful means of shackling the many to the yoke of the few – the knowing and wily few. But how did tradition maintain its grip? And why was it that the subservient mass did not rise up and destroy their oppressors? After all, it had happened in France only seventy years before...

And yet why was tradition – a kind of repetition, really – so right here, for the native peoples...?

'Oh, Come on, Mr Crosby!' Billy's exasperated voice brought Will back to immediate concerns. He looked down, almost surprised to find the boomerang lying at his feet. He picked it up, angled it this way and that, and then hurled it up the sands.

Billy ran after it, his face turned up to the sky. 'You didn't hold it right!' he cried gleefully, following its trajectory.

'Show me, then!'

...And yet they had risen up in the past, his compatriots, so it wasn't for want of trying. Peterloo, Tolpuddle, the Chartists... and the Luddites, even. Today, though, the English populace seemed merely cowed, and acquiescent – obligingly so, even speaking out against those few of their fellows who raised challenging voices, condemning them roundly… For fear of worse, was it? And yet they continued their endless grumbling and complaining about their lot: his army days had given him ample proof of that!

And where did *he* stand? Among the obligingly acquiescent? Leaving it to others to speak out… such as Thomas? Will frowned; well, that, certainly. Yes, those uprisings, in fact, were nothing short of miraculous!

And in Ireland, Thomas had said, when he'd spoken about the poor, the situation had been the same, if not worse. What was it he had said? That the starving people had gone like sheep to the slaughter, the great majority dying, even, in an exemplary, law-abiding manner…?

'Catch it Mr Crosby! Catch it! Oh, you didn't even try…!'

Billy's panting rebuke and stamped foot brought Will sharply back to the present moment, and to the fact that the boomerang had just whizzed past his head. 'I'm sorry, Billy. You're right, I wasn't concentrating.' Will grinned, sheepishly, and went to retrieve it. 'I'll try and do better, now. Promise!'

Billy sighed heavily and backed away to a suitable distance.

Yet after a few more throws – and the temporary closure of the gates of his mind and memory – Will asked to be excused.

'You carry on, Billy. I'm afraid I have important matters to see to…'

It sounded lame, even as he was saying it, but Will felt himself to be somehow on the tip of something, some sort of breakthrough… and whether it came or not, he should at least try to smooth out some of the ruts in his thinking, not least if he was to attempt to be a father to this child in the time ahead.

Billy turned his back, and flung the boomerang away along the shore, trudging after it with his head down, as Will stalked off, guiltily, in the direction of the tents.

Later that day, Will took Thomas to that same stetch of sand where he had failed so conspicuously to measure up to Billy's expectations. They walked near the shoreline, first northwards for a half a mile or so, when Thomas stooped to pick up a large shell, doused it in a rock pool, then slipped it in the deep pocket of his habit, at which juncture they turned back.

'But have you really considered it, Will? The foundations upon which our British way of tyranny rests. Well… have you, now?'

'No… not really.' Will, found wanting also in Thomas's eyes, could only shrug. 'Though I have felt it sharply enough…'

'A small number of institutions, that's all it rests on. And the pomp and ritual and trumped-up mystique that reinforce them, of course; and all the stronger for having existed, virtually unchanged since the Middle Ages, nourishing, incidentally almost, the mystique of "tradition". All meant to dazzle and overawe!' Thomas's face registered his disgust. 'And which are they? Well, first, there's the monarchy, bewitching enough as spectacle, always – like the showy parrot birds here. But, much less perceptibly, as a huge web of controls that… I'm in no doubt at all… will entangle us, even here, at this far side of the world…'

And in that moment, absurdly, Will saw himself as an erstwhile member of Thomas's congregation, agog, awaiting the coming revelation.

'Aye, you're right there,' he grinned, recalling his soldiering days. 'It doesn't take much more than a few brightly coloured costumes and a bit of martial music to dazzle folk!'

'Spectacle – it bewitches them, befuddles brains…' cried Thomas, his priestly passion mounting. 'And equally strong in its grip, with more uniforms, with yet more ritual – he raised his eyes skywards, his scorn palpable – is established religion, with its own insidious web of controls, of course… though subtly meshing at crucial points with those of the crown… Do you see what I'm driving at, Will?'

'Well, the glass is not so dark as it was… Oh, but… sorry to interrupt you, Thomas. Isn't that the matron coming down onto the sand? I don't think she's seen us…' Will smiled. 'She seems to spend a lot of time alone. I swear I've never yet seen her in the company of other women…'

'Aye, 'tis her, right enough.' Thomas peered ahead, slackening his pace. 'A fine young woman, that she is. But perhaps she does not need the company of… others. And yet, when I have, I mean, when I've… found myself in her… What I mean is… she seems amiable, personable, enough…'

Will looked at him, bemused. 'Shall we catch her up? She's walking at no great pace…'

'Ach, no! Let her be if she prefers it that way…'

Will raised a quizzical eyebrow. But then his attention was distracted by a sharp movement to their landward side.

'Thomas, look!' he whispered, pointing away in the trees. 'In that tall one; high up, just above its first fork. Do you see where I mean?' Taking hold of the priest's shoulders he swivelled him round. 'There's a hole, do you see it? And I'm sure I saw…'

'A hole…?'

'Yes. And I saw one of those…'

'Where? I can't… Ah, yes, I see, but…' Thomas glanced back along the sands, at the slowly moving figure drawing further ahead of them.

Will stepped back, the better to observe, and after half a minute he was pointing again, as a flash of colour settled at the entrance to the hole. 'There it is, look!' He jabbed a finger towards it. 'And away he goes… and now there's another one. And it's disappeared inside now…'

'Yes, Will,' Thomas laughed. 'And though they may not be sparrows in spring, their purpose is naturally – obviously – the same! They'll have young in there… they're surely feeding them.'

Will laid a hand on Thomas's arm. 'I know… But is it not strange that these birds, so utterly different from our birds, should behave exactly as ours do? Is that not a proof of… something? Or am I being…?'

'You are! But I see what you're asking… The distance. The differences of… place, vegetation, climate, and what have you… Shouldn't they add up to something quite… different?'

'Yes. That's it. Precisely.'

When the flurry of movement had ceased, they moved off again.
And the matron, Will realised, had disappeared.

'But Thomas, I'm sorry, you were saying… about the Church…'

'Aye, the Church…' Thomas pulled a face. 'With its beautiful,
precise, but moribund Latin tongue… kept alive, Will, not primarily
as communication but as barrier and control. Its language… which
for centuries was also the language of the Law and of Learning: that's
first among its mysteries… and the language of all the others.' And he
smiled his admiration, though whether of that 'tongue' or, perversely,
of the Church's manipulation of it, Will could not be sure.

'…Particularly the Roman one, though the Church of England,
and that of Ireland, are much the same…' Thomas stooped to collect
another shell. 'Latin was the language of all the mysteries to their…
flock, I mean, for they of course, poor souls, had no means of knowing
it… even though they heard it every time they entered a church.
But… not to worry, eh, Will?' And Thomas winked, conspiratorially.
'For the kind, knowledgeable priest was always on hand to interpret
and explain, to be sure he was! Just as he interceded for them with the
saints, or in taking the bread and the wine, which… miraculously…
though he alone took it – so who else could say? – became the body
and blood of Christ! Despicable! Oh yes, Will, the Latin has been
for centuries, and still is for Holy Mother Church, an impregnable
citadel…' And he snorted his repugnance.

Will had neither the knowledge nor the practised imagination to
confirm or reject these arguments, but they sounded right to him;
that they came from Thomas, somehow made them right… But take
heed, he admonished himself, for wasn't that precisely the point
Thomas was warning about…? The friendly priest…?

'…Then, of course, there's the cathedrals… Fortresses, they are,
dwarfing everything about them for miles around, whether in the
city or the country. And they dominate the religious and social
organization of every parish – with their saints' days and the major
festivals in the Church calendar; and through the sacraments and
the confessional… where the ever-inquisitive, busy-bodying parson
or priest comes into his own… By the unrelenting power of all these

instruments, these… tentacles, they dominate the lives of so very many of our countrymen. Ah, but…'

Thomas hitched up his habit and strode over to an outcrop of rocks where he perched, somewhat precariously, on a ledge. 'So are you still following what I'm saying?'

Will sat too, facing the still distant, incoming sea. 'Oh, the Church has a finger in every pie, all right. That I am aware of. Even in places as remote from Canterbury and London as my Whitehaven! And Appleby, Dacre…'

'Aye, Will, and many more than we can name. But as I say, tentacles, rather than fingers.'

The two men fell silent, Thomas twisting round now and then to watch the waves. And inevitably, Will's mind turned to Alice, and he wondered, fleetingly, if she was still in Netherton, the place his sister had mentioned. But before his thoughts could plunge any deeper, Thomas was bringing him back to his own line of thought.

'Then there's the universities, Will. Ages old themselves, and in origin very much the offspring of Holy Mother Church… And behind *them*, the grammar schools and now, the new, grossly mislabelled "public" schools, the only paths into the Universities. And it is these, of course, which shape the future decision-makers in political matters, or religion, or the military, or the public purse. And the only way you can benefit from these institutions is by paying. And that, of course, precludes over ninety per cent of our people, who are destined for… lesser lives.'

Thomas shifted his position for greater comfort. 'Age-old norms, Will. But it's what is happening *here* that concerns me now…'

'Was this what you were leading up to… last night?'

'At one point it was. But then… well, you've seen what manner of man Kemp is; he and his loyal officers. So I decided it would be breath entirely wasted… And in any case, they'll be going back home, sooner or later… Oh, they are, by their likes, good men enough, I don't doubt, but they belong, body and soul, to that rigid, militarised system I've just described. And they'll live out their days in relative comfort within it, believing it to be the best mankind could ever devise! They have just enough education, and wit, to turn it to their advantage, but not enough to know how to question it. They are men without books, Will, and men without books are but sots.' He shook his head slowly, in resignation. 'But Will, it's the people here, on this island, those who have not yet crossed the narrow straits to the mainland, that we should talk to; try and stir their minds, so that once over there they will demand a great deal more... and less, of their new commonwealth. That would be a start.'

Thomas was comfortably launched, Will realised, which suited him well enough. He took out his pipe, glad it had remained in his pocket, and began to fill it with tobacco that was rather past its best. 'But, Thomas, are we not...?'

'The point is this, I think.' Thomas waved his incipient question aside, 'It is in the words... Everything, in the end, comes down to words, you know. Not just what is said, but how it is said and, perhaps most of all, how it is received and understood – which is not always the same thing. Words are power, Will, make no mistake. And those who have few or very few will always be victims... *That's* why we are where we are. And why we will need... new words.'

Will drew contentedly on his pipe, absorbing the priest's words – his tone sometimes forceful, at others almost a whisper. Thomas's world was much narrower than his own had been, yet clearly more deeply entered, more thought about, more... known. And he had an air of assurance that he himself, he was convinced, would never attain, however long he lived.

'The common language of the day – our day certainly, but any other too, I have no doubt – deeply entrenches the unquestioning, untutored mass of people. It entrenches them in the commonplaces, the catch-all phrases, the aphorisms and slogans that speak the narrow values of polite, but essentially un-thinking society: the gin-trap of words, Will! To all intents and purposes, we are talking about a code of acceptances, of unconsidered endorsements of the very tastes and prejudices which restrict our lives at every turn: it represents nothing less than consensus around the *status quo*. And so, the unschooled multitude takes suggestion as... as the lapdog takes its morsels… snuffling and rubbing up against the rich man's feet…'

Thomas spoke on in lilting, quiet tones, as if re-ordering his mind, dusting off ideas from shelves not visited for a while. Will drew on his pipe, then laid it aside, aware that the contentment it induced was not conducive to the concentration Thomas's words merited, and he was in danger of losing out to these… pleasures of the moment.

'…the inexperienced, the untravelled, those who from the cradle have been subjected to… what we were saying before: the liturgy, the sacraments, the expedient wisdoms of the times, filtering down through the different levels of a community; all-pervading in their power to rein in and control. Ah, but – Thomas shrugged – it's getting people to see, to realise what dupes they are! That's the nub of the matter!'

And then, perhaps reading Will's earlier thought, he rose abruptly. 'Perhaps we should be getting back. Oh, but your pipe…'

'Ah, 'tis no matter,' Will laughed. 'In truth, I was too comfortable with it… in danger of dreaming rather than listening.'

'Were you, now! Well, maybe you were too hasty… I mean, the pipe might have profited you more…'

'I think not, Thomas. The pipe has been with me a long time, but I'm still as ignorant as ever I was…'

Thomas looked askance. 'Self-abnegation can destroy a man, Will… Take heed, for 'tis true. But what was I saying…? Ah, yes. You know what I have particularly noticed,' he confided, as they ambled back, 'is that, in the main, it is the generalising absolute that's the problem, the *vatic*, aye *vatic* statement, which makes the one example suffice to explain or justify or condemn the many, thereby seeming to remove the necessity of examining each case one by one, by its own lights. And that, I believe, is the hub of our liberal tyranny with its general stultification…'

''Tis rife in military life, certainly.'

'I'm sure it is. And why aren't our "forces of order" called upon more often to quell and coerce? Maybe because this pernicious, narrowly controlled way of speaking does their work for them… I am just thinking aloud here, but am I right…?'

Will bent down and tapped the cold ash from his pipe. 'Aye, I'd say you are… though I'm not too sure I could reconstruct your argument, if pressed to do so!'

Thomas chortled. 'Well I'm not too sure I could, either!'

'If I have understood aright, you were saying that the common language of the day is, in a manner of speaking… chief among the forces of order. But can that *really* be? Is it *that* powerful?'

Thomas grinned. 'Aye, that's what I'm saying,' he said, looking pleased with himself. 'And I like your phrase, "in a manner of speaking", for it is on that, precisely, that all else turns! The "manner" of speaking, yes. I very much fear that whatever seething, personal anger or bitterness or sense of injustice, our people here have dragged with them across the oceans, will all be dissipated by that all-too-seductive voice of prejudice which, very likely, has been transplanted and already taken root.' His face clouded, betraying a fundamental pessimism.

'So…?' Will began, but checked himself, seeing what now looked like impatience about to break. 'No, go on.'

'If they – but Holy Mother of God, what am I saying…? If we, for we are of them and with them… do not create and possess our own words, then we shall fall back into the old, familiar, comfortable-uncomfortable patterns of before, patterns that express only conformity to the needs, greed and demands of the haves… The age-old dispensation. Showing patience and forbearance in the face of injustice will change nothing. It never has yet, and it never will!'

They walked on, neither seeming inclined to converse further. Will was vaguely aware of the sea and the distant mountains, the latter almost lost in haze. And he wondered at the vastness of it all, and its… what? Its… serene disdain, yes, that was it, its serene disdain for his own seething anxieties – about Alice and Lilian, about Billy, and the future – all set against this majestically indifferent backdrop, its tides and currents, ebbing and flowing and eternally eddying, which includes all else in its heartbeat but not alienated mankind.

And maybe that was what the expulsion from Eden had been all about…

LXXXI

Will pulled back the flap and looked inside, but there was no
sign of Billy.

'Agh, he'll be away playing with his friends, I don't doubt,' Thomas
said, noticing Will's worried frown. 'Aye, look, down yonder! What
did I tell you?'

Thomas raised his hand in response to Billy's hasty wave, and
stood for a moment or two watching, as the boy ducked and swerved
to avoid being caught by a little girl who seemed to be pursuing him.

Will's relief was as obvious as had been his momentary concern,
and, feeling a hand laid reassuringly on his shoulder, he smiled. 'So,
Thomas, given the likely truth of all that you have been saying, what
is to be done?'

'The common man must have his day, Will. Of that I am convinced.
He must have his say, and that is what we should all strive for, with
might and main.' He turned, then, ushering Will inside the tent. 'But
first I'll have to get these boots off!' And he sat down hard, on the
narrow bed.

Will laughed, and sat down too, facing him.

'But to achieve that end,' the priest said, patiently unlacing a tight
double knot, 'the common man must, first of all, above all else, *cease*
to be the "common" man – as we presently understand that term.' He
loosened one, then set about the other boot. 'And… you know, we
must still be few enough, and new enough, hereabouts, to have some
small chance of making these things come to pass, even in Brisbane.'

Will was on the point of speaking – for there were several more questions already forming in his mind, even as his friend was speaking.

Thomas, however, still struggling to remove the second boot, raised his hand to delay them.

'Ah, Will, I know I do prattle on something wildly… It's just that… here, we have the opportunity to heal some of the fracturing that late events in England and Ireland have unnaturally… engineered. Common speech – don't you see? – has been gagged and has been replaced by an argot made up of, well, the dire necessities of living, on the one hand, and a rapacious, machine-driven greed on the other.'

He threw the boots down in seeming disgust, as if they were somehow implicated in those machinations, then he stretched himself out on the bed, sighing his newly won comfort. Yet, almost in the same movement, he was sitting up again, wagging his finger. 'There is only one means of deliverance, Will, and that is proper schooling, especially the *self*-awareness that comes from it. And you know what that means? Schooling taken entirely out of the hands of the politicos, and the industrial and commercial monsters whose craven, restrictive interests it is made, all-too-readily, to serve.' Thomas paused briefly. 'And that, to be sure, means teaching about the world and its wonders, and how to express it in writing and in speech. And not being deprived of that richness so you can be driven, like mules, to drudge in the factories, or the fields, for rewards that beggar themselves. Oh, but the world has to change, Will. Its rhythms must change. And long-locked gates must be flung open.'

The priest's finger finally ceased its wagging. 'And that is why…' He paused, then tossed his head and grinned broadly. 'Yes, I shall shed my cloak and its clumsy magic at the first available opportunity, so I will!'

Will looked at him. 'Are you sure of that, as that magic has been a help to so many, here?'

'Aye, I'm sure of it, Will… Useful though it has been in this … furnace of adversity. It is tainted! It belongs with the myths and mysteries that befog and beguile, and I want to be free of it, free of all that! I want to be able to gain a trust that is mine alone. There will be minds to educate, to lead out of the land of darkness, and… blinded eyes. And that is really where I want to be… in the vanguard of such a new awakening.'

'Aye,' Will laughed, willingly infected. 'And I shall shed the midnight-blue uniform I have not yet worn… Indeed, maybe we should go back down to the rock pool tomorrow, and be baptised afresh…'

'…In the name of the crabs, the jelly fish and the sea urchins, Amen!' Thomas intoned, chuckling. 'Oh, but Will, your journey… I keep meaning to ask you. Did you come across any of the native people? I rather presumed you must have, as you were away so long…'

'And I have been meaning to tell you!' Will smiled. 'But now you've gone and filled my head with all these other things…with your particular call to arms…!' And he leant forward to punch the priest playfully on his shoulder.

By nightfall, Will's mind felt like a battlefield, as Thomas's tightly meshed arguments were compared and fused, wherever they touched, with the emerging vision Tompani's world had seeded in him.

LXXXII

A week later, Will and Billy were standing high above the blowhole, on Whale Rock. The sun, nearing its zenith, dappled swaying leaves all over the rock's surface.

As they had approached the end of the long beach, the little boy had come to a sudden halt.

'I think, Bluebell...' And he had paused, importantly, a hand on the horse's side. 'I think... since we are so near... that Mr Crosby is taking me to see Mr Twopenny's not-quite-magic again. But don't worry, Bluebell. You can rest here.' And he had looked up at Will, his face a confusion of childish plea and a knowingness beyond his years.

And thus Bluebell, as had become the custom for her on these excursions, had been left tethered to a bush at the bottom of the defile, perhaps 'thankful' of the rest, Billy had devised, after her 'tiring' journey – as well as perhaps having no great interest in blowholes! Indeed, this whole expedition to Point Lookout had been urged by Billy, still insisting on seeing Mr Tompani to thank him for the special gift, which had lost none of its magic and excitement for him.

Not that Will had needed much encouragement – mainly because he wanted to see Tompani too, and hear more about him and his people, but also because the castaways in the camp had become very restless again. Most were impatient to be away, unable to comprehend why, when the pestilence had left them, they were still confined to the island. There had been several verbal clashes, which Dr Mallon,

Father Thomas, and he had borne the brunt of, since many still perceived them to be agents of the Authorities on the mainland, whose inaction, and nefarious purposes, were deemed responsible for prolonging their imprisonment.

One man – Will Farmer's neighbour… Albert Woods, was it? – had become a thorn in the flesh of all, making an ugly scene outside the mess tent on three successive days; loud-mouthed, accusatory, totally unwilling to listen to reason. On the last occasion, Will had tried his best to make it clear they all shared his views unreservedly. But the man wouldn't let up and had even slapped his own wife when she'd tried to make him calm down, dragging her away by her arm, cursing at her and pummelling her back as she tried to free herself. Clearly, all Will's expressions of impatience and of scorn for the "Authorities" were interpreted by some as a subtle piece of play-acting: the fiction of Sergeant Crosby had long hardened into fact, in most people's minds. And of course, it was undeniable that the need to maintain order in the community had forced them, Will especially, to tread a thin line…

The blowhole demonstrated its magical power once more, and Billy squealed in delight. Will shook his head, marvelling too at the way the sunlight caught the falling spray.

No. If he had harboured any doubts about renouncing his intended career with the local police force, they would have been dissipated, once and for all, by these latest outbreaks at the camp.

'Come on, Mr Crosby. Let's go.' Tiring now of the blowhole, Billy was angling to be away again, so Will turned away from the sea and scanned the rocky face they must reascend, looking for the most convenient route. But Billy, distracted by an enormous black and white butterfly, dashed away and started to clamber up at once in breathless pursuit, shouting words that were drowned in the crashing of the waves below. Will stood watching, taking as much pleasure in the boy's response to all this newness, this wild grandeur, as in his own. He sat down again on a broad, flattish rock, keeping an eye on the boy, and as he watched, his thoughts drifted once more to the future and what it might hold, once release from imprisonment here removed his last excuse for making no clear decisions about it.

Over and above this dilemma, if closely linked with it, were the changes that had come about, almost as he slept, it seemed, in the way he now saw the world and his own place in it.

Thomas had clarified much for him. And then Tompani had begun to show him a radically different path. And the mingling reverberations of the two had brought about a quite conscious shift in his own priorities, deeply felt, if quite impossible to define, as yet, much less fully grasp in its implications. He glanced up at Billy, dashing first this way, then that in his pursuit, and he recognised clearly enough that the little boy's needs would inevitably determine his own priorities over the next few years. It could not be otherwise.

The child stopped in mid-scramble. 'What is it, Mr Crosby?' he shouted. 'Am I tiring you out? Well, you just sit on awhile, till I get your breath back...'

'Very thoughtful of you, Billy.' Will did not trouble to suppress his sarcasm, though his smile registered sheer delight in the child's impudent wit.

Spotting another, then another of the butterflies, Billy resumed his chase, seemingly trying to go in several different directions all at once.

Just what he himself had been doing in his mind, Will realised. And he sighed deeply at the truth of it. He had come to Queensland to evade all possible contact with Nancy. And the seven years that would finally free him from her were intended, too, as a time of careful, calculating rehabilitation, a time during which he would acquire prosperity and maybe even some social standing, to lay at Alice's feet and demonstrate that he was indeed worthy of her love and respect.

But seven years... Thomas had made him face up to the absurdity of this dream – as had the *karadji*. Alice's seven years would, inevitably, have a different trajectory from his own.

Oh, it was not that Alice and Lilian could not be a part of whatever life he forged for himself here. That was not the problem – or not the whole of it. The real difficulty lay in how to persuade her, for it would take far more than just letters, of that he was certain. They would need to talk face to face, and over some period of time. He would need to hear what she had to say, too, and what sort of life she envisaged for herself. Yet twelve thousand miles separated them, as well as the seven years, and the question of Billy, and, of course, whatever chance pressed upon them all... in the meantime...

Will looked up again, and there was Billy, still in determined pursuit. Yet, fragile and insubstantial as they were, the butterflies managed always to elude him; and the child giggled good-naturedly at his continuous failures, which clearly did not deter him in the least.

'Would you like a try, Mr Crosby? Or are you still too tired...?'

But Will waved him away, too preoccupied by his own particular pursuit to be distracted in the moment.

Surely, he reasoned, what Thomas and Joanna had done before them, he and Alice could do even now. Surely, they could...

Yet the disjuncture... the oceans that ebbed and flowed between them... it was all too real and operated in ways he could never have imagined when he had first formed his plan for their future, in the weeks prior to his release from Carlisle gaol. And the amount of persuasion Alice might need would drown a thousand times in the oceans' vastness...

Billy had finally given up on his butterflies, and was sitting, panting hard, Will noticed, on a rock high above where he himself still sat. 'I think I can see some whales going past out there, Mr Crosby. Can you see them too? Look, there!' and he stretched out his arm, excitedly. 'Look...! And there, as well, Mr Crosby!'

Will strained round to look in the direction the child was pointing. But now Billy was away again, climbing higher, to command a better view, perhaps. Will looked again, but it was hard to say whether the movement of the water was caused by whales or by shoals of rocks, just beneath the surface. 'Yes, maybe,' he called back. 'Maybe they are. I'm really not sure...'

Thomas had also convinced him that, whatever plans he devised for his future, he should first attend to his 'selving' – find his own voice, to then rise up and talk, using *his own words* instead of parroting the shoddy dictums of a polity experience should tell him was quite discredited. 'And where will you find them?' he had asked pointedly. 'From books, man! From the right books. That's where!'

And it was happening, his mind was on the move; he was sharply aware he was understanding things, lots of things never considered before, and seeing the ways in which they connected. And when it all came to... ripeness... if it did... he must surely find a way through the maze he had trod these few years past, since first setting eyes on Alice, to find her once more, at its centre...

Will shifted his position on the rock, but his eyes remained unfocused, resting on the sea. Mere departure from this island offered no guarantees, he knew that; and knowledge alone, however acquired, was no guarantee either. And yet, he was certain, there could be no advancement without it.

Suddenly distracted by a school of dolphins, leaping and plunging as they made their way round the headland, he half turned in Billy's direction, but the boy, all eyes, all awareness, had already spotted them, and was standing as if transfixed, following their passage.

'Are those dolphins, Mr Crosby?' he called down. 'Or are they... swimming rocks as well...?' And he shielded his eyes from the sun's glare, the better to see them.

Will chuckled at the child's endless impudence, his sharpness of mind. And in the moment, he recalled Thomas's declared decision, not long ago, that he would teach Billy the game of chess. And when taxed with Will's obvious perplexity, he had said it would show the boy that the series of accidents we call history was, to the contrary, the unfolding of a finite number of patterns; patterns which, on closer inspection, were invariably shown to have their own inner logic, with the game's rules and set moves determining its course. What was it he had said? That once mastered it bred 'a familiarity that became foresight – Machiavelli's virtue, no less,' and could help release a man from blind bondage. Something along those lines, anyhow. Yet, sceptical though he himself was – for it seemed a huge responsibility to set on a mere pastime – he could not challenge such a claim, being entirely ignorant of the game's intricacies.

'Oh, to be sure – and Will heard his friend's softly lilting tones in his mind's ear – it will take time, of course, but Billy will readily see that the winds are chance, the waves are, the stormy days, and the tranquil', as were all of those natural forces that could ever overwhelm us from one moment to the next...

'Yet, in our dealings with our fellow men,' he had concluded, 'we could all become "grand masters", and rise above the loose conspiracy of control and regulation to possess our very selves! Yes! And that is better by far than being strangled by the rich man's laws and customs...'

Returning to the spur, above the point where the horse was tethered, Will heard Billy's excited cry ahead of him. And for a moment he worried that something was amiss, perhaps with Bluebell herself.

'Billy... Are you alright?'

The boy gesticulated wildly, and then he was off, heading further along the rocky promontory towards its end, stopping every three or four steps to point back along the wide northern beach they had earlier traversed.

'Look, Mr Crosby! Look over there! Are those... are they more whales, or are they... other kinds of fishes... or just more of your rocks? Can you see where I mean?' he asked urgently. 'They're not rocks, I know they're not!' And he pointed yet again, then stood quite still until Will had caught up with him, though every now and again stabbing the air with his outstretched finger.

Will came up behind him and peered over his shoulder into the strong light glancing off the barely rippling, emerald lawn of the sea, almost, he fancied, as far back as Amity. And yes, there in one instant, to be vaporised in the next into a shimmering void, to then return as before, or almost as before, were several elongated, blackish shapes. He scrutinised them for perhaps half a minute and was almost certain they were neither whales nor dolphins; their particular rhythm did not suggest whales.

'Hm. A pity we don't have the telescope from Bluebell's saddlebag, Billy.' But by the time I fetched it, they would have disappeared altogether.' Will stood and stared, shook his head then looked again, moving a little further to his right. 'Ah, Billy, I think they are not sea-creatures at all.'

'Not sea-creatures…?' Billy looked bewildered.

'No. They are moving like canoes… But they are so low in the water it's hard to make them out. I can count… four, maybe five of them, and they are…'

'Are canoes… are they like… boats, Mr Crosby?' Billy asked, a hint of curiosity entering his voice.

'Yes, in fact, they are a *kind* of boat, Billy…'

Billy hooded both eyes with his hands. 'You could be right, Mr Crosby. But… where do you think they are going?'

'Well, I would say… yes, towards Moreton Island. You remember, I pointed it out to you when we were at Amity Point, that day, when…'

'When we met Mr Twopenny?'

'Yes, that day.'

'Mr Crosby…' Billy looked decidedly anxious. 'Is he in one of those coonoos, do you think?'

Feeling acute disappointment for the boy, as well as on his own account, Will nodded. 'Yes, Billy, I rather fear the canoes belong to Mr Tompani and his people, and that for now, anyway, we have missed them.'

'But why, Mr Crosby? Why is he going?'

'He did say they might be moving on soon… And there they go, I think, though 'tis a great pity!'

Billy, keeping his eyes lowered, reached for Will's hand. 'So now I'll *never* have the chance of saying thank you to Mr Twomparmy. Maybe we'll never see him again… Will we see him again, do you think, Mr Crosby?'

Will stood closer, his hands resting on the boy's shoulders. 'Oh, I think we will, Billy, if we really want to, somewhere about these islands. But, you know, sooner or later, they'll come back here. For they always do come back, you know…'

Billy twisted round then to look up into Will's face, tears glinting on his lashes. 'You mean like a boomerlang always comes back? Well, nearly always… but… not if *you* throw it…'

'Yes, Billy…' Will squeezed the child's shoulders. 'Exactly like a boomerang… should.'

The boy looked away, stubbing his toe repeatedly against a rock. Then he turned again to Will. 'Why can they go away from this island, but we cannot? Margaretta's daddy was very angry about it, yesterday. He kept saying that it was "a bloody crime…" What's "a bloody crime," Mr Crosby?'

Will tried hard not to laugh. 'Oh, that's just an angry man's not very polite way of saying "it isn't fair." But… you're not an angry man, are you, Billy? And as for why they can go and we cannot – well, not just yet – it's because they are not subject to… they do not have… the same rules and regulations as we do…'

'What are rules and… regulations, Mr Crosby? Do I have them too?'

'Shhh, Billy, with your interminable questioning!' Will pleaded. 'I'll explain later if you remind me…'

And the two of them stood watching until the boats finally fused with the sea and the sky and vanished altogether. But still they remained, watching.

The green sea was slowly overlaid with a different vision, a long sward of gently swaying grass, sloping away down towards another, lesser cliff edge, far away. And it held a memory, composite, because not of one occasion only, many rather, stretching over a whole summer – a soldier, a woman, and a little girl, walking slowly in the direction of the sea.

Would it ever be enough, Will found himself wondering, just to know that that vision had once been the reality at the centre of his life in the ephemeral, material frailty of his days; that it would remain constant always, at the very heart of him? There were times when the vast distance between the substance of then and the longings of now seemed like a death, very like a death. But he doubted the adequacy of the vision, indeed, was more than half in revolt against it, because he knew now, as he had always known, that it was she, Alice, and only she, who could light up the moment, forever cresting the all-severing waves that rose up between them, braving time, and distance, yet wholly oblivious of her continually renewing presence, at this far side of the world.

Well, I shall make sure she does know. I shall write to her, yes, and make sure she does know. Even though, in the end, it will be she and not I who will decide.

Yes, he would write to her. He would; he must. It would be a start, anyway.

With Billy lolling against him, Will rode Bluebell gently back along the north beach, past Amity Point and down past the spring at Myora, with its painted poles. And he wondered whether he would ever pass this way again. At times he drifted off into reveries of past and of futures, and he continually looked around him, taking in the wispy trees with their silvery-tufted leaves, or the sturdier ones with spikey, fan-like clusters and pineapple-like fruits. And while he did not see any of the big, yellow-crested birds, he could hear their shrill cries, occasionally. Once or twice, the vast canopies of Ridley's Moreton-Bay fig trees were host to the ever-squawking rainbow parakeets. But mostly, Will – and Billy, awake but seemingly content with just nestling against Will – relished the silent unwinding of the late afternoon.

When Will and Billy rode into the encampment, the whole place was humming with activity, people dashing here, there and everywhere, and there was even dancing among the tents. The *Aurora* lay at anchor alongside the jetty, and there were people moving about the decks of the *Emigrant* too, on the far side of her.

There was Mr Jones, walking among the tents, possibly for the first time. Mr and Mrs Parry out walking along the path leading out of the camp – they too, maybe, for the first time. Margaretta, and other children, were dancing together, imitating the grown-ups. The O'Rourke brothers, outside their tent, waved, smiling as Will and Billy rode by.

As they went past where he stood, at some distance, McIlroy turned away, seemingly busying himself with his kit, piled up beside his collapsed tent. Then Ridley and Barney, brimming tankards in their hands, beckoned to him as he rode Bluebell – for the last time, he now realised – towards them.

And then, hand in hand, Will and Billy strolled back through the few remaining tents, to where the hospital tent had stood. And there was the young matron in a chair beside her bags and boxes, sitting – incongruously – just outside the ring that marked where the large tent and its many sorrows had been. And this scene brought to Will's mind the days that had followed the departure of the annual circus, in his far-off childhood, when they had all joined hands and danced about the stained grass circle.

And there was Thomas seated beside her.

Will halted, hesitating. Their conversation was clearly absorbing them entirely. But then both looked up in the same instant and smiled their welcome.

'Will,' Thomas exclaimed, his eyes alight. 'How opportune!' Then he looked into the distance for a moment, seemingly discomfited. But when he looked back, he smiled, and – Will was almost certain – winked at him.

'Miss Labone here – Lillian – like us, has no one to turn to, and I've suggested she come along with us… At least, for the time being, till we all find our feet, you know. Would you, the two of you, be in agreement with that, now?'

The question had little time to hang.

Before Will had managed to salvage thought from surprise, Billy had dashed forward and thrown his arms around the young matron's neck.

'Oh, Miss Labone!' And he whispered something in her ear, something that did not displease her, evidently, for she began to giggle.

'You have our answer, it seems,' said Will, laughing. 'What was that saying, Thomas, about… mouths and babes and sucklings?' And he thought back to the day they'd disembarked on the island, and he'd set disappointed eyes on the already claimed bed in the tent to which he had been assigned… Disappointed? Whoever would have credited it, now?

Stepping back and contemplating the whole scene, Will realised, in one of those rare flashes of self-revelation, that in these moments something vital had been kindled within him, something as yet indeterminate, not quite fully fledged, but real enough.

And this curious sensation brought to mind that instant when the *Emigrant* had left the flat, barely rippling waters of Plymouth harbour and entered the open sea… and the first wave that struck had lifted her, and her rhythm had changed at once as she moved ever forward towards… what? Redeeming his dream, he supposed, redeeming time. And with that sensation now fully awakened and working within him, for the moment, at least, he would be content.

AFTERWORD

The events surrounding the ill-fated voyage of *The Emigrant* from Plymouth to Brisbane, between April and August 1850, are well documented, and have been the subject of historical inquiry.

This story, however – intended, as Auden suggests, as both 'a feigned history and a parable' – engages only minimally with the facts of these histories, which instead offer a helpful 'sometime' and 'somewhere' in which to re-cast the misplaced life of a maternal grandfather I never knew.

Little was known, then, of course, about the causes of typhus, which was treated by sheer guesswork; by quarantining victims from the wider public (as, historically, with all ship-borne diseases) and leaving them to survive as best they could. And thus it is that my chief protagonist spends three months of his life in the makeshift camp on Stradbroke Island.

Did my grandfather make such a voyage? He may well have: the limited evidence I have suggests that William Crosby disappeared off the face of the earth shortly after his release from Carlisle gaol, where he had been committed for bigamy – which is where this story of his begins.

The novel has its geographical roots in my first visit to Stradbroke Island, in 1998. It is a large sand island, a veritable paradise – if inevitably affected by modern-day tourism. It is well wooded, swampy in parts, and has long, golden beaches, as well as a wealth of animal and bird life. Our time there – three days – was all too short but having arrived too early for the ferry back to the mainland, I happened to wander off into the old cemetery, at Dunwich.

The cemetery, which is at the northern end of the small township, is in a lovely, peaceful setting, close to the sea, and it was here that I stumbled across the twenty-six graves of the victims of the typhus epidemic brought by the *Emigrant*, in 1850 – additional to the sixteen who had already died during the voyage out. I cannot now recall quite how soon after that chance discovery the idea of the novel came to me. I do remember, however, being so captivated by that quiet corner of the cemetery by the sea that I made a large painting of it after returning to England. I suspect it was while this painting was in the making that the diverse strands of what became *The Approaching Tide* emerged and gradually came together.

A Note on Typhus

The main focus of this note is the disparity between the realities of typhus as it is understood now and the blind groping towards understanding in the mid-nineteenth century.

Typhus is not one single disease but a group of diseases, all of which are transmitted by bites from infected lice, fleas, or ticks. The most common form is epidemic typhus which, historically, has been known by other names such as camp, gaol, or ship fever, all of which indicate incidence due to overcrowded, insanitary living conditions in which lice and fleas breed easily. And it is this variety which is central to the tragic context of *The Approaching Tide*, both on Stradbroke Island in 1850, and prior to this (between 1846 and 1849), during the great famine in Ireland (from where it spread to parts of England and was known, disparagingly, as the 'Irish disease').

Specifically – as I understand it – this variant is caused by the bacterium *Ricksettia prowazekii*, which enters the blood stream of the common louse (*pediculus humanus humanus*) when it sucks the blood of an infected animal (including human beings). The bacterium – which eventually kills the louse, by passing into its gut and multiplying in its intestinal canal – is present in the faeces of the dying louse, which are the main agent for its transmission to human beings: when scratching a louse bite one rubs the faeces into the wound. This passage and process were not fully understood until the period 1909-16, much too late, of course, for the passengers from the *Emigrant*.

Prior to boarding ships, nineteenth-century travellers often picked up the typhus bacterium during their stay in filthy lodging houses in the main ports. During long voyages, like that to Queensland, there was plenty of time (and the right environment) for unaffected passengers to pick up the infected lice from those who had brought them aboard. On average, it takes ten days or so for the disease to show any symptoms after first infection, so ships were always well at sea by the time an epidemic was detected.

Throughout the nineteenth century (and earlier), it was commonly believed that the disease was airborne (like 'malaria' – literally 'bad air') and that it was also contagious. Strictly speaking, both were wrong although, as the bacterium remained active for several days after the death of the host louse, it could still be transmitted to humans through the dried (powdery) faeces still present in clothes and bedding, especially if they happened to be shaken, sending up clouds of the deadly bacterium, which could then be inbreathed by those close by.

In *The Approaching Tide* I have endeavoured to convey something of this ignorance about the disease, and the guesswork that directed treatment of it. Dr Mitchell, in his insistence on a regime of bodily cleanliness, is on the right track; ironically, though, it is Father Thomas, in one of his flights of 'scientific' fantasy, who almost makes the vital connection between lice, uncleanliness, and the disease.